I0691971

A Will
of Her Own

by

Lynn Shurr

This is a work of fiction. Names, characters, places, and incidents are either the product of the author's imagination or are used fictitiously, and any resemblance to actual persons living or dead, business establishments, events, or locales, is entirely coincidental.

A Will of Her Own

COPYRIGHT © 2016 by Carla S. Hostetter

Cover Art by *Diana Carlile*

The Wild Rose Press, Inc.
PO Box 708
Adams Basin, NY 14410-0708
Visit us at www.thewildrosepress.com

Publishing History
First Mainstream Women's Fiction Edition, 2016
Print ISBN 978-1-5092-0682-7
Digital ISBN 978-1-5092-0683-4

Published in the United States of America

Will Collier shrugged massive shoulders,
no longer built like a butterfly swimmer, more like a
construction worker. His chest had thickened along
with his waist. He seemed to be a solid wall of muscle
now, like his father who had poured iron in a foundry.

"I don't get much chance to travel. I knew a girl
named Kara in college. Want some?" He nodded at his
lunch.

"Oh, yes." Kara did, she really did. She glanced at
the diplomas and certifications hanging on his office
wall. "I went to the same school."

"No kidding. What class?" Will took a Swiss Army
knife two inches thick from his desk drawer and opened
the longest blade. He sliced off a hunk from the uneaten
end of the sandwich, placed it on a napkin, and held it
out in his big hands.

Kara gave him their class year and accepted the
offering. He stared at her ringless fingers. "That girl's
name was—a—Shafer, not Ryder, Kara Shafer. Birch
beer?" He held up a long-necked glass bottle of reddish
brown soda pop. "I didn't drink from the bottle yet."

"Please, I'd like some. Yes, Kara Shafer—a short,
mousey girl, kind of on the plump side, her nose always
buried in a book. Plain brown hair, plain brown eyes,
not much going for her."

"Hey, she was a top student, a real nice girl, and
not bad looking. I would have asked her out, but the
guys kept ragging on me all the time, and I couldn't
take the teasing. They expected me to jump her bones
the first night out and then tell them all the details.
Frank Bragg scared her off. I heard she married some
druggie rocker. Seemed too sweet for that type."

Praise for Lynn Shurr

"Shurr is a wonderful storyteller."

~The Romance Studio

~*~

"Very easy reads, well written, combined with conflict, believable plots and secondary characters that make the story come alive."

~Jane Lange, Romances, Reads and Reviews

~*~

"I love how deep and well written the characters are."

~Juliette Brandt, Paperbacks and Frosting

Dedication

For my very supportive college roommates,
Louise, Faye, and Ann

Prologue
Louisiana Blues

The drive across Texas and Louisiana seemed endless, but Kara steeled herself to cross the Mississippi River Bridge and rest her head on a pillow at the Hampton Inn in Baton Rouge tonight. She sped by flat, featureless land until her sturdy little Toyota mounted the causeway across the great Atchafalaya Basin swamp. The oncoming headlamps of cars, the stars, and the gas flares illuminating stands of cypress trees provided the only light out here. Thumping down from the causeway, her car caught the ghostly forms of grazing white cattle off to the right in its headlights. She entered a tunnel of dark trees looming over both sides of the road. Water glinted at their roots. Far off, a yellow smudge on the horizon signaled a big city ahead.

The music of Paul Simon thrummed in her ears. She'd written some pretty good lyrics herself, not that she'd gotten the credit, but no one beat Paul Simon for sheer poetry. The monotonous trees and the white center line continued hypnotically onward. Kara closed her eyes just for a moment. When she opened them, she was bearing down on a large dark lump in the road sure to tear out her brake lines or destroy the Toyota's undercarriage. The lump raised its head. A large armadillo froze in her headlights.

Kara jerked her steering wheel hard left. The little

car crossed the center line. Trunks of swamp maples and water oaks came up fast. She spun the wheel and headed toward a deep water-filled ditch on the opposite side of the road. Way in the back of her mind, she heard Mr. Wise, her high school driving teacher, say as he snapped on his neck brace, "Never overcorrect, steer your vehicle, keep control."

She nudged the wheel, her hands tight and white-knuckled. The right front tire caught in the soft soil at the top of the embankment. Kara straightened out the Toyota, felt the two outer tires grip the hard surface of the emergency lane, applied the brakes gently, and came to a stop several yards down the road. Heart pounding, she looked in her rearview mirror. The armadillo stretched out like an accordion, waddled to the ditch and slid over the side without a nod of thanks in her direction. A moment later, an eighteen-wheeler doing eighty passed the spot. Her parked car shuddered in its wake.

Kara laid her head on the steering wheel. "Thank you, God, and damn that armadillo. And Jeff Ryder, too." He put her on this road. No, no, he'd fathered her two wonderful children, at least physically. They might grow up to be beautiful and talented like him—and learn from their mother's mistakes. She had no one to blame for this mess but herself.

With trembling hands, she found the battered thermos that rolled under the front seat and poured a cup of black coffee. The thermos with its tacky plaid cover and dented side accompanied all her travels and still kept liquid hot all day and half the night, another blessing—but a wonder she didn't scald herself as the contents slopped over the side.

"Kara, take the plane back to Pennsylvania. Driving cross-country alone is dangerous, and I'm simply too old to raise your children," dear old Mom said, omitting any mention of other stupid acts Kara committed in her life. She'd just wanted some time alone and checking out the condition of the old farmhouse provided a convenient excuse.

So, she'd left Los Angeles and the baggage of a failed marriage, two small children, and a wobbly career as a lyricist, hoping to find sanctuary back on Great-aunt Mary's farm near her hometown of Lost Spring, Pennsylvania, all because of her own willfulness. Not that she hadn't done everything in her power to make the marriage work, but it takes two to do the quick step, and as Jeff so often pointed out, band members never dance with a partner. No, she'd fallen for great sex and a wannabe rocker instead of building a real life with a good man.

Will. Ruefully, she thought of another meaning. She bet Will Collier grew up to be a responsible adult with a real job, a man who cherished his kids and supported them the best he was able. Why couldn't he have noticed her when she kept throwing herself in his pathway at college? Instead, his oblivious indifference caused the biggest humiliation of her young life. Of course, that prank didn't compare to what Jeff had done, but infuriated with her ex, she'd gone way past humiliated.

She couldn't really blame Will for the trick played on her. He probably didn't even know about it. As for her roommates, they'd been ready to lose their virginity and she'd wanted to do the same. All except Faith, of course, who wanted to remain pure for religious reasons, not that she had—given raging hormones and the temptation of slick, college guys. No, she couldn't blame them, only herself for deciding to date anyone who asked and give it up to the first man who showed any promise. Most of them didn't. She'd been more than ready to tumble when Jeff Ryder turned those intense, dark eyes on her.

Enough self-flagellation. Kara put the car in gear and nosed onto the road. Ahead, the lights of the Mississippi River Bridge. Bisecting the nation as it did, the great river seemed to be a clear dividing line between the mad life she'd left in L.A. and the future promise of peace, quiet, and reality she *would* bring into existence for herself and her children.

Like that watershed moment, literally, in college leading to her misguided marriage, crossing the river meant change—for the better, she swore. No one had to dump a bucket of cold water on Kara Shafer this time.

Chapter One
The Sophomore Slump

Seven Years Earlier

Kara Shafer strode along the sidewalk with her new red dress swinging across the hips and thighs she considered a tad too large. Not the prettiest girl on campus, not even close. Her plain brown hair fell fine and straight defying every curling device known to woman, and so she wore it with a fringe of bangs and a simple blunt cut at her shoulders. Her brown eyes matched her hair, but they weren't large or lustrous. She had an okay nose, not hooked or bumpy, but not pert and upturned or straight and aristocratic either. Her mother cited her best traits as her warm smile and her friendly personality. Her roommates contradicted that and gave the prize to her large breasts that bobbed under the halter-top of the killer red dress and forced her to walk more slowly as she approached Heck House. Kara Shafer held no claim to being beautiful, but at this moment she felt like the homecoming queen—because tonight Will Collier *would* notice her.

Kara's feet sweat in the low-heeled scarlet sandals she wore to go dancing. All the spit in her mouth seemed to have dried up. She ran her tongue over her lips coated in a shade of crimson exactly matching the dress that took her friends an hour to find at the

5

drugstore. A pace behind, she heard her three suitemates whispering and giggling and offering words of encouragement.

"Go get 'im, Kara," big-boned, freckled, and good-natured Lulu cheered as if she were at a pep rally. Her outfit, a hot pink skirt and blouse, clashed with her curly red hair.

"You're perfect!" Hannah wore her hair in a short, pale blonde cap that showed off the fine bones of her face. Shedding sixty-five pounds since leaving the farm and coming to college, she looked fantastic in a tight black sheath.

"Your dress is great. I wish I had the nerve to wear something like that," Faith said softly. She had brown hair with more bounce and body than Kara's, pretty hazel eyes, and a very small chest completely covered to the neck by a summery cotton dress she'd sewn herself.

"Here goes." Kara stepped directly in front of Heck House, one of the many off-campus residences for men. Named for its curmudgeonly landlord who never made repairs until all of the students left for the year, the guys who had to live there called the place Hell House. The tenants also implied wicked doings occurred there all times of the day and night, but the girls never met anyone who participated in any such thing. They wrote it off as the kind of "in your dreams" type of bragging college boys did.

With the sun still up on this warm spring evening in mid-May, all the windows of un-air-conditioned Heck House stood open, each one crammed with young men, some of them shirtless, a few of them whistling at the women as they passed. The girls kept their eyes straight ahead. Nearly past the walkway up to the residence, Kara heard someone calling her name, not Will Collier. She'd never spoken to Will directly, but she'd stood close enough to him to recognize his quiet, low-pitched voice.

"Kara! Oooh, Kara Shafer," a strong male voice beckoned.

Kara turned her head. Frank Bragg hung out a second story window. His wide, pale chest filled the frame. He had brown hair streaked with blond, seductive blue eyes, and when fully dressed, looked like a preppy who had accidently landed at this small state college after attending a series of private schools.

Kara heard Lulu whisper, "Isn't he gorgeous?"

"Lookin' fine tonight, Kara Shafer. Come over here for a minute." Frank crooked a long finger at her.

With no desire to impress Frank Bragg, Kara started to walk by. They had some classes together, and she didn't care for him. Bragg, the name fit.

"Will wants to say something to you, Kara, so step right up here." Frank pointed to a place beneath his window.

She hesitated and looked back at her friends. Hannah shrugged. Lulu urged her with a sweep of her hands. Faith said, "Be careful."

Kara went up the walk and moved across the patchy lawn until she stood below Frank's window. She shielded her eyes from a sun low in the sky and searched for Will Collier. Frank Bragg reached behind himself as if to pull someone forward. In a single swoop, he grabbed a small, red ice chest and tossed the contents down on Kara Shafer. She jumped back. The ice water landed harmlessly a foot in front of her, but the backsplash splattered the front of her red dress, creating dark spots that made her body look as if it had been sprayed by buckshot. Cold water dripped from the ends of her soaked breasts, making her nipples pucker beneath the fabric that clung tightly to them.

"Will says you're so hot for him, you need to take a cold shower!" Frank Bragg hooted with laughter. The other guys took up his cry, long arms and hairy torsos contorting in the other windows. Some wit shouted, "You cold, Kara?"

Frank tossed the cooler to someone behind him. "Hey, Vince, go get more ice for the beer."

Kara Shafer stood rooted to the place of her humiliation, her legs too shaky to move, until Hannah shouted, "Shit asses! Come on, Kara."

That's exactly what they were, Kara told herself as she ran back to her friends, all too aware of her jiggling breasts and too-wide hips. She kept going until hidden behind a tall barberry hedge, her face burning as red as its fruit. Unfortunately, she could still hear Frank Bragg.

"Run, Kara, run to Will's arms!" He made loud, smoochy noises that brought more howls of laughter from his housemates.

Out of sight of Heck House now, she slowed to let her gal pals catch up. Long-legged Lulu reached her first and swung a big arm around Kara's shoulders.

"They're just big jerks. Ignore them."

"Yeah, jerks. I didn't see Will anywhere," Faith added.

"Look, I don't feel much like going to the dance anymore. Go on without me. I'll take another way back to the dorm. I need to pack."

"Honey babe, this is the last fling after finals. We have officially survived our sophomore year. There are sure to be some fine parties after the dance. You can pack in the morning. We don't have to be out of the suite until noon. Dance, drink, and forget this," Hannah advised.

"I don't think the water will stain the dress. Look, it's drying already in this heat," Faith said.

"If I looked that good in a dress, I'd wear it with the stains. Besides, the gym will be dark, so who cares," Lulu said. "Really, it could be worse."

"Right, cooler water on a sidewalk is better than a bucket of pig's blood at the prom. If I had supernatural powers, Frank Bragg would be toast right now. I'll walk as far as the union with you, then I'm going back to the room. This was all a silly, foolish waste." Kara flicked at the layers of her skirt.

"Let's stop off at the union and get something cold to drink. The night is young," Hannah suggested. Kara went along with it.

In the student union lounge, she fumbled with the tiny purse hooked over her arm. It contained her student ID, the perfect red lipstick used only once, a comb, and emergency money. She withdrew a dollar bill, but Hannah waved it away. "My treat."

While they waited for Hannah to return with the drinks, Faith and Lulu took seats beside Kara. When a young man dressed in a short-sleeved blue shirt and khakis quick-stepped toward them, the girls stood in front of their friend like she-wolves protecting an injured member of their pack. Grady Spurrier, a resident of Heck House, was coming their way.

Grady slid to a stop. His dark hair was slicked back

as if he'd just gotten out of the shower, and he hadn't bothered to shave. With the glasses he usually wore in class missing, his gray eyes appeared naked.

"I'm sorry, Kara. None of the guys knew what Frank was going to do. Will wasn't even in the house. He left for the dance a while ago."

"They still laughed," Kara said miserably.

"Yeah, Frank can make them laugh, but most of us felt kind of bad afterwards. I came to tell you so."

"Well, thanks." Kara wanted to return the favor, but had to question her motives. Something deep and ugly inside her wanted to deal out a little hurt to someone. "You do know your girlfriend, Madison, is engaged to a guy back home? She just wants someone to fool around with when she's away at college."

Grady's mouth fell open, making the science major look dumb, which he wasn't when it came women. "That's not true! You want to get back at me, and I didn't do anything. I didn't even laugh when that water hit the ground, but I should have." Grady found his glasses in the pocket of his shirt and put them on. He turned on his heel and charged out of the union as fast as he'd come, no doubt hunting for Madison.

"Ooops!" Hannah returned with four dripping, frosty cans of Diet Coke. "Never, never tell a guy his girl is cheating on him. Does no good because he won't believe you, and it flies in the face of sisterhood."

"That's true, but you know who else is right? Frank Bragg," Kara said.

"No way!" Lulu answered.

"I've made a fool of myself panting around after Will Collier—whom I've never met. This is a silly, sophomoric crush. Will wouldn't have noticed me if I'd run naked by that house."

"I wouldn't bet on that—and we are sophomores, after all," Lulu said.

"I'm nineteen, nearly twenty. I never go on real dates because I'm always mooning after Will. And, I've never slept with a man."

"None of us have," Faith said in a low voice, swiveling her head to see if anyone overheard. "I intend to wait for marriage."

"I intend to wait until Gregor buys condoms," Lulu quipped, turning a little pink under her freckles.

"Gregor is always broke, Lulu. You might have to wait a long time. As soon as Bradshaw Coulard Denlinger the Third slips an engagement ring on my finger, I'm going for it." Hannah held out her ring finger.

"I intend to start going out with whoever asks me, and if the vibes are right, I'll do it," Kara vowed. "It's about time I exerted my own will instead of waiting for some guy to notice me."

"You shouldn't throw away your virginity, Kara," Faith responded.

"Only with the right guy. We'll see who's still intact next fall."

"I guess that will be me because I am going to wait."

Hannah passed around the cans of soft drinks. Solemnly, they popped the tabs. Lulu raised her drink. "To finding the right man." They sipped.

"Now, let's go to the dance. To hell with the men of Heck House."

****

In the darkness of the old gym, given over to

intramural sports and dances after the new sports complex replaced it, a rock band pounded away, their words unintelligible, their beat throbbing. Colored lights strobed over the crowd celebrating the end of the term. All of it gave Kara a headache, but other students, already drunk or high, came prepared to party.

Gregor Horvath waited near the doors for Lulu. A son of Russian immigrants thrilled their boy had gotten a music scholarship, Greg stood a few inches shorter than Lulu and probably weighed less, but he'd inherited an old world preference for big women. Besides, Lulu was a voice major. They made beautiful music together, he liked to say. His big, dark eyes took in all of Lulu as the girls approached. He didn't spare a glance for the now slender Hannah or for Kara's big breasts. Greg enveloped Lulu in a full chest embrace and took her out onto the dance floor.

Faith sighed. "Greg is so devoted. Who ever thought Lulu would be the first to have a steady boyfriend?"

"He's great if you want to marry a music teacher," Hannah sniffed. She scanned the mob for Brad Denlinger. The heir to a meat packing business, he'd taken her out three times in the last month. He should have been attending Princeton or Rutgers but didn't have the grades to get in those hallowed halls. A nice guy, Brad was content with himself as is—rich, not brainy. He had blond good looks like Hannah and should have been on a rowing or squash team, but their small state university didn't offer those sports.

Hannah jumped when Brad came up behind her and drew her close. "Hey, my honey, want to dance?"

Hannah struggled in his grasp, batting at his hands

that wandered over her body. "You are so bad, Brad Denlinger!"

Brad appeared pleased to be bad. He'd obviously been drinking but wasn't too sloshed to dance. Being beefier than the diet-reduced Hannah, he picked her off her feet and carried her into the gyrating throngs.

"That leaves us. Want to dance, Kara? In this mob, no one will notice we don't have dates."

Faith wedged into the bumping, grinding crush. Kara followed. As she spiraled toward the band, she saw Will Collier up near the stage. He danced with an athletic-looking blonde woman who had the shoulders of a butterfly swimmer.

Will specialized in the butterfly on the swim team. He owned the wide shoulders and slim hips that proved it. All six foot two inches of him cut through the water with the grace and speed of a dolphin. He shaved his sleek body like most of the swimmers, but wore a cap over his curly, light brown hair that turned naturally golden over the summer when he worked as a lifeguard. Will refused to get rid of his thick sideburns even though his teammates said he'd take a couple of seconds off his times if he did. Under his heavy brows, the strobe lights glinted off blue eyes the same color as the bottom of the diving well at the natatorium. He had a straight, aristocratic nose, and the full lips to go with it. For a man with the coordination of a sea creature, he danced rather awkwardly on land, looking at his feet and not his partner.

Kara didn't care. She was no great dancer herself. Being only five-four, she doubted Will could see her or the red dress in the mass of people on the dance floor. From her safe position, she admired the way his tight black T-shirt spanned his chest and back, how snugly his jeans fit his ass. Not that she only lusted after his body—Will Collier majored in mathematics. He possessed a brain under all that hair. Quiet, perhaps shy, unlike Frank Bragg, he didn't date a lot. Kara found him so very appealing. She'd let herself dream about Will Collier one last time, and then, tomorrow, pack her bags, go home, and start dating any man who noticed she was alive.

Chapter Two
The Last Virgin

Fall Semester, Junior Year

Kara lay in her single bed separated from Lulu's by the space of two night tables. She'd been the last one to check into the suite. Her parents insisted on taking everyone to dinner, and she unpacked and got ready for classes afterwards. That left no time to catch up, really catch up.

"So, did you and Gregor do it this summer?" she asked into the darkness.

A white shape in a summer nightie, Lulu shifted in her cot. "Let's just say he had a summer job playing piano and dancing with old ladies at a resort, and his parents have this little vacation cottage they call a *dacha* nearby in the Poconos."

"And…"

"I managed to get away from watching my younger brothers and sisters for one whole weekend. My parents weren't too happy about it, but they'd promised to pay me, and let me have some time off. I chose to spend that time with Gregor."

"How was it?" Not a casual inquiry on Kara's part.

"Glorious. Greg got a kitchen helper to buy a bottle of wine. When he got off for the evening, we went to the dacha and sat outside drinking, looking at the stars, making out, you know." In the other bed, Lulu's freckled arms wrapped herself in a hug.

"Don't know." Kara stared at the ceiling, no stars glowing up there.

"Anyhow, he gave me a present all wrapped up with a bow: a jumbo box of condoms." Lulu sighed.

"How romantic."

"It was, sort of. Showed he cared. The bed was kind of musty, but after a while, we forgot all about it. I left a stain on the mattress that I hope his mother never sees. We flipped it over. Anyhow, before I left, he took me to meet his parents."

"How were they?"

"Well, I think his dad likes me. He said I was a big, healthy woman, not like most skinny American girls. His mother not so much, but she came around after I sang some German *lieder* for her. His father plays the balalaika, and his mom said she once had a voice just like mine. She cried."

"Oh, the power of music. How did your family like Greg?"

"Haven't had the nerve to introduce them yet, but I must because this is it. He's the one. And the sex is great."

Kara wished her roommate hadn't said that. It only confirmed she was missing out on life. "One down, three to go."

"I wouldn't say that. Faith got in last night. Did you notice how depressed she seemed?"

"I didn't have the chance."

"You know she got a job as a counselor at that church camp on Lake Ontalonee this summer. She met another counselor named Christopher and fell for him hard. He got in her pants before the Fourth of July. Since camp ended, guess what? He doesn't call, he doesn't write, and he won't answer her emails."

People opened their hearts to Lulu because she never judged and always joked when the occasion called for some levity. Kara wished she had that ability, but no. She took emotions and turned them into poems, often sad. Faith's summer qualified for an opus of its own. "Poor Faith! She wanted to wait for marriage. At least, Hannah and I are still striking out in the same league."

"I wouldn't bet on that. You were asleep in bed last year by the time we got in from that party Denlinger took us to at his frat house. If Hannah and Brad didn't do it in one of those upstairs rooms, I'll be damned. Fourth date, and you know what that means. Put up or it's over. I notice Brad called as soon as he got in today. I hear they went sailing on his family's Flying Scot this summer."

"How did Brad like her family's farm?"

"Let's just say he likes to ride, but doesn't muck out stalls. The Schmidts weren't too crazy about him. How'd your dating scheme go?"

Kara squirmed in her bed. "Not too well. I did go out a total of six times with three different guys."

"Sounds like a good start to me."

"Not really. I met the first fellow at the pool snack bar. He kept coming back to buy small items and get change. Finally, he got up the nerve to ask me out. We went to a summer theater play, and out for ice cream at one of those hokey old-fashioned parlors. I ordered a cashew butterscotch sundae with whipped cream and a cherry. He got a scoop of vanilla ice cream and told me how nice it was to go out with a girl who wasn't watching her weight."

"Boo! Hiss!" said Lulu, ever on Kara's side.

"Yeah, our first and last date. Who orders one scoop of vanilla ice cream unless they have the personality of Bob Newhart? Mid-summer, I went to our family reunion barbecue at Coocoosing Meadows. One of my cousins brought along an unshaven friend riding a big Harley hog. He gave rides on his motorcycle to all the girls, but he asked *me* out."

"Lucky you. Because of your vow, you went with him, right?"

"I did. We sort of had a good time just riding out in the country and stopping for cheese steak sandwiches and the best french fries I've ever had at this little place he knew about."

"No dietary comments, that's good. I'd love to have a cheese steak right now." Lulu's stomach rumbled. She must be on another one of her crash diets that never worked, Kara figured.

"He asked me to a party the next night and picked me up on his bike. Let me wear his leather jacket, too. We got to this rundown house way out in the boonies. Harleys are parked everywhere, loud music, biker babes giving tongue on the front porch. A guy asked if I wanted a drink, and I told him I'd like a rum and Coke with a twist of lime."

"Ah, the Cuba libre, your drink of choice."

"I'm fairly sure he didn't know what a Cuba libre was. Anyhow, he knocks the top off a glass Coke bottle, pours half the soda onto the ground and refills the bottle with rum. He said he was clean out of limes. I sort of wedged myself in a corner and sipped, trying not to cut my lip on the glass."

"They still have Coke in glass bottles?"

"Mexican cola. Probably the same with the cocaine some of them were snorting."

"And then, and then?" Lulu asked, dramatically.

"Pot smoking, all sorts of drugs—no, not me taking them—and very hairy, tattooed people drinking shots off a woman's stomach. I was scared to death. My date came up beside me and shouted, 'Boo!' I spilled my drink all over both of us. When I asked to go home, he took me. One of his buddies shouted as we left, 'Where'd you find that prissy little virgin, Jax?' Does it really show that much?"

"Don't worry about it. Most of the women at that party were probably pros. That means you did go on three dates with someone else. See, music majors have great math skills."

Lulu's chuckle warmed the room and lifted Kara's gray mood a little. She might as well tell the rest of story and get it over with.

"Yes, a guy who goes to Drexel. I met him online, one of those dating services. You get five contacts, you know, but I only heard from him. I guess I'm not very appealing even in cyberspace."

"I guess you didn't lie on your form like everyone else does."

"Anyhow, we did the dinner and a movie, dinner and necking on Skyline Drive, dinner and getting a motel room. We made out for a while on the bed, and then, I just couldn't do it. We ended up watching a movie on the television. Afterwards, he took me home. He didn't call again." Kara punched her pillow a couple of times and tried to relax into the hollow she'd made with her fist.

"I'd say you were lucky you didn't get raped this summer."

"That, too. They were all decent guys, even the biker. I guess for two years I thought I'd save my virginity for Will Collier, and I can't let it go that easily."

"Aren't you over Will?"

"Oh, I am. I didn't drive past his house in the city even once. I stayed away from his swim meets and the pool where he usually works. Not that it mattered. He wasn't swimming this summer. Will had a job doing surveys with a construction crew."

"So you did ask about him."

"Absolutely not! The information came to me unbidden. I worked the snack bar during our pool's swim meet, and two fellows from one of the teams came to stoke up on carbs after their events. While I got their hot dogs, chips, and drinks, I heard one of them say they would have won the relays if Will Collier hadn't been doing construction surveys all summer. I couldn't exactly drop their food and plug my ears with wax penny candy Coke bottles, now could I?"

"I guess not. You'd have to drink all the stuff out of those little bottles just to get the wax, and by then it would have been too late."

Lulu let loose with one of her booming laughs. She could have shilled for a comedian by sitting in the front row and laughing at his jokes. No surprise she'd been named for Lucille Ball, another notable redhead, but everyone called her Lulu—which suited her totally.

"I know. I'm ridiculous."

"No, no, girl. You simply haven't found your

Gregor Horvath yet. Keep trying."

"I intend to." Kara pulled the covers over her head to end the conversation.

Chapter Three
The Poet

Spring Semester, Junior Year

Kara passed an uneventful semester break. She caught up on sleep, filled her stomach with favorite childhood foods that went straight to her hips, and brought home perfect grades—though her parents had no idea what their daughter would do with A's in Irish Literature and Early English Sagas. With no desire to teach, Kara didn't know either. Well aware that a person could starve to death doing what she dreamed of—writing poetry and stories, she didn't have to make a decision on her future for another year and a half. Thank heaven for that.

After the break, the girls switched rooms with Faith now bunking with Kara. Hannah, true to her word, wore a beautiful two-carat engagement ring presented to her by Bradshaw Coulard Denlinger III at his family's Christmas Eve gathering. Hannah described the event all to her friends—from the immense limestone mansion sitting on acres of untilled farmland allowed to return to forest for seasonal hunting right down to the gilded seafood forks the Denlingers used to eat their shrimp cocktails. With the wedding date set for the following December, the Denlingers offered to pay for most of the expenses. The Schmidts refused this arrangement at first, saying they could afford a small wedding with the reception in the basement of their Lancaster Lutheran church. Intimidation won out when they received the Denlingers' proposed guest list of three hundred. The ceremony would be held at the Episcopal church in Bryn Mawr with a large reception afterward at their country club.

Around the same time, Gregor gave Lulu a ring with a stone so small that most people didn't think the band had one at all. He'd asked permission of her father and mother before going ahead with the proposal, which won over the McFarland family entirely. Lulu's father made them promise to finish college before marrying and a year and a half hadn't seemed so long to wait.

Regardless, Hannah and Lulu were often absent at night. Their grades slipped slightly as their fiancés took up more of their time. Faith and Kara, the unchosen, by sharing a room, managed to get a good night's sleep without someone slipping in early in the morning to get ready for class. Celibacy had its benefits in good grades and healthy habits.

Faith came out of her funk over her summer romance and re-dedicated herself to celibacy before marriage at Christmas in front of her church youth group. During the holidays, Kara went out a couple of times with a boy she'd known in high school. He sent her emails and texts now and again, but she hadn't cared enough to answer them with more than a line or two.

As for her dating plan upon return to campus, Kara went out with a freshman who got up the courage to ask out a junior. Sweet and funny and happy to make do with a goodnight kiss, he'd caved in to all the jokes from his buddies about dating a cradle-robbing cougar who didn't put out. They'd gone their separate ways. She concentrated on her studies instead of men to such an extent that when she ran bodily into Will Collier on the narrow third-floor staircase to the English and Math offices, the collision hadn't been intentional.

Will mumbled, "Excuse me," in that low, sexy voice and moved on, hardly looking her in her face.

By the time Kara managed to get out a "No problem," his long legs had carried him halfway down the stairs. She admitted she'd sniffed the air and taken in his clean scent of chlorine and aftershave as he passed, but she hadn't gawped after him, just kept trudging toward her receptionist's job in the English department.

Spring break came and went with Faith building homes for Habitat for Humanity. Hannah spent the time in Aruba with Brad's family and returned with a toasty tan. Lulu made Russian Easter eggs with Greg's mother and took some home as gifts for her own family. Kara avoided the guy she knew in high school and ate enough of her mother's home cooking and Easter candy to put on five pounds she now had to lose before summer. On the whole, she was disgusted with herself.

Kara emptied a bag of foil-covered chocolate eggs into a candy dish, hoping her friends would finish off the temptation, while Faith went on and on about working for President Jimmy Carter's organization. She'd signed up for a missionary trip to Haiti where she would help at an orphanage during the summer.

"Not only will I be helping the poor, but working with the children will be a great experience to put on my resume as an elementary school teacher. What are you doing this summer, Kara?"

"Same old, same old, running the snack bar at the pool."

"Why don't you come to Haiti with us?"

"I really need the money. Besides, how will I continue my dating plan if I'm looking after little black orphans?"

"You don't need a man to make you happy." Faith, so earnest, bobbed her head and looked at Kara with light-filled hazel eyes.

"Absolutely. So, do you want to go to a poetry slam with this old maid?"

"I don't think so. I hate the smoke, and all the poems seem to be about sex even when they're not."

"Right again," Kara agreed. "Well, I must go for my American poetry class and write a critique. Later, okay?"

****

Kara found two of her classmates at a small table in the coffeehouse. She ordered a double espresso, afraid the milk in a latte would put her to sleep, but there wasn't much chance of that. A young black woman, the first poet up, ranted loudly about inequality and black men. Her short orange dreadlocks shook with her passion like tiny flames. Each word she punched out came accented with foot stomping and clapping hands. She got a nice round of applause, much clanging of spoons against coffee cups, and some snapping of the fingers by old-timers. A slim white boy, possibly still in high school, took the floor next. Kara believed his poem to be about the pain of being homosexual, but wasn't quite sure. The listeners applauded politely.

A college student made his way to the stage. Several young women sucked in their breath. He stood behind the mic, caressing its neck with his long, pale fingers. Smoke swirled in the spotlight, ringing around the leather aviator's jacket and white silk scarf he wore over a snug black T-shirt and jeans. He stared directly at his audience with luminous dark eyes under brows that were two straight black slashes across his pallid forehead. High cheek bones, hollow cheeks, straight nose, sensuous lips, two days of attractive beard stubble, and the whitest smile Kara had ever seen captured the attention of every woman and some of the men in the room. His hair shone blue-black, brushed back and hanging straight and long past his shoulders. He had the lean, lithe body every passionate poet should possess.

"Who is he?" Kara murmured.

"Jeff Ryder," signed one of her classmates. "He makes the critique worth writing."

"*A Song for Beautiful Women* by Jeff Ryder," he began. "You and You and You/ Though you may not know it/Are beautiful women," he said in a baritone rich as hot chocolate.

Jeff Ryder pointed his pale finger around the room, picking out the black woman with her orange dreads, one of the college professors well into middle age, and Kara Shafer. She could have sworn that finger pierced her heart because after that moment she could barely make sense of the rest of the words of his poem. Dutifully, she wrote in her notebook, "Jeff Ryder transfixed the audience with his ode to women."

When he finished, silence, a collective sigh, then wild applause filled the coffeehouse and shifted the smoke making a halo around his head. The poet accepted with a deep bow that sent his silky hair cascading over his shoulders. He flicked it back and gave the stage to a stout older woman who soon had the audience laughing with a comic piece about menopause. Jeff, accepting congratulations from admirers, moved through the jam-packed tables. As he passed Kara, one of her companions snagged the edge of his jacket. He stopped.

"Hey, Lilah."

"We have an extra place, Jeff," she claimed, though utterly untrue.

Mugs and notebooks cluttered every inch of the tiny table, and all three chairs were taken. Kara wondered if the other two girls, who obviously knew Jeff, expected her to leave. She started to get up, but Lilah reached over to the next table and helped herself to a spare chair vacated by a person who'd gone to the restroom and placed it between her and the other students of poetry. Jeff squeezed into place. Slim of build, he was shorter than he appeared on stage, perhaps five-eight. A waitress rushed to his side, and he ordered a double espresso. Kara couldn't help but notice they preferred the same drink, dark and bitter, not the fluffy cappuccinos the others sipped.

"You're new here. American Poetry II, huh?" Jeff Ryder nodded at her notebook. "Helps to fill out the audience. So, what's my critique?" He made a grab for her notebook, but Kara hugged it against her chest.

"I called it transfixing."

"No lie? Then it will be even better set to music. I test my lyrics here." Jeff reached into the pocket of his battered flight jacket and withdrew a card.

Kara read it—*Jeff Ryder and the Ryders of the Night*—another wannabe rocker. State had an excellent music school that spawned groups of all kinds. Need a string quartet for your wedding? Call the music school. Want a band for your bar? Check the bulletin board in their lobby.

Kara started to hand the card back, but Jeff Ryder pushed it into her palm. "No, keep it. It has all my contact numbers and an email address. We're playing at the Hot Spot this weekend. I should have *Song for Beautiful Women* ready to go by then."

"Oh, I don't turn twenty-one until June." Kara lowered her eyes.

"Look, when you get there, sit at a table and order a soft drink. The place is always jammed, and they don't have a bouncer. Leo, the owner, is pretty lax about carding. Besides, the worst that can happen is that you'll get thrown out. Ah—I don't think I got your name."

"Kara, Kara Shafer."

"Kara, I could see your smile all the way from the stage. I'd like to see it again Saturday night. Gotta split." Jeff chugged down the hot coffee as if it were ice water.

"I guess we all need to get back to studying."

"Hell, I'm flunking out. My only A's are in music, and my dad said he won't pay any more tuition unless I bring my grades up, but, man, music is all there is. I guess I could have gotten into Julliard if my high school scores hadn't sucked. This will be my last semester at State. The Ryders are going on the road. I turned twenty-one in February, and the rest of the group is seniors or dropouts. My great-granddad used to say,

'Free, White, and Twenty-one'. I never knew what he meant until now. I can go anywhere, do anything I want. This was his flight jacket from WW II. Cool, huh?"

He took Kara's hand and squeezed it. "I *will* see you there Friday night."

She steamed hot all over like the espresso machine behind the counter. Her last crush had been an all-American boy oblivious to her smile. Now, some failing poet-rocker made her heart go pitty-pat. Kara Shafer, you have poor taste in men, she told herself. "Maybe," she said—transfixed.

****

Kara folded her hands, beseeching or maybe praying. "Please come with me, Faith. You turned twenty-one in March."

Faith shook her head with finality. "You know I don't do the bar scene. Ask Lulu or Hannah. It would be safer to have some men along."

"Hannah and Brad are going to a country club dance. Lulu and Greg are getting paid to sing at some kid's bar mitzvah party. Please, I can't go alone."

"I'll make a deal. If I do this, you go to church with me on Sunday. You know I get tired of going alone, too."

"Deal." A little religion wouldn't hurt, might help. "Should I wear my red dress? It's been hanging in the closet since last spring."

"To church! Absolutely not."

The look on her roommate's face nearly made her laugh, but Kara held it in. "No, to the Hot Spot."

"I think that's overkill, but do what you must." Faith rolled her eyes. "This isn't really a date, you

29

know. Jeff Ryder is just drumming up an audience for his band. He probably hopes you'll come with a bunch of friends."

"I would if they weren't otherwise engaged. Get dressed. His band comes on at nine."

Faith sighed, stripped down to her underwear, and sorted through her closet. She pulled out a black knit with a turtleneck and long sleeves, slid it over her head and hung a few gold chains around her neck. "There, good enough for Jeff Ryder?"

"Perfect." Jeff wouldn't notice Faith at all. The dress might have been sexy if Faith had any breasts to speak of, and less narrow hips, but as it was, the garment sort of hung on her like an empty sack. Yes, Perfect.

****

The friends arrived at the Hot Spot in Faith's old, used Kia her parents provided to make student teaching easier for her in her senior year. They parked in a big gravel lot already close to full. The Hot Spot consisted of nothing more than a big metal building with a brick façade and a glowing red neon circle with the words, HOT SPOT, blinking on and off in yellow in its center. No one guarded the doors, but Kara noticed anyone approaching the bar got carded. She and Faith took seats at a table stripped of all but two chairs and sitting in the middle of the audience, well protected by mobs of people on either side. The first band packed up their gear, and drinkers crowded to the bar.

"Get me a rum and Coke, Faith, and something for yourself." Kara pressed a ten-dollar bill into her roommate's hand.

"I think you're going to owe me more than one

Sunday in church."

"Sin now, be saved later. Go!"

Fighting the thirsty throngs, Faith stayed gone for ages. Kara watched the Ryders take the stage and begin setting up their amps and instruments—drums, two electric guitars, and a keyboard. The band finished tuning up by the time the drinks arrived.

"Thanks. What did you get?" Kara took her drink, squeezed the lime into it, and stirred with the little plastic straw.

"A cherry Coke." Faith took the wrapper off the top of the drinking straw. Before she could put it to her lips, Kara switched straws and tossed her lime into Faith's soft drink. She plucked out a maraschino cherry by its stem and immersed it in her rum and soda.

"Hey, that's the best part," Faith said, protesting the loss of the cherry.

"It's all mine now, and if anyone asks, you have the rum and Coke. I have the cherry cola."

The club owner mounted the stage and took the mic. "Back by popular demand, the rocking-est band in town—Jeff Ryder and Ryders of the Night."

He flipped the mic to Jeff who held it close to his lips and breathed, "You—and you—and you / Are beautiful women." The band contrived an echo effect on the "yous" and several pounding chords between each phrase. Jeff's finger pointed right, then left, then directly at Kara, at least she thought so. The song took off with a heavy beat, Jeff making love to his guitar and every woman in the audience. When the final note faded, female shrieks of lust filled the void.

Kara craned her neck to see around a tall, broad-shouldered guy strangling the necks of six beer bottles in his large hands as he passed to a side table. She realized a moment later Will Collier had been this close to her, and she hadn't cared. Evidently, he worked on getting quietly drunk with some of his swim team buddies off in a corner.

"Thank you, all you beautiful women," Jeff murmured into the mic. "That one was for you. Here's one for the guys." The Ryders launched into a well-known raunchy standard.

"Wow," Faith said, "he's exactly the kind of guy my mother always warned me about."

"You know it. I think I'm going to need another drink. This one evaporated when he started to sing."

"If you get drunk, don't expect me to carry you back to the suite or clean up any puke, Kara Shafer."

"With luck, you won't need to. Jeff Ryder will be taking me home. Let's dance."

They pushed to the dance floor in front of the stage. Kara threw her arms above her head and let herself jiggle. Both she and Faith danced with a few stray men and didn't return to their table until the break. Kara shooed Faith to the bar for another round of drinks. Nothing remained in her glass but the cherry and some melting ice. Waiting, she toyed with the stem when a hot body pressed against the back of her chair. She gazed up into the dark eyes of Jeff Ryder, or she would have if he hadn't been wearing shades.

He took Faith's chair and mopped his forehead with the end of the white silk scarf. In the other hand, he held a sweating bottle of beer. He upended it into his mouth. Kara couldn't take her eyes off the pulses of his Adam's apple as he swallowed. Jeff slammed the bottle on the table when it was empty. Unlike most of the guys she knew, he didn't follow that performance with a burp. Instead, he gave her that glistening smile, pointed to the maraschino cherry, and asked, "You want that?"

"It's all mine, and I'm not giving it away."

"Trade you for my scarf."

"Don't you need it for your act?"

"I have a bunch of them."

"Okay, then." Kara lowered the cherry into his mouth. He closed his teeth over it, and she snapped the stem.

Jeff Ryder sucked on the fruit. Slowly, he took his scarf and wrapped it around Kara's neck. She inhaled his musk. He pulled the ends toward his face, drawing Kara along until their lips touched. He gave the cherry back. She swallowed so hard the cherry went down whole. Faith arrived. Kara groped for a drink and gulped it down.

"Next time, you go! Someone pinched me in that crowd, and I have a bruise the size of a quarter on my rear end," Faith said with disgust.

"Your butt is so tiny I'm surprised anyone could find it. What I would give to have your hips. Oh, Jeff, this is my roommate, Faith Harvey."

Jeff nodded. "Jeff Ryder—with the band. And there's nothing wrong with your hips, Kara Shafer. They're womanly. I'll bet they are a handful. Got to get back. Stick around after the last set, okay?"

"I'll be waiting. Faith, too." That would show him she wasn't easy—maybe.

"Great. Faith, too." Shaking his mane of blue-black hair back over his shoulders, Jeff made for the stage.

****

The Ryders packed up at midnight, and another band took their place. Kara drank four Cuba libres, sure she'd danced them off. Regardless, Jeff held her elbow as they walked to the band's van. Sober as a nun at midnight mass, Faith followed

The drummer, a big fellow already going soft around the middle, packed his equipment. He wore his bleached hair in a crew cut, making his pumpkin-like head seem even larger. The keyboard man, skinny, dark, and hook-nosed, could have been Jeff's much less attractive younger brother. He leaned against the van and smoked a cigarette.

"Meet the band, Kara. My drummer, Baxter Legg, who prefers to be called Buzz Light. This is Rico Vega who works the boards. Bass guitar and backup is Eric Larson, better known as Deuce. Where the hell is Deuce?"

"He said he had some place to be." Rico Vega shrugged. Since Kara was obviously with Jeff, he eyed Faith up and down and shrugged again indifferently.

"Want to get something to eat?" Jeff offered.

"Our car is over there." Faith nudged Kara in the right direction.

"We can all go in the van and bring you back later to pick it up."

"Sounds great!" Kara clambered into the front seat as Jeff held the door for her.

Faith shook her head, but got into the backseat next to Rico. Buzz Light settled himself down amid the equipment in the rear. As they pulled out of the lot, the sweet, mellow scent of marijuana rose from the drum section. They drove an Omelet Shop out on the highway. By the time they got seats at the counter, Kara felt light-headed from her drinks and the pot fumes. Faith ordered coffee and waffles to soak up the alcohol for both of them while the band members tucked into platters of eggs and sausage. Kara paid for their food since none of the men offered. They took the long, long way back to the parking lot.

The van came to a stop at a deserted picnic area on the outskirts of town. Buzz lit up a fresh roach and offered it around on a clip. Rico took a drag and passed it on to Jeff. He offered it to Kara, but she shook her head, and Faith, looking as if she held a live cockroach, passed it back to Buzz.

"I like to come here after a gig and look at the stars. I'm inspired by heavenly bodies." Jeff slid his arm around Kara's bare shoulders. Far in the rear of the van, Buzz snickered.

Jeff ignored their audience. He pressed his lips lightly on hers. She responded by licking the outline of his mouth. In a moment, they were trading tongue. With one hand, Jeff released the single button holding up Kara's halter-top. He gave her a very thorough breast exam with both hands. She could feel the light calluses built up from playing the guitar rasping over her nipples. One of his hands moved under her skirt. She opened for him and tried to lose herself in the sensation of his long fingers probing and stroking, first through her panties, and then inside of them. Jeff climbed over Kara and pressed her back into the seat, his erection hard against her center.

So, this was it, her first time—awkward and embarrassing in the front seat of a battered van with the odor of pot in the air and another couple tussling in the backseat. No upstairs room in a frat house, no mildewed mattress in a Poconos' dacha, no flowery meadow at a Christian summer camp for Kara Shafer. At least, she'd be able to say she'd done it with a man ten times as pretty as her.

A foot against the back of their seat jolted them both forward. Faith and Rico wrestled for supremacy. "I said put that back where it belongs!" Faith ordered.

"Hey, anybody want a condom? I got two I'm not using," offered Buzz. Two foil packets landed in the front seat.

Jeff picked one up and tore the wrapper with his teeth. He whispered in Kara's ear, "You on the pill, sweetheart?"

"No," she answered in a small voice.

"Shit! I don't trust these things. My brother always used a condom and still had to marry his girlfriend when he was twenty. Now he has two kids, a mortgage, and a job selling suits at Men's Warehouse, and he's not even twenty-five. Look, baby, I don't want to ruin my life—or yours either, so this stops here." Jeff Ryder flung himself back into the driver's seat.

"Ah, fuck! Not pepper spray," Rico said. "I'm done wit' you, too. We should let 'em both walk home."

"I'd rather!" Faith snapped.

"No, we'll take you to your car. No more side trips, I promise."

Jeff Ryder started the van, giving Kara time to pull her dress both up and down. She found her panties on the floorboards and struggled into them without lifting her skirt. They parked next to Faith's car. Jeff gave Kara a lingering kiss against its door as Faith put away the pepper spray she'd kept handy, and Rico cursed softly in Spanish.

"No hard feelings, baby," Jeff told her. "Maybe some other time when we don't have so much company."

He opened the car door for Kara and buckled her into her seat. "Take care, sweetheart." In the moonlight, his grin glittered with all the magnetism of a vampire.

Kara watched him in the side view mirror until their car turned onto the street. Faith fumed, but Kara dreamed of a chance to be alone with Jeff Ryder, beautiful Jeff, who'd stopped out of consideration for her and told her to take care.

Chapter Four
The Deflowering

"I cannot believe you went parking with Jeff Ryder," Lulu was saying. "Don't you know about him, girl?" They sat in the suite's small living room on the cracked cushions of the shabby green Vinyl sofa while waiting for Faith to finish dressing up for Jesus on Sunday morning.

"We met at the poetry slam. I know he is incredibly sexy and very considerate when it comes to women," Kara replied.

"Everyone in the music college is aware he's flunking out and—and—he does drugs. That's why he wears sunglasses to class, so you can't tell his eyes are dilated. He comes from this filthy rich family who lives on the Main Line in a mansion, and they are about to disown him for wanting to be a rock musician." Lulu imparted her knowledge with her arms crossed under her chest and a tone of dire warning in her alto voice.

"I know he writes beautiful poetry, and except for that one toke, he didn't seem high to me."

"Kara Shafer, you should stay away from that man." The arms unfolded and a finger wagged.

"I think he'll be staying away from me. He doesn't do girls who aren't on the pill. Are you, Lulu? I know you and Greg must be using something."

Lulu's face turned same shade of red as her hair.

"Since we got back to school, I went over to Planned Parenthood. Neither Greg nor I can afford not to finish college. Hannah is taking them, too, in case Brad gets carried away before the wedding."

"Planned Parenthood, you say."

"Ah, Kara. You don't have to. Jeff Ryder has moved on for sure. He probably isn't used to the virginal types."

"Thanks a lot, voice of experience. Just keep reminding me that I'm the only virgin left in the bunch."

"Look, sex isn't all that great." Red washed over Lulu's face again. "Okay, I'm lying. It's the best free thing in the universe, but I found the right guy, that's all. You should wait."

"Thanks for the advice, Mother Lulu. Where did you say Planned Parenthood is located?"

Reluctantly, Lulu wrote down an address and handed it to Kara just as Faith stuck her head in the doorway.

"You ready for church, Kara? Lulu, are you sure you don't want to come?"

Kara put the scrap of paper into her purse right beside the dollar she took along for the offering. "Lulu needs her rest after singing all evening. Hannah spent the night at Denlinger's, so it's just us. Let's get this over with."

They walked across campus to the High Street United Church of Christ and were given a friendly greeting and a program by the ushers. A fair number of students attended. One group moved toward the center of the pew to give Faith and Kara room to sit.

While Kara marked the first hymn with her

program, Faith gave her an elbow in the ribs. "Whoever said it isn't worth getting up to go to church? Look ahead and to your right. Isn't that Will Collier?"

It was Will, all right. Imprisoned between two people as tall and broad as himself, they could only be his parents. As if he knew someone talked about him, Will glanced back toward the girls. Even two rows away they could see his blue eyes were bloodshot and deeply shadowed.

Faith whispered, "Must be wonderful having your parents catch you with a hangover."

"Let's thank the Lord ours live far away and call before coming."

"Amen to that."

They stood for the opening hymn, and the service proceeded. Kara daydreamed of Jeff Ryder and the pleasures of the flesh during the sermon. She forked over her dollar gladly and made her fast escape when the benediction concluded. She nearly put the address of Planned Parenthood in the collection plate. Wouldn't that have been a hoot?

The minister tended to gab and held each person captive by the hand as he spoke to his retreating congregants. He told Faith at length about their youth group especially for college students while Kara, having slipped past the greeting, waited impatiently outside on the church steps. Will Collier attempted to do the same thing, but when the light of the spring morning hit his eyes, he winced and stumbled into Kara. His parents passed the clergyman with a quick handshake and a "just visiting" once Faith got out of the way.

"Sorry," Will mumbled.

"Forget it, Will," Kara replied. Now that she'd lost interest in him, her words came without effort.

"These girls friends of yers, Will-yum?" his mother said.

On the alert to save her son from bad women, she gave the young females a basilisk stare with pale gray eyes so sharp Kara looked down to make sure all the buttons on her blouse remained closed. Mrs. Collier stood close to six feet tall, raw-boned with large, sloping breasts. She had her coarse salt-and-pepper hair drawn back into a bun at her nape like a granny. The severe style made her large Roman nose more noticeable, as did the deep lines bracketing a hard mouth adorned by a slash of red lipstick. Hands as large as her son's clasped a big black handbag immense enough to assault any felon who might try to snatch it. Her dress was a drab navy blue and plain. Her shoes looked as if they had been recommended by an orthopedist. She did not smile when she questioned her son.

"Ah—yes, I guess." Will squinted against the sunlight.

His father came up and pumped both of the girls' hands. "Always glad to meet Will's friends, especially the pretty ones."

Mr. Collier had the same height as his son, but brawny and big-bellied instead of buff in body. Muscular forearms covered with sandy hair bulged from his short-sleeved dress shirt. He'd shucked his suit coat and loosened his tie immediately after exiting the church. His blue eyes were merrier than his offspring's, and his curly, light-brown going gray, close-cropped hair receded at the temples. Will Collier favored his father in looks, thank heaven.

"Would you lovely ladies like to join us for lunch at the High Street Diner?" Will's father invited.

His mother frowned. "We were gonna have a nice, quiet Sunday dinner with our son, but ya can come along if ya want to."

Kara decided to put Will out of his misery as he shifted his feet and searched for an escape route. "Thank you, but we have other plans, Mr. and Mrs. Collier. It was nice meeting you."

"Likewise," snapped Mrs. Collier, herding her men down the stairs and away from the other women.

"I cannot believe you passed up a chance to eat dinner with Will Collier," Faith said, amazed.

"I'm no longer interested," Kara answered and meant it.

****

She'd been to Planned Parenthood, read their literature, and participated in a group discussion about the need for birth control and the dangers of contracting sexually transmitted diseases. Kara had kept her appointment with a recommended doctor for a checkup, been lectured again, and finally obtained a prescription for the pills. She couldn't start taking them until she had a period, still a week off, and she'd never been more irritable with PMS. For two weeks, she avoided the coffeehouse and stayed away from the Hot Spot. Finals approached, and she should do great because all she did was study.

Whether from stress or plain good luck, her period came a few days early. Kara started her testing drugged with cramp and bloating meds and counting off the five days until she could pop that first pill from its little plastic ring. Time was running out. Once finals ended, the students scattered, and Jeff Ryder's band would hit the road. She could have left for home on Thursday afternoon because she had no finals scheduled Friday. Faith and Hannah had already decamped, leaving a grumbling Lulu behind to study for her last exam. Kara took her first pill that morning and went to the coffeehouse that night looking for Jeff Ryder.

She found him there, not performing, but handing out badly printed flyers giving the dates and places the Ryders of the Night would play over the summer. He wore his shades and a white silk scarf over his usual black clothes and failed to notice Kara when she entered the room. Kara salvaged one of the flyers being used to soak up a ring-shaped puddle on a café table. It noted the band's first stop as Baltimore, but by July, the Ryders should arrive in Reading, just ten miles from her home in Lost Spring. Someone snatched the flyer from her hand.

"Have a fresh one, Kara Shafer. Will I be seeing your smile across the room at one of our gigs?" Jeff Ryder stood so close she could feel his body heat.

"I live near Reading, a little town called Lost Spring. Yes, I'll try to come."

"I've done all the damage I can here. You want a coffee or some food? I'm heading up to the High Street Diner to post a few flyers."

"Sure, I'll go along. My finals are over. I'm free."

They swung along the main drag, pausing whenever Jeff felt moved to staple another flyer to a telephone pole. Following the old brick pavement past trendy shops catering to students and more upscale restaurants where their parents took them to eat eventually brought them to the cheap and old-fashioned diner where Jeff scarfed up Mom's meatloaf and mashed potatoes, and Kara ordered a toasted cheese sandwich that came with a mound of fries her hips simply didn't need. Too preoccupied rehearsing lines in her mind announcing she was now birth control safe, she failed to keep up much of a conversation.

Jeff didn't seem to notice. Energized by the thought of going on tour, he ate the large lump of meat sitting in tomato sauce like a pool of blood as ravenously as a panther in the zoo and ordered a large slice of apple pie with ice cream for dessert. Kara on the other hand grew so nervous she finished all the fries she intended to leave on her plate automatically dipping them in a swirl of ketchup. The cheese oozed from the last triangle of her sandwich as she raised it to her mouth and headed for her chest. She flicked out her tongue in time to catch the rich, yellow glob.

Jeff Ryder stopped in mid-sentence and stared at her mouth. "I never knew eating a cheese sandwich could be so sexy," he claimed.

"I'm on the pill now," she answered.

"Well, we have the whole night ahead of us, and you, Kara Shafer, are too fine a lady to do it in the front of a van. I know a place on the edge of town where we can get some privacy."

"The Piney Woods Motel?"

"You know the place. Been there often?"

"No, never. Other people I know go there—for privacy."

"Let's find the van. I know I left it near the coffeehouse."

Jeff paid their bill. Kara snuck back while he went

into the restroom and left a tip because he hadn't added anything to the tab for the waitress. She wanted everyone to be happy tonight. They went back down High Street faster than they'd come, tripping over cracks and snapping twigs off of bushes that grew too close to the sidewalk. The van stood in plain sight half a block from the café. The drive to the Piney Woods proved fast and brief.

Kara slouched down in the front seat as Jeff paid for a room with a credit card he said his dad would repossess once his son made it clear he wasn't coming back to college in the fall. Jingling the key, Jeff moved the van to a space in front of lucky number seven. Lucky for him. After helping Kara out, he rummaged under the backseat and came up with a half empty bottle of Bacardi rum and a roach of marijuana.

"Refreshments and entertainment," he said.

Jeff left Kara standing in the middle of the room while he went to fill the plastic ice bucket and get two Cokes from the vending machine next to the office. The Piney Woods offered clean orange chenille bedspreads, white unfitted sheets, and tired furniture circa 1968. The night table had a ring eaten through the varnish exactly the size and shape of a rolled condom. The maid had placed a clear glass ashtray over the spot, but that only magnified it. The old couple who ran the place made most of their income off of college students. They probably figured there was no sense in replacing the table when the same incident would happen again. Kara waited perched on the edge of the sagging mattress, unsure if she should take off her clothes and slip under the covers or let Jeff undress her.

She didn't want to appear too easy, so she

continued to sit on the side of the bed, wiping her sweaty palms on the tangerine-colored spread. Finally, she kicked off her sandals. Jeff returned and made drinks for both of them in two plastic cups. He held up the roach.

"Now or later?"

"Later." Kara figured this might be her first night for many new experiences. She wasn't a smoker or into drugs, but she did gulp down that drink.

Jeff put an arm around her and sucked her lower lip into his mouth. "You're tense," he said after a while of oral exploration.

"I'm a virgin."

His arm dropped. "I've never done a virgin."

"Well, you have the chance now. I guess you've been with a lot of women."

"Hell, yes. I mean I started at fifteen. This senior thought I was hot. She had a bedroom on the first floor of her parents' house, and she'd leave the window open for me. She went to the prom with someone else though. I wrote a poem about that once—about being good enough to sleep with, but not good enough to take to the prom—from the guy's point of view. Then, a couple of other girls in high school. We have women who follow our band—not as many as you would think—and you have to be careful of those because of the diseases they can give you. I'm real careful who I go with."

Jeff wiped his hand across the bedspread and fumbled in his hip pocket. "I have condoms."

Suddenly, Kara realized she made sexy Jeff Ryder nervous. But, he was The One. She didn't want him to have second thoughts or be unable to perform. She began to unbutton her blouse, letting it hang open over the pink satin bra with no padding because she didn't need any. She'd made a special trip to Victoria's Secret in the nearest mall for the underwear of her deflowering and intended to get maximum impact for the price. She wiggled out of her jeans to reveal the matching panties with lace side panels and a strip of pink satin in the middle. Jeff watched with interest. She put a hand on the lump in his crotch and rubbed it lightly.

"Better not do that," he cautioned. "Lie down. I'll give you a massage."

The first part of giving a massage involved unhooking her bra and pulling the panties down over her buttocks. He did knead her shoulders, his erection prodding between her legs as he leaned forward. He worked down to her waist and even rubbed her ass thoroughly before sliding a hand between her legs. The panties came all the way off. The bra slipped aside as Kara turned over, her eyes closed, her breathing ragged.

Jeff inserted one finger inside her, stroking carefully as if he tested a new musical instrument. He strummed her soft, slick folds with his thumb and laughed softly when he found the sweet spot and she bucked. He moved a second long, slim finger to join the first, and when he had Kara writhing, he took his hand away, applied his condom, and re-entered with his penis.

She gasped. He stopped. "Did I hurt you?"

"No, not much. Just move, move."

Kara pressed her hands against his backside and urged him on. She felt full and uncomfortable, but another tightness built low in her pelvis. Forgetting about being gentle and careful, Jeff closed his eyes and rocked on. She pushed back. He breathed hard now, and when Kara made a soft cry and dug her nails into his back, he didn't seem to care. He rode on and on until his sweat dropped on her chest and, gasping, he collapsed against them with his ear pressed against the beating of her heart.

When he caught his breath, he said, "That was the best I've ever had."

"Me, too," whispered Kara as she stroked the blue-black hair splayed across her breasts.

****

Lulu had the kindness not to wake Kara when she left for her final even though she burned with curiosity. True, during finals people came and went at all hours in the dorm, but for Kara to come in at dawn was a first. She'd heard her fumbling out of her clothes and into a nightshirt. When she looked in on her, trying to be a good roommate, Lulu noticed the pink panties stained with a deep maroon streak on the floor. No sense in letting good underwear be ruined. She snatched them up and put them in the sink to soak in cold water.

Kara was up when Lulu returned with a bag of oversized blueberry muffins, two coffees, and a sure A in her advanced vocals class. She handed Kara one of the thick paper cups and placed a muffin on a napkin.

"Spill it."

"The coffee?" Kara said innocently. She gulped the hot beverage as if her mouth were very, very dry.

"I'm the one who put your panties in the sink, roomie. Sooo, I deduce you found Jeff Ryder ready, willing, and able."

"Smart thinking, Sherlock. He was The One. We went to the Piney Woods Motel."

"He spent the big bucks for your first time. I can appreciate that. Greg and I had to make do with the dacha and a lumpy mattress."

"Paid for it with his father's credit card. We had something to drink—and then we did it."

"What do you think?" Lulu peeled the wrapper from a muffin and broke off a piece.

"I think I'm sore because we did it more than once—and you were right. Sex is the greatest free thing in the universe. Makes you hungry, too." Kara devoured a muffin. "I need to get dressed and finish packing. My mother is going to be here with a borrowed Volvo station wagon to pick up my junk in a couple of hours."

"Volvo. That always sounds so obscene. When do you think you'll see Jeff again?"

"Probably never. He's leaving for a gig in Baltimore and touring around all summer. I doubt if he will even call before he goes or get in touch with me later, you know, like Faith's fellow," Kara said as if she were too sophisticated to care.

The phone rang. Lulu grabbed it first.

"Madam Lulu's Chicken Ranch. We pluck 'em, you fuck 'em. Yes, Kara is available."

"That could be my mother!"

Lulu grinned, showing a blueberry caught in her teeth. "Could be, but it's not. Hang on, Jeff. She looks fine to me, glowing even." Lulu tossed the phone to her roommate and settled in to listen.

"Yes, I'm fine. A little sore. It's nothing. I know you have to get on the road to Baltimore. Don't worry about it. Yes, I'll see you in Reading, if not sooner. Bye, Jeff."

"Be still my heart." Lulu clasped her freckled hands across her chest. "A man who calls afterwards to make sure you're okay."

"Didn't Greg?"

"We were still together afterwards, all weekend. So, when are you going to see the sexy, rich, poetic druggie, Jeff Ryder, again?"

"Like I said, probably never." Kara gathered the paper cups and the muffin wrappers, shoving them all into the last trash bag to go to the dumpster before they left for the summer.

Lulu watched as her roommate hauled out the garbage. Considerately, she bagged the wet panties in plastic and shoved them way down inside Kara's open suitcase where her mother wouldn't see. Somehow, Lulu didn't believe her roommate. She and Gregor always found a way to be together. So would Jeff and Kara.

Chapter Five
Summertime

Kara accepted two dates in the month of June from guys who hung around the pool snack bar as if they could sniff out the loss of her virginity the way flies found bodies in which to lay their eggs. Maybe she projected a more worldly confident personality now because both men tried to go too far on the first date. She'd scraped them off, and they hadn't asked her out again. This didn't surprise her.

The constant stream of emails and texts plus the occasional postcard from Jeff Ryder did. The band did well, attracted a following. Jeff wrote that since he'd met her, he'd become inspired. She was his muse. He'd written a song for her that she'd hear in July when the Ryders of the Night played Reading.

A muse? Her? Plain old Kara Shafer with the nice smile, good personality, and slightly too big butt? She would not fall in love with Jeff Ryder. He was only her current crush like Will Collier had been the year before. Besides, no way would Jeff Ryder love her back if it came to that. Too bad no one else appealed to her.

She marked off the days until July first on the snack bar calendar, measuring the hours passing by bags of penny candy sold and cherry Popsicles ordered from the wholesaler when the kids began to complain only orange ones were left. Jeff Ryder blew into town at last and called her from the joint out on the Kutztown Road where he performed that night. He had to spend the afternoon dropping flyers around the campus of Albright College, the state school up the road, and the technical college, hoping to attract summer students, but then, he would be free until nine when the band was scheduled to start. She got off at six and called home to say she'd be going out with friends.

Jeff Ryder appeared even better than he did in her nightly dreams. With his blue-black hair grown one month longer, he'd tied it back with a thong. Shades in place, he had three days growth of dark stubble that showcased his perfect smile, and somehow, he found the time to take a tan that covered his poet's pallor. He said she looked great, too. He liked that she wore her hair a little longer and her tops and jeans a little tighter to show off her—assets.

They went for cheese steak sandwiches and real milkshakes at the place Kara knew about from last summer's adventure with the biker and joked about having onion breath and not caring because they tasted the same. Kara knew about a grove that provided some privacy—because one of her pushy dates had taken her there.

After reassuring Jeff that she still took the pill, they spread a blanket over the grass and had sex like long lost lovers, which was sort of what they were, kind of. The second time, Kara asked permission to be on top. Jeff Ryder laughed out loud and told her she had no need to beg, she could do what she wanted to him. Fascinated by the patch of dark hair on his chest, his long, lithe limbs, she reveled in the power she seemed to have when she stroked his manly parts to attention.

Mounted up, she tossed back her hair, closed her eyes, and rode him until they were both satisfied—as if she had been doing this for years. Finished, sweat cooling their naked bodies, they rolled apart and watched the sun set through the trees.

"You're so tight, and your reactions are so pure, you make all other girls seem like skanks," Jeff said. "Stay this way forever."

"Well, thanks, I guess. You're wonderful, too."

Jeff swatted her nicely rounded backside. "Mosquitoes are coming out. We'd better get dressed."

****

Jeff arrived ten minutes late for the gig in yet another metal building sitting in another gravel parking lot. Named rather prosaically, Burger's Roadhouse, its lot held a clutch of motorcycles and was just beginning to fill with the small cars owned by college students on summer break and a few trucks driven by local farm boys. The bouncer at the door asked for Kara's license and noted she'd turned twenty-one just last week.

"I didn't know that. I should have brought you a gift. I do have a gift, my song for Kara Shafer," Jeff Ryder said.

He led her to a table right in front of the bandstand where the Ryders of the Night sat looking surly because the manager just chewed their asses about the music starting late. Jeff soothed the boss man's temper with his Main Line manners and a promise to play an extra half hour for free. The Ryders grumbled, got up, and took the stage.

Jeff breathed into the microphone in that low, sexy voice of his, "Ladies and gentlemen, I'd like to start out tonight with an original song written for this lovely lady sitting at the front table. Then, we'll do some of your favorites. Pass us a note if you have a request."

He snapped his fingers three times to give the band a starting point. "I met her after school, and I knew that she was cool—but imagine my surprise—when she turned out to be a—HOT VIRGIN! HOT VIRGIN!"

Kara covered her face, but Jeff came off the stage and peeled her fingers away from her blistering red cheeks. He put the mike to her lips. "Sing it, baby."

"Hot virgin," she sang in an off-key, quavering voice.

"Now everybody! HOT VIRGIN!"

The bikers at the table across the dance floor raised their beer bottles in her direction. Kara prayed that none of them were the guy she'd gone to that scary party with last summer. She didn't recognize any familiar tattoos. The entire crowd roared HOT VIRGIN now. The lyrics extolling her unexpected enthusiasm in bed went on and on and on with the chorus coming up all too frequently.

When the ordeal ended, drinks began to appear magically at her table—a frosty beer, a tequila shot, an elegant martini with two olives—along with notes saying, "How about it, honey?" and "Meet you in the parking lot in five" or "I'm driving the red Corvette." Kara figured if she drank all the alcohol provided, she might be able to black out her embarrassment.

Jeff swooped down to scoop up the notes and shred them on stage. "No way, she's my HOT VIRGIN. Find your own." Humping his guitar, he plowed into an encore. The audience laughed.

The band started another song, and dancers got up to bump to the beat. Kara downed the tequila shot, which burned all the way to her belly and attempted to put out the fire with sips of the cold beer. At this rate, Jeff would have to drive her home and pour her out on her parents' doorstep. Since she'd been marked as Jeff's girl, no one asked her to dance and getting drunk became a very real possibility. Still, she paced herself and just finished the martini when the band took a break and Jeff came to sit with her.

"I guess liking this is an acquired taste," she said, sucking on an olive to get the flavor out of her mouth and trying not to look like she wanted to be somewhere else.

"You weren't embarrassed, were you? My song was supposed to be a tribute," Jeff said. "Let me get you a rum and Coke. I know you like the sweet drinks better."

"Well, you did sing it like you hadn't had sex since the Piney Woods Motel."

"I haven't. I leave the skanks for Rico and Deuce. All Buzz ever wants is a dime bag of pot."

"You really haven't been with anyone for over a month?" She searched his face for signs of lying. Hard to read his eyes in the dark cavern of the roadhouse.

"No. You?"

"Of course not."

"Kara, since I met you I've had all kinds of luck. Songs pop into my head begging to be written. Club owners seek us out instead of the other way around. Hell, my dad didn't even cut off my credit card, and we've been sleeping in motels instead of the van. I don't want this to end."

"Us or your lucky streak?'

"Both. Say, uh, we play here on the Fourth in the

afternoon. Then, I have a mandatory performance at my folk's house for a barbecue. Want to go meet the source of my funding?"

"Odd way to put it, but yes. Lulu tells me you live in a mansion on the Main Line."

"On a side street really. It's a big house, but not a mansion, befitting the orthodontist to the rich, my dad, Jules Ryder, DDS, better known as 'Jaws' to his friends."

"That explains your fabulous smile."

"I get free whitenings."

"Can't wait to meet a man called Jaws."

"Be careful he doesn't eat you alive. He's already swallowed my brother and sister and regurgitated them in his own image."

"Ugh."

"Yeah, ugh. Gotta go start another set. Don't go anywhere."

Jeff started the second set with *A Song for Beautiful Women* and pointed to Kara first.

****

Allison Ryder met her son and his friends at the door. A well-kept blonde patrician housewife, she checked out Kara from top to toe while greeting the boys and pointing them toward cold drinks and hot hors d'oeuvres on the patio. Buzz Light pounded across the oriental runner in the hallway and out the French doors at the rear of the lovely limestone colonial with two white pillars at its front entry. He left a lingering smell of pot behind in the flower-scented air. A huge bouquet of tropical blossoms in a blue and white china vase graced a hall table with little bowed legs and clawed feet.

Kara had dressed for inspection in good tan slacks, a one-hundred-percent cotton fitted sleeveless blouse of deep blue, carefully ironed, and a white cardigan hung over her shoulders in case the evening became cool— nothing too tight, too tacky, or too synthetic for the Main Line. She hoped Mrs. Ryder would not suspect the sandals came from Shoe Town. Allison's painted toenails peeped out of similar sandals, though she probably picked hers up in Florence on her last trip to Italy.

"Kara, Jeff has told us so much about you—how nice you are, how intelligent, and pretty."

She guessed herself to be all but the last. "Thank you for having me over, Mrs. Ryder."

"Alli. Call me Alli, but please don't call my husband Jaws. His name is Jules, a perfectly good name. Come meet the rest of the family."

Since Jeff had abandoned her to his mother, she followed Alli out onto the flagstone patio.

"Look, Kara, little crab cakes." Buzz held two in his hand and chewed on a third.

"Good sangria, Mrs. R." Rico Vega topped off his balloon glass.

"I wanted to make you feel at home, dear," Allison said.

"You know I come from Philly, right?"

"Yes, but I want everything to be perfect for everyone."

Jeff and Deuce sat on a glider with pale beige cushions that probably had to be replaced every year. They moved to make room for Kara who accepted a sangria poured by Rico. On the edge of a large manicured lawn, Jaws, orthodontist to the rich, toiled over a large stainless grill as bright as an adolescent's braces. He basted split lobster tails with butter and lemon juice and checked on the contents of a large boiling pot.

From a distance, Dr. Ryder looked like a larger, less refined version of Jeff. He dressed in topsiders, khakis, and a turquoise golf shirt rather than all black. His dark hair was slick and combed back, long only on top, and he had probably shaved around noon. He turned his large, dark eyes on the group occupying his terrace. Clearly, Jeff had inherited his father's coloring, but his mother's light complexion and slighter build. Jaws turned and waved to his audience. He'd covered his clothing with a barbecue apron shaped like a shark. A stuffed cloth leg dangled from a pocket in the white appliqued teeth.

"Steamers and tails are about ready. I hope you brought an appetite."

He cupped his hands around his mouth and shouted the same message toward the rear of the long lawn where a rustic cottage with gingerbread trim housed the riding mower and yard tools. A thin young woman walked a toddler around a goldfish pond with a small bubbler in the center. A handsome man, a younger Jaws, chased a four-year-old across the grass, caught the little boy and swung the child up on his shoulders. The small, perfect family joined together at the pond and headed in for dinner.

A timer went off in the kitchen, and Mrs. Ryder rose. "The cheese petit fours are ready. You must eat them while they're warm. I wish Steven never bought that apron for his father. It's in such bad taste. Our son and daughter-in-law, our grandchildren, Steven,

Brooke, Schuyler, and Trenton," she informed Kara about the approaching group.

Alli whipped into the house to save her hors d'ouvres and returned with a tray of what looked like tiny cakes but tasted like bleu cheese. Her eldest grandson insisted on having one and spit it out on the lawn when he discovered the cake wasn't sweet. Alli frowned at her grandson as Schuyler also resisted a cherry tomato and a celery stick from the vegetable tray, but finally accepted a baby carrot and a plastic cup of caffeine-free diet cola to wash away the taste.

"It's always best to eat outside when children are involved," Alli remarked. "They make such a mess."

The toddler settled into a high chair and gnawed a chicken drumette along with some chopped cantaloupe from the fruit tray. The rest of the family and friends gathered at two picnic tables covered with checked linen cloths held down at the corners with little pewter weights shaped like ladybugs and honeybees. Alli lit the candles under individual warmers with a long match and poured melted butter into the small pots while her husband forked nets of corn and cherrystone clams on to each plate, adding a curved half of lobster tail, nicely grilled, on the side with his tongs. He put on his oven mitts, removed foil-wrapped potatoes from deep in the grill and heaped them on a platter to be passed.

"Everyone have drinks? Good. Dig in before the grub gets cold," he said.

Grub? Lobster was a treat ordered in a restaurant only on birthdays in Kara's world. She saved that special pleasure for last and daintily plucked the small clams from their shells with a tiny silver-plated fork topped with a real seashell. Down the table, Buzz extracted the meat from his lobster with a thumb and dipped the whole tail in melted butter that dribbled down his chin when he ate. Deuce and Rico knew how to use forks. Deuce even knew about dinner conversation. With his short dirty blond hair and light eyes, dressed in khakis, a casual cotton shirt and loafers without socks, Deuce came closest of all the band members to fitting in at a Main Line picnic.

"So, wassup, Dr. R?"

"Big news. Steven has been promoted to manager at his sales job. When he gets a few more years of experience under his belt, Brooke's father and I are going to see about financing a nice little haberdashery for him right here in Bryn Mawr."

"Haber-dash-ery, huh?" Buzz said slowly.

"A men's clothing store, idiot." Deuce gave the drummer an elbow in the ribs and caused Buzz to swallow the clam he was rolling on his tongue too suddenly. Deuce pounded his back until the coughing stopped.

Across the table, skinny, pale, and rather plain Brooke Ryder appeared thoroughly grossed out. She'd filled her plate with raw vegetables and fruit and declined a potato. For the daughter-in-law of an orthodontist, she possessed bad teeth, not crooked, but yellow as if the enamel had thinned. She wore her sandy hair very short, accenting the hollows in her cheeks, and had toothpick legs and almost no breasts at all. Seated between Jeff, who had been shunted to the far end of the table by his mother, and her husband, dark, hardy, and as good looking as Dr. Ryder had probably been in his youth, Brooke seemed like a smear of light mayonnaise between two hunks of rye. How she managed to give birth to two robust children, Kara had no idea.

"So, what does your father do, Kara?" asked the orthodontist.

"He's a supervisor at one of the mills in Reading. My mother is a bookkeeper there. She does payroll."

"That must be difficult to keep track of—all those deductions and such. You know, Jeff could have gone to Julliard if he'd gotten better grades," Mrs. Ryder said. "Our daughter, Jennifer, is backpacking in Europe this summer. She's going to be a dentist like her father."

Was Mrs. Ryder merely filling her in on the family history or implying if Jeff had gone to Julliard he would have met a better class of people than her and the band members? A drop of melted butter from the morsel of lobster Kara lifted to her lips splattered on her blue blouse. What a klutz she was compared to the elegant Allison.

"Oh, I should have provided lobster bibs. I'm so sorry, dear. I think it will come out with a little pre-soaking. Do you have brothers, sisters?"

"Two sisters. The oldest married a military man. He's a captain now. They're stationed in Germany. My younger sister starts college this year at Albright. She wants to teach French."

"Teaching is always a good profession for a woman. That way they have the same time off as their children if they continue to work after marriage. Do you plan to teach, Kara?"

"Perhaps in college if I can get an assistantship to go to grad school. What do you do, Mrs. Ryder?" Kara answered, a little tired of the interrogation.

"Me? Oh, I have my clubs—garden, bridge, crafts. I serve on a number of committees—beautification, cancer society, heart association. Does anyone need more melted butter? Seconds on the lobster? We have plenty." Allison Ryder rose to get these offerings from the grill and her husband took over like a tag team champion.

"Jeff has one year to get this rock band nonsense out of his system, then, snip, snip, we cut up the credit cards. What do you think of that?"

"I think if he really wants to pursue music as a career, he will find a way to do what has to be done. He does have talent and writes his own songs. Have you ever listened to them?" Kara picked up the correct fork and dug it into her baked potato.

"It's not my kind of music. I prefer classical. I play classical music in my office. It soothes the patients, and those kids won't hear it anywhere else. You know, Jeff could have gone to Julliard and played with a symphony orchestra. We never should have bought him a guitar. A trombone is a fine instrument, or a French horn."

Good, Dr. Ryder hadn't heard *Hot Virgin*; bad that he didn't support his son's choice with anything but money. Kara found that very sad. Neither of her parents had gone to college, but they told her whatever she wanted to do was fine with them so long as she could make a decent living. They still had her younger sister to put through school. Kara had been given four free years to finish college. After that, her life was her own.

Dusk set in by the time Mrs. Ryder served the angel food cake iced with real whipped cream and stuffed with a strawberry puree. Brooke and Kara helped her clear the tables while the men mellowed out with cold beer, declining hot coffee, as they sat around the tables playing desultory rounds of black jack in which everyone but Deuce soon lost interest. Allison Ryder ventured out to light decorative containers of citronella to ward off mosquitoes, and Kara found herself alone with Brooke who seemed to be staring at the butter stain on Kara's blouse.

"If I had breasts that big, I'd probably tip over."

Kara nodded, not knowing what to say.

"I only had good breasts when I nursed the boys. As soon as I stopped, they just shriveled up and hung there like two fried eggs." Brooke watched her sons chasing fireflies on the lawn under the supervision of their grandfather.

"So you're telling me not to nurse?"

"No. I'm telling you not to get involved with Jeff Ryder." Brooke took a sip of the unsweetened iced tea she brought inside with her. "This is one fucked up family. You know, I was the girl next door—for real. I had this tremendous crush on Steve all through high school."

"I know how that is." Kara kept her eyes on the seafood forks that had to be washed by hand while Brooke shoved the butter ramekins none too gently into the washer.

"Finally, Steve noticed me one summer when he had nothing better to do. We used to have sex out in the storage building—on the lawnmower if you can believe it. That's where we conceived Schuyler. The condom broke. Oops, you're a daddy, Steven. If I were born poor white trash, I could have had my baby single or put it up for adoption or gotten an abortion, but the

Schuyler family takes responsibility for its actions—since the days of the Revolutionary War—as does the Ryder family—since the days of Ellis Island."

Brooke selected a remaining celery stick from the leftovers on the relish tray and tapped it against her thin lips. "You know, the Ryders are only first generation WASPs. When Alli traced her husband's family tree for the Daughters of the American Revolution, she only got as far as 1900 when a Polish Jew named Meyer Ridensky dropped from the branches. He changed his name to Michael Ryder and married an Irish Catholic lass. Their Catholic son brought home a Scottish Presbyterian war bride, and since he didn't give a damn about religion, Jaws out there was baptized a Protestant, which made him eligible to marry the blonde Anglo-Saxon Episcopalian he met while in dental school. All Alli can do is pretend it isn't so. She's a stone cold bitch," Brooke said viciously. She crunched down hard on the celery and swallowed.

"She's been fairly nice to me."

"Wait. Just wait."

Not wanting to hear more, Kara said, "So, is your son named for your family?"

"Yeah, we do that here on the Main Line. We saddle kids with names like that and marry for them, too. I suggested Meyer for a first name. Alli just about had a cow."

"You have beautiful children."

"And a rented townhouse near the mall where Steve works. If we behave and stay together, we'll have a haberdashery someday—whether we want it or not."

"The second child couldn't have been an accident."

"Could have been, but wasn't. Steve cheats on me.

He loves Schuyler so much I thought another child would bring him back. I stopped taking my pills. He hasn't forgiven me yet. Excuse me. I have to go throw up."

"Are you sick? You gave most of your food to Buzz."

"What a pig. Just watching him made me want to upchuck. Kara, you've heard you can never be too thin or too rich. All I've got is thin. That's what my shrink keeps saying is the problem." Brooke fluttered her fingers at Kara as she entered the guest powder room.

Kara went outside to escape the sounds of retching coming from the spotless little bathroom she'd used earlier with its violet-patterned wallpaper and a gardenia-scented candle and matchbook on the back of the commode. She joined Jeff stretched out on a blanket under a beech tree.

"In half an hour, you'll be able to see the public fireworks from here. Claim your spot while you can." Jeff patted the blanket.

Kara lay down beside him, her arms behind her head. "Brooke is in the powder room throwing up. Did you know she's bulimic? I can't figure out how she gave birth to two such healthy, normal children."

"Brooke's a mess, but all that stuff started after she finished nursing Trent. She was a chub in high school, slimmed down in college enough for Steve to take an interest. She gained the weight back after she had Schuyler. Steve, well, Steve goaded her about it. Didn't help that he was banging the skinny chick who works at the earring stand in the mall either. When another kid didn't bring him back, I guess she figured being thin would. Sad, bony bitch."

"Couldn't you talk to your brother and get him to help her? She is the mother of his children."

"She sees a psychiatrist. Her parents pay for it. Look, Steve stays in a marriage to a woman he never loved but wanted to screw for a while. He's a good father. That's the best he can do."

"Did you know Schuyler was conceived in the tool shed—on the riding lawnmower?"

"No shit? You're still on the pill, right?"

"Same as last night."

"When it gets dark and everyone is watching the fireworks, why don't we give that a try?"

"Dream on, rocker boy."

"Look, the first skyrocket."

All eyes turned toward the streak in the sky that burst open into a cascade of silver and gold. When the rockets exploded as fast as popcorn thrown into a fire, Jeff tugged Kara's arm. She went with him, not wanting to draw attention by resisting. Once through the doors of the little cottage, which looked like a plain metal shed on the inside, Jeff settled himself on the seat of the mower and sat Kara on his groin. He unbuttoned her blouse and unhooked her bra, letting her breasts free fall.

"We aren't going to do this, Jeff."

He didn't answer, his mouth being on her breasts, his hands busy fondling them. By the time he shoved her slacks and panties down to her knees and unzipped himself, she'd forgotten about arguing with him. She stood up on the fenders to mount him, threw her head back, closed her eyes, and enjoyed. Jeff gripped her buttocks, murmuring that he loved a good handful. The fireworks reached the grand finale just when they did.

They kept going after the last explosions petered out, trying for two.

The shed door swung open. Kara stared directly into the wide, shocked blue eyes of Allison Ryder. Desperately, she tried to pull her bra down over her breasts and fasten it from behind, a mistake because they kept falling out the bottom. Inside of her body, Jeff's penis shriveled to boy size.

"Get dressed and come to the house. I'll expect you in five minutes," Mrs. Ryder ordered. She made her queen-like exit, closing the door behind her. Like naughty children, Jeff and Kara hung their heads and obeyed.

In the interrogation room, otherwise known as the study, with the door closed, Mrs. Ryder sat behind her husband's large desk and berated the young couple standing before her on the oriental rug like criminals taken up in a raid.

"If I called your parents, Kara, and told them how I caught you, what would they say? I thought Jeff was bringing home a nice girl, not some band groupie."

Even though her face burned, Kara raised her head and faced the judge. "I am not a groupie. Jeff and I are both twenty-one. I'm on the pill. We're in love." Jeff sucked in his breath, but she went on. "I think my parents would say we're old enough to know what we're doing so long as we're careful."

"Kara, I am sorry for calling you a groupie, and I think, a slut earlier. You know, dear, it is up to the woman to say no, to be the one in control because men have no brains between their legs."

Jeff snickered. "You know what great-granddad always said—free, white, and twenty-one. We're free, and we're leaving. Come on, Kara. I can't take any more of this crap."

His mother appeared as shocked by the word 'crap' as she had been by catching them in the act. Allison Ryder dug her nails into the edge of the desk and watched them go, an expression of disgust marring her beautiful, waspish face.

Jeff gathered his band members, two drunk on the free beer, one not, and lifted Kara into the front seat of the van. On the way back to Reading, the guys in the back zonked out.

"I'm sorry, Kara. My mother had no business walking in on us like that. She sure didn't need a hoe or a rake at ten p.m. at night. I'm sorry she called you a groupie and a slut, and I think I heard the word whore once when she was ranting."

"Went looking for a rake and found a ho', I guess." Kara offered him a small, pained smile.

"Forget what she said. You sure handled her and that threat to call your parents."

"Jeff, she doesn't know my father's first name and probably not the town we live in unless you told her. What was she going to do—slide the tines of the cocktail forks under my nails until I divulged their number? As for myself, maybe I am those things. Two weeks ago, I said I'd walk home if the guy who bought me a nice dinner didn't take his hand off my chest. With you, I'm absolutely wanton."

"Well, you aren't a slut or a whore. You're smart and you're fine. You're a hot virgin, my hot virgin."

"Not a virgin anymore. Just hot for Jeff Ryder. Where is that bucket of cold water when I need one?"

"We can go back to Bryn Mawr. I'm certain my

mother has ice water in the refrigerator as well as in her veins and would be glad to throw it on you just to watch the steam rise."

"I don't think I can ever show my face there again."

"Sure you can—if you love me like you said you did. Love makes it all right."

"The question is—do you love me?" She studied his face in the on-again-off again glare from headlights in the other lane. Jeff kept his eyes on the road.

"Kara, I let the other guys have any groupies who came our way when we were on the road this past month. I've never sung better. When I get together with you, we screw like rabbits in the springtime. If that ain't love, I don't know what is."

Jeff put an arm around her shoulder, his hand resting on her breast, and drove one-handed. Not exactly a lyrical declaration, but as good as she was likely to get for now.

Chapter Six
Going to the Chapel

Senior Year

Jeff Ryder roared in and out of Kara Shafer's life three more times over the summer. Each appearance led to maniacal sex that left her hot and bothered for days afterwards. She turned down dates to keep herself available for Jeff.

Back at college, the same story retold. She might as well have been a nun in a scriptorium surrounded by her books and papers when Jeff was out of town. When he returned, she threw off her nun's habits and became Jeff's insatiable lover. Lulu shook her head over this. Hannah, oblivious, continued the countdown to her December wedding, and Faith urged Kara to attend church.

The only time Kara did go to church she stood by the altar holding Hannah's flowers while the wedding ceremony progressed. Horrified to see Jeff's parents sitting on the groom's side, she strained to keep a carefully neutral expression. Jeff, himself, played elsewhere. At least, her parents hadn't come. Thank God for that!

At the reception, Mrs. Ryder, cordial as ever, said how lovely to see Kara again, all the while staring at the strapless burgundy sheath the six bridesmaids had been required to wear. Being big busted, Kara showed a great deal more cleavage than the other attendants. She tugged up her top. Alli's cold eyes searched below the waist looking for a baby bump, Kara guessed.

At Christmas, Jeff had a gig in the Poconos at a ski lodge boasting one hill and a snow machine. The management wanted to draw a younger crowd. The band got a small chalet to use as part of the deal. Kara and Jeff had a bedroom all to themselves. She and Jeff emerged for food and bathroom breaks. Her family thought she'd gone on a ski trip with the entire Ryder family.

For a gift, Jeff gave her a CD the band recorded to sell after performances with *Hot Virgin* and the *Song for Beautiful Women* on it. Kara presented Jeff with a framed poem she'd written herself and transcribed with a calligraphic pen. She'd done ink sketches of falling leaves, snowflakes, spring flowers, and a burning sun in the margins of the handmade yellow paper. It read:

I miss you in the springtime
when the flowers all abound.
I miss you in the summer
when the sunshine burns the ground.
I miss you in the autumn
when the withered leaves fall down.
I miss you in the winter
when the icy gales come round.
I miss you.

"Corny, corny but sweet. Thanks," Jeff said. "Don't take this one to the poetry slam. They'll pelt you with their biscotti."

"You hate it. Give it back. I'll get you Taco Bell gift certificates or something else useful."

"No, I think I can use this. Teenage girls love simple rhymes they can sing to their boyfriends or copy in their diaries. I could use this for a chorus." Jeff hummed a few notes under his breath.

"Keep it then. At least, I know what not to do next year." Kara stopped talking. Next year, she'd be in graduate school, and who knew where Jeff would be.

"About next year…"

Here it came, Kara Shafer about to be dumped. She squeezed her eyes shut as if that would keep her from hearing.

"What are your plans?"

"My plans? I've applied for an assistantship in English literature at the University of Delaware. I guess I'll teach a few freshman classes, work on my master's degree."

"Wouldn't you rather go on the road with the Ryders—my luck, my muse, my Kara?"

"Your easy lay? Jeff, I have no musical talent whatsoever, and none in poetry, evidently. My parents worked hard to put me through college. I can't toss it all to be your perpetual groupie."

"Think about it," Jeff Ryder said. "Do we have time for one more before you go?"

****

Thinking about being with Jeff occupied Kara's thoughts whenever schoolwork allowed her a chink of time to fill. She managed to meet him during spring break in Pensacola, Florida, where plenty of college girls were ready to take her place in Jeff's bed. The other band members took their pick of women who didn't mind baring their breasts when they were sodden with drink—or not. When they parted again, Jeff told her the band wouldn't make it back north in the next few months. He said he'd try to be there for her graduation, but he didn't arrive to meet her parents or pose for a picture next to her in cap and gown.

Will Collier stood with his proud parents a few feet away from Kara's group after the ceremony. Mr. Collier, jovial as ever, asked her father to take a picture of the mother-son-father combination. He returned the favor for Kara's parents.

Will, looking down at what appeared to be hiking boots sticking out of his academic robe, mumbled, "Summa cum laude, nice going, Kara."

"In English literature, Will. A magna cum laude in math isn't too shabby."

"Yeah. Good luck with teaching or whatever."

"Same to you."

In the two years since she had gotten over Will Collier, this was their longest conversation—ever. They went their separate ways.

****

Despite the occasional phone calls and infrequent emails, Kara knew the affair had ended. She tried to be happy for Lulu and Gregor at their wedding in June as she stood with Hannah and Faith, garbed in what could only be described as some kind of Russian peasant outfit—a poufy skirt and floral embroidered corset worn over a low-cut white blouse. Lulu's mother bought into the folk festival theme entirely. All the girls wore their hair down around their shoulders like maidens of old, though there wasn't a maid amongst them. They sported headpieces of wheat stalks, symbolic of fertility, and dried strawflowers. The bouquets matched.

Selections from Tchaikovsky—that greatest of Russian composers—played before, during, and after the ceremony, in a perfectly normal Presbyterian church in western Pennsylvania. Somewhere, the Horvaths found a reception band that could play both contemporary wedding music and polkas, mazurkas, and whatever songs Russian peasants danced to. Kara suspected they also played Jewish weddings and did gigs in the Poconos. Still, the band filled the vast, barn-like hall the McFarland family rented with sound, and the place supplied plenty of room for dancing.

The wedding band provided an emcee who encouraged numerous toasts to the bride and groom. Guests became more forthcoming about this gesture as copious amounts of cheap champagne lubricated their throats. Champagne consumption segued into tossing back icy cold vodka shots. Mr. Horvath taught the Presbyterians to shout "*Gorka!*" after every toast.

Kara leaned over to Greg at the head table. "Doesn't *gorka* mean bitter, as in Gorky, the famous Russian author?"

"Yeah, and don't ask me why they shout that at weddings. I only know if we had gone Scotch-Irish, I'd be wearing a kilt right now instead of this nice, leg-covering tuxedo."

Lulu's mother had sewn the bridal gown, obviously an act of love. Lu appeared statuesque and happy with her red hair stuffed under a tiara and veil and very flushed from honoring toasts and shouting *Gorka!* along with everyone else. Her only concession to folk peasantry costuming was the large bouquet of wheat and dried flowers lying on the table in front of her. The florist, not knowing quite what to do with a Russian theme, totally ignored the June date of the occasion and went with a harvest festival look that repeated itself in sheaves of the same assortment on all the tables.

Mr. Horvath, a big man with a round head and slanted Mongolian conquest eyes, came to their table and put his arms around Lulu and Greg, giving each a boozy kiss on the cheek. "When we eat, Gregor? You know, in Russia we party two days, maybe all week. You Americans, you don't know good time."

He helped himself to Lulu's champagne and shouted, "*Gorka!*" The Presbyterians shouted back and beckoned to the waiters for refills.

Lulu said, "I think we do need to eat something."

The food, plain but plentiful, had a ham and a roast beef anchoring the ends of the buffet table. Tiny cabbage rolls and *piroshki*, some stuffed with meat and some stuffed with fruit, piled high on platters along with the regular wedding fare of crustless triangular sandwiches and chicken drumettes. One small iced bowl of genuine Russian caviar the Horvaths had been saving for the occasion graced the very center of the spread directly in front of the largest wheat sheaf.

Brad Denlinger, red-faced with drink and separated from his own bride, did not distain the offerings even though his own nuptial feast had featured surf and turf individually served on gold-rimmed china. Seated with the Horvaths, whose nearest relatives were still in the Old Country, he seemed to have made friends with Gregor's father who pounded him on the back each time he passed. Big enough to handle that, Brad was certainly no snob. "*Gorka!*" he cried as he raised another shot to his lips, ignoring Hannah who shook her head "No!" from her place at the bridal table.

Midnight approached with the newlyweds preparing to leave in the limo and Mrs. McFarland running around desperately trying to find enough designated drivers to get everyone home safely. Kara's parents left right after the cake was served. Her mother had seized the car keys early on, and reminding Kara of their two-hour drive on the turnpike to get home, made an early departure with her slightly wobbly husband.

The wedding party trouped outside to toss handfuls of birdseed on the departing couple. As Lulu and Gregor sailed off into married life in their yacht-sized vehicle a man dressed all in black and riding a motorcycle pulled up in front of the hall on his panting machine. He wore no helmet. Kara thought the guy must have a death wish, but not her problem. As maid-of-honor, she needed to help Mrs. McFarland distribute the centerpieces and find more sober drivers. Conscious of her duties, Kara wasn't nearly drunk enough to be tempted by any of the tipsy music major groomsmen anxious to prove they weren't gay.

A leather-clad arm snaked around her waist. "Hey, baby. Some dress!"

"Jeff, you came!"

"Yeah, we're playing down the road. I borrowed the cycle to use during the break. Guess I'm late."

He followed Kara inside the hall where the caterer boxed wedding cake and leftovers. Mrs. McFarland, her faded red hair flying in little wisps around her freckled face, trotted right over and tried to get Jeff to take a centerpiece.

"You must be Kara's young man. Please fill a plate before they pack it all away. What a shame you missed her parents. Here, take them some flowers tomorrow."

She shoved a sheaf of wheat and strawflowers into Jeff's arms and hurried away to help Mr. Horvath fill the trunk of his car with leftover champagne and vodka bottles.

"Looks like I missed a good party."

"We had plenty to eat and drink, and music you wouldn't believe. Why didn't you tell me you were nearby?"

"I couldn't have come anyway." He shrugged. "You going home tomorrow?"

"Yes, Faith and I are staying with the McFarlands tonight. Tomorrow, we go to Lost Spring. Faith got a job in my hometown teaching third grade. She's going to stay with my folks until she finds a place of her own. I'll hang around until August, then go down to Newark and find an apartment near the campus. If you stopped by for a quickie, I don't have the time." She said those words but could already feel the heat building between her legs under the layers of poufy material.

"I guess the only way you'd come on the road with us would be if I married you. You'd want all this?" He gestured toward the post-wedding chaos of caterer's helpers collapsing tables and bagging *piroshkis.*

"I could make do with less. Is this some weird sort of proposal, Jeff?"

"I got this yesterday." He held a plain gold band in his open palm. "We can go down to Elkton, Maryland. They have a forty-eight hour waiting period and a bunch of wedding chapels. We could check into a motel, enjoy ourselves, get married on Wednesday, and be in Cleveland for our next gig by Friday."

"Gee, you make it sound so tempting."

"You've got the dress already." Jeff flicked a

finger at her poufy skirt. "And a bouquet that won't spoil."

He unloaded the sheaf of wheat and dried flowers into her arms and smiled that perfect smile of his. Did she have the will to do this wild and crazy thing or not? She'd never been wild except with Jeff and certainly not crazy. Two years of grad school loomed ahead like a great, gray iceberg she must circumnavigate in order to teach at the college level, one of the few ways to get a job with an English degree. Now or never, Kara Shafer.

"Pick me up at the McFarland's house tomorrow afternoon."

"That's a yes, then?"

"That's a yes."

The long kiss that followed made Mrs. McFarland, bearing a paper plate filled with leftovers, veer in another direction, but she waited for the couple to come up for air and thrust her offerings on Jeff. He ate in a hurry, then disappeared into the night, a study of black on black, riding a motorcycle.

"Have your parents met this young man, Kara?" Mrs. McFarland questioned in a well-meaning, motherly way.

"No, but I've met his. They live on the Main Line and have plenty of money."

"That's good, then. Maybe you can get a house near where Hannah and Brad are living if you intend to marry the boy someday."

"Oh, I intend to—someday."

Chapter Seven
Love and Marriage

Kara Shafer didn't wear the poufy dress to her own wedding. She drew Faith Harvey into her plans to elope, asking her friend to call home and explain that Kara didn't feel well and would stay a few extra days at the McFarland's to recover. They'd believe Faith since she wasn't much of a drinker, but were realistic enough to assume their daughter had a hangover from the festivities and felt too sick to come to the phone. Kara also asked Faith to be her maid-of-honor at the Elkton wedding chapel as they sat in the McFarland's kitchen that could have passed for a set in a 1950's sitcom.

Shoving aside a half-eaten ham sandwich on dark rye—part of the wedding feast—she begged, "Please! I don't want to remember Buzz Light holding my bouquet."

"This is a bad, bad, bad idea, Kara. Your parents would want to attend even if this is spur of the moment." Faith licked the icing from a piece of nuptial cake off her fork and pointed the tines at Kara.

"I've loved Jeff Ryder since the first night I met him. My parents will try to make us wait."

Faith gave her the eye roll. "You think? You believe they might want you to wait until you have your master's degree, and Jeff has a real job."

"I'm paying for that master's degree by myself,

and Jeff does have a real job. It's just not a traditional one."

"Yeah, being a rock star is a real grounded ambition. Playing in local clubs is about one step up from playing in a garage."

"He has real talent, Faith."

Succumbing, Faith nodded. "Okay, I'd better go along to make sure he does the deed."

In the end, Faith Harvey followed the bandwagon to Elkton and helped Kara find a dress at the nearest mall. The outfit, filmy and layered, had a misty floral pattern. Kara showed good sense and sound practicality since she could wear this dress for other occasions she pointed out to Faith. As for the bouquet from Lulu's wedding, the colors didn't match, but, oh well, better than nothing. When Jeff arrived with a white orchid to replace it, Kara gifted him with that smile he could see from the stage when he performed.

The Justice of the Peace, a middle-aged woman in official robes, tried to make the service special for them by giving a brief sermon about the meaning of love and marriage. Kara, standing with her hand shaking in Jeff's, probably heard one word in ten. The justice frowned when Jeff produced only the one ring, but went on to wish them all the best. After Faith took a few pictures with her camera phone, the woman directed them to a nice restaurant where Jeff urged his new bride to order the lobster and told the rest of the band to watch the prices. Faith, not very hungry, had grilled flounder.

Afterwards, they made the dreaded phone calls. Dr. Ryder and Alli didn't ask to speak to Kara. The words Jeff's bride could make out were "crazy," "irresponsible," "pregnant," and "on your own." Jeff hung up.

"That went well. We may be crazy, irresponsible, and on our own, but at least you aren't pregnant."

Kara's parents did not shout. Her mother cried. Her father told Jeff he didn't think much of a man who would marry a girl without ever introducing himself to her family. Both made Jeff promise to take good care of their daughter.

Her younger sister got on the line and asked if Kara was pregnant. Mom wanted to know. "Okay, not pregnant, just crazy. Yeah, I know, crazy in love. Good luck, then. Oh, and Mom says whatever happens, you can always come home."

Her sister hung up. Kara felt as if she were suddenly in free fall with only Jeff Ryder to hold her hand.

By Thursday night, Jeff and the Ryders of the Night, plus one, arrived in Cleveland. On Friday when they went to see the Rock and Roll Hall of Fame, Jeff's credit card had been cancelled. Kara wrote a check on her small bank account for the admission. She worried that afternoon at rehearsal.

Jeff tried to work her into the act. After a brief session at the mike, the unanimous opinion of the band: she had no talent for singing.

"I told you this," Kara said, red in the face from her humiliating flat-note failure.

"Maybe she could like wear skimpy clothes and bounce a tambourine on her hip," Buzz Light suggested. "You know, add a little eye candy. She ain't too bad looking."

"Where are you—back in 1965? No one uses

tambourines anymore, hophead." Rico Vega waved a hand in front of the drummer's red-rimmed eyes.

"Look, guys, I don't want to be your Yoko Ono," Kara intervened. "I'll just sit around and applaud loudly to encourage the crowd."

"Yoko who?" asked Buzz.

"The broad who broke up the Beatles, man," Deuce answered.

"Yeah, don't be her. Don't break up the band."

Kara moved off the stage and over to a table. "Go ahead and practice. Don't mind me."

She recorded the session on her phone. Maybe they could use the replay to improve. Jeff sat with her for a moment.

"I know you're worried, babe, but we get six hundred dollars for this gig."

"That won't go very far toward food, motels, and gas if you only play on weekends."

"Hey, Boris, come on over here." Jeff beckoned to the manager away from an inventory of the bar stock. "Could you use us next week for maybe a two-hour set Monday through Thursday, two hundred a night?'

The man with the brutal, broken-nosed face of an ex-boxer shook his head. "Not enough business. I don't even know if you're a big enough draw for the six hundred I agreed to pay you for the weekend."

"You'll get your money's worth."

Jeff went back to rehearse with a vengeance while Kara sat at a table in an empty bar in Cleveland and wrote the University of Delaware using stationery from the motel.

I greatly appreciate your offer of an assistantship in English literature to the University of Delaware, but

I've married recently. My husband's career involves frequent travel, and he wants me by his side. I regret having to inform you that I'll be unable to use the assistantship and hope that another graduate student might be able to put it to use at this late date. Sincerely, Kara Shafer (Ryder)

Boris lugged a carton of bottles past her table and out to the alley. The exit door slammed as if punctuating her letter.

****

On Saturday night, or rather Sunday morning, as the band packed their instruments, Kara went with Jeff to the office to collect the performance fee. Boris sat emptying the till and counting the cash, putting the twenties into stacks of one-hundred dollars. He picked up three piles and thrust the money at Jeff without taking his eyes off the rest of the night's take.

"This is only three hundred. We agreed on six for the weekend."

"Take it or leave it. You're not that great."

"But we agreed on six hundred."

"Get out before I call the bouncer."

Rico, Deuce, and Buzz crowded in behind Kara. Deuce moaned, "Not again."

"Didn't you get him to sign a contract, Jeff?" she asked her new husband.

"No. The agreement was verbal. You heard him the other day. He agreed on six hundred."

"Prove it or get out." Boris began to pack banded stacks of bills into an overnight deposit bag.

Kara reached into her purse, withdrew her phone, and turned up the volume so the whole group could hear. Boris came across loud and clear with his

83

unmistakable foreign accent—"I don't even know if you are a big enough draw for the six hundred I agreed to pay you for the weekend."

"We'll leave, but we'll come back here with the police to collect the rest of the money. I hope nothing else illegal is going on in here. Who knows what they might find?" From the dark corner where she passed the night, Kara had observed packets of white powder changing hands and a few drinkers who might, or might not, have been underage.

Boris reached deep into the moneybag and took three hundred dollar bills out of the bottom. Rico snatched them off the desk. "Hey, I want a receipt for the entire six hundred, greaseball."

Kara wrote one out on another sheet of motel stationery and passed it to Jeff to sign. The band left immediately afterwards, headed for Akron, intent on driving all night in case Boris claimed connections to the Russian mafia.

"First you face off my mother, now this." Jeff stared at his bride as if he had gotten a wedding gift box whose contents he didn't wholly expect or understand.

"In Akron, we'll find a library and run off some standard contract forms. I'm sure we can get them on the internet or from a book. This should never happen again."

"I'm with you there, Kara," said Buzz Light, already rolling his relaxation for the night as he leaned against his drum in the rear of the van.

"You have no musical talent at all, but you do have balls, Kara. You know what that makes you?" Deuce drawled from his position directly behind her in the van.

"No." She stared out the windshield into the night, watching the cat's eyes embedded in the road wink as they streamed by. Maybe that made her an interloper, a problem, a Yoko Ono.

"A manager," Deuce answered.

Chapter Eight
Five Years on the Road

Kara's job was simple enough. When the Ryders of the Night arrived in a new town, usually on a Monday, they checked into the cheapest motel with a free breakfast. While the band members got some sleep, she went from club to club playing their CDs for managers and trying to get one of their contracts signed. Once she'd booked a gig she went to the local library and made flyers to spread around on bulletin boards, telephone poles, and windshields. If they stayed in one place long enough, she spent time calling ahead, visiting the next town down the line, handing out the PR packages she'd put together, trying to arrange bookings or at least appointments so they wouldn't arrive cold in the next place.

Kara Ryder realized she had become more than a manager. Den mother might be an apt word. She cared for the Ryders when they came down sick. Once, she'd found a free clinic that treated Rico for a case of syphilis, and she'd transported the bulky Buzz to the emergency ward for a stomach pumping, saving his life after he'd consumed a bad mix of drugs. She often caught Deuce, the most civilized of the group, with his hand in the communal cash and shamed him with a lecture about the evils of gambling.

She'd soon learned she must be in control of their

cash flow or else the money earned poured outward into each band member's vice. Rico wanted to show the ladies a good time. A slot machine or video poker attracted Deuce as much as any blonde or redhead, and sometimes, not often, he won. Buzz Light enjoyed his pot and any other recreational drug that came his way. Jeff forked over any amount for a new demo or to people who promised him a big break—and then disappeared from their lives. The bank account had her name on it now and at her insistence only her name.

Not that Kara didn't have a weakness of her own—and she knew it. He went by the name of Jeff Ryder. While she wanted to do a circular tour doubling back on towns they'd played already where getting them booked wasn't as difficult, Jeff desired to move ever westward, sure he needed a fresh audience and a new scene to be discovered. Fame awaited just over the horizon, and Jeff always chose to go in that direction. The longest they stayed anywhere was six months in Austin, Texas, a year ago. That idyllic period when Kara thought the band might settle down cost them their keyboard man.

Rico formed an attachment to one of his lovely ladies, this one a Tex-Mex beauty with soulful eyes and a papa with a Mexican restaurant. Lupe lingered after one of the Ryders' early gigs and invited them all to chow down on leftover specials, rice and beans, and warm tortillas. Her burly father and her four brothers, who waited tables and cooked, but might have been *banditos* in another time and place, made it very clear to Rico that he couldn't toy with Lupe.

Whether lured by the unattainable or really in love this time, Rico stayed behind when the band packed for Vegas. While not thrilled by their daughter's choice of a Philadelphia Puerto Rican rocker, he was at least Catholic and Hispanic. Lupe's papa promised to allow his son-in-law to start a house band to entertain on weekends and serenade the customers on special occasions. Jeff and Deuce kidded Rico that he'd have to give up the keyboards and buy an acoustic guitar to play *Celito Lindo* for the diners. They promised to be back in town for the wedding.

Kara painfully excised one quarter of the funds from their bank account and gave Rico his cut. He kissed her on the cheek. "You take care of the band, Mama Kara, and look out for yourself because you know this showboat won't." Rico punched Jeff on the arm, and they shook goodbye.

The boys in the band began calling her Mama Kara ever since she'd lined them up to dole out a weekly allowance after clamping down on finances. At first, they used the term sarcastically as in, "May I have an extra five this week, please, Mama Kara?" That changed when she went to the mat for the Ryders, or rather to the top of a Florida bar, entering a wet T-shirt contest for the sake of the fifty dollar prize, two bottles of rum, and a tray of chicken wings—oh, and a dry T-shirt—when the band was down on its luck, and the bank balance almost at zero.

They found another keyboard man who couldn't wait to get the hell out of Texas and moved on. Terry, so achingly young he called her Mrs. Ryder, claimed to be twenty-one and produced a questionable driver's license to prove it. Quiet and intense, he wore his headphones in the van so he wouldn't have to talk. When he played, though, his hazel eyes glazed over and his shaggy brown head bobbed in time to the music until it seemed he wasn't there at all and his long-fingered hands channeled some late, great piano man.

Playing lounges and small venues on the edge of the strip, the band stayed seven months in Vegas, so long they rented a shabbily furnished two-bedroom apartment for six months. With the lease nearly up, the nightly debate centered on whether to sign up for another six or hit the road to Seattle or L.A. Jeff voted for moving. Terry backed him. Kara and Deuce wanted to stay. Buzz refused to cast the deciding vote because he simply didn't give a shit as long as he had shit. After five years on the road, the wear and tear showed. Another break was inevitable.

When Jeff demanded the band head to L.A., Deuce bowed out. He'd been offered the job as a lead singer in a house band with steady pay and benefits. At twenty-eight fucking years old, playing Vegas, both the band and the slots, was his idea of paradise. They could go on without him. Jeff wavered for the very first time. He asked Deuce to wait a couple days before accepting. Though Kara preferred staying in Austin to stepping over drunks and avoiding tapped out gamblers begging for change in Vegas, she'd settle anywhere with Jeff if only they could stay in one place.

That night as she sat writing poetry in a marble back notebook in the back of the lounge where the Ryders slammed away on their instruments, Manny Lomax came into their lives. The lounge owner hadn't wanted a rock band, but the group he'd hired didn't show—probably going someplace with better money for the night. He asked Jeff to tone down the music, and so her husband crooned *A Song for Beautiful Women* and ended the set with *Miss You*, the softly sung song he created from Kara's corny heartfelt poem. Men winced when he sang about flowers abounding, but their honeys snuggled closer and said they felt exactly that way. The CD with *Miss You* on it generally sold like single red roses at the end of the show.

Jeff breathed into the mic that the band would take a short break, and he wished all the beautiful women out there could stay the night. Flipping his blue-black hair that now hung to mid-chest back over his shoulders, he left the stage, pausing along his way to Kara's table to speak to some of his targeted ladies and urge them to buy a CD. Without an invitation, Manny Lomax took the seat between Kara and Jeff.

"I'm an agent—always looking for new talent. One of my groups is playing nearby, but to be honest, I can only take so much of that screaming. I slipped in for a drink and I start thinking—look how that guy has every woman in the place half in love with him. Jeff Ryder, good name, great hair. My card."

Kara snatched it from the table. "You work out of Memphis, Mr. Lomax?"

"Heart and soul of the music industry. You with him, babe? Because you are laying on a gold mine."

She'd heard this before, only not so crudely put. Next, he asked exactly how much gold the mine possessed. He wanted a check to cover making a demo and other expenses. So many towns, so many similar scams.

"No thanks. I manage Jeff and the Ryders. We do pretty well on our own."

Lomax shrugged. He wore an expensive gray suit with a pink shirt, a polka-dotted tie and pocket square that didn't flatter his shifty eyes, sharp chin, and cheesy little moustache. The ensemble made the agent resemble a sideshow barker trying to lure the hayseeds into a freak show.

"Suit yourself. Give me a call if you ever get to Memphis. Got to go buy some earplugs and get back to my boys." Manny Lomax vanished into the night as quickly as Santa Claus on Christmas Eve.

"Kara! This could be it." Jeff had that look again, the kind that led to fights over the bank account.

"Let me find a library and check him out. We've gone this route before, Jeff. One more day won't hurt."

"If he checks out, we head for Memphis."

Kara sighed. "Sure, if he checks out." These guys never did.

****

Much to her astonishment, Manny Lomax turned out to be a real agent with a web site and a creditable list of groups and single artists he represented. Kara had heard of a few of them. She printed out the information for Jeff. That night, they voted again on where to go next. All hands went up for Memphis except the one belonging to Deuce.

"Go on without me. This is only another long shot, and there's no place else I want to be than right here where the action is."

Kara carved another quarter out of the funds in their bank account, enough for Deuce to renew the lease on the apartment if he wanted to keep it. They parted not as cordially as they had from Rico.

"Screw him," Jeff grumbled. "He'll be broke and attending Gamblers Anonymous by next year. We can pick up someone in Memphis. The place is probably crawling with backup men. We leave on Monday as soon as we wrap this gig."

"Jeff, I have a physical scheduled the end of next week."

"Cancel it."

"Jeff, I can't get a new prescription for birth control pills without it."

"Do what you always do. Find a sympathetic druggist and tell him you're on vacation and left your pills at home. That's always good for one month. We'll be in Memphis in a few days."

She had a few pills left, then her period for a week. That never turned Jeff off, the safest time, he always said, but he didn't have the bloating or the cramps to contend with. Her cramps were not helped by riding for hours in the old van, but this wouldn't be the first time she'd taken one for the team. Kara packed for the trip, and the Ryders headed out of Vegas on a chilly desert morning in February.

****

The ten year-old-van broke down along Interstate 80 and had to be towed to the only garage in a place Jeff described as Nowhere, Utah. Parts, the codger running the gas station said, must be brought in from Salt Lake. That would take about a week. The band stayed at a run-down motel that still styled itself as a motor court and charged the strangers as if they were staying at the Hilton. The sole diner in Nowhere served only decaf coffee, but copious breakfasts of bacon and eggs and hash browns with a stack of pancakes on the side allowing the band to skip lunches.

The parts came in late on a Friday. The repair shop closed Saturday, and no one worked in Nowhere on the Sabbath. On Monday, the mechanic discovered the wrong parts had been sent. For an extra fee, Elder Smith would send his grandson to Salt Lake to get the right ones. The Ryders paid up. They offered to play at the grange hall, but were told the devil's music wasn't welcome—now if they had been a country-western band of the clean variety, might be a different story.

Kara inquired discreetly of a waitress at the diner where she might get a prescription filled. By mail, mostly, for the chronically ill, she answered, Salt Lake for everything else, but she could recommend some good herbal cures for anything minor. Jeff asked Elder Smith's grandson where he could buy condoms. Salt Lake, of course, but he'd ask around among his friends. Generally, the denizens of Nowhere considered the unavailability of condoms as a deterrent to sin, he explained. Just before the band pulled out of town, the boy showed up with two rubbers that looked as if they'd been in someone's wallet since World War II. Jeff slipped him a five like a drug deal was going down.

Once on the highway, Buzz stretched out in the back of the van and lit up a roach so short he needed his clip to hold it.

"Didn't want to get busted in Nowhere. Those were some very conservative folks. You think Elder Smith and that old dude at the garage have more than one wife?"

"No, I don't think that, but I'm positive they have lots of children," Jeff remarked wryly.

He'd been edgy all week without sex or music to keep him occupied. He wrote a facetious country/western song called *I'm Stuck Here in Nowhere, and Nowhere's the only Place I ever Been* to pass the time. Played on a borrowed acoustic guitar, the little ditty turned out to be a big hit at the diner and got him a free meal and some applause. Several people tried to convince him abandon rock entirely for a new career and convert to Mormonism. No one in Nowhere seemed to get the joke. Jeff coaxed some money out of Kara to buy the guitar just in case they ever got stuck in Nowhere again.

"I don't give a fuckin', shittin' damn," Terry snarled. Chills and sweats rocked his body.

"We can stop in Salt Lake and find a doctor," Kara said.

"Just get me out of frickin' Utah."

"Here, man. Chill." Buzz offered Terry his stubby toke with great reluctance.

Terry smoked it down to ash and got a little calmer. At the first sizeable town in Wyoming, they stopped for a leg stretch and gas. Despite a bitter wind, Terry walked off down the street leaving the others to huddle over cups of hot, fully leaded coffee in the convenience store. The layover lasted much longer than anticipated, but Terry finally returned feeling better. He threw Buzz a small sack of weed he'd picked up wherever he'd gone. "Thanks, man. Returning the favor."

Traveling over the Rockies in a strong wind turned out to be no joke. The currents pushed the van to the edge of the road more than once. When, they reached the foothills, Jeff declared himself done for the night. They found another sad little motel and checked in, Jeff springing for two rooms because the price was right. They sat on a bed that offered magic fingers massage, but had a broken coin box. Kara rubbed Jeff's neck and shoulders, her soft breasts pressing against his back.

Jeff grew hard and the two ancient condoms

burned a hole in his pocket. He used the first one to get rid of his frustration, ramming himself into his wife's body over and over again until she cried out. Kara used the second condom to sheath him later in the night as she settled herself on top of his body and leaned over him, her hair so long now, the strands made an intimate curtain around them, like a waterfall he often said, though its color was still more like muddy brown water. No money for highlights or coloring.

When they both climaxed, her before him, thanks to her own efforts, Kara lay against Jeff's chest until he slept. No sense waking him to say the second condom split along the side during the height of their mad ride. She flushed it along with the other and burrowed in beside him.

****

The snow started as they crossed the Nebraska line, and when visibility went to nothing, Jeff pulled off the road and got rooms in the only kind of motel they could afford anymore. This trip ate up the bank account in big gulps what with van repairs, extended layovers, and no paying gigs. The blizzard shoved snow up against the motel door and by morning showed no signs of stopping.

Buzz used his bulk to bully his way to the vending machines and retrieve survival rations of stale honey buns, chocolate bars, and icy packs of peanuts. The soft drinks, frozen in the can, pushed up the tops of the aluminum. He let the cola and orange crush thaw in the motel's plastic cups and handed around slushies to go with the rest of the meal. On the second day, they drank tap water as cold as the snow outside their window and breakfasted on bags of corn chips.

That evening, Jeff made his way against the wind to the small café attached to the motel and asked permission to sing for tips and burgers. The clientele seemed to be mostly stranded truckers and a few families driven off the road by the weather. He played *Time in a Bottle* and *Miss You* and learned truckers could have a sentimental streak and be generous tippers. When he did the ballad version of *Beautiful Women,* the only women he could find to point at were the lone brassy blonde waitress way too old to be a bombshell and labeled Maydell on her name tag, a tow-headed little girl snuggled in next to her tired mother, and the driver of a big rig he thought was female, but wasn't quite sure. That got a big laugh just about the time lights went off.

The waitress lit little votive candles in glass holders surrounded by bottles of ketchup, sugar holders, and sticky, plastic honey bears, letting Jeff play a while longer before she sent the audience and him back to their rooms with orders to sleep bundled up. She'd try to have some kind of breakfast available in the morning for those who wanted it. Putting together some ham sandwiches, Maydell added a few overripe bananas in a paper sack, and pushed half a huckleberry pie soaking through its crust Jeff's way.

Just outside the café door, the female trucker waited. "You gonna be lonesome tonight, pretty boy? I like your hair."

"Got a wife and some friends waiting for dinner." He held up his paper sacks. "But, ah, thanks for the compliment."

Jeff tapped on the door behind which Buzz and Terry had started a blizzard party of their own, both already stoned. He offered the food. Buzz grabbed the sacks, gouging out a piece of huckleberry pie with his hands, and Jeff decided to stay a while. After a night like this when he, Jeff Ryder, lead singer of Ryders of the Night, had prostituted his music and gotten an offer to prostitute himself, well, he deserved a little recreation. Besides, he'd run out of condoms again in a place he christened in his mind as Bumfuck, Nebraska.

****

When Kara woke, she felt Jeff already inside her, pushing away with a loopy grin on his face. "Kara, my love, my luck, my muse."

"Jeff, do you know what you're doing?"

"Oooh, yes, and it feels so good."

She should have bucked him off. He let cold air in under the layers of coats, thin spread, blankets, and sheet covering her naked body. His hair hung over his face, not a waterfall, but more a dark forest surrounding him, his face like a pale moon above her, and she let him continue. He took forever, then rolled off when he finished and went to sleep without bothering to tuck himself back into the jeans he hadn't taken off. Kara did that service for him.

She wondered if his dick froze off would they have any reason to stay married? He'd never cheated on her in the past five years as far as she knew, but then, Kara always waited for him at the end of each gig. Often, he'd want three climaxes before being able to settle down after performing, and he did have a horror of STDs and pregnancy, she'd learned rather quickly. Still, if she felt used, she got some pleasure out of it.

He'd roused her enough that sleep wouldn't come again. Kara got up, dressed quickly in the frigid room, and put on one of the coats. She opened the drapes. The snow had ceased falling and allowed a full moon to shine down upon its pure white surface. By this reflection of light, she wrote a poem in her notebook about her lover rising over her like the moon above the white drifts.

That finished, she tried to remember what Hannah and Lulu said about getting pregnant. Fairly sure Hannah, giving in to the imperial wishes of the Denlinger family after she'd finished upgrading their computer system and bringing Denlinger Meats into the twenty-first century, took six months to get pregnant after going off the pill. Maybe, Hannah hadn't tried very hard. Her daughter, now two, came into the world with white-blonde hair, big, blue eyes and an excellent nanny waiting.

Lulu, on the other hand, recently gave birth to her third child. She told Kara she'd gone off the pill on their first anniversary. Why not? They both had jobs in the same school system. Greg taught high school music and conducted the marching band for extra pay. She rotated around the elementary schools in the district giving music appreciation lessons to the smaller children. Lulu conceived within six weeks and gave birth to a fine little boy she wanted to nurse—which called for using alternative forms of birth control. One year and nine months later, she had her second son whom she'd nursed until she discovered she gotten pregnant with her third. When Kara asked how often she'd had her period over the last five years, Lulu answered, "What's a period?" Lu now gave piano and voice lessons at home to save on child care costs. She seemed happy regardless.

Kara received Facebook photos of Hannah's golden child and Lulu's three mischievous sons, the first two dark and round-headed like the Horvaths, the last, red-haired with goggling blue eyes. She'd been caught in a wave of envy that gradually receded as she chanted her mantra of the last five years. Kara Shafer, you are married to a handsome, talented man and have an exciting, unusual life. Poor Faith teaches third grade in a town no bigger than the one she grew up in and has neither husband nor child. Kara Shafer is a lucky woman. Repeat. Repeat again.

Still, if a child came along accidentally, would that be so bad? A child needed a stable home, a safe place to grow up, not late nights and the second-hand smoke of barrooms. She and Jeff could settle somewhere near a city with an active music scene. Jeff would continue to play, and she'd find a job that offered health insurance and paid enough for a house note. She'd wait and see, but she wouldn't be careless again.

Kara woke as the snowdrifts gave birth to a pink and perfect dawn. The electricity hadn't come on, but the eighteen-wheelers warmed up in the parking lot making the whole building throb. One by one, the big rigs bulldozed their way onto a road the snowplows had been over once and headed for the interstate. Jeff, Buzz, and Terry slept on. Kara waded through the snow to the café and accepted a bowl of cold cereal and a cruller covered in powdered sugar to go with warm apple juice poured from the bottle. She asked where she might find a pharmacy, and the waitress pointed the way down a snow-clogged street.

After wading through the drifts, Kara found the place closed due to the power-outage. She took a chance and crossed the street to a neighborhood bar. That dive was open. The owner swabbed the floor with a mop and a bucket of cold water giving off stinging ammonia fumes. Some of his patrons had stayed the night and left a mess behind. She asked to use the bathroom, and careful to avoid the wet spots, ducked into the men's room and bought as many condoms as her change would purchase.

She returned to the motel wet to the waist and in need of dry clothes. The guys were up along with the hood of the van exposing a stone cold dead battery. The manager tried to help them jump it, but the cursed piece of junk wouldn't hold a charge. Kara reluctantly gave Jeff a signed check to buy a new one at Western Auto. After two hours, the three men got the battery installed. They revved the engine and kissed Bumfuck, Nebraska, goodbye.

The condoms lasted until they reached Des Moines where Kara begged a month's supply of emergency birth control pills at a clinic for the indigent. The package lay unused in her purse as she awaited a period. With all the crises, the skipped meals, the stress of this journey that should have taken days and lasted weeks, no wonder her body was confused. Still, each time she opened her purse to dole out a few more dollars of their dwindling supply, the pills lay there a guilty reminder of being late.

The Ryders of the Night turned south after Des Moines and followed the Mississippi to St. Louis. They arrived broke and went from club to club trying to find enough work to buy the gas to take them to Memphis. Finally, the owner of a biker bar agreed to let the small combo set up in a corner. Without Deuce as a backup, the band had a thinner sound, Kara thought, but Jeff shouted out *Hot Virgin* for the first time in weeks and got those who listened to shout back, instant gratification, the kind Jeff loved the best. After the gig, he and Kara argued so loudly Buzz and Terry said later they heard them clearly through the walls of the cheap motel.

"There are plenty of clubs here. We should stay a month and build up our bank account. Mr. Lomax won't be impressed by a group that arrives broke and needs money to find a room." Her words.

"If Manny works with musicians, he should be used to that. I say we go tomorrow." His belief.

"Jeff, I'm tired, worn out. I don't feel well." Kara burst into genuine tears.

Jeff blinked. Kara never cried, always on his side, a real trooper.

"Okay, we'll rest up and stay another week or two."

The Ryders found a good gig and ended up staying a month. Kara banked all the money she could, cutting back sharply on the cuts she gave to Buzz and Terry. Buzz used his share to get his head shaved since his grown-out flat top flopped down in his face. With a bald head, a big belly, and a dime bag of pot, he did a fairly good impersonation of a Happy Buddha sitting behind his drum kit. Though the last five years had been lean, Buzz's stomach expanded to vast proportions on the junk food he craved and no amount of nagging from Kara convinced him to try the salad bars at inexpensive steak houses along the road.

Terry cursed Kara out and wanted a bigger cut. She denied him and went off to the Laundromat with a sack of soiled jeans and T-shirts, a five-dollar bill, and the room key in her hip pocket. When she returned, her purse and Terry were gone.

Jeff found her purse minus the band's stash of cash and checkbook in the motel dumpster. Desperately, Kara phoned the branch of the national banking system she used in St. Louis. With the account flagged, Terry beat it out the front door during a signature check and left the checkbook behind. He'd gotten a hundred in cash from a clerk at a small grocery store, who failed to ask for any identification for a fifty dollar purchase consisting mainly of booze and candy. As for her birth control pills, they probably lay under a layer of garbage in the dumpster. Kara didn't bother to mention their loss. She knew by now she had no use for them.

The remnants of the band crossed the Mississippi Bridge into Memphis the next day. All three of them checked into a single room at a decent motel with plenty of free mini-bottles of shampoo and conditioner. Jeff washed his hair. Kara blew it dry, and brushed the black strands until they shone like the mane of a high-priced stud horse. Her husband put on the least worn of his clean black clothes along the beat-up bomber jacket and white scarf, even though he stepped out into a city where spring had arrived with mountainous azaleas in bloom and street side planters filled with pansies and snapdragons.

"My lucky clothes and a kiss from my muse, Kara baby. That's all I need."

Jeff craved a lot of luck. The kiss went on and on. He rubbed his hands across breasts so tender Kara wanted to pull back but didn't. Buzz merely kept flipping through television channels. He'd seen the kind of kisses Jeff gave Kara often enough. Evidently, it did nothing to arouse him, and a lot of time had passed since they stayed in a place with cable. Give Buzz MTV and a vending machine stocked with fresh Twinkies, and you got a happy man. Both he and Kara stayed behind when Jeff went off to seek fame and fortune with Manny Lomax.

Chapter Nine
Walking in Memphis

Unfortunately, Death also found the Ryders in Memphis, Tennessee. While Jeff kept his appointment with Manny Lomax, Kara called home. She tried to do this once a week, but with the constant travel and money and morale low, she'd skipped the last month. She prepared funny stories about their stays in Nowhere and Bumfuck since she knew her parents would be worried. She'd leave out the part about having one of the band members steal their meager funds for liquor and drugs. Here they were in warm and sunny Memphis, safe and sound. They planned to stay a while—she never got the chance. Her younger sister answered the phone none too cordially.

"Where are you? Why haven't you called! Mom wanted to contact the FBI to find you."

"Memphis. We just got here. Hey, I've only been out of touch a few weeks. What's the big deal?"

"Dad died on Monday. One of those freak March snowstorms blew in, and you know Dad, he wouldn't pay some kid to shovel the walks. He said he had nothing better to do with his time since the mill closing pushed him into retirement. Massive heart attack. Mom found him in a snowdrift when she went to call him for lunch. So, you just get your wayward butt back to Pennsylvania. Dawn and her family are on their way from Fort Bragg. The funeral is tomorrow at three at the UCC in Lost Spring."

"Tell Mom I'll be there."

Kara hung up. She had nothing else to say to her sister. Dad usually answered when she called, saying aye-yie-yie in his funny Pennsylvania Dutch accent in answer to her smoothed over and prettied up accounts of life on the road. She never asked her parents for money no matter how bad the situation and they never reproached her for making a poor choice in life. Her father—only sixty, and she hadn't seen him face to face in two years. He should have been around to see Jeff make it big, to see his next grandchild.

"Buzz, I have to fly home. My dad died on Monday. That means I'll have to use your share of the money in the bank account. I'm sorry."

"S'all right, Mama Kara. You go." Buzz nestled deeper into the four pillows on his bed and opened another bag of corn chips. A litter of snack wrappers and soda cans accumulated around him as if he were some bum sleeping in an alley, but his total, matter-of-fact acceptance made her burst into tears.

"Hey, hey." Buzz Light swung his massive thighs off the bed. He gathered Kara into his arms and let her cry against his big, warm, gurgling belly until she pushed away and went to wash her face.

She soon discovered the fiction about airlines offering special fares to the bereaved. The last minute booking on a red-eye flight leaving at eleven p.m. with a lay-over in Chicago and a slingshot flight out at six a.m. to Harrisburg, the closest airport to her home town cost twice the amount of a normal pre-booked flight, but she had her plans in place by the time Jeff returned full of enthusiasm from his meeting with Lomax. He failed to notice her puffy eyes or the small, packed suitcase sitting by the door.

"We are on our way, babe!" Jeff twirled Kara around until she felt nauseous. "I auditioned at Manny's studio. He says he'll take me on, but not as a rocker. He wants to repackage me solo as a ballad singer doing love songs if I tone down some of the ones I've written. He wants more songs, and he'll cut a demo and start getting me bookings."

"Huh?" said Buzz, shifting in his nest of debris. "What about the Ryders of the Night?"

"Buzz, big guy, you might not have noticed that you are the only Ryder left. A drummer can find lots of work in Memphis—so, no worries. Manny has a couple of apartments he keeps for his clients to use. You'll stay with us until you get on with a new group."

"Sure, okay." Buzz sank back into his mattress.

"Jeff, I have to leave tonight for home." Kara waited for the reaction. It came as quickly as a nuclear reaction.

His pale face darkened. "You can't leave me now, Kara. You're my luck. This time I'm going to make it big, no, huge!"

"My father died. I have to leave tonight to get to the funeral on time. There isn't enough money for both of us to go."

"Too bad it wasn't my old man. We could have saved the plane fare and used the inheritance. Your father wouldn't have wanted me at the funeral anyhow. Every time we passed his way, he'd stare at me like he wished I'd fall off the bandstand and break my neck." Jeff whipped his long hair around, lashing the air.

"He never said anything bad about you, Jeff." Or about anyone else. It wasn't his way. But Dad might have thought it.

"Yeah. Just a feeling I had. Considering that my folks told me not to come home until I settled down and made something of myself, your dad was a pretty solid guy. So, go. Tell your mom I'm sorry. By the time you get back, I might be recording."

Jeff drove her to the airport in the old van late that evening. Kara Ryder took with her an overnight bag battered by travel and filled with nothing but jeans and t-shirts and a navy blue suit she wore when trying to book the band at the better establishments. She found the suit, a real bargain, at Goodwill in Austin.

When the plane touched down in Harrisburg, she knew her sister would meet a woman who'd lost the ten pounds so annoying in college, and then another ten from skipping meals when money became scarce. That woman had plain brown hair parted in the middle and grown down to her waist because she hadn't had a haircut in five years. When she braided it and pinned the coils at her nape for the funeral, her eyes and mouth might seem too big for her angular face. The smile that could light up a room would be absent.

Chapter Ten
Home Sweet Home, Pennsylvania

Kara sat sandwiched between her two sisters, Dawn and Joy—as she had always been—in the first row of chairs at the funeral home. Her mother preferred to stand right next to the coffin, as close to her deceased husband as possible, to greet the mourners, but Kara had thrown up her tea and toast that morning and didn't think her legs would hold for any length of time. Friends passed along the line of sisters, patting their hands and murmuring, "Good man", "fair and honest boss", "a neighbor who was always there to help when you needed him", depending on the relationship to their dad. Everything they said was true of the man who lay in the coffin dressed in his good gray suit, the same one he'd worn to his early retirement party.

The strong scent from a large pot of Easter lilies Faith brought made Kara slightly dizzy. Faith whispered she would see Kara at the church before moving down the line. Hannah sent an enormous basket of mixed spring blooms and Lulu a wreath of carnations because neither could get away to attend. The combined fragrance of these and other floral tributes made Kara feel like she'd been chained to the perfume counter at Bloomingdale's to be assaulted by atomizers filled with their strongest products. No one else appeared to notice the reek.

Kara's neck ached from the weight of the braided hair pinned at the nape, and she still felt queasy. Her mother told one last visitor Mike had said more than once that he would die if he couldn't work, and he had—just a year and a half after the mill closed. Ancient Great-aunt Mary hugged the widow and said, "I know. I know. It's hard to lose such a wonderful man, Della."

The funeral director announced in a low, modulated voice, "We're going to close the casket now. If you'd like to take a final moment with your loved one before going to the church, please step forward."

Her sisters stood, and Kara did, too, wobbling a bit. Dad did look at peace, though the funeral home styled his hair wrong. He'd worn his prematurely white hair combed to the side, not straight back. What a time in life—in death—Kara corrected herself—to try a new hairstyle. She'd never see his kind gray eyes again. Michael Alan Shafer's middle daughter tried to recite a final prayer for the man whose tombstone would say it all, "Beloved husband and father," but nothing came into her mind except, "I'm sorry, Dad. I'm sorry I've made a mess of my life and haven't been to see you for two years. I am so sorry."

She started to cry into a shriveled tissue twisted in her hands and then, her knees gave way. The funeral home attendants, always on the lookout for the faint, caught her before she hit the ground. Seated with a cup of hot tea and honey pressed into her hands, she barely realized what had happened. Her two sisters looked on as if she'd planned the collapse just to be the center of attention. Early this morning, Joy sniped on the way home from the airport, "Dad always loved you best.

Glad you could make his funeral."

Boxed in her own grief and guilt, Kara heard barely a word of the service at the UCC. March winds whipped around the gravesite in the old cemetery behind the church where some of the founders of Lost Spring lay buried—and now her father. The remnants of the snow that brought about his death lingered in the shade cast by the tombstones. From this side of the hill, far off across a countryside patterned with pasture, fallow cornfields, and white drifts, Kara saw the roof of the massive dairy barn where her dad milked cows as a youngster. He'd enjoy that view, she knew. She hadn't thought to bring a coat and shivered violently by the time each member of the family dropped a white carnation onto the dark casket lid before being taken away in the limousine to where the guests waited at home.

Once in the kitchen, her mother heated up a can of chicken noodle soup, the comfort food of Kara's childhood, and pressed her daughter to eat it. People milled in the dining room and the living room and the hallways, waiting for the family to make its appearance while Mrs. Shafer fussed over her middle child.

"Mom, people are waiting for you to come out so they can start eating," Joy said peevishly.

Her fiancé had provided the funeral meats. Arlen Frey managed his family's market not far from the church. One of the oldest families in Lost Spring, the Freys competed with larger chain stores on the basis of their homemade Lebanon baloney, ring bologna, scrapple, fresh pork sausage, smoked hams, and bacon. People drove from the city to stock up on their wares. The guests waited to dig into the display of Frey cold cuts fanned around the large party trays. Church members brought cold and hot potato salads, macaroni and cheese, kraut and sausage casseroles, platters of pickled and deviled eggs, and a big basket of good rye and hard rolls among other offerings. Kara sipped soup and tried not to think about all the other food.

"Go ahead, Mom. I've been on my own for a long time now. I'll be fine."

"That's right. What is it like being the wife of a rock star, Kara? You haven't told us," Dawn snipped. She'd put on forty pounds after giving birth to two children and eating away her anxieties while her husband served in war zones overseas. Her brown eyes, the same shade as Kara's, appeared sunken and small in her round face surrounded by short hair going gray early.

"What is it like being married to a general, Dawn?" Kara shot back.

"You know Gid is only a major."

"Exactly. Jeff sings for a living. He isn't a star." Kara bit off each word and spat them out in Dawn's direction.

"Stop it! I'm ashamed of all of you, squabbling on the day of your father's funeral. He hated when you argued. Dawn, Joy, stop picking on your sister. Anyone can see she's expecting," Della Shafer snapped. "She doesn't need any more stress. I'm going to greet the guests. The three of you make up."

Della straightened her small, soft body, patted her sleek cap of silver hair, dabbed at her dark brown eyes with a handkerchief, and walked out of the kitchen with her arms held out. "Thank you for coming, my dears!" No doubt where Kara got her warm smile.

"Are you?" Dawn stared at her middle sister, looking for signs.

"Really?" Joy, the slim, pretty one, echoed.

"I think so. I'm not sure. I haven't taken any tests."

"I passed out during an officers' wives club tea when I was expecting Mikey and a couple of times when Megan was on the way. You're pregnant all right," Dawn offered in reconciliation.

"Does Jeff know?" Joy asked, finding this more interesting than cold cuts.

"No. I haven't mentioned the possibility yet. I can't be more than two months if it happened in Nowhere or Bumfuck."

"Where was that?"

"Never mind."

"Well, I'm going to the drugstore for a pregnancy test kit right now," Dawn said, grabbing her purse.

"Please, not today. Tomorrow, okay? We should go out and accept condolences. Let today be about Dad."

The three sisters made their entrance out of the kitchen together and went to separate parts of the room to accept the warm-handed pats and hugs of the mourners. Kara found herself with a plate of cold macaroni and cheese in hand on the far side of the dining room when she came to one of the chairs pushed up against the wall. She sat and began to peck at the macaroni with a plastic fork when yet another hand, this one large-veined and age-spotted, reached out and touched her knee.

Great-aunt Mary drank coffee in the corner chair. Her eyes, the Shafer family shade of gray, were sunken in a mass of wrinkles giving her the appearance of an old, wise tortoise at the age of eighty-two. She wore her white hair cut short with a little fringe of bangs. She'd often said she hadn't the nerve to bob her hair until Pop Shafer, Kara's great-grandfather, passed away.

Mary spent her youth and part of her middle age taking care of widowed Pop, including the trying two years after he'd suffered a stroke at the age of eighty. In return, she'd been left the house and barn and twenty acres of farm land while her two remaining brothers divvied up the rest of the acreage, sold out, and retired to Florida after forty years of work in the mills.

Mary, though, surprised everyone by going out and getting a job at the now defunct Five & Dime store in the city instead of cashing in on her inheritance and following Earl and Clyde to the Sunshine State. She retired at the age of seventy-five as head of the notions department, rented out her land for hay and corn production, and still kept a single cow in the huge barn, saying she could never adjust to the taste of store-bought milk.

"Your dad was my favorite nephew, Kara. He always came when I needed help. Just last spring, he replaced the stones nice and solid in my wall along the drive after the heavy rains washed them out. What a good, good man. You know, he had to grow up fast when Roy and your grandmother died in that car wreck back in '69 and him only twenty-one and newly married."

Kara nodded. She'd heard this family story many times.

"And you, always visiting when you could. So caring, like your dad. Oh, how I've enjoyed all those postcards you've sent me. I still have every one of them. I never got to travel. I needed to work if I wanted to hold on to what was left of the farm. Then, I just got too old. It must be exciting seeing all those places." A little glitter shown in those old tortoise eyes.

"The traveling gets old after a while, especially when you have no place to call home, Aunt Mary."

"Your home is here in Lost Spring, Kara. I know your dad worried about you, taking off with that band."

Kara closed her eyes getting ready for the guilt trip. She put down the fork full of cheesy macaroni before it reached her mouth.

"But you know what he said to me as he repaired that wall? He said, 'Kara seems all soft and sweet, but she possesses a will of iron when something really matters to her. I know we couldn't have talked her out of going off with Jeff. If she must rebuild her life some day, she'll do it as solid as this wall. Mark my words. But, I still get to worry because I'm her father'."

"That sounds like Dad. I think my wall is crumbling." Kara began to cry again. No one stared. Those closest to her murmured sympathetically.

"There, I didn't mean to upset you. I only wanted you to know your dad supported you all the way. Let me get you some nice hot coffee and a piece of this raisin pie—funeral pie Pop always called it back in my childhood, what with people dying in the winter of pneumonia and no fresh fruit available, back before penicillin, you know."

Kara offered her a watery smile. Aunt Mary excelled at family history diversions. "Thanks, but no coffee. I can't stand the smell of it right now."

"But, we always sat on the back stoop and had our coffee when you visited. I know just how you like it, black and hot. I still take mine with just the fresh cream since we always had plenty of that on the farm. Now, I sit mostly out front facing the river. Ever since Clyde and Earl sold out to Walmart I can't stand seeing the glow of that place beyond the windbreak Pop planted before I was born. Ach, that building is like a Gee-deed big dog with a litter of ugly pups gathered around sucking off its tits. The lights are on all night long outshining the stars. What kind of people shop at two in the a.m., anyhow? Glad I still have a cornfield and a pasture between me and them. Walmart put the Five & Dime out of business, you know."

Kara wasn't too sure about that last statement. People simply ceased to going into the city when shopping centers spouted up where dairy cattle once grazed. She found herself smiling more broadly. Some people, like beloved landmarks, never changed. Gee-deed was Aunt Mary's euphemism for goddamned since she never swore.

"I'll try the pie."

Aunt Mary bent over slowly and picked up a plate of at her feet. She pinched up a sweet crumb fallen from the pie's topping and popped it into Kara's mouth. "Good, ain't?" she asked before tottering off to fetch another piece.

People like Aunt Mary with their ways and speech were dying out, too, like the Five & Dime. Kara's father said Mary had been forbidden in the county schools of her time to speak the Pennsylvania Dutch dialect she'd learned as a child. All he retained from his grandparents was the accent and a handful of cusswords they didn't want him to use. How strange he'd gone before his elderly aunt who dwelled in the past.

Mary returned with the pie. "Eat up. Raisins have lots of iron. That's good for the baby."

"Did Mother tell you?" Kara took a bite of the pie, which seemed almost supernaturally sweet.

"I may be an old maid, but I been around farm animals and expectant women all my life. I know the signs."

"You've never been alone, though," Kara said, deflecting the direction of the conversation.

"No, never alone. People said I'd be murdered in my bed for taking in folks who needed a place to stay, but I said, heck, I ain't got nothing for them to steal. Why would they kill me?"

At least two of Aunt Mary's homeless people died in her guest room, going to their rest like wounded animals who sought out a safe place to close their eyes. The ensuing autopsies caused no end of trouble as if she'd poisoned them like the old ladies in *Arsenic and Old Lace.* Then, she'd paid for the cremation of their remains and scattered the sieved ashes on her garden. "To dust thou shalt return" was Aunt Mary's motto. You might as well do the earth some good in the process. She wanted the same for herself when her time came. Dawn and Joy as children refused to eat any of the vegetables Mary brought from her garden, though their father said they were being foolish. Because Dad called her sisters foolish, Kara gobbled the sugar peas, sweet white corn, and string beans without a qualm.

"None of my strays ever stayed all that long. I'd feed them up, and when they got stronger, they went."

Kara nodded. The bums Aunt Mary collected in Reading were happy to go to her place in the country for a free meal and a clean bed, although they weren't too crazy about her home remedy lice treatments that burned like hell. Since Mary's place also had a policy of no alcohol, tobacco, and any drugs stronger than aspirin, they'd leave soon enough. Dear Aunt Mary.

Kara finished her pie. "I guess I should go mingle, Aunt Mary. Great seeing you again. You never change."

"Ach, the big change is coming for me, but I'll be around a while longer. You come by and visit before you leave, hear now? I have tea if you can't handle coffee."

"I will."

****

Dawn, being the oldest and a natural organizer, went to Geiger's drug store as soon as it opened the next morning at eight. She bustled into the kitchen clutching the small plastic bag. "That nosey Jay Geiger tried to wheedle which one of us needed the kit." She handed the test to Kara.

"Oh, no! He'll think it's for me—that Arlen and I have to get married," Joy moaned. "He'll spread that all over town because he's such a jerk."

"Old Mr. Geiger was a gentleman. Too bad his son inherited the pharmacy," Kara's mother remarked. "Here, Kara, eat some toast before you go pee on the stick."

"I shut Jay down by asking why he still isn't married. It could be for any of us except Mom."

Sometimes, her sister's sharp tongues put themselves to good use. Kara peeled off the wrapper and began reading the instructions as Joy protested.

"You're too old, Dawn, and everyone knows Kara can't support a child and that life style of hers," Joy

117

whined.

Instead of getting into it with her youngest sister, Kara retreated to the downstairs bathroom adjacent to her parents' bedroom, but she heard Dawn say, "I am *not* too old to have more children." She shut the door. Her flow didn't want to cooperate. Fear held it in. "Face it," she commanded herself. Be the stone wall not the crumbling plaster. A trickle wet the stick.

By 8:35, the trio of women confirmed Kara's pregnancy. Her mother insisted she stay over and see an obstetrician, while Kara demurred by saying she didn't want to spend the cash on changing her plane ticket. Dawn changed the ticket, and her mother paid for it. Della Shafer already lobbied for Kara to come home for the birth.

Though she had to wait a week for the appointment, the results reassured. The doctor proclaimed Kara healthy, if a little underweight and iron deficient. Vitamins and iron pills easily remedied that. She should come back in a month for another checkup, or see a doctor where she lived. Della Shafer hugged her middle daughter and said, "And so, life goes on."

The telephone rang during this touching moment. Kara half expected to hear Jeff's voice, he'd been on her mind so much, but the person on the other end of the call turned out to be her mother-in-law, whose voice she didn't recognize at first.

"Is this the Shafer residence?"

"Yes," replied Kara with caution, surely a telephone solicitor or some realty ghoul who wanted to see if her mother might sell her house now that she was a widow. She'd had one of those calls already.

"This is Allison Ryder. I need to get in touch with Jeff and Kara. Would you have their current address?"

"This is Kara."

"Oh. I want to speak to Jeff."

"Jeff is in Memphis. I'm here because my father passed away recently."

"I'm so sorry to hear that of course. But the reason I called is because we have a bereavement of our own."

"Not Jaws, I mean Jules!" Jeff's wish come true, possibly. He'd regret his words, Kara believed. No one really wanted their father dead.

"No, no. He's a healthy as ever considering his lack of regard for diet and exercise. Our daughter-in-law, Brooke, is gone."

"Brooke? Was she in an accident?"

"Not an accident. A heart attack."

"But she wasn't more than thirty."

Evidently, no further details would be forthcoming. "Regardless, she's dead. Can you be here for the funeral in two days? What about Jeff?" Alli asked in that cold, clipped upper crust way of hers.

"He's working with a new agent. I'm not sure he can get away. This may be his big break."

"Oh, of course—the big break." The barely suppressed sarcasm zinged over the miles. "You come then. Here are the directions."

Kara scrambled for pen and paper while her mother looked on, puzzled. When the call ended, Mrs. Shafer asked who on earth that had been.

"Jeff's mother. Brooke Ryder is dead of a heart attack. The funeral is in two days. I have to go. Will you lend me a car?"

"Certainly I will, but I simply don't believe this.

I've sent that family a Christmas card every year for five years, inviting them to stop by and including our address and phone number, and this is the first time that woman has called. Some people!"

Some people indeed, and Kara got the privilege of facing them alone.

****

Clad in a new black dress purchased by her mother that probably wouldn't fit in a month, Kara went to her sister-in-law's funeral. Mercifully, they'd gone closed casket. She soon knew why. Despite years of therapy, Brooke Schuyler Ryder finally starved herself to death. Steve Ryder, however, looked like an ad for masculine health, prosperity, and pulchritude, as he stood between his sons, aged nine and seven, all dressed in identical black suits with a fine chalk line as befitted the owner of the Main Line Haberdashery. The third row of the church held his staff, two tailors, a gay salesman, and a nubile, red-haired bookkeeper fresh out of secretarial school.

The service went full Episcopalian Mass with communion and brief eulogy for a short life. Brooke Schuyler Ryder, devoted mother, helped her husband build his new and successful business. She would be missed by all. End of a short story.

Kara met Brooke's family after the service at the catered reception in the Schuyler family home, another lovely, limestone manse next to the Ryder's house. Mrs. Schuyler, looking at Brooke's in-laws with angry eyes, remarked that the Ryder men were tough on their women. Why, even Allison Ryder with her fine patrician features was beginning to appear haggard. Kara seemed like a nice young woman. She should be careful of her health.

In the first year of her marriage, Kara sincerely tried to keep in touch with Jeff's family. She called. They wanted to speak to Jeff who didn't want to speak to them. Like her mother, she'd sent cards, but none came in return, even when they stayed a while in some location where the band gained a small following. Today, all Kara could do was circulate around the room expressing regrets and more regrets for Jeff.

Chapter Eleven
Down and Out in Memphis

"Manny got us a two bedroom apartment. He said Buzz could stay with us until he finds another band. He'll ask around if anyone needs a drummer."

"You won't need one?" Kara asked.

Jeff hadn't shut up about Manny's munificence since he picked her up at the airport. Her mind dwelled on the two funerals, and he didn't ask about those.

"No. Manny wants love songs from me, a whole repackaging of my image, he says. No more rock."

"You're giving up rock! I thought rock was your life."

"That won't bother me if I sell a million albums. We restyled and recorded *Song for Beautiful Women* already. We're calling it *You* on the demo. *Miss You* didn't need much work, but he wants a few new songs from me. We'll fill out the disk with standards."

Jeff pulled into the lot of an apartment building reminding Kara of the Lorraine Motel where Martin Luther King, Jr. had been assassinated—two stories, long open balcony running past the numbered doors, not in the best neighborhood. Graceland's Gates said the sign arching over a courtyard of cracked concrete, but neither Elvis nor salvation seemed to be hovering around. A black teen playing hooky skateboarded without a helmet in an empty swimming pool fenced with some low timbers and a padlocked entry. The kid could break his neck in there, and no one would notice, Kara thought as she turned away from the scratching sound of the skateboard descending into the deep end. Death stayed on her mind, and she couldn't seem to shake off morbid thoughts.

Jeff parked the band van among the other faded rusty cars, hauled her bag up the metal staircase and stopped at the first of the doors. Buzz, a fried chicken drumstick in his greasy fist, let them in.

"Great to have you back, Mama Kara. Jeff doesn't do laundry. There's a great fried chicken place down on the corner. Neat, huh? I saved some for you."

"Good to see you, too, Buzz."

Like Great-aunt Mary, Buzz never changed. The vast purple T-shirt covering his belly was mottled with food stains and saturated with the odor of pot. Kara accepted a piece of chicken and ate it along with a small cup of slaw and a unbuttered roll since the airline offered only a cup of lukewarm tea on the flight. Jeff waited impatiently for her to finish. The bones of his meal rested in the sink waiting for someone else to take them out to the trash along with an array of other garbage. The greasy food and the smell from the sink made Kara's stomach roil, but she managed to keep the meal down.

"Say, Buzz. Kara and I are going to turn in early." Jeff nodded his head toward the outside door.

"Ah, sure, Jeff. I'll just take my smoke outside." Buzz exited. The metal stairs vibrated when he took a seat at the top.

"Can you believe this place came with a king-sized bed?"

Jeff threw open the bedroom door. The big bed filled the room, leaving space only for a dresser that looked like it had been purchased at a motel going-out-business sale and a pole lamp circa 1975. Jeff flopped down on the pea-green spread and put his hands behind his head.

"I am beat from a day at the studio, but that doesn't mean I'm not happy to see you."

He opened his jeans to prove it and beckoned his wife to cover him. Kara shed her jeans and panties. As she straddled him, Jeff drew off her T-shirt and unsnapped the bra that cut into the tops of her swollen breasts. He rubbed his hands over the two red marks, and she shivered.

"Two weeks of Pennsylvania Dutch cooking and you've gone up a bra size, I'd say." He weighed her breasts in his hands. "Let's check out that butt."

Jeff cupped her bottom, urging her to take him all the way in. "Getting nice and round like it used to be. I guess I don't feed you enough."

Kara ignored his teasing. Although being on top let her set the pace and was supposed to be empowering, she often felt Jeff simply had a lazy streak and didn't want to do the work for all the pleasure. Tonight, tired and depressed from her trip, and full of tension about what they had to discuss, she simply wanted him to finish fast. She wished they'd talked first, but maybe sex would make her news easier to accept. Kara pumped with her thighs until Jeff came fast and explosively. She rested for a moment on his chest, then dismounted and curled against his side.

Jeff still had his eyes closed, the heartbeat beneath Kara's ear gradually going back to normal.

"Manny says having a wife is a liability to my new image. But, I tell you, baby, I needed you right here these last two weeks."

"Jeff, we're starting a family."

"No, babe. Now that *would* be liability. We can't afford a kid, and Manny sure isn't going to pay for hospital bills. I already owe him big time for this place and the studio time and the demo."

"Jeff, I'm pregnant."

The muscles of his chest hardened against her cheek. "Can't be. You're on the pill."

"I would have been if you'd stopped along the way long enough for me to get some."

"We used protection."

"Sure, fifty-year-old condoms. And then, there was the night in Bumfuck when you came back to the room high on something Terry and Buzz gave you. I guess you don't even remember that occasion."

"Bumfucked! That's how I feel right now." Jeff withdrew his arm from around Kara and sat up. "You have to get rid of it. This can't happen now. I'll ask Manny where you can go. He might be willing to pay for an abortion."

"I think it's too late for that. It's time to grow up and settle down in Memphis if you want. You can do your album and promote it right here. You said Memphis is a good music town."

"Let a doctor tell you if it's too late."

"I saw a doctor back home. The baby is due in early October. I'm going to have it."

"You know what Brooke did for Steve?"

"Starved herself to death so he could fuck someone else? Don't count on my doing that."

"That's not what I meant. Brooke had serious head problems. When she found out he was screwing the new bookkeeper, she went off the deep end again, but before that, she had an abortion because Steve didn't want another kid a couple of years back. Steve said getting an abortion is no big deal."

"They had two other children, and this is a big deal to me. I'll be twenty-eight by the time the baby comes. Most of my friends have children. You tell me this is your big break. Then, we should be able to do this."

Jeff turned his back on her and slid under the green spread. "I need some sleep. We'll talk about this in the morning."

Kara lay awake. Buzz came in, raided the refrigerator, and went to his room. What kept going around in her head wasn't her fight with Jeff, but her last visit to Aunt Mary.

As promised, tea had been served along with a plate of crisp, buttery sand tart cookies, each one dusted with cinnamon-sugar and half a walnut pressed into the center. They sat on the back stoop. In the daytime with the barrier of trees and fields, they could barely see the Walmart, though the occasional blat of a horn told them some driver got pissed over being cheated out of a parking space close to the door.

"It's better in the summer when the trees are in leaf. Can't hear the noise so much," Mary said.

They walked out on the back lawn and found a patch of crocus, purple and yellow, pushing out of the earth despite the chilly air. Three crows flew by, hungry for spring crops. Their shadows passed over the two women.

"Death comes in threes," said Aunt Mary. "I might

be next. You tell your baby about me some day and about this place, no matter where you end up."

"I will," she promised. Unless Kara held strong, death number three would to be her baby.

****

Jeff left early. Buzz stayed in his room. Kara took out the garbage and cleaned the small kitchen and living/dining area. The bathroom was disgusting with two men using it for a couple of weeks and not bothering to so much as wash the toothpaste spit out of the sink. Or, maybe the place had been disgusting when they moved in. Regardless, Kara walked until she found a store with cleaning supplies, stocked up, and hauled the cleansers back to the apartment. The brown stains wouldn't come out of the toilet bowl, but the rest of the fixtures cleaned up well enough.

Jeff didn't come home for lunch, didn't call. She made herself a sandwich of smoked turkey from an open package in the refrigerator and popped the top on a fizzing ginger ale that soothed her stomach. After eating, she sat at the kitchen table and wrote a poem about death. Then, she flipped to the front of her notebook and read her foolish poems about love straight through until she came up against death again. One poem was missing, the one she'd written on the way to Memphis, the one about her lover being like the moon over snow.

Jeff didn't come home for dinner. Buzz remained quiet in his room. Strange—hunger should have gotten the best of the big guy by now. Possibly, he wasn't even in there. Maybe he'd gone out while she went to the store. She needed something to do, and this would be a good time to flush out his room. She knew how

Buzz lived.

Kara knocked and got no answer. She opened the door. Buzz still slept in a room darkened by aluminum foil tapped over the window. The odor in the small space was rank as if raw sewage had leaked through the walls. Vomit rose in her throat, and she turned away from his bulk under the blanket, crunching chip bags and candy wrappers under her feet as she rushed to escape the odor.

Kara stopped in the doorway, a hand over her mouth. Buzz was a champion snorer. She'd heard him often enough through thin hotel walls and in the next bed a few weeks ago. The only sound came from a large roach scuttling out of the mouth of an empty beer can and racing across the snack wrappers to the darkness of the closet. Pinching her nose and moving back through the debris of junk food, Kara pushed the filthy blanket aside and placed a hand on the drummer's forehead like a mother testing a child for fever. Cold. Buzz Light had passed in the night—the third death.

****

Kara called 911 and tried to contact Jeff. She found Manny Lomax's business card stuck on top of an old-fashioned wall phone in the kitchen but got only an answering machine when she dialed. The ambulance arrived, bringing all the unemployed residents of Graceland's Gates to their doorways. They watched with avid curiosity as the medics transported a gurney up the staircase and into the first apartment, breaking up the monotony of their day.

"What happened?" she asked the medics.

"Guy this big—could be a heart attack even at an early age. Maybe an OD. Did he do drugs, ma'am?"

"Just pot, usually. When—will you know?"

"There has to be an autopsy in a case like this. We must wait for the coroner and the cops before we can remove him. We're sorry for your loss, ma'am."

The police and the coroner showed up a half hour later. They took pictures and pawed through the trash and took the sheets after Buzz had been rolled onto the gurney, even though they suspected no foul play. She could pick up a copy of the police report tomorrow afternoon. The officials were sorry for her loss, too.

The coroner remarked, "Your husband was a big fellow."

"He's not my husband, just a friend who stayed with us. An old friend. His name is Baxter Legg, but he went by Buzz Light."

"You know of any next of kin?"

"No, he never mentioned any. I do have his social security number. He played drums in our band. He didn't have much money."

"State will bury him. Won't be the first musician to die broke in Memphis."

"We'll take care of the arrangements. Will we be able to get a copy of the autopsy report?"

"In a few days. Things are always backed up at the morgue."

"Thank you for coming so quickly."

"Our job, ma'am."

The attendants strapped down the remains of Buzz Light covered decently with a clean sheet. They ran into trouble getting the body out the bedroom door.

"We could scrap the gurney and use a body bag."

"None big enough. Big push on the count of three."

They repeated the process at the front door while

Kara watched, thinking how easily Buzz for all his size passed through that door only yesterday. Now as a pile of dead meat slopping over the sides of a gurney, he became nearly immoveable. The medics began easing the gurney down the stairs. Halfway, the bottom man lost his grip. The gurney rolled right over him and bounced to the bottom, skewing and turning over on the concrete like a dead bug with its feet in the air. Buzz, a big fan of slapstick and the Three Stooges, would have loved his exit. Kara hoped he watched from somewhere, high as a kite and having a big belly laugh.

Kara went back to the silent apartment and into the room where Buzz Light expired. She picked up the trash on the floor, aired out the room, bundled the dirty clothes flung into a corner, and sprayed for roaches with a half empty can of Raid she found under the kitchen sink.

Kara kept cleaning, washing and drying and folding Buzz's oversized clothes in the small apartment Laundromat, then stowing them neatly on the closet shelf. She found another set of linens in the hall closet and remade the bed with a bottom sheet and a blanket. The top sheet she draped over the drum set that took the place of furniture in the room. Going out to the living room, Kara lay on the shabby, fake leather sofa and cried the only tears that would be shed for Buzz Light.

****

Jeff found his wife asleep on the cracked black Naugahyde divan. An old movie played on the small TV, flickering in the three a.m. darkness like a virtual fireplace. The apartment smelled clean for the first time since he'd moved in. Shaking Kara's shoulder, he bundled her up, still half asleep, against his chest.

"Sweetheart, I'm sorry I didn't call. I played a solo gig tonight, last minute. Manny set it up. Look, I got paid in cash." Jeff unloaded a handful of bills onto the wobbly coffee table. "Things are going great, babe. You know that poem you wrote about the moon. I had to change it around a little, you know, so it sounded like a man telling the story. It goes like this now—*She rises above me/ her face is like the moon/ in the darkness/ but she'll be going soon. I've given her my life/ but we cannot stay together/ she's a rich man's wife. In the darkness, oh, in the darkness...*" Jeff sang, thrumming his fingers against the table for accompaniment.

He gave Kara one of his perfect, heart-melting smiles, bright even in the dim room illuminated only by the security lights bolted to the apartment block. His wife's eyes, looking a little puffy, remained half-closed.

"Manny loves it. It's going on the album. Big bucks are coming our way, but just now, we have to be careful. Manny said he'd give me the money for the abortion. If I'm seen with a pregnant woman, all his hard work building me up as a heartthrob will go down the toilet."

Kara pushed away, stood up, brushing off his hands. "I'm supposed to be happy because you took my poem without asking. I'm supposed to be joyous because you want to flush our baby. I guess I should stand up and do cheers because Buzz died today, and he won't be in your way anymore."

"Buzz is dead?"

"In his bed of a heart attack or overdose, I don't know. But I am sure of one thing, Jeff. Buzz Light is going to be the last death."

Chapter Twelve
Life Goes On

Kara placed the laundry basket on the fifth step of the staircase and rested her bulging belly on top of the clean clothes. In the shade of the stairwell, her downstairs neighbor, Jacquetta Hawkins, sat enjoying the mild October afternoon from the comfort of a plastic chair with a pillow stuffed behind her back.

"You know I be helpin' you, honey, if my back warn't so bad," Jaquetta remarked.

Kara smiled down on the old black lady, a hard-working woman all her life only to end up with a shitty apartment and three worthless sons who visited when her disability check arrived. But, who was she to judge? Jacquie cajoled two of her boys into hauling the newly painted crib and baby dresser up the stairs to the bedroom for the price of a pizza lunch when they stopped by on the first of the month. Spots of the pale yellow paint still dotted the cement where she and Merita Sanchez from across the way freshened up the second-hand furniture. All Jeff did was haul the new mattress from the van.

Kara took as deep a breath as she could and lifted the basket up another few steps. The contents consisted of hand-me-down baby clothes washed with Ivory Flakes and Snowy Bleach. The women in the complex gave her a shower back in September with gifts consisting mostly of disposable diapers and baby wipes, but they also cleaned their closets of boxes of newborn onesies and fancy infant dresses barely worn with the understanding she would pass the clothes to the next person who needed them.

"I'm okay, Miss Jacquie. It just seems like this staircase used to be shorter."

"That the way it be the las' month. You about ready to pop."

"Can't happen too soon."

Kara attained the landing and dragged the basket to her front door. She heaved it and herself over the sill, carrying the clothes the rest of the way to the room where Buzz Light had died from choking on his own vomit. That's what the coroner's report said. Hopefully, they would be out of this place before the child could ask what the small plain cardboard box on the closet shelf contained. Buzz remained with the Ryders until Kara could find a next of kin to accept his ashes.

They sold the drum set to repay Manny for the cremation costs. The bed remained, now covered in yellow gingham to match the little dresser and crib and the cushion on the rocking chair. Jacquie had sewn simple pocket curtains of the same material on her machine to put on the window. A teddy bear mobile hung over the crib and more stuffed bears sent by her older sister squatted on the pillows of the bed. She'd made a cheery place for her child with Jeff griping about the expense every step of the way.

Her husband needed his money for leather pants and a new guitar and a more reliable ride. Kara pointed out she had gone her entire pregnancy wearing unzipped jeans and Buzz's immense T-shirts. She went to the free clinic for checkups and signed up to endure natural childbirth under the tutelage of a midwife in a birthing room to save on money, not because she wanted to do it that way. So, he could just shut up.

As strained as their day-to-day life became, Jeff still came to her after a gig in the early morning hours wanting sex. These last few months, he'd had to do it sitting up or doggie style, but that didn't slow him down. She should be grateful he wasn't taking his lust elsewhere.

As Manny placed Jeff in better and better clubs, she stopped going to the performances. Around her sixth month, she'd shown up wearing one of those tight, stretchy tops that showed off her baby bump and gone to give Jeff a big kiss after he made his way through a morass of grasping women wanting to touch him to her table in the rear. He hung a white silk scarf around her neck, drew her close and whispered, "You can't come here like this." His adoring fans thought how kind of him to make a pregnant woman feel like she still had sex appeal. They tweeted that all over the internet. No harm done to his image, but she stayed home after that.

Kara put the tiny clothes away and sat for a moment in the rocker. She needed to make a second run and get her ugly maternity underwear out of the dryer before the local pervert helped himself. He possessed no taste whatsoever. She'd already lost two of the big cotton bras the store clerk assured her could be used for nursing as well as proper support plus one of the huge white panties with the stretchy panel in the front. Jeff loathed the underwear and said she could have worn her old bikini pants. Usually naked in bed when he came home, he didn't see all that much of the stuff. She ignored this criticism.

Weary, she pushed against the arms of the rocker, got to her feet and dragged the laundry basket back to the washateria, as some of the tenants called the small, steamy room filled with machines and a few big drum dryers. With the next load so light, she had no reason to expect anything would happened on the return trip, but Kara felt something give at she mounted the stairs.

Old Jacquie said, "Either it rainin' out of a blue sky or yo' water done broke, honey. Better call an ambulance."

"No, that's too expensive. Can you get Merita? She has Manuel's truck today. The guy who hires day laborers picked up him up."

Jacquie got to her feet with the help of a cane and slow as a possum crossing the interstate, made her way across the weedy courtyard to the opposite block of apartments. Kara stood dribbling on the staircase until she saw Merita come to the door, retreat, and return dangling the keys to the truck. Carefully, she made her way to the apartment, dripping as far as the hall closet where she stuffed her pants with washcloths. She made a call to Jeff, getting Manny's answering machine as usual, and left a message to meet her at the hospital.

Seizing the packed bag sitting inside her bedroom door, Kara went out. Merita and the truck with the camper back that looked as if it had last been used to smuggle illegal aliens across the border waited for her at the base of the stairs.

"Ai-yi, get in. You leakin', *querida*." Merita leaned over to open the door, her broad, brown face full of concern.

"Maybe I should get more towels."

"*No problemo*. We already got a blanket across the springs. I wash it later. *Andalé*, Karita."

Kara no sooner settled herself on the uncomfortable springs than Merita peeled out of the parking lot while Jacquie and Merita's two big-eyed children watched from the safety of the doorway. The suspicious-looking truck and the reckless driver got the two women a police escort to the hospital before they were six blocks on their way and pulled over for speeding.

****

Eight hours later, the baby still hadn't come. Doing her huffing and puffing, Kara lay hooked to an IV drip and a monitor. The midwife, kindness personified, rubbed Kara's back and smoothed lotion over her cramping belly, things Kara knew Jeff was supposed to be doing. He showed up around dinnertime.

"Hey, babe. Just got the message from Manny. How's it going?"

In the midst of a contraction, she tried a smile that came out as a grimace.

Jeff shook his head with mock pity. "Not my idea, sweetheart. Yours."

When it appeared the baby wouldn't come before midnight, he left for his gig after feeding his wife a few ice chips.

The infant girl, as if waiting for her father's return, finally entered the world at three in the morning after a twelve hour, drug-free, excruciating labor. Jeff arrived in time to witness the miracle and mess of birth. His expression said he wanted to puke, and he passed on the honor of cutting the cord. He held his daughter momentarily like someone put a dog turd in his hands.

The midwife pointed out the baby's shock of black hair and lusty cry as if she felt the need to prove paternity, taking back the child before he dropped her. Jeff spoke up only when the midwife began nursing instructions.

"No. She isn't nursing. Those breasts belong to me."

"Jeff, it would be cheaper and better for the baby if I..."

"No. I'm saying no."

Kara accepted a shot in the rear to stop her milk and keep her husband happy, though the midwife scowled. The next day, Kara stood in their kitchen pouring formula from cans into little plastic bottles while Jeff complained about the price of infant feeding and the baby's name.

"Mari Della. No one names kids Mari anymore."

"In honor of my great-aunt and mother. Mari spelled with an I sort of modernizes the name, don't you think?"

"You could have called her Mari Juana in honor of old Buzz and that wetback who drove you to the hospital and almost got you killed." Jeff snickered at his own wit.

"You said you didn't care about the name—and where were you when I called?"

"In the studio. You can't just ditch a recording after you have all the musicians and sound people lined up."

"Exactly when is this album coming out? It's taking longer than my entire pregnancy." Kara rinsed the empty can and took great pleasure in crushing it as she placed it in the trash.

"We needed to make some changes. Christmas, we

plan to promote it for Christmas sales. You know—a gift for lovers. After that, I'll need to go on tour. I'm opening for Mandi McDonald. You remember her, don't you?"

"Barely, as in barely clad. Didn't she burn out a long time ago?"

In the nursery, Mari woke and wailed. Kara grabbed one of the bottles and started for the bedroom with its changing table and cushioned rocker.

"Jesus! We can't even have a conversation anymore without being interrupted by the kid. You probably aren't interested anyhow." Jeff rose from his slouch on a kitchen chair and opened the refrigerator. "Nothing but formula in here. Where's the beer?"

"Go out and get some!" Kara snapped. With her bottom aching and her breasts leaking a little despite the shot in the behind, she paused in the doorway. "I do want to know all about Mandi and your tour right after I get the baby settled."

Rummaging in her purse for a twenty, Jeff found the cash and pushed past her without another word.

Chapter Thirteen
A Merry Little Christmas

Manny Lomax credited himself with brilliance as an agent. He'd paired Jeff with another of his clients, Mandi McDonald, whom he discovered at sixteen years of age and most willing to do anything to succeed. Her scantily clad body gyrating through one music video after another proved a great deal more spectacular than her voice. With her streaky blond hair whipping around her head, full lips pouting in her round face, smoldering eyes heavily outlined in black, and her navel, pierced with a cross on a ring, ever exposed, Mandi danced through many a boy's wet dreams and probably through those of older men as well.

Upon meeting her, Jeff said diplomatically that she'd always been one of his favorite performers. He didn't mention she'd been a fantasy of his middle school years. Mandi had more mileage on her than the Ryders' old van, Jeff eventually told Kara. The pop singer at the age of nineteen married her bodyguard and gave birth to a child that interrupted her career. By twenty-one, she divorced the husband who stole from her and married one of her dancers. She gave birth to another child and at twenty-five, got rid of the dancer for cheating on her with another man. Past thirty with her cigarette-damaged voice gone and her body going, Mandi turned to Manny Lomax for rebranding and a comeback tour.

Manny got her nipped, tucked, and sucked down in size. He glitzed her up again and chose songs her smoke-roughened voice could handle. Wisely, he hired a troupe of dancers who made Mandi look good even when she drank too much and fell all over the stage. Best of all, he paired her with Jeff Ryder, his spare darkness and rich voice contrasting nicely with her glitter and bump and grind.

Manny Lomax was a master of the game, and the master was being kept waiting while Jeff's sad, long-haired wife said goodbye and begged a kiss for the red-faced infant daughter clutched in her arms. Too bad the kid looked so much like the father, or he might have been able to drive a wedge into that unfortunate marriage and set Jeff free to roam among the many women who would want him. That always made for good publicity.

Feigning disinterest, Lomax shamelessly listened in on the prolonged farewell. Always good to know what speed bumps lay ahead on the long road to stardom. Some he could smooth out, some not.

"Jeff, can't you wait until after Christmas to leave?" Kara begged. She lowered her voice, but Lomax possessed the hearing of rodent outwitting a cat. "We haven't had sex since the baby came. It's okay to go ahead now. I told you that last week."

A good agent could use that information somewhere down the line. Lomax stared straight ahead as if deaf in one ear.

"Manny says we need to get some rehearsal time in with Mandi on the big stage. We open in Los Angeles on New Year's Eve. I want you to come out for the first show, maybe get a place out there since we'll be playing the west coast and Vegas."

"Take your Christmas present, then, from Maridel and me." She thrust a small box into his hands. "It's a cell phone for calls just between the two of us. If this phone rings, I'll always be on the other end. No one else. I can send you pictures of Maridel too."

"Cool." Jeff accepted the gift, but didn't unwrap it. "I wish you wouldn't call the kid Maridel. Sounds like an amusement park."

"We're living in the south now, Jeff. When I told everyone I'd named her Mari Della, they used both names and then shortened it to Maridel. I think it's kind of cute."

"Whatever. I have to go. Manny is waiting."

Kara glared at the agent with the face of a blood-sucking ferret sitting behind the wheel of a Lexus. He smiled back showing small, sharp teeth. His eyes, black, beady and alert sat above a sharp nose and thin little mustache. His quick, nervous paws tapped the steering wheel impatiently. The wife could be trouble, but nothing the great Manny Lomax couldn't handle.

Kara held up the baby for Jeff to kiss. He hesitated, finally laying his lips briefly on the fragile forehead of the sleeping child. The baby didn't wake.

"She won't know the difference if I'm gone, Kara. You're the one who gets up all night and answers her every beck and call."

"She'll notice when you're gone soon enough. So will I."

"Merry Christmas, sweetheart." Jeff managed a farewell kiss, a brief brushing of the lips.

Unable to stand the delay any longer, Manny's

fingers hit the horn for one sharp blast. Jeff Ryder came running.

****

On Christmas Day, Kara called her mother early. Her mom had an invitation to dine with the Freys. The Freys planned to have a fresh turkey as well as a pork crown roast, her mother said. Joy, like Kara's old roommate, Hannah, would never lack for meat in her life. Once more, her mother bemoaned never having seen her new granddaughter in person, and now Kara talked about moving to the west coast. Kara and the baby should have come home for Christmas. Hadn't she offered to send the plane fare?—which Kara had been too proud to accept or to ask for her mother's help with the baby in the shabby Graceland's Gates apartment.

So instead of dining with the Freys, Kara Ryder now stood in the bald backyard of a run-down frame house in Memphis watching Manuel Sanchez and some of his brothers barbecue a *cabrito,* the headless carcass of the young goat very reminiscent of a large dog. The Mexicanos and their guest had already dined on turkey with a chocolate mole sauce at noon. They passed baskets of fresh, hot tortillas for scooping up the refried beans, yellow rice, and corn laced with red and green peppers, saving the *cabrito* for an evening treat.

Indoors, a number of motherly women exclaimed over Maridel's mop of black hair and passed her from hand to hand for inspection. "And look at my *niño*, bald as a buzzard," one of Merita's sister-in-laws said, laughing. Merita nudged Kara, hovering anxiously over her baby, making sure no one dropped the child.

"Go outside, Karita, and call your man. Maridel, she be okay."

Kara took the hint about being insultingly possessive and went out to the relative calm of the space where all the men gathered to drink Mexican beer around the barbecue pit. The yard had better reception anyhow away from the hoard of children beginning to wind up for piñata busting.

Her phone rang so many times, she became certain the artificial voice telling her to leave a message would soon kick in, but at the last moment, Jeff picked up the call.

"Merry Christmas, sweetheart. Guess where I am?"

"With Mandi," she said dully.

"And her two obnoxious sons. One is a bully, and the other is almost certainly gay. If we had to have a kid, I'm glad it's a girl. That's not the good part. I'm lying beside Mandi's heated pool drinking mimosas and taking a tan. We haven't had dinner yet, but the first course is shrimp cocktail. There's a tureen of caviar and those dry melba rounds just for snacking."

"Great. Is anyone else there?"

"Sure. Manny and some of her dancers, the two ex-husbands who don't get along with each other or Mandi. It's a real sideshow. Did I tell you Mandi's grandfather was one of Musical McDonalds, Virgil and Luther, big on the country circuit in the Fifties? Virgil had this mended harelip and didn't sing, but played a shitload of instruments. Lute had the voice. Their kids formed a gospel group, and little Miraculous Mandi McDonald sang with them. Hard to believe by what she's wearing at the pool today, big ass hanging out like two hams on either side of thong and caviar caught deep in her cleavage. Family disowned her when she started acting out and ran off to be a pop star. Man, I wish you were here. You could write a funny poem about it."

"Actually, I find all that kind of sad."

The sound of a large splash obscured his next few words. "Jesus, that older boy is the size of a walrus and has about the same manners. Look, Kara, I want you to come out here. We can stay in the hotel for a while, but I have a line on a house way better than that dump in Memphis. Just get on a plane and come."

"Jeff, what about the crib and my rocker and all the things I have for the baby?"

"Christ, you are hard to please. Suit yourself. Stay there, or pack up the band van and haul the baby junk out here."

"I can handle it, Jeff. I'll see you soon."

A swarm of children exited the house following the bearer of a brightly colored star-shaped piñata on the end of a rope. After tossing the rope over the limb of a leafless hickory, the bashing began with many shouted directions and squeals of terror when the first boy started to flail his stick at his crowd of cousins.

"Where in hell are you?"

"I'm with the Sanchez family. They were kind enough to invite me and Maridel. Your daughter is a big hit with all her black hair."

"They don't have enough black-haired kids of their own? Gotta go. Just get yourself out here one way or another. Merry Christmas, Kara."

"I love you, Jeff," she said, but he was gone.

A tiny girl beat at the piñata now. Her uncle lowered the star-shaped object to allow her to tap at it with the bat. When another boy took over, the uncle raised it up again, prolonging the excitement.

Battered and excited pretty much described how Kara felt. Jeff wanted her in L.A., but with a child in tow, she couldn't simply jump into the old van and head out of town on an impulse. She'd need to have the tires and belts checked, make sure they had enough cash for the gas, stock up on formula and diapers. Still getting up with the baby at night, her energy ebbed at an all time low. Just thinking about the to-do list made her tired.

A tall youth took his turn at the piñata. When his uncle jerked the rope, the boy leapt up and took a mighty swing. Brightly wrapped candies burst from the papier-mâché star. The children scattered. Spats broke out, and the watching mothers went to make sure each child got a share. One of them deposited Maridel in her mother's arms again. The commotion woke the baby who cried for her bottle.

Kara went inside and sat in a sagging chair in a back bedroom, giving the baby her formula while trying to carry on a conversation with a nursing mother who spoke very little English and lay on the bed, when the second commotion broke out. A uniformed man flashing a badge and shouting, "INS," came to the door and motioned the women and babies from the room.

In the living room, Merita and her female relatives clutched large purses to their chests and gathered their children around them. Through the window overlooking the backyard, the men stood stark still, their hands behind their heads. Two officers guarded the rear gate.

"Everyone outside, you hear? *Comprendé?*" the INS officer ordered. His words were repeated in Spanish by a slim Hispanic woman, also in uniform.

Out in the yard, the officer said, "Sorry to ruin your holiday, folks, but we got word there are illegals at this address. Let's see your papers." The translator echoed his words.

The women began hauling work cards and birth certificates from their purses and waving them in the faces of the guards. "Born in the U.S.A.," some said, pointing to their children. In the chaos, two men made it over the low backyard fence. Kara with nothing to show pretended not to notice, but one of the gate guards took off down the alley after them

"Okay, okay, one at a time. Line up."

Kara, holding her baby to her chest, waited sixth in line.

"Papers? Birth certificate for the baby?"

"Papers?" she parroted.

The translator repeated the question in Spanish.

"I'm sorry. I don't speak Spanish."

The agent sneered and leaned toward the translator. "I don't know. She's brown and brown. Might just be a light complexion. The kid has all that black hair and dark eyes. Maybe she's Anglo married to one of the daddies."

"Excuse me," Kara interrupted. "I speak English perfectly well. I'm not married to any of these men. If you let me get my purse, I have a driver's license, but I'll have to go back to my apartment to get the baby's birth certificate."

"Check her license," he told the translator.

In a minute, they were back in the yard with the translator holding the license up to the light. "Looks good, chief."

Merita and her children passed muster, thanks to

her credentials showing proper employment as a cleaning lady for two prominent Memphis families and the birth certificates of both her son and daughter, citizens of the U.S of A. Not so lucky, Manuel stood with his hands bound behind his back, along with several other men who wouldn't be eating *cabrito* tonight.

"The baby could belong to one of the others. You guys put the men in the wagon. Luz, you take her home and check the birth certificate. *Feliz Navidad*, one and all. Now I can get home to my own dinner," the lead officer said.

"*Por favor*, please. I say *adios* to *mi esposa, si?*" Manuel asked.

"Go on. It's Christmas."

Manuel leaned over so his wife and children could kiss him. He whispered something in Merita's ear, then joined the line of men being pushed toward a van. The translator tugged Kara's arm and took her, the baby, diaper bag, and car seat to an unmarked car. Kara gave the woman her address.

"This is terrible. How can you work for the INS?" she quizzed the translator.

The woman shrugged. "My mama came here nine months pregnant. I was born in this country. I got to stay. My papi was sent back. I think having someone who speaks the language helps them. I do a good job no matter what anybody says about me."

Back at the apartment, Kara produced the baby's birth certificate only recently arrived only in the mail.

"I thought you were legit, but the chief likes to be thorough. Does that baby belong to any of the men back there?"

"No. My husband is Jeff Ryder, a singer. He's out in L.A. right now. Maybe you've heard of him?"

"Can't say that I have. They'll need me back at the processing center. Merry Christmas, Mrs. Ryder."

As Kara walked the officer to the door, she noticed Merita and her children arrive in Manuel's big truck. She continued down the stairs and across the courtyard.

"What will they do to Manuel?"

"*Nada*. Send him back to Mexico. He say for me to move. Let him know where we go. He be back."

Despite the sad ending to the day, she gave Merita a hug and thanked her for the invitation. On the way back to the apartment, she realized how on her own she truly was. Jeff dwelled in L.A. and might as well have been in Mexico for all the good he did her.

By mid-week, Kara got the old van serviced and closed out the small bank account in Memphis. Jacquie summoned her sons again, and they loaded the secondhand dresser into the rear, slung her rocking chair over the back seat, and shoved the disassembled crib into the space Buzz Light once occupied. She filled the floor space with a case of formula and sacks of disposable diapers, boxes of baby clothes, and her own battered suitcase. After emptying out the refrigerator, she gave the contents to the Hawkins boys sure they'd only use the six-pack of beer Jeff left behind.

Manny rented the apartment, not her. Let the agent who paired her husband with Mandi McDonald take care of the utilities. Across the way, Merita Sanchez loaded up the camper truck. Both of them were starting over.

Chapter Fourteen
On the Road Again

Kara remembered her father always said never go back the way you came. She would make no stops in Bumfuck or Nowhere on this trip. She sought Route 40, paralleling old Route 66, and drove flat out for over two days with Maridel beside her in the backwards car seat. The baby should have been in the rear seat, but with that space crowded full of shifting belongings, the infant was better off where her mother could see her. Besides, Maridel provided company. Kara smiled down at her daughter who turned her head toward her mother's voice and tired very hard to focus. At eight and a half weeks, the deep blue eyes of her birth had darkened to Jeff's shade of intense brown. She'd be a beautiful child, far prettier than her mother.

Amarillo, Tucumcari, and Albuquerque disappeared in the rearview mirror. They passed through the striking landscape of northern Arizona, finding the air surprisingly chilly. Piñon pines dotted the red hills and canyons. Kara promised Maridel that some day, when not in such a hurry to reach Daddy, they would stop to see the Petrified Forest and the Grand Canyon. When the baby cried for a bottle or a diaper change, Kara took a break wherever they were along the road.

The last day turned scary as they crossed the

Mojave Desert with plenty of water and fuel in a very old van. The great emptiness made Kara all the more aware a small life depended on her and only on her. She stopped in Needles to get gas. The place that routinely registered the hottest temperatures in the States wasn't so awful in the wintertime. With a beautiful sort of desolation all around, Needles turned out to be an oasis in the desert.

The station offered gas, hot and cold drinks, snacks both salty and sweet, and a rack of tabloids by the checkout counter. Kara found herself looking at her husband stepping out of a limo with Mandi McDonald. The former teen star's belly might have bulged over the top of her very tight, very low cut rhinestone-studded jeans, but her breasts appeared big, high, and firm in a hot pink sequined halter top. Implants, of course, Kara told herself. She hoped the glaze of lust in Mandi's eyes proved equally false. Jeff didn't smile, but he did look gorgeous, all lean and longhaired. The caption read *New Man for Mandi?* With her old plaid thermos refilled with coffee, Kara forged on making great time across the desert, finally turning off Forty, south to L.A.

The freeways of Los Angeles inspired their own kind of terror, four, sometimes six lanes across, all full of cars filled with people in a suicidal hurry to be somewhere else. By the time Kara parked the decrepit van in front of the hotel, her hands had stiffened from gripping the steering wheel so hard. As she removed the baby's carrier, a snooty doorman told her she couldn't park there. He reminded her very much of the bar manager who tried to cheat the Ryders of the Night so many years ago. She drew herself up, tossed him the keys, and handed him her last five-dollar bill.

"Then find a place for it, Buster. I'm checking in."

She marched through the lobby, shabby suitcase in one hand, brand new baby, carrier, and diaper bag in the other. Every woman in Los Angeles except her seemed to be tall, blonde, and sun-kissed. Their kind lounged all over the place, waiting by the huge jardinières filled with tropical flowers, draped on the red microfiber sofas and chairs, laughing on the arms of men as good-looking as themselves. Feeling small and scruffy, Kara placed the baby carrier on the check-in counter and waited for someone to offer assistance. The staff, consisting mainly of more beautiful women, seemed intent on serving men in expensive suits. She pounded on a call bell. Its sharp *bing* brought her a short, balding, and rather annoyed male clerk.

"May I help you?" He peered at Maridel as if she were Kara's pet poodle. "Adorable," he drawled in a way indicating he used the word far too often.

"Thank you. Would you call Jeff Ryder's room and tell him his wife is here? That's Ryder with a Y."

"I'm well aware. Name."

"I'm his wife, Kara Ryder."

"So sorry, you aren't on his call list." The clerk had a short, pudgy nose, yet he managed to look down it.

"Jeff has a call list? He may not be expecting me until tomorrow. I made very good time. Please ring his room."

"Mr. Ryder seems to have many wives. I'm afraid I've heard this one before. He is sleeping at this time of day and doesn't want to be disturbed."

Kara bowed her head, overwhelmed by a stark realization. Like the plumber's wife who never gets her pipes cleaned, she'd had to buy Jeff's album at a music store in Memphis. An entire rack of them displayed with a cutout of Jeff leaning against it took up its share of floor space. Her husband wore a black leather jacket and pants with a red shirt. His signature white silk scarf hung over his shoulders. One lock of his blue-black hair hung down his chest as if the photographer had placed it just so. His perfect smile seemed to say, "Buy my album and take me home." She didn't know that Jeff had already gained a sight-recognition type of celebrity despite the middle-aged woman who said in passing Jeff Ryder could put his shoes under her bed any day.

Maridel woke up and scrunched her eyes against the bright light of the lobby. She stretched her tiny limbs and began to fuss. In a short time, she'd be in full demand mode for a bottle of formula.

"Sir, this is Jeff Ryder's child, and she owns a voice as loud as her daddy once she gets going. She might need a diaper change, and I am perfectly willing to do that right here on this counter while she screams if you don't call Mr. Ryder's room immediately."

The clerk placed a call. Kara hoped not to security. He spoke politely to someone on the other end of the line. "So sorry to wake you, Mr. Ryder. A woman with a baby wants to see you. She says her name is Kara."

Maridel stiffened her legs and grew red in the face. She wailed into the receiver. Kara resisted the urge to pick her up and offer comfort.

"He says that scream sounds familiar." The way his brows rose, Kara supposed he believed Jeff fathered Maridel, probably out of wedlock. The clerk wrote a room number on the inside of a small folder. "I'll have to unlock the elevator for you. This way—Mrs. Ryder."

Maridel continued to shriek on the ride up to her

father's floor. Her mother told her, "Good work, babe. You'll have a bottle and a clean diaper in a few minutes. Try to tone it down for now."

Maridel didn't quiet. As they approached Jeff's room, the door opened before them. "Hellfire, Kara, this is the executive floor. I could hear you coming all the way from the elevator."

Her husband seemed as dark and poetic as ever. She took his face in her hands and laid a kiss on his lips so hard he stumbled backwards. "Yeah, I'm glad to see you, too. But, ah, it's hard to concentrate when the little fire alarm is going off."

"Fire alarm? Oh, the baby."

"Give me a while to wake up. Go lie down. Get naked."

He'd come to the door in only a sagging pair of pajama bottoms, his black hair tangled and wild. She ran a hand across the patch of dark fur on his pale chest and down his center line toward his navel. She felt his response pressing hard against her before her fingers reached the spot. "Keep that thought. I won't be long."

Naturally, the diaper had to be a poopy one, and Maridel cried the entire time it took for the change. Kara sat on the closed toilet and gave the baby her bottle. After several minutes of frantic sucking, the infant quieted, finished her meal, produced her burp, and fell bonelessly into sleep. With the baby settled into her carrier again, Kara tiptoed out into the dim center of the suite.

Heavy curtains kept out the hazy California sunlight. She used the light from the bathroom to guide her past an impressive desk, a set of comfortable chairs, a table, and seating that could be used for dining, and a kitchen/bar area to the closed door of a bedroom. Opening the door, she went to the bed. Carefully setting the baby carrier off to one side, Kara undressed and slid in beside her sound-asleep husband.

****

When Kara woke to the sound of Maridel's fretting, Jeff was gone. She scooped up the baby and patted her back while she went to the drapes and opened them to the red sky of sunset. She showed the baby the view. "Looks like the Ryders finally made it to L.A."

She stripped Maridel of a wet diaper in the luxurious private bath attached to the bedroom and got her another bottle. The platform tub offered whirlpool nozzles and a tempting array of first class bath products. Kara took a good look at herself in a wide mirror with enough lighting to put on stage makeup.

In her haste to join Jeff, she'd driven into the night on each portion of the journey and fallen into a budget motel bed as soon as the baby settled. Out of habit, she shoved the little soaps and shampoos into her bag before she left and took a quick wakeup shower in the morning before pushing on full of whatever free breakfast the motel offered.

The bathroom lights showed off the dark circles under her eyes, the greasy hair with small, stiff patches where the baby had bubbled on her. She threw on the T-shirt she'd been wearing when she'd arrived in the lobby. The black tee had belonged to Buzz and honored The Grateful Dead. She certainly looked the part, but she wasn't grateful. Beneath the shirt, her breasts looked soft and saggy in their cheap cotton bra. She prayed they were done leaking now that she'd be sleeping with Jeff again. Thank God the room had been dark when Jeff opened the door.

"Want to see your mommy take a remedial bath, Maridel?"

The baby kicked her feet and watched as her mother turned on all the jets in the tub and dumped in aromatic bath salts. Kara shucked the T-shirt and lowered herself into the hot water. After a while of purely luxuriating, she ducked her head under the water and lathered up with a heavenly papaya-mango shampoo. While she rinsed out her long locks, she played peek-a-boo with Maridel who stared intently as her mother with the strange white foam on her hair disappeared and reappeared looking more normal each time.

"Where's Mommy? Here she is." Her baby smiled for the time. "Aren't you wonderful?" she told her daughter.

Getting out of the tub, Kara assessed herself again. Her breasts remained big and blue-veined from giving birth. She stood sideways. Her stretched belly looked like she carried a child in the fourth month of pregnancy. She sucked it in. Well, for all that, she could still see her ribs. Quickly, she covered herself with a thick terry robe hanging on the bathroom door. Kara combed an expensive cream rinse through her tangled strands and rubbed a little of it into her pubic hair which had finally grown back beyond the prickly stage after the hospital shaving. She thought Jeff might enjoy the scent.

The suite door opened and closed. The bedroom door followed. The bathroom door banged back on itself. Jeff Ryder kept right on coming. His baby daughter smiled.

"Look, Jeff. Maridel is smiling," Kara said to his reflection in the mirror.

Jeff's arms reached around her and untied the robe. She wanted to cover her breasts and belly, but he didn't seem to notice their sad condition. The robe hit the floor. He turned her and raised her onto the counter between the two sinks. He unzipped and plunged between her legs. Kara's eyes opened wide. Like the first time all over again, she thought, not expecting the small amount of pain.

"Jeff, ah, Jeff. We should… We need…"

"Yes, we do need. Sorry, babe, I couldn't wait. I thought about this all through rehearsal. I had to hide my woody behind the guitar. Just let me, then I'll take care of you, I promise."

Alert and happy, Maridel with wide, dark eyes watched her father finish. Lots of motion kept her attention. The baby gurgled and grinned.

"Wrap your legs around me. We're going for a trip."

Kara held on tight as they crossed the bathroom and fell across the king-sized bed. Jeff licked her breasts and worked his fingers in her swollen pubis. She came as quickly as he had after nearly three months of abstinence. In the bathroom, Maridel fretted for the mother who'd disappeared from view.

"Jeff, I need to get the baby—though I'm not too sure I can walk."

"She'll be fine where she is for a while."

He began kissing her neck. Give him another half hour and he'd be ready again. Kara knew her man. She shoved at his shoulders, and reluctantly, Jeff let her rise and bring the carrier into a dim corner of the room.

"She should go to sleep soon for a few hours if we give her a little quiet."

Kara snuggled into a place on his shoulder. "You really did miss me. You and Mandi aren't an item, are you? I saw some tabloids on my way out here showing the two of you together. They said you were her new toy boy."

"Manny says the publicity is good. I wouldn't lay a hand on that old whore. She sleeps with her dancers. It's a miracle she isn't HIV-positive yet. The one thing I love about you, Kara, is that you've never been with another man. You're still clean and sweet and only for me after all these years." Jeff smoothed her hair back and kissed her forehead. "Going around with a rising star is good for Mandi's image according to the Man. So, we go out and make the scene together, but not tonight!"

"She isn't that much older than we are, and frankly, I worried. She looks fairly lush in those pictures, and you haven't shown much interest since I had the baby." Kara reached down and stroked Jeff's penis. It jumped in her hand. "I've missed this big guy very much."

"And he missed you. This is much easier now that the baby is out of the way. You don't feel quite the same though, not as tight."

"Well, yes to both, I guess. You don't squeeze seven pounds of baby out a tiny hole without stretching. But, it was still good for you, wasn't it?"

"So good I'm ready to do it again."

She could tell. Not a good time, really, to say he needed to use a condom as a precaution, not with Mandi McDonald waiting in the wings.

Chapter Fifteen
California, Here We Are!

What a hellish mess! Kara stood in the deluxe bathroom again, surrounded by mirrors. Squeezed into her killer red dress, the same one she worn in college and brought back to Memphis after the funeral, she'd hoped to wear it out somewhere with Jeff before she got too big to fit into it. Her breasts bulged out of the sides of the halter top, and the waist fit so tight she couldn't breathe. No way could she wear it for the opening on New Year's Eve. Glad Jeff had gone off for one more lighting check, Kara peeled the disastrous dress off of her body. She needed to shop and quickly.

Sorting through the contents of her suitcase, she realized she'd spent the last nine months in rags. Her jeans were distressed because she had worn them to shreds, not because she bought them that way. All the T-shirts belonged to Buzz. She had about as much chance of being waited on in the chic stores around the hotel as the hooker in *Pretty Woman*. What to do?

She dressed her baby in an adorable pink outfit, certainly used Baby Gap, and put a kooky little hat on Mari's black hair. For herself, Kara selected her rattiest jeans and a black T-shirt with most of the logo washed off and knotted it across her middle to show a little belly. She took off her thin wedding band and put it in the pocket that had no holes. With the small amount of cash Jeff left for her, Kara went to a shop in the arcade off the lobby of the hotel and purchased oversized sunglasses. She flung her hair back and, hauling her child, she stepped out in her worn Huarache sandals to take on the first dress store in the arcade.

No one rushed to serve her. Kara sorted through dresses on the racks. Each garment seemed too small. Reluctantly, she went up a size. She slung three possibilities over her arm and started for the dressing room. A quick clerk intercepted her and counted the dresses she wanted to try on.

Not the red one. It showed all her leftover baby bulges. The hot pink sequined number, a la Mandi McDonald, fit like a tube sock. Sighing, Kara pulled the plain black dress over her head. The modest scooped neck flattered as did the little capped sleeves with their lettuce edges. The swingy skirt bore the same edging and came just to her knees. She suspected the dress was meant to hit mid-thigh on a taller person but didn't care. Another point in its favor, the skirt also hid her hips and thighs, which reappeared with the birth of the baby. Kara hadn't worried about those parts of her anatomy for all the years on the road with Jeff, and now here they were, back again and rounder than ever. With her long hair, she seemed to be nineteen again, maybe a good thing. Obviously sold on the new look, Maridel smiled up from her carrier.

Kara took the dress to the counter. The very thin, impeccably dressed clerk helped a woman who must be Somebody. She took her time, making small talk and wrapping each purchase carefully in tissue. Kara toyed with a display of glass-beaded chokers that shone like dewdrops caught in a black spider web. Like the dress, they were way overpriced but pretty. Poor women in China probably churned them out for fifty cents each.

At last, the clerk, her very white smile vanishing, turned to Kara. "How will you be paying for that, miss?"

Kara darted a look over her shoulder, then raised her sunglasses just a bit. "Don't you know who I am?"

"No. Cash, check, charge, or debit?"

Kara placed the baby carrier firmly on the counter. She took off Maridel's droll little hat and showed off her shining black hair. "I'm the mother of Jeff Ryder's love child. You may charge the dress and this necklace to his room."

Kara snatched up one of the beaded chokers and placed it on the dress. "I'll need a pair of dark hose, and those in a size seven." She pointed imperiously toward a display of strappy Italian dress sandals and prayed that the things would fit without being tried on. "This, too." She added a tiny black evening bag with a gold chain handle.

The clerk balked. "I'll have to clear this with Mr. Ryder. I've seen him in the mall, but you weren't with him."

"He's at rehearsal right now. Try Mr. Norman at the front desk. I believe he'll vouch for me."

The clerk took her suggestion. Kara could hear Mr. Norman say, "Her again!" very loudly, but the sales person wrote up the purchases with no more fuss or insult. Before she left the shop, the woman who assisted her so reluctantly put the phone to her ear again. Kara caught the words "love child" and "Ryder" and smirked. Evidently, news traveled fast in L.A.

Pleased with herself for the moment, Kara took her

purchases back to the room. Jeff would freak when he saw the five-hundred dollar tab added to his account, but the mother of his child should be treated well. Now, that was a new and novel thought.

****

Nervous about leaving the baby with a hotel-supplied sitter, Kara tried to give instructions to a squat Hispanic woman who seated herself in front of the hi-def TV mounted on the wall and said, "So little, they no trouble," with barely a glance at Maridel, asleep in a portable crib.

"Her formula is in the bar refrigerator, and the diapers are in this bag." Kara set the diaper bag down pointedly next to the woman, who nodded without taking her eyes from the crystal clear image of a show broadcast from Mexico. "I'll be at this place."

Kara waved a slip of paper giving the address and phone numbers of Jeff's venue and her cell phone in front of the sitter's eyes. The woman grabbed it from Kara's hand. The scrap obviously blocked her view.

"Sure. I unnerstand. Everything be hokey-dokey. You go now."

Out in the hall, Kara patted the tiny purse. The cell phone barely fit inside on top of the key card, the ticket and stage pass, a lipstick, comb, and cab fare. Jeff had ducked in long enough to give her the tickets. He never ate before a show, but told her to order room service as he ran his fingers along the small naked spot between the knotted T-shirt and her jeans, saying, "Later."

Nervous about leaving the baby and the "later," she'd barely forced down a California club sandwich, oozing with avocado and shrimp, and a glass of iced tea. Taking a deep breath, she took the private elevator to the lobby crowded with New Year's Eve revelers and an excess of people with cameras. Out one corner of her eye, she noticed the salesclerk from the dress shop and started to wave, willing to let bygones be bygones. The woman pointed a long-nailed finger at her, and suddenly the camera-wielding men engulfed Kara.

"Is it true that you are the mother of Jeff Ryder's love child?"

"Ah, yes. I'm the mother of his child. Please, let me pass. I don't want to be late."

"You're going to his opening tonight? Where's the baby? Big bucks for a picture of her." One of the most aggressive men shoved a card into Kara's hand.

"Yes, of course I'll be at the opening. Jeff gave me tickets. Maridel is with a sitter. Please, let me pass." She flapped the card at the hoard.

"Out! All of you, out!" Bless his tight little heart, Mr. Norman, still on duty, came to the rescue. "I'll call security, and you can spend the night in jail if you continue to disturb our guests. Out now!"

Swept along in the wave of paparazzi heading for the wide glass doors, they continued to shout in her ears. "What's your name, doll? How long have you and Jeff been involved? Does the baby have your last name or his? How do you spell Maridel?"

"Ah, I'm Kara Ryder—Jeff's wife, not his lover. No, I mean his wife and his lover. M-a-r-i-d-e-l. It's a nickname."

"A nickname for what?"

"Cab! Oh please, a cab!" She implored the snooty doorman. "Big tip later, I swear."

He imposed his broad epauleted shoulders between her and the mob and blew his brass whistle. A cab streaked to the curb. The doorman helped her into the vehicle. The paparazzi went scattering to their cars. The hall where Jeff and Mandi performed wasn't far from the hotel. Kara asked the cabby to take her to the stage entrance. She paid the man an entire twenty with shaking hands and didn't ask for change. Once inside the stage door, she showed the guard her pass and asked him to locate Jeff.

"He's busy. You the wife? You're in the second row. Place is filling up. You better get to your seat. Down those steps to your left. Watch you don't trip on the cables."

Kara took her seat. Still shaking, she calmed by the time the lights went down and an announcer appeared stage right to welcome the audience to Mandi Mania with Jeff Ryder. Blackout, moody blue lighting, stage left. And Jeff sat on a stool making love to an acoustic guitar. "This is for all the beautiful women out there. You know you are all beautiful to me," he said in that voice like melted chocolate.

He followed his opening with some standard love songs and did *In the Moonlight* toward the center of his set. He wrapped up with *Miss You* and one last song—for Mandi, he claimed. The chorus sounded familiar to Kara though she'd never heard this ditty. The words definitely came from a juvenile poem she'd written shortly after meeting Jeff. "You are a fantasy—for a plain girl like me", but "plain girl" became "poor boy."

Jeff turned toward the stage and veils of curtains opened. Mandi McDonald bounced down a flight of golden stairs, her stomach held in by extra-strength red spandex, her breasts not really moving along with the rest of her body. She tossed her blonde, bewigged head and lip-synced her way through one of her early hits, all the while weaving through rows of male dancers who put on quite a good show. No one seemed to mind she wasn't really singing.

"Whoa, I need to catch my breath for a minute. Let's bring Jeff Ryder back out for an encore and give him a big hand." Mandi held out her arms toward the wings.

Jeff got both applause and screams from the women in the audience. Kara overheard a disgruntled date who'd paid big money for seats this close to the stage grumble that Jeff was probably a pansy. His girlfriend punched him in the arm.

Jeff and Mandi did a duet version of *Miss You* while gazing into each other's eyes. Mandi toyed with the ends of his long, black hair. His rich baritone covered her smoke-roughened voice like syrup poured over gravel. With each verse, they moved farther apart, Jeff's hair sliding through her hands, until Jeff faded offstage and Mandi ended in the opposite corner.

"Jeff Ryder. Don't you just love that hair?" Big applause. Many screams. "And now a special delight. Let's watch Mandi's Men do their thing."

The dancers performed a long and sexy routine. Finally, Mandi came back and sang *Is That All There is Is?*, only the chorus and the part about first love gone sour. The song suited her post-thirty voice. Mandi's Men cavorted around her illustrating the need to keep dancing and having a ball no matter what life throws at you while Mandi reprised the chorus over and over again, not much worse than many recent songs that seemed to have only four lines, Kara thought.

During intermission, she found Jeff chugging a

bottle of water backstage. "What do you think?" he asked.

"The women are crazy for you, and the men are jealous."

"Great! Come on and meet Mandi."

Not in her dressing room, they found her smoking a cigarette in the alley. She also had a drink, but her beverage of choice wasn't water. Her sons stood nearby. She quizzed them on the show. "What part did you like best, Houston?"

"The dancing. I want to dance with Mandi's Men someday."

Mandi shrugged. "Like father, like son."

"That's 'cause he's a fag, Mom. Baby Huey is a fag. You were the best part. Jeff is probably a fag, too," a very chubby boy spoke up.

"I'd like you to meet my wife, Austin." Jeff presented Kara to the family group.

"Okay, so you're not a fag. My mom still sings better than you."

"He's very loyal." Kara excused the boy's rudeness.

"He knows his daddy doesn't pay any child support. I'm Mandi, of course." Mandi gave Kara an air kiss, her hands outspread to hold the cigarette and the vodka bottle away from their bodies.

"Austin and Houston. You must be from Texas."

"Hell no! I'm from Tennessee. Those are the cities where my kids were conceived. I hear yours is Maridel, but I can't place it."

"It's a nickname, not a place. I wouldn't have named her for the place, believe me."

"That bad, huh?"

"We weren't playing big cities then." Brief flashes of Nowhere and Bumfuck passed through Kara's mind.

"You were in his band?"

"No, I served as manager until Manny took over Jeff's career. Now Jeff uses yours."

"Must be tougher than you look. Nice meeting you. I got to squeeze myself into something gold and tight and change wigs. Enjoy the show." Mandi trotted back into the theater with her sons at her heels like hungry pups trailing their bitch mother.

"Good meeting you, too," Kara called after her.

"What do you think?" Jeff whispered.

"Old beyond her years."

"Like dog years. Look, get a cab back to the hotel after the show. Mandi takes a long time to come down after a show, and she always wants company. I'll see you when I see you, sweetheart."

The second half of the performance went about the same as the first: lip-syncing, dancing, one real song, more dancing, and Jeff helping Mandi close at one minute to midnight with a reprise of *Fantasy*. They bowed hand-in-hand.

Jeff tossed his white silk scarf Kara's way. Mandi thew a red one toward the other side of the audience. Kara raised her hand, but the slick fabric sailed over her head and was snatched from the air by two women who fought over it like rabid raccoons over a rotten fish. Raccoons, now where had that come from, Kara wondered? Must be their eye makeup. The scarf tore in the middle, and they both had a souvenir.

Jeff and Mandi urged the audience to count down to midnight. On the stroke of twelve, the false ceiling opened. Confetti, balloons, and streamers rained down on the crowd. On stage, Mandi laid a big kiss on Jeff. By the look of her hollowed cheeks, she was the one Frenching. The two raccoon women hugged. Couples smooched. Kara stood alone. The stage door guard got her a cab, and she went back to her baby.

The sitter dozed, but Maridel still breathed, the first thing Kara checked. An empty feeding bottle sat on the bar, and the waste can held a wet diaper. Kara shook the sitter awake, paid her, and saw her out. She took off the shoes that pinched and the pantyhose that held her belly in, hung up the overpriced dress, and got into bed naked to wait for Jeff.

He came in reeking of smoke around three a.m. Kara, up and wrapped in the terry robe, sang Maridel softly back to sleep. The charm of the scene was lost on Jeff. His eyes had that dilated, glazed look, and his smile was as goofy as if he'd spent the evening with Buzz and Terry again. He tugged at the tie to the robe.

"Just a second, Jeff. I need to put the baby down."

"Yeah, she's definitely in the way, sweetheart. Come right back here." He patted the sofa. Kara put the baby down and with her robe hanging open, returned to Jeff. He took her on the sofa far from the drawer in the bedroom where Kara had stocked the condoms.

****

Manny Lomax went out early looking for reviews the day after the New Year started. Mandi McDonald had been entertaining, the critics said, but not fresh, and way past her prime. One credited Jeff Ryder with a great voice utterly wasted on the schlock he poured out, but women adored him. He definitely had a solid career ahead. Manny could live with this. None of the critiques would kill the show.

His beady eyes drifted across the news racks, looking for more papers that might have given his clients space. What he found, he didn't like. A gaudy tabloid showed a front-page picture of little Kara Ryder resembling a big-eyed doe about to be torn to pieces by the hounds. The headline splashed across the page read *Jeff's Secret, Secluded Wife and Baby,* the subtitle— *Does Mandi Know?*

Manny Lomax firmly believed any publicity was good publicity, but that little bitch probably cooled Jeff's career down a notch simply by existing—or rather letting her existence be known. The agent had so carefully cultivated the Mandi-Jeff myth, and now, Jeff Ryder appeared to be a cheating bastard. Women didn't go for that. Jeff might have to start off the New Year doing damage control instead of lining Manny's pockets.

Chapter Sixteen
California Girls

Kara, boxed in between Manny and Jeff, held the baby wrapped in a blanket, hidden from the photographers. The men promised the press conference wouldn't last more than fifteen minutes. Jeff at his most charming, wide white smile gleaming, read his statement telling the world that he and his lovely wife, Kara, had been married six years. Mari Della was their first child. Kara had stayed behind in Memphis while he rehearsed the show with Mandi, but as everyone could see, she and the baby came to be with him at the opening.

"Kara, yo! Over here! How do you feel about the relationship between Jeff and Mandi?"

"Mandi and I have met. While she is certainly a woman capable of getting any man she wants, I am quite sure her relationship with Jeff is only professional."

Someone in the rear of the room said, "Yeah, right," but another reporter cut him off.

"Kara, could we see the baby?"

Reluctantly, she turned back the flap of blanket hiding Maridel's small face. Supporting the baby's head with her hand, she held her child toward the crowd. Maridel experimented with one of her gummy smiles. Lights flashed, cameras whirred, people jockeyed for position to get another shot of the kid with all the black hair. Maridel screwed up her face and began to cry. Kara cradled her against her shoulder. The press conference was over as far as she was concerned.

"Kara, are you and the baby going on tour with Jeff when the show leaves L.A.?"

"I don't really know. I—"

Jeff cut in almost surgically. "Kara managed my former band, the Ryders of the Night. She understands about the need to tour, but taking a baby along would be difficult. We'll do what is best for Mari Della. As for Kara, she remains my inspiration, my muse. Mandi and I are friends and co-performers as we have been all along."

Manny filled the remainder of the time plugging the show. When the photographers called for more pictures, Jeff put his arm around his wife and flipped the blanket off the baby's face again. They left the platform and vacated the room by a back door.

"You done good, Jeff." Manny patted his star on the back. "Now, all those females out there are going to see you as a devoted husband and father. They can pretend to be married to a guy like you. Let's get Kara out of the hotel and up to the house before any of these guys catch on that she won't be staying. She can't buy so much as a stick of gum in the lobby without getting her picture taken if we don't move quick."

The old van waited for them patient as a draft horse, already packed with Kara's things. The bandwagon toiled through the traffic with Jeff behind the wheel and Manny following in his own car. They exited onto one of the canyon roads outside of the city and took a winding path up above the smog line. The road, lined with stucco and frame houses sitting precariously on tiny lots with cliffs above them and cliffs below, grew steeper. To Kara, the dwellings resembled the kind of places she'd seen moving down hillsides propelled by mud slides, but the lawns bearing short, green grass in January seemed encouraging. Jeff pulled into the concrete driveway of a unit and parked next to a sturdy new Toyota bearing dealer's plates.

"Home, sweet home, babe. The Toyota is yours. Merry Christmas." Jeff tossed her the keys to the new car. "Three bedrooms, two baths, and a price tag you wouldn't believe for a place like this. When my career really takes off, we'll get something better—with a pool."

"It's fine. It's great, our first house."

"And you get to buy all the furniture and decorate while I'm on tour. I told you that you didn't have to bring that used crap from Memphis." He jerked his head toward the baby's dresser and unassembled crib in the rear of the van.

"Well, we would have needed something to start with anyhow. I can help you unload, but first, let's pick out a room for Maridel."

They walked through the modest one-story home. Kara dropped her suitcase in the master bedroom. Jeff would want a king-sized bed so this space didn't require much in the way of furniture. Choosing the middle bedroom, close to theirs, for the baby, she and Jeff lugged in the dresser, crib, and rocker while Manny waited impatiently. The men went off to attend to business in the city, leaving Kara with a half-assembled baby bed, a cell phone, and a cranky child.

"Looks like you and me, Maridel. I wonder if they

deliver pizza up here." Patting the fretting baby, she moved into the small kitchen, thankful the last owners left the appliances and curtains. The electricity and water had been turned on. She picked up a phone book from the counter. Chinese, Italian, Thai, Greek, everyone delivered. Kara skimmed over the oriental offerings. No need to select the cheapest noodle dishes on the menu anymore. Her stomach growled for shrimp, beef, pork, and crisp vegetables.

"Okay, then. Happy Family for me and formula for you, California girl."

****

Driving Manny's car, Jeff returned in the late afternoon. A small moving van followed and parked on the street. Two men unloaded the predictable king-sized bed, hauled it into the bedroom, assembled the pieces, and left. Jeff and Kara engaged in sheetless sex on the bare mattress while Maridel napped. Afterwards, they emptied the old bandwagon of its contents.

"A guy from the Baptist mission will be coming for the van tomorrow. I donated it for a tax write-off," Jeff remarked off-hand.

"Oh," said Kara, suddenly as bereft as if she'd lost an old friend. She'd lived in that van, slept in it, had sex in it, and the old bandwagon hadn't let her down when she crossed the desert. Like Buzz Light, whose ashes traveled along with her, she and this van hadn't been apart for six years. In a way, the old rust bucket was more reliable than Jeff. Her eyes watered.

"It's only a van, babe. Here is your checkbook. Go wild. I'll probably stay in town tonight. How about trying out that mattress one more time?"

They did.

****

While Kara did enjoy buying big at Rooms to Go and getting Maridel a spiffy stroller, she wished Jeff had come along to help her pick and choose. Ha! At best, Jeff was an impatient shopper. He became restless waiting for her to buy milk at a convenience store. For the first time, she regretted not having the kind of wedding that would have supplied her with sheets and towels, matching dishes and dinnerware, the kind of wedding her sister would have in May.

Day by day, the house up the canyon became more and more of a home. Kara moved the baby into the third bedroom while she painted the child's room a pale yellow and hung the curtains Jacquie had made. She could have gotten better, but the hilltop was a lonely place where most residents left for work early and returned late to disappear into their houses without a word or a wave to their neighbors. She missed the soap opera lives of her friends in Memphis and their warmth and willingness to share and help out.

Jeff visited most afternoons while Maridel napped. When Kara pointed out what she bought and how much had been accomplished, he commented, "Nice" or "Great" and led the way to the bedroom. Too tired after a show to make the drive, he said, Jeff usually stayed in the city at night.

He wasn't happy when she brought up the subject of using condoms. "We should be careful until my body gets back to normal, and I can start using the pill again." She smoothed a rubber over his erection.

"So you weren't on the pill when you got here in December?"

"No, but don't worry. Mari was only two and a half

months old. I shouldn't have been ovulating yet. Relax. Enjoy." She certainly tried to do that, too.

By the time the Jeff and Mandi show took off for San Diego, San Francisco, Portland, and Seattle, Kara felt worn out and worried. She found a pediatrician for Maridel immediately, but put off going for a final checkup with an obstetrician month after month. She was so tired, and her post-natal period refused to arrive. Might be leukemia—or another baby. Which would seem worse to Jeff? Hard to say.

Finally meeting her next-door neighbor, the thrice divorced, extremely thin, blonde, and tan mother of two teenagers, Kara spilled her fears in Barb's messy kitchen over coffee that gave her heartburn.

"Here." Barb yanked a telephone book out from under a pile of fashion magazines. "This is my pap smear and breast man. He's good looking, too. Gives you something nice to stare at while he's working under the sheet."

Maridel began to cry in her carrier while Kara wrote down the number.

"You need to give that kid some rice cereal. That 'only formula' for six months is a crock. Her bedroom is right next to mine, and I know she still cries at night. Hungry is what she is."

Barb's daughters who dressed in Gothic black but spoke more like Valley Girls arrived home from school, not on a bus, but in the neat little convertible they'd guilted out of their father. "More power to 'em." Barb added more sweetener to her coffee. The teenagers dumped their backpacks in the entry and stormed the kitchen for rice cakes and diet soft drinks.

"Do either of you babysit?" Kara asked, very

hesitantly.

"Like, no!" answered the younger one. "Dad pays his child support."

The older girl, a diplomat despite her nose ring, said, "Your baby is cute and all, but no, we don't do that." Both of them took off for the private paradises of their bedrooms equipped with computers, televisions, and iPods.

"If you ever get in a bind, bring her over," Barb offered. "Second thought, call first. I might be entertaining one of my gentlemen friends." Barb flicked the ash of one of the two cigarettes a day she allowed herself into her saucer.

"Thanks for the offer. I'll call for a doctor's appointment and try that rice cereal on Maridel. Sorry if she's keeping you awake."

Barb shrugged. "I don't do much sleeping at night. Guess you don't get to nap in the afternoons with that handsome man slipping in and out of your place."

"My husband, Jeff."

"Sure, honey. Whatever. Come over anytime. Call first."

As she left, Kara wasn't too sure she was glad to know Barb. Still, she'd received some good ideas she would never have gotten from her other neighbor, Mr. Matsumoto, a reserved gentleman of oriental extraction, who nodded at her when she took the baby out for air. He lived alone and seemed to spend most of his time manicuring the sand and rocks that made up his small front yard and pruning its contorted bushes with a tiny pair of shears. A dutiful son with a wife and two grandsons came every Sunday and took Mr. Matsumoto away for the afternoon, returning him after dinner. Kara was distressed that she knew this. Didn't she have anything else to do with her time but watch her neighbors come and go?

Barb's gynecologist couldn't take Kara for two weeks. By that time, she felt better and slept more. The rice cereal did the trick. Barb knew lots of tricks, judging by the variety of men who sought her company. Kara told Mr. Matsumoto about the cereal when he remarked the baby's cheeks had filled out like ripe plums. "Rice good for babies," he said, going back to the endless raking of a yard disturbed by the winter rains.

When the day arrived, Kara loaded Maridel into her car seat and went off to keep the doctor's appointment. She found Dr. Feingold to be handsome, very professional, and totally sympathetic. She confessed she'd never gone for her three-month checkup, engaged in unprotected sex with her husband when the baby was two and an half months old, and hadn't had a normal period since Maridel's birth as if the man were a priest instead of a physician. What sort of penance might come her way?

Her confessor gave the doctor's classic answer. "Hmmm. Let's take a look."

Even though Dr. Feingold warmed his hands before proceeding, Kara remained as tense as she'd ever been with her legs spread. More "hmmms" came from under the sheet as he asked a few simple questions, pressed her abdomen and bobbed up occasionally to give her a reassuring smile. She dressed, gave blood and urine samples, waited, and was shown to the doctor's office.

"Congratulations. I'd say you're three months

pregnant with another beautiful child." Dr. Feingold nodded toward Maridel who had been very patient during the whole examination.

"Oh!" The word came out as a squeak as her throat closed up, and she began to cry. "My husband didn't want the first beautiful child. How could he not want her?"

Dr. Feingold handed her a tissue. "Men," he said with a certain amount of disgust. "I can recommend a clinic that will give you a second opinion and consider you for an abortion, but I really feel you've passed that point in time, Mrs. Ryder. Are you in difficult financial circumstances? We can allow you to pay for your care and delivery over time." He hesitated. "We do arrange private adoptions now and then. As I said, your daughter is a beautiful child. We would have no trouble placing her or the new baby."

"No. We can afford two children, and if Jeff doesn't like it, he can take his business elsewhere." Kara mopped her tears. Just maybe, it wouldn't come to that.

****

This kind of news should not be told over the phone, Kara rationalized. Jeff called once a week from wherever the tour landed. He told amusing, rather cruel anecdotes about Mandi who was so taken with a hired chauffeur in San Francisco that he'd been made a part of her entourage.

"His name is Jerrell, two e's, two r's, two l's, but I can't help thinking of him as big, black Jumbo. This guy must be six-five, two-fifty, all muscle, shaved head, and one gold earring. Mandi's first husband said he's done time for assault, but Mandi thinks of that as a plus.

He scares the shit out of the paparazzi—and me. The best part is I don't have to spend the evening with Mandi after the show."

"Are you lonesome tonight?" Kara asked, a little coy.

"And horny. Why don't you find a sitter and visit me some time?"

"I'll see what I can do," she promised.

In the end, she had no one she knew or trusted enough to leave Maridel with for an hour let alone for a long weekend. Besides, the baby grew more charming with each passing day. As she reached six months, Maridel crept along on her belly and sat up with some support. She loved everyone who paid attention to her and vocalized with a large range of babble words meaning absolutely nothing. Like her father, she seemed to enjoy the sound of her own voice.

Mari could pry a smile from Mr. Matsumoto when her mother took her out for a walk. The Goth Valley Girls were so charmed they offered to watch her for one Saturday afternoon so Kara could go shopping—for really nice maternity clothes, a fact she kept a secret.

"Like we totally understand why you need to go shopping, Mrs. Shafer," Molly, the tactless, said, staring at Kara's mom-jeans worn out in all the non-cool places with her kohl-ringed eyes.

Kara attempted to buy maternity clothes a size smaller than she currently wore, but the cheery saleswoman patted her stomach and said, "We're already showing, and we need room to grown."

Alone in the dressing room regarding herself in the merciless mirror, Kara admitted the truth. She hadn't shown very much before five months the first time, but now she popped out at the beginning of the fourth. She'd reverted to big T-shirts and half-zipped jeans for the last few weeks, but Jeff would notice. She'd planned to take the black New Year's Eve dress on the visit to Jeff, but found it already too snug in the chest and waist.

The saleswoman went to search for something dressy and returned with a stretchy gold garment, boldly Veed in the neckline and taut across the belly. "In L.A., we don't hide our pregnancies, we flaunt them," she said.

"Do you have this in black?" Kara asked, showing her uncertainty.

The clerk laughed and went off to try again. The final selection was midnight blue, high waisted, and showed off her full breasts. She'd be able to wear her $500 accessories with it and probably use the dress after she gave birth, too. Somehow, Kara couldn't surrender her Pennsylvania German practicality to free-spending California ways. She added some black leggings with a belly pouch for the baby and a few oversized shirts to her purchase. For the time being, half-zipped jeans and big T-shirts seemed the way to go. Jeff was used to seeing her that way. She bought Maridel a full week's worth of new duds from a fancy baby boutique next door, much more fun than outfitting herself.

By the time Kara returned home, Maridel possessed painted pearl pink fingers and toenails, and a new do of spiky black hair tipped in crimson thanks to her sitters who seemed to feel they had a doll to dress up. The baby wore the jeweled leather dog collar usually found on Barb's nervous teacup poodle.

Meredith and Molly, delighted with their new toy, handed over their punk version of Mari reluctantly. With a little washing, all the improvements were reversible, and Kara could only be grateful the baby hadn't picked up fleas from tiny Tutu. She started packing for their visit to her baby daddy, Jeff.

Chapter Seventeen
The Emerald City

Kara and Maridel got on the plane for Seattle with a full suitcase. They deplaned at Sea-Tac, searching for Jeff Ryder. He waited with his long hair pulled up under a ball cap and dark glasses hiding his soulful eyes from his wife. Looking sort of scruffy with two days growth of beard, he wore blend-in clothes. A man that could only be Jerrell stood with him, covering his back.

The first words out of Jeff's mouth: "You brought the baby!"

Maridel had been sharing her smiles with all and sundry, but now she took one look at her father's face stubbled face, grabbed a fistful of her mother's long hair and hid herself in Kara's shoulder. When she turned her head halfway to look again, the fistful of hair went into her mouth to be covered with drool.

Jeff gestured. "Can't you stop her from doing that?"

"A hazard of motherhood. Be glad this isn't cereal and egg yolks breakfast. It washes out, Jeff."

"Well, I don't want her to get in mine."

Help came from an unexpected source. "Give her to me, little mama. I don't have no hair for her to mess wit'."

Jerrell, the ex-con chauffeur held out his arms and laughed when a long string of drool landed on his skin-tight, black tee. Maridel appeared fascinated by his dark skin and the swirling pattern of tattoos on his arms. She gave Jerrell a delighted smile and reached for his gold earring.

"Uh-uh, baby girl. We best be going, Jeff."

Jerrell tucked the small suitcase under one arm, ignoring its little wheels, and started up the concourse with Maridel peering over his broad shoulder at her parents. He secured them in the back seat of a Mercedes with heavily tinted windows and spun them through Seattle traffic to the downtown hotel. Giving the keys to a lackey to park, Jerrell escorted them through the lobby and up to the door of their suite.

"Tell you what, little mama. Give Miss Mari to me, and you and Jeff have yourself a—conjugal visit. We go and see Mandi, baby girl. She got sparkles in bot' her ears."

"Ah, she needs to go down for a nap soon. Her bottles are in the bag. She likes to be rocked…"

"Don't you worry. I helped my mama raise eight befo' I got in trouble wit' the law. We jus' down the hall."

Jeff hung a Do Not Disturb sign on the door handle and kicked the door shut. They left a trail of clothes to the bed, not that either had much to shed. With Kara's jeans already half unzipped, Jeff had them and her T-shirt off and the big, white maternity bra unhooked before they got out of the lounge area. He filled his hands with her breasts, all the while backing his wife toward the bedroom. She was naked of clothes as they fell on the bed, and he had only to pull off his jeans since he'd evidently been going commando in anticipation of her visit.

His hand encountered the wet patch in her hair. He hesitated, then brushed the hair aside to kiss her neck, also a little damp where the baby nuzzled. Switching sides, he kept on coming, a little rough with his beard against her tender breasts. Lying flat, Kara didn't feel quite so dumpy. Jeff in his haste made no comments about her body. Only after the second time when they lay spent and sweaty, did he run his hands from her chest to her belly and remark, "Still haven't lost that baby weight. You can use the gym here."

Kara turned on her side away from him and drew her legs up to her stomach.

"Come on now, don't get angry. You don't do angry well," Jeff cajoled. He started to stroke her hair and stopped. "If you're going to be mad any way, I could do without the baby spit, too. Ah, shit, stop crying."

Her shoulders shaking, Kara answered. "That's not fat, Jeff. It's your baby, your second child. If you hadn't been in such a hurry last New Year's Eve—just like now…"

"Damn, Kara, I always trusted you to take care of things so I wouldn't have to. You know that. True, you warned me in Bumfuck, but you didn't say a word in L.A."

He sat on the edge of the bed, his back to hers. "What's with you? Suddenly you got this earth mother business going on."

"Maybe I'd rather take care of children for a change instead of grown men."

Jeff pulled on his jeans. She hoped he'd get caught in the zipper, but he didn't. Stalking to the bar in the living area, he cracked open a mini-bottle of Crown

Royal, poured it over ice from the bucket and tossed it down.

"I guess you aren't drinking," he sneered as his wife emerged from the bedroom wrapped in the hotel's terry robe. She gathered her clothes as she went along. "That explains the ugly bra, too."

Kara said nothing. When she found her shirt, she went back into the bedroom and dressed. She stood at the door while Jeff unscrewed another little bottle. Seizing the handle of her suitcase, she said, "Maridel and I will be out of your spotless, gorgeous hair as soon as I can get a flight."

She went down the hall dragging the bag with one squeaky wheel and rapped on Mandi's door. Jerrell used the peephole, then opened up. Maridel lay asleep on his big shoulder.

"Come on in, little mama. Missin' yo' girl?"

"Yes. We're going home. Mind holding her while I book a flight?"

"That you, Kara, doll?" Mandi called in her rough voice as she made a raid on her own bar. Without her stage makeup, she had a hard face for a woman under forty. "I haven't been smoking around the baby, honest to God, but since I ain't the one pregnant, I am having a little drinky."

"How did you know?"

"Jerrell said he thought so. You had that look, that little bulge, those big knockers. Come on in."

"Jeff is upset."

"You won't keep a guy like Jeff by cranking out babies every year, honey, not when twenty-year-olds are throwing their panties at him on stage."

"I'm going back to L.A. Jeff can do whatever he

wants."

"Oh, baby, that's no way to punish a man. Mandi will tell you what to do. Just let me get on my shopping disguise. Jerrell, you mind watching that child a while longer?"

"We be fine."

The famous Mandi McDonald stuffed her bleached hair under a red wig and topped it with a straw cowboy hat. She covered the trademark navel pooching out over her jeans with a leopard print big shirt, put on a denim jacket against the Seattle chill, and shoved her bare feet into a pair of lizard-skin boots. Even though the day was gray and drizzly, she added oversized sunglasses

"Good to go," Mandi asserted and led the way.

People wearing all-weather coats and business clothes stared as Mandi and Kara passed, mostly at Mandi's outrageous outfit.

"Damn, it's hard to hide when you're a celebrity. I think I saw an expensive jewelry store in that little mall under the monorail station. Yep, there it is. What's the best gift Jeff ever gave you?"

"Maridel, but he isn't happy about it."

"No, no, no. A material object, girl."

"The Toyota and the house."

"I'm not talking about middle-class transportation and a tract home."

"My wedding ring." Kara held up her hand to show the plain gold band.

"You are not getting my point." Exasperated, Mandi stomped her boot into a puddle and kicked up some water.

Searching for a better answer, Kara jumped back to avoid the splash. "He did write a song for me once, and he does set my poems to music."

"That last could be considered stealing from you. Cheap bastard." Mandi charged through the doors of the jewelers. The clerks jerked to attention and searched around for security just in case the bizarre, ballsy woman turned out to be a problem.

"Pick out something nice, baby, something real nice. I'll see it's taken out of Jeff's cut for the show. Whoa! Do you like this ruby and diamond necklace?"

"Where would I wear it?"

"To the show tonight."

"I won't be going."

"Oh yes, you will. Better pick out something else before I tell them to wrap this up."

Kara peered around desperately. She spied a simple, pear-shaped diamond displayed on a black velvet cord with the price tag discreetly turned downward. If the stone had been set in a ring, it would have covered her finger from its base to her knuckle. Under the lighting in the locked case, the diamond sent off multi-colored sparks of light.

"That's nice, tasteful," she told Mandi in a weak voice.

Showing himself to be unafraid of eccentric rich clients, a clerk rushed to the case. "Would you like to see the stone more closely? As you can tell, this diamond possesses perfect color and clarity and a magnificent cut. If you wish to examine it, you may use my loupe."

Although the clerk addressed Kara, Mandi took the loupe and eyed the diamond with the scrutiny of an appraiser. "Yes, very nice, a small inclusion near the top by the setting, but nice. Price?"

"Ten-thousand."

"Wrap it up." Mandi tossed him a platinum card. "And leave it on that cord."

"Yes, certainly, Miss McDonald. I am so sorry I didn't recognize you when you came in," the clerk fawned as he read her name.

"That's the point of the wig, brother. There had better not be any photographers waiting for me and my friend when we get back from visiting the Space Needle, either."

With no extra charge for the cord or the elegant box, Mandi shoved the necklace carelessly into her big tooled leather bag. She insisted Kara ride the monorail to the Space Needle since they were so close anyhow. As they strolled around the observation deck admiring a misty view, Mandi did most of the talking.

"So, now you have a nice souvenir of Seattle, should have been an emerald though, and got in a little sightseeing. What else did Jeff say that set you off besides not wanting another kid?"

"He said I had baby spit in my hair. Jeff can be very fastidious about some things." Kara patted the strands that hung over her shoulders self-consciously.

"Yeah, I noticed. Big confession coming up. I did hit on your husband when Manny first put us together, but we aren't cut from the same cloth. I like mine down and dirty, and he likes his nice and clean."

"Oh, he will go down on me. It's just since the baby came, he…"

Mandi threw back her head and belted out a laugh. "Not what I meant, Kara, honey. Anyhow, Jeff and me never happened. Just wanted you to know. How about some coffee since you can't drink?"

They traveled down to the base of the Needle, then up again to the restaurant level. Mandi demanded a seat by the window and called for coffee. The waiter offered a dessert tray for their inspection.

"You had lunch, doll? Me neither. What the hell, Manny will never know. Give us two pieces of that key lime cheesecake." Mandi up ended the contents of a pink packet of sweetener into her coffee.

"You know what I like about black men, Kara? They appreciate a big booty and don't mind a little body fat. I tell you, Jerrell is a find. Austin gives him respect because Jerrell demands it. Jer is teaching Huey kickboxing because he says the boy will need to know how to defend himself. You know what he did time for? Beating the crap out of the man who knocked up his fourteen-year-old sister. You can bet he was nobody's bitch in the slammer. Now, that's a man."

"You aren't scared of him?" Kara savored another forkful of the pale green cheesecake, though she'd opted for tea.

"Did you see how he was with your baby? That's how he treats me—unless I ask for something different. Jerrell may be the One."

"Or the Third," Kara said without thinking.

Mandi laughed again, loud enough to turn heads. "I like you, girl, now that we know each other better. Yes, my life is a mess and so are my kids. Now, about that baby spit remark. When's the last time you had a haircut?"

Back at the hotel, she insisted the beauty salon work Kara into their schedule. She left a big advance tip, but told them to charge Jeff's room for the hair and makeup.

"Take my key, and come change in my room. I'll be gone by the time you get out of here. Order room service. Feed and burp that baby *before* you get dressed. Jerrell will sit for you. My boys will be back from that indoor pool by now, but I'll make sure they don't torment your kid. Knock 'im dead, tonight."

Mandi peeped cautiously out into the lobby. "You know that fucker at the jewelry store didn't call the reporters. I think I'm kind of disappointed in him. Later, doll."

Kara watched Mandi go much as she would have a tornado receding into the distance—with great relief. In a few minutes, she observed six years worth of hair hit the floor of the salon. A quick and talented hairdresser cut in shaggy bangs and layered her straight brown hair to end just above her shoulders.

"Some red or blonde highlights to set this off?" he suggested.

"No, I don't think so. This is enough of a shock for now."

"Lia will do your makeup."

"Oh, you got natural shine," the little Korean lady said. "You don't need much this stuff. I thin your brows some. Nice arch. Pretty brown eyes. I bring them out. You want makeup for keeps, I add to your bill."

She went to work with a tiny razor and soft brushes of all sizes. In the end, Kara bought the overpriced makeup and added it to Jeff's room tab. She looked like a stranger—a great looking stranger.

At Mandi's room, Jerrell jumped up alert when Kara opened the door. For a moment, he didn't recognize her. A smile spread across this wide face. His gold-capped tooth glittered. "Lookin' good, little mama. Austin, Houston, say 'Good Evening' to Miss Kara."

Mandi's sons barely looked up from a violent video game, but both said, "Evening, Miss Kara.'" Jerrell did good with those kids.

Wide awake, Maridel watched the kick-ass colors speeding by on the screen. She seemed uncertain when her mother picked her up, but soon snuggled in for a bottle, not recognizing the hair or the eye makeup, but responding to her mother's voice and scent and softness. The baby didn't settle until the loud game was turned off when dinner arrived: enormous designer cheeseburgers for Jerrell and the boys, fresh salmon grilled on a plank for Kara.

Jerrell ordered a crib along with the meal. They put the baby down in a darkened bedroom and closed the door as Mandi's sons turned back to their game. Jer suggested strongly the boys watch a Disney movie before bedtime, and they did.

Kara put on her high waisted midnight blue dress, carefully lowering it over her hair and makeup. She regarded herself in the mirror. Head on, she didn't appear pregnant. Jerrell came up behind her holding a black cord in his hands. She jumped, couldn't help it. He was one scary looking dude.

"Don't forget yo' bling, little mama." He fastened the diamond around her neck. "The cab is waitin' for Cinderella. I will escort you out."

Jerrell turned toward the boys. "And you two, don't move an inch while I'm outta here. That baby better not be cryin' when I come back."

"Yes, sir," Austin and Houston answered.

Jerrell offered Kara his arm, and away they went.

****

Thanks to Mandi and not to Jeff, Kara had a seat in the front at the concert. The show went much the same as the opener, perhaps even smoother. Kara believed Jeff had turned his smile upon her several times during his act. During the finale, Jeff let various pieces of female underwear and one jock strap flung onto the stage lie at his feet without picking them up. He threw his scarf, and it sailed like destiny on white wings toward Kara who caught it with both hands. Feeling rather naked without her cloak of long hair, she draped the silk over her shoulders.

Using her pass to go back stage, she waited in the shadows while Jeff signed autographs for some privileged fans and gave out a few pecks on the cheek. He glanced her way more than once. Certainly, he could see the white of the scarf and the glitter of the diamond hanging near her cleavage. Finally, Jeff moved her way.

Just before she stepped from the gloom of the wings, he said, "You have the warmest smile I've ever seen, my lady. I could see it burning from the stage." He bowed gallantly, allowing his dark hair to swing forward to shade his pale face.

"Oh, Jeff." Kara came out into the light.

"Kara, my God! What have you done to your hair? Are you wearing Mandi's jewelry? That better not be yours."

"See, no more baby spit. I thought you liked the new style. You kept smiling at me during your acts. As for the diamond, Mandi bought it for me, but she said it would come out of your share of the gate." Kara touched the ends of her hair, then brought her hand down to finger the diamond. She tried to summon that smile again. It simply wouldn't come to her lips.

"I thought you were some rich bitch who could help my career. As for that slut picking out your jewelry…"

"I'd remember Mandi is the star here, and there is no show without her, Jeff. Sorry you don't like my hair this way. I do. It's much more practical." Kara slid the white silk scarf off her neck and balled it in her first.

"I meant you should wash it more, not hack it off, and get a nanny for the kid so you wouldn't have to carry her around with you everywhere. You know, Kara, you've really screwed things up royally. Forcing two kids on me, throwing my money around, cutting off your hair so you look like some middle-aged housewife."

Jeff's gaze had rested on the slight bump of her belly, but now it traveled up her torso, to her swollen breasts, the diamond teardrop sparkling between them. He regarded her lips, outlined and red, and her eyes, deftly shaded to make them look bigger.

"Go back to the room, Kara. We might as well make the most of your visit."

"Go to hell, Jeff Ryder. Take your scarf and…" Oh, so many choices—hang yourself, shove it up your ass, or—"shove it down your throat." That phrase made it all the way to her lips.

Kara turned on her high-priced, hurting heels and, stumbling over cables and around the work crew, found her way out of the theater. The private floor of the hotel rested quietly. Mandi must not be back yet, Kara thought. She let herself into the star's suite. Jerrell, who'd been watching TV in a dim room, jumped up.

"It's only me Jerrell—Kara. Mandi and her entourage should be along shortly. I wanted to check on the baby, then I'm going to get a room for us downstairs."

"No need, little mama. Mandi don't bring all them folks over no more. Jerrell can bring her down jus' fine wit' a nice massage, a little lovin', a warm bath. She don't need the booze and the pills, and no other man but me. You stay wit' us. Thangs didn't go so good wit' Prince Charmin?"

Kara pressed her fingers against her eyes. If she started to cry, she'd look like the raccoon-eyed women who had fought over Jeff's scarf on New Year's Eve. "No, Jerrell, they didn't. Thanks for asking—but I believe you mean Prince Charming."

"No, ma'am. I meant what I said. I always figured Jeff Ryder for some kind o' ass wipe."

Not out of the mouth of babes, but an ex-con, Kara had to agree with him.

Chapter Eighteen
Help!

The hills covered in golden poppies and yellow mustard that delighted Kara and Maridel on their long walks turned seer and brown by the middle of May. On any given day, the puffs of small brush fires could be seen from their hilltop. Kara bought the baby a small wading pool. Maridel, buttered with sunscreen and wearing a cotton sun-hat and nothing else, sat inside a plastic ring in the water, slapping her hands against its surface and pursuing a flotilla of plastic toys. Her mother lounged nearby in a wicker chair purchased from Pier I. The cliff looming above the small plot provided a bit of shade for her and the young lemon tree Kara planted, enchanted by the idea that citrus could be grown in her own backyard.

Her neighbor, Barb, sat in the duplicate chair and drank the iced tea she doctored with a slug of booze brought from her own house. "I know you're pregnant, but we don't all have to suffer, now do we? Better get a sprinkler, hon. Keep your lawn watered in case the brush fires come this way. I got mine on right now. You should have a hose to wet down your roof, too."

Barb's sprinkler squirted across the lawn. Her girls blasted some loud song that could be faintly heard even with the windows closed and the air conditioner on. Barb, between boyfriends and very bored, proved to be a fund of practical suggestions.

"Where's lover boy been keeping himself?" Barb drew on a cigarette after flicking its ash into a large conch shell Kara used to decorate the porch table. Barb put on five disgusting pounds according to her since her last lover left, and she'd gone up to a pack a day smoking it off.

"I told you Jeff is a musician. He's on tour." Kara didn't add that his calls came few and far between since their argument in Seattle. Someone kept her bank account plump, whether Jeff, Manny, or Mandi, she didn't know.

"Wait a minute here." Barb put her deeply tanned hands to her forehead and rubbed as if she were receiving a psychic message. "Kara Ryder. Jeff Ryder. Why didn't you tell me I live next door to a celebrity? I remember all that secret baby crap. You telling me that's the secret baby sitting right over there peeing in her pool?"

"Jeff wasn't that much of a celebrity back in January. You couldn't have seen him more than a few times before he went on tour."

"No, but I appreciate a good-looking man when I do see one. What is Jeff Ryder's wife doing stashed away in some canyon development?"

"He bought the house in my maiden name so Maridel and I wouldn't be hounded by the press. Manny said the paparazzi wouldn't think to track me down out in the suburbs."

"Sounds like you're still a secluded wife with a second secret baby on the way. That's good about the house, though. If yours is the only name on the mortgage, you won't have to sell if you get divorced."

"Who said anything about a divorce?" The dreaded word entered Kara's mind and stuck there.

"Not me. I've been around the block a few times, is all. Good-looking rock star on tour with Mandi McDonald, right? Things do happen." Worldly wise, Barb flicked her ashes into the shell again and took another slug of enhanced tea.

"Not with Mandi. She has her own man. He's big, black, and very protective."

"I'm just saying—put as much stuff in your own name as you can. You never know. I got to go, kid. Wait until I tell my girls that Mandi McDonald is sleeping with a black man."

"Barb, I'm going to be out of town for a couple of weeks for my sister's wedding back in Pennsylvania. Could you keep an eye on my place and uh—hose down the roof if the fires come this way?"

"For that piece of gossip, I'll water your lawn, too. And I'll give you a call if that husband of yours sneaks home. Gotta go primp. I have a date with a guy I met online." Barb crushed her cigarette butt against the pale pink wall of the shell and headed home. As she opened her door, a new song leaked out, a love ballad by Jeff Ryder sweet as cherry limeade and just as artificial.

****

Kara left a message telling Jeff where she'd be for the next two weeks along with her mother's number, but he didn't call, even to wish Joy well on her marriage. What Kara dreaded most about being alone at the festivities wasn't Jeff's absence. All the old biddies would smile at Maridel, chuck her under the chin, and in the same breath remark on Kara's sixth month belly. Girls today relied too much on the pill, they'd say, and didn't know how to tell a man 'no.'

At first, Kara felt slighted about not being asked to be in the wedding. Joy said both her sisters were on the move too much to get to fittings, and she chose three college friends for her bridesmaids. Now, she was grateful. She'd gotten a dress in a summery melon color that hung straight from the shoulders and ended just above the knees. It blended with the shell pink of the bridesmaids' gowns and her mother's pale rose suit. In Lost Spring, PA, people still did not wear black or white to weddings. Wearing white upstaged the bride, and black was the color of mourning. The common wisdom said one wore black only if really unhappy about the marriage. Beware a mother-in-law in black.

Feeling like the watermelon in the fruit centerpiece, Kara sat with a cake plate balanced on her stomach and watched Joy, gray eyes shining, her newly streaked blonde hair coming out of its pins, twirl by in the arms of her groom. When Kara turned her head to see who held Maridel at the moment, her chin brushed across the daisy corsage pinned to her shoulder. She didn't feel as fresh as those flowers anymore.

Many women stopped by to coo over the baby and give the young mother birth control advice, locking the bedroom door being a favorite. Kara was overfull with advice—and the excellent prime rib, swirled browned mashed potatoes, and baby green beans of the nuptial feast. Some people still picked at the grapes and cheese on the appetizer table, but not Kara.

Her old college roomie, Faith, sank into the chair next to her. Faith had finally escaped Uncle Byron who took up ballroom dancing in retirement and was always on the hunt for someone to dip. A drum roll summoned all single women to the center of the room for the throwing of the bouquet.

"Go on, Faith. You don't have to sit by the wall with me."

"I'm too old to compete with Joy's friends. You know we'll be thirty next year, and there's not a man in sight for me."

"It's that vow of chastity. Scares them off."

"By the time I figured that out, all the good ones were taken. I envy you, married to an exciting man like Jeff, having an adorable baby and one on the way. You know Hannah has two girls now, and Lulu is working on number four. Of course, I never would have had the nerve to elope. Maybe I should have let Rico go all the way that night in the van." Faith, thin and as modestly dressed as ever, came late to the reception at the country club after picking up at the church and delivering the altar flowers to patients at a nursing home.

"Only if your true dream was to own a part share in a Mexican restaurant in Texas and have a large family. Rico's wife gave birth to a boy last year and is expecting twins. Don't envy us. You're a career woman, not an old maid."

Faith shook her head. "Lost Spring still has old maids. I'm an old maid school teacher in a town where most men marry when they turn twenty-one if they didn't marry right out of high school."

"You can always come back to L.A. with me. School will be out soon, and I could use the company." Kara bent over awkwardly and set her cake plate on the floor.

"No, I grew up in a town like this. It's what I'm

used to, and the church depends on me year round to help out. You should ask your mom to visit you now that the wedding is over and Joy is moving out. She'll be lonely."

"Mom? She recovered from Dad's death more quickly than I did. She's joined a dozen clubs and groups since she retired, not like Dad who just wanted to work on his house and yard. Besides, my guess is she'll say someone needs to be around to look after Great-aunt Mary."

"Does Mary look like she needs help?"

They both watched the elderly old woman doing a slow, stiff-armed waltz with Uncle Byron.

"No. That is one woman who can take care of herself. I can guarantee she was a career woman before they were invented. Tough old bird, tougher than me."

"I'll look in on Mary from time to time. Ask your mother to visit you. I think it would do you both good."

Kara thought Faith's eyes appeared sad with longing as she watched the bride and groom dance, the bridesmaids scrambling for the tossed bouquet. She wondered what Faith saw in her eyes.

****

Kara and her mother stowed the remnants of the table flowers not taken by aunts and cousins in the back seat of Faith's car next to the leftovers bound for the soup kitchen. Faith kept nudging her friend to say something to Della.

"I will. I will."

"You will what?" asked Della as she set a box full of cake slices on the floorboard.

"The Ryders want me to visit them tomorrow and bring the baby. Want to come along? None of my memories of Jeff's family are very fond."

"I invited them to the wedding. They replied that they had other plans, but did send Joy an entire place setting of that expensive china she picked. Most of our relatives gave her a cup and saucer or a single plate—so overpriced. I suppose the Freys will fill in the settings for them. I can always give them serving pieces for Christmas."

"Will you go with me to Bryn Mawr?" If she had this much trouble getting her mother to make an hour's drive, how could she ask her to come to California?

"Oh, certainly, dear."

****

The only noticeable change in the Ryder home was the flowers in the blue and white bowl now filled with zinnias and small sunflowers instead of tropical blooms. Allison Ryder greeted them at the door and reached for Maridel.

"Come to Alli, Mari. Such a sweet, old-fashioned name. She reminds me so much of Jeff as a baby, but of course, girls are so much easier to handle."

Maridel turned shy and burrowed her face into Kara's chest.

"Yoohoo, Mari," Alli tried again, wiggling her fingers.

Maridel clung tighter to her mother. She wanted this stranger to go away.

"Let's sit down. She'll warm up after a while," Della Shafer said. "She took some time to get used to me, too, but now we get along fine. It's hard having grandchildren you don't see very often."

"This is my first granddaughter, but not my last," said Alli, leading the way to the formal sofa sitting to one side of the limestone fireplace. She sat in a Queen Anne chair and offered refreshments already set on the coffee table. Maridel lost her shyness and strained toward a plate of small pink cakes.

Kara settled the baby next to her and gave her one of the cakes on a cocktail napkin to keep her busy. "We don't know if this one is a girl. I asked the doctor not to tell me."

"Oh, I meant Melanie, Steve's fianceé. They had the ultrasound done last week. We're having a small wedding ceremony here in the garden next week. I hope you'll stay around to attend, Kara. We tried to contact Jeff, but you know how that goes, and time is a-wasting after the paternity test came back. Not that we had any doubt. Steve and Melanie became very close after Brooke died. She comforted him."

"Red hair, bookkeeper? Yes, I remember her from the funeral." Kara nodded.

"Jennifer and her dentist are expecting, too—a boy."

"With her dentist?" Mrs. Shafer choked a little on her hot coffee.

"I should have said our son-in-law, the dentist. Jen got halfway through dental school and decided to marry instead of completing her degree, but we still have a second dentist in the family. It seems all of our children are reproducing this year—though Kara's pregnancy came as a surprise. Jeff never seemed fond of children."

"You never know until you have one," Kara evaded as she sipped tea poured from a round pot in the silver service. Maridel squirmed. Leaving a trail of pink frosting behind on the fabric, she slid down the pale brocade of the sofa and flung herself toward the tray of cookies. Kara grabbed her just in time and resettled her child on one knee.

"Lace cookies," said Mrs. Shafer. "These are very hard to make. Mine always fall apart."

"I let mine harden draped over a broom handle. You must work very quickly to get them off the pan. I hope you don't let the baby have too many sweets, Kara. Jules wouldn't approve, and he'll be home from the golf course soon," Alli said as Kara let Maridel have one of the lace cookies which crumbled all over the pale green carpet.

"Ah, no, I don't. She's restless after the long drive. I'll walk her around a little."

Kara let Maridel dangle from her fingertips. The child strained forward toward a new goal, a small table displaying a herd of Swarovski crystal animals. Kara walked the baby around the table and turned her back toward the sofa, but Maridel balked. Her mother picked her up and showed her the animals from a distance.

"Pretty, but mustn't touch." She squeezed Maridel's hands slightly. "Mustn't touch."

Maridel smiled beautifully showing off her four teeth but never taking her eyes from the glittering bibelots. She kicked back against her mother and launched herself through the air, landing on the table, spraying shards of crystal animals everywhere. The display table tottered and fell taking Maridel with it. Kara scooped up her child and examined a bleeding knot on the baby's head. She pried open a little fist and extracted the broken neck of a crystal swan. When Maridel saw the blood on her hand, she screamed louder than she had before.

"Thank God my cleaning lady is still here! There's

blood on the rug, and my collection is ruined. That child is undisciplined and destructive just like Jeff and his brother. Always breaking my best things. I don't know how much more I can take from children!" wailed Alli.

"I'll replace every one of them. Just give me a list," Kara swore as she applied a napkin to the baby's cuts.

"Some of them aren't made anymore. Ada, come quickly before the blood seeps into the rug!"

A stout woman in a white uniform arrived with a broom, dustpan, and a squeeze bottle of stain remover. She swept and spritzed as more blood dribbled on the carpet.

"Allison!" Della Shafer snapped. "We need to take the baby to the emergency room. Where can we find one?'

The cleaning lady answered. "Get back on the highway toward Philly. You'll see a hospital sign a few exits down. I hope the kid is okay." In an undertone she added, "At least I won't have to clean these little frickin' dust catchers anymore. She should have kept 'em in a case."

"We're going now, Allison. We'll let you know how the baby is." Della steered her daughter and the wailing child to the front door.

Cradling the head of a crystal teddy bear in her palm, Allison Ryder shot her a look that said she didn't care, and Della Shafer gave her a look right back that said she did. Kara's mother drove the car like she piloted an ambulance. In Kara's belly, the unborn child kicked and turned with the rush of adrenaline. Maridel continued to cry and bleed through the wad of cocktail napkins Kara held against the toddler's head.

In the emergency room, a nurse shaved away a patch of Maridel's black hair, cleaned and numbed the area. A doctor checked the wounds for glass, sewed up the head gash with seven tiny stitches and bandaged the little hand. He ordered an x-ray. About the time Kara and her mother should have been heading home after strong cocktails concocted by Jules and a delightful gourmet meal prepared by Allison Ryder, the X-rays came back negative, and they were released to fight the Philadelphia traffic.

"Back to the Ryders?" Della Shafer asked.

"No, home." Kara dialed her cell phone and got her brother-in-law on the other end.

"Let everyone know the baby is fine, Steve. Mari got seven stitches and an X-ray, but she's sleeping in her car seat now. I'm covered in dried blood, so we're heading back to Reading. Oh, best wishes to you and Melanie. I need to return to California, but I'll send a gift. It's no trouble. Say hi to everyone for me. Okay. Bye."

"Not going to the wedding?"

"No way in hell. Say Mom, I could use a little company in L.A. Would you come back with me and stay until the baby is born?"

Kara waited for a string of excuses. Her mother had obligations. All her friends lived in Lost Spring. Her church and her husband's grave and her weekly hair appointment were there.

"I haven't felt more useful since your father died than I did today. The Freys took over the wedding plans and my daughter—because of my bereavement, they said—pushed me aside as if I should spend the year dressed in black and weeping for a time I couldn't bring back. Planning the wedding would have made my life easier, not harder for heaven's sake."

Della Shafer heaved a sigh, never taking her eyes off the freeway traffic. "With working and putting you girls through college, your dad and I never had the time or the money to travel. We figured we'd to do that when he retired, but never got the chance. You know, I think it's time I saw the Pacific Ocean. Getting away might be a relief from people asking me how I'm doing all the time."

"You might have a hard time seeing the beach through the smog, and the traffic to get to the coast is terrible."

"Are you trying to talk me out of coming?"

"No. It never snows, and I have a lemon tree in my backyard."

"Terrific. We can make lemonade." Della Shafer drove happily toward the sunset.

Lynn Shurr

Chapter Nineteen
Lemon Tree

Kara toiled up the hill from the little pocket park situated halfway down the canyon road. She'd pushed Maridel on the baby swings and let her daughter show off her new running skills by chasing the vicious-looking seagulls that made a mess of the place. Her daughter had gone from taking a few tentative steps at ten months to full speed by eleven. Kara couldn't keep up with her, not with baby number two still in utero.

This one seemed to be bigger than Maridel. The infant pressed mercilessly against both Kara's bladder and her diaphragm, making her pee if she coughed and keeping her constantly short of breath. The doctor told her walking would be good for the swelling in her ankles, but Kara swore the hill got higher every day. She had no energy and remained tired all the time, a consequence of having babies too close together, she'd been told by Barb and other founts of knowledge, but not her mother.

A motorcycle passed the stroller, not a big Harley hog like the one Kara rode on in college, but a little neon green Japanese model that whined like a mosquito as it passed. The rider's long, dark hair streamed out behind him from under a space-age helmet. Maridel pointed at the cycle with delight and cried, "Dat!"

The bike did a U-turn and came back to stop beside

them. Jeff Ryder took off his helmet and cocked his head at his wife. "Jesus, Kara, you're huge. I recognized the kid, but thought she was with a nanny or someone."

"Welcome home. You look great, too. I'm surprised you recognized Maridel. You haven't seen her since March. As for me, this is how women look just before they give birth. Oh, right. You weren't around much the last time."

"I see women get bitchy, too. I'd give you a lift, but I don't think the cycle could handle it. As for the baby, you send me enough pictures on that camera phone for me to keep up with her."

Maridel reached a hand toward the alluring neon green cycle. She paused in her effort to escape the stroller and turned large dark eyes on her father. When he didn't smile, she slumped down in the stroller and closed her eyes. The stranger still stood there when she opened them a moment later and hid behind her hands in another attempt to make the unfriendly stranger go away. Daddy was a picture in her room, not a man dressed in black leathers holding a scary hat. She whimpered.

Kara continued to toil up the hill with Jeff walking his crotch rocket beside them. The California sun beat down on them. Kara felt dizzy and short of breath by the time they passed Mr. Matsumoto's place and turned into her driveway. Her mother bustled out to help with Maridel.

"Who's your friend, Kara? Oh, it's Jeff, of course. Jeff Ryder. You look hot. Come sit on the patio. I have the fresh lemonade ready." Della Shafer took her grandchild from the stroller and led the way.

It occurred to Kara that in all the years she'd been married, Jeff had met her mother only four times, when they played near Lost Spring. Her parents made the effort to come hear the Ryders of the Night, though hard rock wasn't their style of music. Holidays, the band had always been on the road grabbing up the good gigs festivals offered.

No wonder Della treated him like an honored guest, bringing out a plate of chocolate chip cookies and suggesting she run next door to Barb's and borrow a beer if he would prefer that to the lemonade. "It's made with our own lemons," Kara's mother burbled.

Could her mother be star struck? Kara felt sick.

"That stick in the ground actually grew lemons?" Jeff gestured toward the young tree, which did look like a leafy umbrella stuck in the soil.

"Yes, four large ones. Will you be staying for dinner? I'm making meatloaf."

"Meatloaf is good. This is my house, you know."

"Of course it is. It's just that you aren't in it very often." Della Shafer turned on her heels and went into the kitchen. The sound of the food chopper started up a second later. Kara smiled. Nope, Mom wasn't star struck.

"I can't believe your mother is still here. When did she come—back in June sometime?" Jeff stretched out his leather-clad legs. Maridel, hiding behind Kara's chair, peeked out, got brave, and dropped a bedraggled stuffed dog into Jeff's lap. The toy was well-chewed about the ears.

"What should I do with this?" he said.

"Tell her it's a nice doggie and give it back."

"Nice doggie." Jeff gingerly held out the scruffy

toy by its hind legs. Maridel snatched it back.

"Go take doggie to Granny, Mari." The toddler headed for the kitchen where her grandmothr opened the screen door.

"Don't you want to know how the tour is going?" Jeff gulped down half his lemonade. From his expression, he would have preferred the beer.

"I've been following the reviews. Chicago—*Mandi and Jeff have lost their Magic.* New York—*Has-been and Wannabe Combo adds up to Mediocre.* I'm sorry, really I am."

"It's your fault, you know."

"Mine! I haven't been near you since spring."

"After your little visit to Seattle, Mandi became very cool toward me. You killed our chemistry on stage. I guess you heard Jerrell knocked her up. Now, we have to retool with less dancing for Mandi and new costumes because she'll be showing before we do our final gig in Vegas. My part hasn't changed that much, so I took a break to come to see you."

"That's nice," Kara replied indifferently.

"I could be doing other things. Manny wants to hook me up with one of his new clients, Kristal Pickens. She grew up as part of a Christian family gospel group but wants to break away and go out on her own doing country-western. Manny thinks we could do a great duet album that might cross over on both the pop and country charts."

"Sounds good for your career."

"Damn right, it is. Manny looks out for me. How do you like my bike? I bought it this morning."

"I think a man with two children should stay away from dangerous toys, Jeff."

"Like I couldn't catch a disease from that ratty toy dog! What you mean is your bank account will dry up if anything happens to me."

"Yes, Jeff. I've become accustomed to a life of luxury." Kara gestured to the toy-strewn yard overshadowed by the cliff.

"Fuck you, Kara."

"That's what you really came for isn't it, Jeff? Safe sex. Let's get to it then. I haven't had any in a long time either." She pushed up from her chair.

"You think I can get it up with a kid running around and Della making meatloaf in the kitchen? You think I want to screw a mother?" He said the last as if it were a dirty word.

"Suit yourself. I'm going in to lie down."

****

Jeff followed. By the horrified look on his mother-in-law's face, the old biddy heard every word. She clutched her grandchild to her chest as if he were some sort of pervert who would hurt the kid. That didn't stop him from going to the bedroom where Kara had sloughed off her sandals and leggings, underwear, and huge knit top. She lay on the bed, her white belly rising like a full moon in the dimness. He kicked the door shut and locked it.

"You know movie stars don't let themselves get that big. Julia Roberts had twins, and she didn't get as huge as you. You should have hired a trainer to keep yourself in shape."

"Well, Jeff, I'm the mother of your children, not a movie star. Take it or leave it."

"You haven't let your hair grown out."

"Take it or leave."

"You really know how to get a man excited."

Kara didn't bother to answer. She knew him too well, his hang-ups and his appetites. He unzipped his leathers and still in his boots and jacket, knelt on the bed. He sank his fingers into her belly and his sex between her legs. The cold of the metal tabs of his jacket pressed against her skin. The baby inside of her kicked in protest, but Jeff pumped on, oblivious to her or her condition. Love.

They'd done this so often and so well, her body responded. She closed her eyes, and let herself go. The orgasm arched across her body before Jeff finished, withdrew, and went into the bathroom. Water ran. He came out angry, wiping his hands on one of her carefully selected towels, which he threw into a corner.

"I'm through with you and your disgusting rug rats, Kara. Any time you want out, go see a lawyer," he shouted.

Jeff exited as he had come, by way of the kitchen where Della stared at him in disbelief. He scooped up his fancy helmet and left through the garage. The whine of his bike diminished down the hill.

****

Kara lay on the bed and wondered how many other times she'd been merely a receptacle for his needs and deluded herself into thinking it was love. This might be the last time she made love with Jeff Ryder. Strangely, the thought didn't devastate her as much as it should have.

The aroma of onion-laced meatloaf wafted into the room. She listened to Maridel babble to her mother and heard the reply as if Della understood every word. Love of family, another kind of love altogether. She drifted off to sleep free of Jeff Ryder.

By the time Kara came out of her room, Maridel sat in her highchair eating mashed potatoes, ground meat, and gravy with her fingers as her grandmother tried to shovel in spoonfuls of strained peas. Kara stood there in her voluminous nightgown.

"Sorry. After all that, I fell asleep, and let you deal with Jeff and the baby."

"He left right after—well, you know—and Maridel was a little angel. That man doesn't deserve my grandchildren."

Kara laughed sharply. Liquid trickled down her leg. In all the years she'd been married to Jeff, her mother never said a word against him, no matter what she thought. Her daughter was a grown woman who could take care of herself, but to disparage her grandchildren, to call them rug rats, Jeff had added the last straw to the camel's back.

"I hope he breaks his neck on that motorcycle," Della said.

"I didn't hear any sirens, but don't worry, Jeff will self-destruct one way or another. Besides, I think he did me a favor and popped this big balloon. Finish feeding Maridel, then see if Barb or one of her girls will watch her. You and I are going to the hospital."

Chapter Twenty
California Dreaming

Alan Marcus Ryder came into the world at 6:15 a.m. on September second after ten hours of labor, during which time his father was nowhere to be found. Kara tried his cell phone—the one she gave him in Memphis—several times. Jeff didn't pick up. No matter. Preparing for the birth as carefully as she had once managed the band, she'd ordered an epidural and a single room in the private wing of a hospital used to protecting celebrities.

She had a photographer known for taking head shots of aspiring stars on call. The day after the big event, Kara summoned a hairdresser for a wash and trim. Barb came over with her makeup kit and fixed her face, erasing the pale, bloated aftermath of birth from the neck up. Her mother brought a quilted bed jacket of pale blue that looked like something Lucille Ball or Grace Kelly might have worn after they gave birth. Kara didn't know such items existed anymore and wondered if her mom had picked it up at a vintage shop. The quilted silk smelled vaguely of mothballs. Baby Alan, swaddled in a yellow blanket, prepared for his first photo session. No more secret Ryder babies!

Kara's room filled with flowers as they waited for the man to arrive—a basket overflowing with blue blossoms and baby's breath from Mandi and Jerrell, two-dozen yellow roses from Manny Lomax, a Tele-Flora bouquet from the residents at Graceland's Gates Apartments, and three-dozen red roses, supposedly from Jeff, delivered at the same time as Manny's arrangement. Faith sent a pale blue teddy bear holding a balloon bouquet, Hannah a classic yellow and white arrangement, and Lulu a black bear gripping a plastic guitar. Obviously, her mom called everyone listed on her cell phone with the news.

"Your sisters said they would see what you needed later. Oh, and Yukio sent this." Della held out the gift like a treasure. Mr. Matsumoto had entrusted her mother with a simple ikebana creation consisting of one unopened spear of blue iris with a white camellia and three green leaves at its base, all set in glistening gray pebbles held by a small black bowl.

"He said to tell you the iris represents your son, and the white camellia is the purity of your motherhood." Della set the small gift on Kara's beside table.

"Not exactly an immaculate conception, but please thank him for me. I don't know about you and Mr. Matsumoto, Mom. First, he teaches you the tea ceremony and takes you to visit the Japan center. Now this. Is he trying to win your favor?"

"Don't be ridiculous. Yukio and I are two widowed people who want some company. Still, I have read *Shogun* and wondered about those pillow books."

"Mom! I lived next to the man for months and never knew his first name."

"Well, you're married and far too young for him. There, have I taken your thoughts off your stitches?"

"Completely!"

The photographer arrived and set up his lights. He'd been instructed to distribute the baby pictures to any outlet he thought might be interested. In return for his services, any profits were his to keep. Baby Alan slept through the photo shoot, his tuft of black hair standing out against the yellow blanket telling the whole world Jeff Ryder had a son.

****

Jeff got the news from the cover of an oriental tabloid on the streets of Bangkok, an appropriately named city. Bang Cock, how Buzz Light and Rico would have hooted at the pun. The teeming metropolis offered up all manner of sex for very reasonable prices, more for custom orders like his. The first girls brought to him were far too young. He made it clear he didn't do children. Making a sign, curving his hands over this chest, he indicated he wanted women with breasts, but they must be untouched. Apparently, virgins over the age of thirteen were as scarce in Thailand as they were getting to be in the U.S.

The next two candidates presented, sisters, possessed small breasts the size of Satsuma oranges and heavy makeup to make them appear older, but their long, silken black hair made up for that. The hotel doctor assured "Mr. Wright" of their virginity, health, and cleanliness. Jeff couldn't decide between them, so he kept them both. Fresh and young, they would help him recapture that feeling of total possession he'd once had with Kara, untouched by any other man.

But now, his male child came sliding out of the womb where only he had been before. The pimp, counting his money, bowed and congratulated his client on the birth of a son.

****

During her recuperation, Kara worked on her poetry. She wrote a bitter piece entitled *Receptacle of Need* and another called *Advice* based on Barb's philosophy. The refrain went like this:

Get the house in your name/ Buy a car and do the same

Ask for jewels/ Don't be a fool

Stash your cash—for the marriage crash!

Whether she suffered from the baby blues or a sense of impending doom, Kara needed to shrug off this sinking feeling and make an effort to save her marriage. Of course, being referred to as Jeff Ryder's estranged wife in the gossip magazines didn't help. Whether Manny or Jeff started the rumor, she didn't know, but for a change the tabloids told nothing but the truth. Never seen together, obviously she and Jeff were no longer a couple. The press still hadn't figured out her canyon address, or maybe she wasn't important enough to be worth the effort. The paparazzi hounded bigger celebrities.

She declined to nurse and hired a trainer named Raoul to whip her into shape as soon as the doctor cleared her for exercise. By the time Jeff's show closed in Vegas, she wanted to be slim and sexy. By the end of November, she knew she'd never meet the deadline. She'd lost her baby weight and firmed up what could be firmed. That didn't include breasts, evidently. Her childbearing hips were still—well—willing to bear children, and the small curve of her stretch-marked belly over a solid base of muscle proclaimed she had. Raoul did give a wicked massage, though.

As she lay on the table feeling his hands work on

her shoulders and slide down the sides of her breasts, Raoul said, "Kara mia, some women are meant to have curves. A man who doesn't appreciate this is a fool. I am no fool."

Not for the first time she felt his erection prodding her thigh, but she always ignored the compliment. "Thanks, but no thanks. If I'm doing this for Jeff, I don't want to blow it."

"Understood, but disappointed. Only plastic surgery will give you the results you desire."

"Do people in L.A. have plastic surgery before they turn thirty?"

"All the time, Kara mia. I believe you to be my only totally natural client."

"Truly?'

"Yes." He kissed the top of her head. "I would like you to remain that way."

Barb, showing off a prominent breastbone and a flat belly in a cropped top and her stringy tanned legs in short shorts, always managed to be out watering her lawn when Raoul folded his massage table and went on to his next client. She stood admiring his tight buttocks as he bent to slide the table into his van. Kara came out in a robe to give him a check for his services. As Raoul pulled from the drive, Barb sidled over and elbowed Kara in the ribs. Water dribbled from the hose and ran down the sidewalk.

"That Raoul is to drool for. You two getting some revenge on Jeff, the absent?"

"No. I'm trying to get in shape so Jeff won't be absent. Does that satisfy your curiosity?"

Leathery-skinned Barb laughed. "You should be hiring in a private investigator to have Jeff followed. In the end, that would be a better investment. I had an affair with my trainer when I was married to the girls' father. He caught us in the act, and threw me out on my butt. Stupid me, I confused lust with love and married the fitness freak. Lost my alimony and for what—buns of steel? Turned out my second husband cheated on me with more than one of his clients. That's where the PI came in. I got a share of his business when we split and squandered it all on a no-good who started eyeing my daughters as soon as they hit puberty. Got the house and the car when I kicked his ass to the curb. Wake up, get a PI, and start socking away some cash."

Barb turned a spray of cold water on Kara and sent her running for the second time in her life, another wake-up call.

Chapter Twenty-One
The Marriage Crash

When the killer red dress fit halfway decently, Kara prepared to take on Jeff in Las Vegas. She wore high heels to show off her molded calves, and let the teardrop diamond swing between her breasts on a golden chain. She went on the pill, the kind that promised no periods. Jeff should like that. Her mother stayed behind and took care of the kids. He'd like that even more. She'd allowed her hair to grow a little longer, but she didn't intend to go back to her old, lifeless style. Ready to roll on New Year's Eve, she'd done all she could.

Kara dined early with the Ryders' former keyboard man, Deuce Larson. He appeared lean and desperate like a man who inhaled second-hand smoke nightly and remained up to his neck in gambling debts. Both were true. Kara wrote him a check. He thanked her, took the voucher with sweaty hands, and shoved it in his jacket pocket. "The thugs I owe swore they'd break my fingers if I didn't pay up soon."

"It's Jeff's money. Thank him."

"Jeff turned me down last week. He won't be happy about this."

"I'll be happy if you promise you'll get help, Deuce," she said. "I don't want to be carrying around your ashes, too."

"Still got old Buzz with you?"

"I don't know what to do with him. If only I'd checked his room sooner."

"He grew up in foster care. If his high school band director hadn't noticed he was big enough to carry the base drum, Buzz would have overdosed before he turned eighteen and been buried by the state. You were the only one who ever cared enough to try to get him to cut back on food or drugs. Jeff never gave a crap about anyone but himself, Kara baby. You were always too nice for him."

"I did everything for him of my own free will, Deuce. Nobody's fault but my own."

Deuce squeezed both her hands. "Let me warn you, Jeff has been seen around with some ditzy blonde on his arm."

"Kristal Pickens. They're going to record together. I'm hoping this is just another one of his agent's publicity stunts."

"I don't know. She looks at Jeff like he walks on water. Take care of yourself, Mama Kara."

"Oh, I am. I took some advice from a friend. You'll notice on the check that my name is the only one on this bank account." Kara gave her old friend a sad, sad smile.

****

Kara didn't bother to ask for a seat in the front row. When Jeff threw his white scarf into the audience, three women built like sumo wrestlers fought over the silk and tore it to shreds. Mandi took her bows a little stiffly over a belly in its fifth month of pregnancy. She looked great though, glowing, as people would say, in a long red gown that showed off her full breasts and draped elegantly over her stomach. While Mandi's Men still cavorted around her, the star had dumped her juvenile hits for torch songs that better matched her mature smoky voice. Kara thought Mandi had regained some of her range once Jerrell convinced her to give up the cigarettes and most of her other bad habits. Kara clutched the backstage pass sent to her by Mandi McDonald.

Midnight arrived. Confetti and streamers floated in the air and stuck in Kara's straight brown hair. On stage, Jeff gave Mandi a farewell peck on the cheek and moved toward the wings. At the back of the audience, Deuce Larson kissed Kara on the lips and wished her luck. She started for the stage as nervous and unsure as she'd been on the evening she and her roommates strutted past Heck House. That ended badly. What a time for a humiliating memory to return.

She found Jerrell and Mandi first. They traded hugs and air kisses all around.

"You are splendid, Mandi. I wish I looked that good the last time I saw Jeff."

"You didn't have my wardrobe and makeup people, Kara, doll baby. This is all your fault, you know. After seeing Jerrell with your little girl, I wanted to give him one of his own. I imagine by my ninth month I'll be fat, sloppy, and bitchy, too."

"Is that what Jeff said?" Kara stiffened.

"We're all fat and bitchy in our ninth month. That's what I told *him*. Besides, look at you! I never dropped baby weight that fast. You're fabulous. Do you have any pictures of the kids?"

She showed some of Maridel with her three-month-old brother to Mandi. She'd made the prints for Jeff if he had any interest in them.

"Aww, Jerrell. That's what our little girl will look like this time next year."

"I think she definitely gonna have curlier hair and a nice ghetto tan, baby."

Mandi punched Jerrell in the arm. "How about coming back to our suite, Kara. We're breaking out the sparkling cider. Want to see what I'm going to wear for the wedding tomorrow? You have to come to the ceremony, but don't tell anybody. Jerrell wants to make an honest woman of me before the baby comes."

"I don't go for this baby daddy crap. Mandi is gonna to be my wife, not my ho'." Jerrell slung an arm around the star's thickening waist.

"How do the boys feel about the wedding?" Kara asked.

"Their attitudes are comin' along. Austin asked to be sent to a military school. He wants to make a career o' the service, and his daddy is happy the boy won't be raised by a black man. Huey said it was fine by him if I married his mom so long as we settle down somewhere wit' a fine arts school and ballroom dancing lessons. We're thinkin' New York."

"Come on big, black, and gorgeous. Let's go up to the room. I don't want to sleep through the ceremony tomorrow."

Mandi cocked her head at Kara, nodding across the stage where fans mobbed Jeff to have their programs signed. Kristal Pickens stood close to him signing her name under his because Jeff passed all the programs to her whether the fans requested it or not.

Kara took a deep breath and hoped she wouldn't pop out of her dress top. Child bearing made her boobs flabbier, but not any smaller. She started across the curtained stage to join the group adoring Jeff Ryder. He saw her before she got halfway. His signature white smile vanished. The crowd around him thinned as guards shunted people who'd gotten their autographs back into the hall. Kristal Pickens dug her fingers into Jeff's arm as if he might run away without her.

Run, Jeff, run, Kara thought. Your little mama is back in town.

Her husband gestured to the guards who herded some disappointed fans toward the doors. By the time his estranged wife arrived, he stood alone with Kristal.

Kara sized up the competition. Kristal Pickens, a slim, anemic-looking blonde with fair hair cascading down her back, owned small, perky breasts shown off nicely by a white lace stretch top, long-sleeved and high-necked, and ornamented by a small cross on a gold chain. Her jeans topped a pair of tooled leather boots with pointy toes. Kristal's eyes, big and scared, were a pale, watery blue. The newly fledged country-western singer stood as close to Jeff as she could and still be a separate person. No more than eighteen, Kara figured.

"Kara," Jeff said coldly. "I'd like you to meet Kristal Pickens. Kristal and I are going—"

"To make an album together. I know, you told me. Nice to meet you, Kristal."

"And you, too," the blonde twanged nervously. She glanced at Jeff and hung tight to his arm.

"No, Kara. Kristal and I are going to be married as soon as our divorce goes through. I've waited to file until the New Year. I didn't want to ruin anyone's holiday. I gave you every chance to file first. I think we can do this no-fault by mutual consent, don't you?"

He seemed puzzled when Kara addressed Kristal instead of him. "How long have you known, Jeff?"

"Oh, 'bout six months," Kristal Pickens said in her hillbilly accent.

"How long have you been sleeping with him?"

Kristal colored so red the flush could be seen beneath her white lace top. "Honest to God, not very long, just this last month since I turned eighteen. He wouldn't touch me before then. But we're so in love."

Kristal tried to look Kara in the eye, but her gaze quickly drifted down to Kara's hands and settled on the pictures of Maridel and Alan gripped between her fingers.

"Are these your babies? They're beautiful. I'm sooo sorry. I didn't mean to be a home wrecker. I wasn't brought up that way. But we're in love."

"Come on, Kristal. She knows the score." Jeff turned to leave. "If you'd fixed yourself up like this before, Kara, we might still be together."

"I was nine months pregnant the last time you saw me, Jeff."

"You didn't have to be," he shot back.

"Now, Jeff. The Lord don't like that talk. Please, ma'am, if you could just let him go real quick. I hate livin' in sin and bein' an adulteress. It ain't right, I know."

"Were you a virgin before Jeff got to you, Kristal?"

Kristal studied her pointy boot toes. "Yes, ma'am, but I got overcome with love. Jeff says I have the warmest smile he's ever seen. He—he wrote a song just for little ole me. It's called *Hot Virgin*. Jeff wants to record it, but it's real naughty."

"Really? I'll tell you what, Kristal, I'll release Jeff

as quickly as I can. Lord help you."

Kara pivoted on her high heels and, straight-backed, walked away from Jeff Ryder. Her heart still beat as regularly as if she didn't care. After a moment, she realized this was so. Her heart went out to Kristal Pickens. "Run, Kristal, run."

Chapter Twenty-Two
Making Lemonade

Barb, naturally, knew exactly which divorce lawyer to call. "He handled my second divorce. Wish I'd shelled out the dough for the third one. The man takes a big cut, but he is worth every penny."

She hired Prater Wolfe. Surely, Kara simply imagined his canine teeth grew longer than normal because of his lean face and sly grin, but she was certain about the avaricious gleam in his golden-brown eyes. Like all his kind, Prater Wolfe went right for the jugular. Considering the adultery, considering the children, considering the years when Jeff's good wife lived in poverty and managed his band, considering the lyrics he'd stolen from Kara's notebooks, his client should get—everything.

Of course, she didn't. But as her poem said, Kara asked for the modest canyon house, her car, all the unneeded and unnecessary jewelry she'd purchased since Alan's birth, the money in her bank account and half of that in the one she and Jeff held jointly, and a whopping amount of child support which her husband fought tooth and nail. Jeff held up the proceedings regarding his songs as well, refusing to admit he'd used Kara's poems for lyrics in his songs.

"Kara can't sing. She can't read music. Hell, she can't keep a beat with a tambourine. These songs

226

wouldn't exist except for me. Besides, her poetry stinks."

He raked his blue-black hair and pulled some out between his fingers. Kara believed his hairline showed signs of receding and relished the thought of a balding sex symbol.

The evidence lay on the long mahogany conference table—Kara's pathetic marble back notebooks where she'd poured out her heart, marked at the places where poems had been torn out and at other spots where Jeff photocopied the original poems for his own use.

"You can't prove the torn pages were used by me to write songs or that I photocopied any of the others."

Actually, Prater Wolfe's expert could. He'd compared the words and cadences of Jeff's lyrics to Kara's other poems and found dozens of similarities. Deuce Larson flew in from Vegas to testify—for a nice stake and a chance to stick it to Jeff. He testified all the members of the Ryders of the Night had seen Jeff using Kara's notebooks, often ridiculing the poems, but picking out the choicest ones for the band. Rico, not eager to get involved or leave El Paso, his wife and three kids, gave a deposition to a Texas lawyer.

"I don't see why I have to support those kids for the rest of my life, either. I didn't want them. She did. She's the one who tricked me into fatherhood."

Through the glass walls of the conference room, Kara observed Kristal happily playing with Maridel and Alan in the waiting area. The innocent hick assured Kara the children would be welcome to visit her and Jeff at the new place they were building outside Nashville. They'd have ponies and a swimming pool there. She'd be a loving stepmother.

Sitting next to his client and rhythmically thumping his fingers against the boardroom table up until this point, Manny Lomax covered his gleaming ferret's eyes with his hands. "May I speak to Jeff alone?"

Kara, the lawyers, and the expert filed out. Maridel ran to her mother and hugged her legs. Kristal handed Alan to Kara and said she needed to go to the little girls' room. Prater Wolfe drew his client closer.

"If he balks again, we bring out the investigator's report."

"Everyone knows about Kristal. She and Jeff have been on the cover of every tabloid on the racks."

"They don't know about the two hootchie-mamas he keeps in Thailand. Eighteen, my ass. There isn't an eighteen-year-old virgin in all of Thailand, and we know that's what he paid for. Those girls are fifteen and sixteen, and I have the birth certificates to prove it."

Kara swore Wolfe started to salivate heavily just contemplating the kill. He wiped his mouth with a red pocket square.

"I don't want to use that evidence for the sake of the children. Someday, they'll want to know why we broke up. If I have to take a little less, so be it."

Inside the glass room, Manny Lomax gestured toward Kara and the children. She thought she could read at least one word coming out of his thin lips. It was "asshole." Jeff looked petulant and unrepentant. The tirade went on. Finally, Jeff nodded. The group was summoned back to the negotiating table. Manny took Prater Wolfe aside and held a whispered conference. More nodding.

"We agree to the child support. As for the songs, we'll offer one quarter of future royalties, and Mrs.

Ryder's name credited as lyricist," Jeff's attorney offered.

"Half the royalties," Prater Wolfe countered. "And what about past royalties? In my view, he owes her for plagiarism."

"A third of the future royalties and a public admission that Mrs. Ryder wrote the words to the said songs—along with label recognition."

"I don't think—" Prater Wolfe started to say, but Kara put her hand on his arm.

"It's enough. I want this done."

Prater Wolfe made it so. He shook the hand of his client in parting. "It's been a pleasure, Mrs. Ryder. So many women come to me looking like the deer caught in the headlights, and let themselves be run over, but you were tough. I have to say I admired the way you transferred all that money and got credit in your own name by buying jewelry and paying off the bills before any of this started. Nice work, very nice."

Not sure she enjoyed the compliment, Kara answered, "Let's just say I had some good pre-divorce advice, and it wasn't as if I didn't see that eighteen-wheeler coming down the pike."

"I like a woman with guts and intelligence." The lean-faced lawyer looked at her speculatively. He shook his head. "Too bad you lack the killer instinct. We could have destroyed Jeff Ryder."

"Jeff Ryder will destroy himself, and his blood won't be on my hands."

"Ah, well, call if you need my services again."

"Heaven forbid!"

Jeff slouched toward the door, his long blue-black hair shining over his shoulders. He did a half-turn toward his ex-wife and gave her a dazzling farewell smile. "We had some good times, Kara."

"Let's say my life wouldn't have been as interesting without you, Jeff. And thanks for the children. They're the best work you've ever done."

Jeff stalked out of the room and into Kristal Pickens' consoling arms. Manny Lomax leaned over the table and held out his thin, nervous fingers. Kara hesitated and finally accepted the gesture by taking his hand.

"Only a schmuck would say he didn't want his kids. I have three of my own. Yeah, I thought a pregnant wife was a liability to his career. I tried to keep it quiet, but you got to admit, I saw you were provided for."

"Yes, I'll always remember Graceland's Gates Apartments."

Manny shrugged. "Jeff wasn't a star then. How could I know if he'd make it big? You can only invest so much in a client. If I'd known you were the one writing his lyrics—maybe I would have tried harder to keep you two together. You got any more stuff? I know a few people."

"Sorry, I sent the last two to Mandi McDonald."

A few things are even more satisfying than a good divorce settlement, Kara discovered. Mandi, itching to write her own songs, set *Receptacle of Need* to music. The lyrics suited the somebody-done-somebody-wrong voice of her thirties. *Advice*, however, touched a chord among divorced women everywhere with its rollicking lyrics. Mandi's pop version went to the top of that chart, and a country-western rendition done by a well-known, big-haired, big-busted blonde, knocked Jeff and

Kristal's love duet clear out of first place in Nashville.

Kara had run out of room in her last notebook. Time to start a new one.

Chapter Twenty-Three
Home Again, Home Again

Kara Ryder, safely arrived in Lost Spring, sat on Aunt Mary's small, shaded front porch and watched the Tulpehocken Creek flow between tree-lined banks on its way to mate with the Schuylkill River at Reading. The sturdy, square, fieldstone house stood on a high bank above the macadam road leading to a four-lane bypass. Farmers used to travel this path taking their produce, milk, and eggs to market in the city. A couple of joggers ran along the old tow-path where mules once pulled canal boats in the distant past. The runners reached the red covered bridge and thumped across its ancient timbers to continue their exercise on the other side of the creek.

Newfound prosperity in Berks County centered on outlet stores housed in the abandoned mills provided funding for a park on all the land between the road and the river. The recreational area continued across the now preserved and off-limits-to-cars red bridge to acres of open land on its far side. The Tulpehocken ran so clean since heavy industry went belly up that its waters now harbored trout clearly visible against its pebbled bottom. Hidden by the twisted grapevine that grew on a trellis, Kara sat on the front stoop of a hot piece of real estate.

Developers wanted Aunt Mary's pastures. The

county made a move to suck the property into the park system if donated. A good contractor might update the interior of the farmhouse and turn a big profit selling a refurbished place built in the 1700s to the up and coming rich. Aunt Mary, now nothing but ashes in an urn on the mantel and an indomitable spirit existing elsewhere, would definitely return to haunt her if Kara entertained any of these offers.

Kara picked a few autumnal grapes from the arbor. Most of the big blue Concords had dried on the vine or split and fallen to make food for wasps and ants. Mary would have plucked them by now and made her famous jelly. Kara squeezed the thick skin until the insides popped into her mouth. She sucked the fruit from the seeds and spit the pits into the yard just as she had when a child visiting the farm. Once renovated—and the house did need work, tons of work—this place could be a real home. She'd hire electricians and plumbers, but wanted to do some of the work herself, get her hands dirty, and make the house hers.

The farmhouse was both better and worse than Kara remembered. As an adult, she appreciated the big stone fireplace in the mudroom whose side door led directly to the German-style bank barn three times the size of the house, but the antiquated oil heater in the earthen-floored basement appalled her. A potbelly stove too heavy for Aunt Mary to move, squatted in the front parlor and vented through a boarded-over fireplace that hadn't seen a flame in years. Instead, its lids, like all the counters in the kitchen, provided shelving for her aunt's china rooster collection. The figurines gathered dust on their proud, feathered tails and shiny red combs.

Thinking of dust, Kara recalled her aunt's last

wishes—that her ashes be scattered on her garden. She hadn't done even that small service yet for the woman who thought her great-niece might need a place to call home. By the time a passing jogger observed Aunt Mary facedown in her tomato patch and called an ambulance, the old lady's spirit had flown the coop. The EMTs had to pry the hoe from her hand. Kara, in the midst of an ugly divorce, missed the funeral service, which shamed her, doubly so when the attorney called to inform her Mary Shafer had made her the sole heir to the estate. She'd seen it coming, that old lady, Kara's future need to return to her roots.

Kara rose out of the sagging cane seat of the old rocker and went back through the house after locking the front door with a big, old-fashioned key. The central hall and staircase were dark from both the ancient paneling and the lack of electric light, but October sun flooded through the windows of the enormous kitchen overlooking Mary's garden and the pastures. Every detail of the place said big, hard-working families ate enormous hearty meals here in this warm, west-facing room. These folks hadn't the time to entertain in fancy dining rooms or sit idle on their porches, though they'd built the back porch larger than the front to accommodate corn shucking and bean snapping out of doors.

Kara searched the kitchen drawers, watched by the beady, black eyes of a hundred porcelain, glass, and china roosters. She finally found the local telephone book under the big base of a handsome, plaster Rhode Island Red. Mary's attorney told her she should have the place surveyed and subdivided into plots if she intended to sell off any of the land. With Jeff lagging in his child support and royalty checks on her songs uncertain from quarter to quarter, she supposed she must subdivide to make the place habitable for her children.

Kara flipped to the yellow pages. "Surveyors—Land" yielded a dozen and more firms in that line of work. Acme and AAA Surveyors obviously chose their names to get first placement in the listings. The third down sprang for a small box ad—Collier and Schultz, Property & Mortgage Surveys, Subdivision Layouts, Topographic Surveys, Environmental and Archaeological Studies. They seemed to fill any bill.

Kara punched the number into her cell phone since the attorney cut service to the big black wall phone months ago. On the third ring, a woman answered. The secretary set up an appointment for the following day and gave directions about which off-ramp to take that would bring Kara into the city. Collier and Schultz operated out of the bottom floor of an old brownstone near City Park.

"Thank you. The last time I lived in the area the bypass didn't exist, just the old traffic circle on Penn Avenue, and that's gone."

"For some time now," the secretarial voice told her.

"Will I be meeting with Mr. Schultz or Mr. Collier?"

"Oh, old Schultzy passed away several years ago, and Mr. Collier took over. He kept the name—good will and all that—but Mr. Schultz hadn't gone into the field for a couple of years before he died. Mr. Collier will be out on a job all morning, but he'll see you right after lunch."

"Great. You've been very helpful. I'll be there."

Kara closed her phone. Hmmm—good will and all that. Collier and Schultz, Surveyors. Okay, she'd stirred old memories and must satisfy her curiosity. She turned to the white pages and let her fingers run down the entries for "Collier." A William Collier still lived on Thirteenth Street. Could be Will's father and mother. Didn't matter because she wouldn't call the number. Oh, what the heck. She dialed. An older woman answered with an irritated "hello," as if the mere act of answering the ring constituted a great burden.

"Is Mr. Collier home?"

"The dead one or the live one?"

"Ah—the live one."

"No, he's at work where he should be. If y'er selling something, we don't want any."

"No, no."

"We don't give to charity, neither. My son ain't exactly Bill Gates, so don't bother us no more."

The receiver slammed down. That hadn't gone well, to say the least. If her old crush, Will Collier, still lived with his harpy mother at the age of thirty, she should be glad he didn't answer. Curiosity satisfied, Kara went out the back door of the farmhouse, turned her car around, and headed down a drive so old the wheels of wagons and the tires of tractors had pushed it down deep between two high embankments. She'd spend the night at her parents' old house, which smelled musty after being closed for over a year but at least had a functioning heater.

****

Kara arrived early for her appointment with the surveyor—early enough to allow for getting lost, early enough to find parking on the street two blocks away, and early enough to interrupt Mr. Collier's lunch. As soon as she opened the door off the foyer of the brownstone with "Collier and Schultz, Surveying Services" written in gold letters on the glass, she smelled onions, red sauce, and beef. Kara followed the scent across the room, past a vacant secretarial desk to an inner office with its door open a crack.

She peered inside. At a battered desk, a large man sat hunched over a foot-long sub sandwich packed to the top of the roll with thin-sliced steak and fried onions. She could see only the top of his head covered by thick, sandy hair, cropped short and bearing sweat marks, probably from the yellow hard hat hanging on the rack behind him. He glanced up, his pool water blue eyes under heavy brows implying, "Who the hell are you?" because his mouth was too stuffed to do so. A dab of tomato sauce marked his strong chin.

"Omigod! Is that a V & S steak sandwich with fresh cut fries and a birch beer? I haven't had one of those meals in eight years, maybe longer. I was always dieting in college."

The man nodded, trying to swallow a gob of meat too fast. He made a choking noise. Kara dashed behind the desk and pounded his back between his two broad shoulders.

"Enough! I'm good!" The surveyor dropped his sub back onto its white paper wrapper and held up his hands in surrender. "I'm guessing you didn't have lunch."

"Ah, no. I thought I'd get something after my appointment with Mr. Collier." Kara edged back around the desk and faced the man she'd recently pummeled.

Dear God, he still wore his hair with those long, curly sideburns. "You're Mr. Collier, Mr. Will Collier?"

He nodded again, wiping those sculptured lips with a wad of paper napkins. Kara pointed to his chin, and he mopped up the tomato sauce, too. He consulted a desk calendar with daily appointments marked on its pages.

"Please sit, ah—Mrs. Ryder, Kara Ryder, my one o'clock appointment." Will glanced at a wall clock that clearly showed 12:50 to be the time.

"Sorry about this. I was laying out a new development off the Lancaster Pike this morning, and my road back to the office took me right past V & S. I'm running a little late. Here, let me open a window. The onion smell is probably driving you nuts."

"Oh, no. Don't bother. A guy I dated once introduced me to V & S sandwiches. Aren't they great? And birch beer, you can hardly find that outside Pennsylvania Dutch country."

Will Collier shrugged massive shoulders, no longer built like a butterfly swimmer, more like a construction worker. His chest had thickened along with his waist. He seemed to be a solid wall of muscle now like his father who had poured iron in a foundry.

"I don't get much chance to travel. I knew a girl named Kara in college. Want some?" He nodded at his lunch.

"Oh, yes." Kara did, she really did. She glanced at the diplomas and certifications hanging on his office wall. "I went to the same school."

"No kidding. What class?" Will took a Swiss Army knife two inches thick from his desk drawer and opened the longest blade. He sliced off a hunk from the uneaten end of the sandwich, placed it on a napkin, and held it out in his big hands.

Kara gave him their class year and accepted the offering. He stared at her ringless fingers. "That girl's name was—a—Shafer, not Ryder, Kara Shafer. Birch beer?" He held up a long-necked glass bottle of reddish brown soda pop. "I didn't drink from the bottle yet."

"Please, I'd like some. Yes, Kara Shafer—a short, mousey girl, kind of on the plump side, her nose always buried in a book. Plain brown hair, plain brown eyes, not much going for her."

"Hey, she was a top student, a real nice girl, and not bad looking. I would have asked her out, but the guys kept ragging on me all the time, and I couldn't take the teasing. They expected me to jump her bones the first night out and then tell them all the details. Frank Bragg scared her off. I heard she married some druggie rocker. Seemed too sweet for that type." He handed Kara a thick white coffee mug filled to the brim with the reddish foam of birch beer.

"Fries?" Will held out a small paper boat of wonderfully greasy potatoes.

Kara took a long one and nibbled on the end to avoid a reply. Will's blue eyes opened wider. "You *are* Kara Shafer. I used to imagine… Never mind. Why didn't you tell me right up front?"

"Still embarrassed about the bucket of cold water, I guess. Sorry I hounded you for a couple of years in college. And I'm not stalking you now, honest to God, I'm not. I've inherited an old farmhouse and some acreage along the Tully. I might need to sell off part of the land for development in order to save the rest. I need a surveyor to do the plats for me. Once I show you the boundaries, I won't hang around unless I'm needed."

"You don't have to be there—but I might enjoy the company."

Kara blinked. Had Will Collier learned to flirt in the last eight years? She knew she hadn't gotten any better at it. Kara finished the fry and bit into her portion of the sandwich. Tomato sauce and steak juices slid toward her chin. She tried to catch them with a flick of her tongue. Will stared for a second, then dabbed her face with one of the paper napkins. He leaned halfway across the desk, his eyes on hers.

"Yoo-hoo! Mr. Collier, I'm back from lunch. Better air out that room before your one o'clock gets here."

Will sank into his chair. "She's already here, Mrs. Fischer. Turns out she's an old friend from college."

"Now isn't that nice?" Sadie, the secretary, opened the office door wide enough to accommodate her round, stubby body. She bobbed a head covered in springy blue-gray curls at Kara. "Would you like me to make coffee?"

"That would be great. Close the door on your way out."

"Won't be but a few minutes." Mrs. Fischer pulled the door to, but a small crack remained.

"Sadie's been here forever, knows everything about the business. I couldn't do without her." Will got up and shut the door tight. "She's one of Mr. Schultz's cousins and a friend of my mother. When old Schultzy offered me a partnership, Sadie came with the business and the stipulation I wouldn't let her go for someone younger. She does know the job even if she is slowing down a little. Sometimes, I feel like she's spying on me."

"And reporting to your mother." Kara gave a little sigh and sipped her birch beer.

"Exactly."

"You still live with your parents?"

"Only my mother." He glanced away and grew a trifle red in the face. "My dad died a few years ago of a heart attack. Believe me, I don't eat these subs very often. Ma packs my lunches, usually. You saved me from finishing the whole thing. Anyhow, I taught high school math for a while and worked for Mr. Schultz during the summers like I had since college. I leased an apartment and had a fianceé, one of the gym teachers at school. Her name was Corky."

Kara nodded. She always knew Will Collier would end up with someone tall, athletic, buoyant—and probably blonde. "What happened?"

"Dad died suddenly. My mother went into a deep depression. I'd go over and find her asleep on the couch, still in her nightgown, no food in the refrigerator. She was a great cook. My dad always said so. She used to make these immense meals, and there she was living off cornflakes, wasting away. The doctor said she needed companionship, but she wouldn't consider something like assisted living. So, I moved back in, and now she cooks for me."

"What happened with your fianceé? Someone actually named their daughter Corky?"

"Corinne, actually. She hated her given name. Corky suited her better. She had lots of pep."

"Pep?"

"You know, energy. Corky said she wouldn't share

me with my mother and wanted a home of her own—outside the city, way outside. About that time, Mr. Schultz's emphysema got worse. He couldn't go out to the job sites any more. He offered me a partnership. I was uncomfortable being around Corky after the breakup, and having those teen-age girls rubbing up against me all the time didn't help. I coached the boy's swim team. Corky coached the girls. We had to ride the same bus to all the events. Real awkward. I took Schultz up on his offer. Pays better than teaching, and I don't have the problem of having an oversexed piece of jailbait, accidently on purpose, peeling off her swimsuit in front of me."

"That really happened to you?"

"More than once."

"What did you do?"

"Walked—no ran—in the other direction. Nothing scarier than a naked, under-aged girl when you're a male teacher."

"Good for you. To be honest, my mother is living with me right now, too. She's taking care of my kids, two of them, a boy and a girl, aged one and two."

"Kids, huh, little kids. So did you marry a rocker?"

"Oh, yes. Ever heard of Jeff Ryder?"

Will snapped his fingers and pointed at her. "Married Kristal Pickens last month in an Appalachian mountain ceremony. Her entire family sang at the wedding. Jeff's two-year-old daughter served as a flower girl and scratched her behind during the ceremony. Cute picture in the magazines. Sorry, my mother loves tabloids. Those rags are all over the house. Sometimes there's nothing else to read in the bathroom. Damn!—you're Secret Secluded Wife. I didn't recognize you without the long, long hair."

Kara took a turn at blushing and hanging her head. "Stupid, deluded wife was more like it. Mari's petticoats itched her legs. Jeff thought she had worms and wouldn't hold her on his lap or touch her hand at the reception. He's not much of a father. Thank heaven Maridel is too young to remember. And Kristal Pickens, sweet but no brains at all between those two shell-like ears. She wanted both children in the wedding and little Alan to be a ring-bearer when he's just started to walk. I had to go to the service to mind the children. Now, Kristal thinks we're best friends."

"Oh, Ma's gonna love this—if it's all right to tell her."

"The whole world knows. Why not?"

"Yoo-hoo! Someone get the door, please. I have the coffee tray in my hands, and I thought I left it open just a bit when I went out." Will turned the knob. Mrs. Fischer bustled in. "Coffee with two non-dairy creamers for Mr. Collier. How about you, dear?"

"Black, just black."

"You got it. Help yourselves to the sugar-free mint cookies. I picked them up while I was out. Do you want me to dispose of the rest of that sandwich? Lunch time is over."

"Sure. Take it," Will replied a little resentfully. "Shut the door on your way out, Mrs. Fischer. Mrs. Ryder and I have business to discuss."

The secretary closed the door with just enough bounce that it sprang open again, leaving a crack a few inches wide. Will shook his head at Kara.

"I guess you're pretty well off now," he said in almost a whisper. He looked around his office as if seeing for the first time the muddy boots in the corner, the bright yellow theodolite he used for surveying propped in the corner, the hard hat and safety vest hanging from a wall peg, and the adjoining work space with its computers and drafting table and the deluxe copier he had to rent to own.

"Actually, I'm having a little cash flow problem at the moment. Jeff is behind on the child support, and the royalties, well, never mind. I can pay for your services. When can you start?"

"Not for a couple of weeks. I have to finish surveying the development I mentioned. If that's a problem, I can recommend another outfit."

"Life isn't lived without problems, Will. I've learned it's all in how you handle them. Here are the directions to the farm, and my cell phone number. Call me when you're ready."

Chapter Twenty-Four
Jiggedy-jig

In two weeks, more eager than she ever thought she'd be to return to Pennsylvania, Kara accomplished miracles. Leaving her car parked in the drive of her parents' home, she rousted her sister for transportation to the airport. Joy, irritable in the early stages of pregnancy and morning sickness, groused the entire time.

"I hope this means you'll let Mom come home. After all, you've practically made her your unpaid nanny and hogged all her attention for the past year."

"Come on, Joy. Until you got pregnant, you could have cared less. You were too busy honeymooning with Arlen and decorating your new house to pay any attention to Mom. You know she does what's needed. I mean she had Dawn and her kids live here while Gid served overseas, drove them all the way to Valley Forge when they needed to use their military benefits. That's just Mom—and I did need her very badly."

"Sorry. Having to eat dry crackers before I get out of bed drives me—well, crackers. I hope Arlen doesn't plan on having a big family."

"You didn't discuss this before you got married?"

"Sure, in the abstract we want three kids. But this is the upchucking reality. Yours didn't exactly seem planned to me, especially that second one."

"No, they weren't. Having children probably ended my marriage, and you know what? It was a good trade."

"So now you're the rich divorcée and can afford a nanny to watch your children while you bask by the pool in the California sun."

"I won't need a nanny, and I don't have a pool. I want to come home."

Joy shot her a skeptical glance. "You're really going to fix up Aunt Mary's old wreck of a place? All those china roosters gave me the creeps when I was little, not to mention the scary people she took in all the time."

"Let's just say both the roosters and the people were colorful. Yes, that's what I plan to do. I've already contracted with Collier & Schultz to survey the farm in case I have to sell off some of the land to pay for the renovations."

Joy may have been pregnant, but she was still quick. "Collier? Didn't you have a crush on a guy named Collier in college?"

Pointedly, Kara stared out the window at the neatly shocked corn in the fields of Amish farms and the fruit stands with orange pumpkins piled roof high, pots of yellow mums posed on hay bales around their base.

"You remember that? I hardly did."

"Right. You made me drive past his house in the city with you at least once a week when you were home for the summer. I'm sure it was just a coincidence you developed a sudden interest in swim meets. Are you stalking him?"

"No! I didn't even know my surveyor was the same person until I got to the office. Doesn't matter though. He lives with his mother who broke up his last romance. I probably had a narrow escape in college."

"Yeah, like he ever paid any attention to you. What a bod, though."

"He's more rugged now. I think he was a little shy in college."

"Don't expect me to feel sorry for you. You ended up with gorgeous Jeff Ryder."

"Jeff, the plagiarizing poet. How lucky was I?"

"At least you traveled. I went to college in Reading and right after that, I met Arlen. The only place I've ever been is Hawaii on my honeymoon." Joy pulled up in front of the terminal. "Mind if I don't get out?"

"No. Thanks for the lift. I'll see you in two weeks. Mom and the kids will be with me."

"Great! I can practice on yours. Anything I can do between bouts of puking while you're gone? Drive by Will's house? Swing by his surveying sites? Make sure no other woman comes between him and his mother?" Joy's mockery could suck all of her namesake trait right out of a situation. Poor Arlen.

"Cut it out! I haven't had sex since the day before Alan was born, and it wasn't very satisfying. That's probably why I found Will sort of appealing, even with the mother problem. Horny, I guess."

"Now I do pity you because that's pathetic." Joy dumped her on the curb and opened the rear of the big SUV to allow her sister to grab her bags. She was gone before Kara walked through the automatic doors of the small airport.

****

Removing her mother from California proved to be more of a problem than selling the house. Naturally, Barb knew the exact realtor Kara should contact to sell her house fast after a divorce. The amazing part was the modest canyon home went on the market for $500,000 and sold in a week for $475,000.

Kara scented the other problem as soon as she saw Mr. Matsumoto had driven her mother to LAX to pick up her up. Her quiet California neighbor rarely took his Honda out of the garage except for trips to the grocery store. A nice but solitary man, Kara thought he should remain that way.

"My pleasure to help," he kept saying, stumbling over the "l's" just a bit and bobbing his head when Kara thanked him for the ride and the assistance with her suitcase.

She discovered more warning signs at her house. Della Shafer had taken up oriental brush painting. A lovely Ikebana arrangement of chrysanthemums and driftwood occupied the center of the kitchen table. A plastic tray of sushi surrounded by baby food jars sat in the refrigerator.

"Going home? This is your home, Kara," Mrs. Shafer said. "Surely you don't mean to live in Mary's ancient house. Sell the place. We can put in a pool right here."

"You know I've always loved the farm. I might have to sell off some of the land to keep it, but…"

"No, you won't. Look here." Della held out several business envelopes and flapped them in her daughter's face.

Kara sorted through her mail. "Three months back child support from Jeff and two royalty checks—big royalty checks from *Advice* and *Receptacle of Need*. What have you been up to, Mom?'

"I called Prater Wolfe—as you should have done

the first time Jeff missed a payment. A good attorney can't be put off by excuses like 'I need to pay the tennis court contractor' or 'You don't want to ruin Kristal's wedding by putting me in jail.' Mr. Wolfe said he'd have Jeff picked up for non-support and would make sure the press knew the time and place." Della Shafer dusted off her hands as if disposing of filth. "So there."

"Thanks, I guess. What about the royalty checks?"

"Mr. Wolfe asked for an accounting, and the checks showed up. Of course, we'll be getting a big bill for his service, but isn't he worth the money?"

"I hope he didn't offend Mandi and Jerrell over the royalties."

"That's show biz." Della dusted her hands again. "Do you really want to leave all this sunshine and go back to shoveling snow and coping with the oil heater in the basement? Just think about it."

"California has never felt like home. I can't imagine raising Maridel and Alan here and having them turn out like Barb's girls—especially Alan."

"Barb's kids are just teenagers acting out. They'll grow out of it."

"You said they were sluts."

"Irrelevant. Today, they're watching the babies. We'd better go pick up the kids before they're corrupted. Honestly, Kara, I thought you—of all people—would know to look past the piercings and the clothes to the real person."

"Speaking of real people. What have you and Mr. Matsumoto been up to while I was gone? The house has taken on a distinctly oriental aura."

"I'm just experiencing a new culture, that's all."

If only, thought Kara, as they went next door to

reclaim her children.

Barb's girls had spiked Maridel's black hair with gel again and put temporary tattoos of butterflies on both her shoulders. Unfortunately, their own tattoos were real—a rose in the curve of one nubile breast and a sunburst around the exposed navel of the older girl. Alan toddled around with mini-spikes and a tat of a spider on his forehead. Mari played with a naked Ken doll.

"Look, we taught Mari how to defend herself from pervs, Mrs. Ryder. Show your mommy what to say and do if a bad man grabs you, Mari," Molly said.

Kara's sweet little girl shrilled, "Bad man! Go away! Bad man!" Then, she bunched her tiny hand into a small, hard fist and socked the Ken doll in his bald, plastic crotch.

"Great, huh? She really likes doing that."

"I don't know where I'm going to find sitters like you back in Pennsylvania," Kara said, shaking her head in wonder.

****

Their departure was rending. Kara hadn't made many friends during her stay in California, but Barb, her girls, and Mr. Matsumoto saw her little family off at the airport. She'd been trying to make her mother smile by touting the first class seats purchased for the trip— across the aisle from each other, Mom, big wide cushy seats—attendants waiting on us hand and feet—little booties, warm washcloths, champagne.

Mrs. Shafer answered with a "hmpf." "How welcome will we be once the kids start crying or acting up?"

Kara gave up and prepared to feed all her carry-ons

through the x-ray machine—the bloated diaper bag and her purse swollen with children's toys and pacifiers, a overhead bag containing her good jewelry, clean underwear, and enough clothing to get through a few days if her luggage got lost. Mr. Matsumoto stood by her mother, enduring the long line with patience. He carried a large shopping bag, and now that they were about to part from his company, he drew out a gift wrapped in silk scarves and presented it with a slight bow to Della Shafer. She unknotted the scarves and opened the sturdy box inside. As a guard rifled through her large purse, her mother's eyes went wide.

"*Shunga*," Della murmured. "Twelve of them."

"Often brides of royalty would bring them to their husbands. To remember me by, Dera."

"Wherever did you find them, Yukio?"

"The internet. I ordered from Japan for you."

"Oh!" Della Shafer's eyes filled with tears. Right there in line, she laid a kiss on Mr. Matsumoto's lips that caused him to step back with astonishment. "I won't forget. Please, please write, email, call whenever you can."

Mr. Matsumoto nodded and stepped aside, his yellow-brown complexion distinctly flushed. Indifferent and bored, the guard ran the box containing Japanese erotic art through the machine without lifting the lid, checked Della's purse and waved her through.

"He calls you Dera?" Kara asked her mother. "What's with that?"

"Yukio has some trouble with the double ells in my name. He wasn't born in California, you know. He made such an effort to get my name right I finally told him I found Dera charming, and he should just call me that. That's all there is to it." Della fluttered a small goodbye wave at Mr. Matsumoto. He answered it with one raised hand and a sad smile.

Barb's girls put down the toddlers who ran through the metal detector as if their mommy might abandon them to the teenagers forever, a very scary thought. Barb waved a hand sporting inch-long acrylic nails painted gold.

"Stay strong, Kara babe. Stay strong. And keep in touch. If you meet any gorgeous guys, you run them by Barb first—save yourself a lot of grief."

With that advice ringing in her ears, Kara officially started her new life.

****

At the Harrisburg airport, Joy and Arlen waited at the gate. Joy had driven Kara's Toyota with its two car seats, followed by Arlen in their big SUV, followed by a white truck with mud caked on its tires, all parked in a row. Kara took a turn being flustered as she struggled with Maridel, her purse, diaper bag, and hand luggage while her mother carried Alan and the gift box of *Shunga*—okay, dirty Japanese pictures.

"A gift for me?" Joy held out her hands but got Alan instead.

"Absolutely not. A gift for me. I shipped you a crate of citrus before I left. I am going to miss that lemon tree so much." Della teared up again.

"Guess I should have brought lemons." Will Collier stepped from behind Arlen and Joy. Not that he'd been hidden. He stood a head taller and a foot wider than Kara's sister and brother-in-law. Still dressed in a flannel shirt over a white tee, khaki work pants, and high laced boots coated with mud, obviously, he'd come directly from a job site.

When he called Kara's cell yesterday during the frenzy of packing to say he'd be free to begin her job on Friday, she told him she wouldn't be in PA until the four o'clock flight the next day. Could they meet after she settled in? Alan had been screaming because Maridel divested him of a favorite stuffed animal, the well-chewed dog both of them loved for some reason. Kara was sure the shrieking made a great impression. Now, here he stood, holding out a bouquet of autumn flowers purchased from one of the farm stands and a white paper bag reeking of onions and leaking small drops of red sauce from its bottom.

"Welcome back to Pennsylvania, Kara." Will leaned over and pressed a light kiss on her cheek.

Maridel pushed him away with two tiny hands. "That daddy kissed you, Mommy," she explained to her speechless mother. "You don't know him. Bad, bad."

Teach a child to deal with molesters, and this is what you get, thought Kara. "I do know him, Mari. Say hi to Mr. Collier."

Instead, Mari buried her face in Kara's shoulder. Seeing she didn't have a free hand, Will tucked the bouquet into the crook of her arm and held up the dripping bag. "A V & S steak sandwich and fries. I know they barely feed people on airplanes anymore. I thought you might be hungry."

"Oh, we flew first—" Della started to say, but Kara nudged her with an elbow.

"That was so kind of you. The children will enjoy the french fries on the way home." The flowers in the crook of her arm dropped until she held them against her body by the blossoms. The scent of crushed mums filled the air and mingled with the smell of the fries.

"Oh, here, let me take the girl." Will held out his brawny arms.

Maridel raised her head long enough to say, "Don't take french fries from strangers, no, no, no."

"Or not. How about your luggage and the diaper bag?"

"Thanks. I guess we should go to the baggage area."

Kara let him take the handle of the small rolling bag and sling the powder blue diaper bag over his broad shoulder. He snapped the handle on the bag and stowed it under his arm. The group moved up the concourse. Joy hung back and let Arlen and Will go ahead. The men exchanged names and occupations.

"My Ma gets your Lebanon baloney all the time," drifted back to the sisters.

"Gee, none of the contractors on our new house ever brought me flowers and a sandwich. He must really want your—business," Joy said with a smirk.

"Oh, shut up. I think he forgot I'd be arriving with two tired children and my mother. We aren't in college anymore. My boobs are sagging, my waist and hips are bigger. What could he possibly want with me?"

"So, his waist is thicker, too, but I must say his hips and shoulders still look pretty good from this angle. Remember, he lives with his mother. You've still got an edge, kiddo."

"A kid sister is such a comfort to have."

"That's why you prayed to God for one, as Mom always told us."

"Be careful what you pray for. That's my advice to you."

Now that Will had moved several feet away, Maridel tugged on her mother's arm. "French fry?"

"If you sit quietly in your car seat. Now be good for Mommy. It's been a long, long day."

****

The October sun hadn't quite melted the rime of frost from the fallen autumn leaves when Will pushed the doorbell. Bundled in a quilted robe, Mrs. Shafer answered the door, and let in a gust of cold wind.

"Mr. Collier? Didn't Kara tell me you were meeting at the farm around nine? It's only seven."

Will stood on the doorstep, the chilly air finding its way into his denim jacket, and held up a bakery box. "Been up since five. I brought breakfast. I thought we could eat, then get an early start on the survey."

"I'm not sure Kara is dressed yet. The children got her up at six, and we just finished giving them some oatmeal. The highchairs haven't arrived, and we had to hold the children on our laps." Della glanced at the gluey, gray stains on her pale blue robe. "This may not be a good time."

"Look what I found." Kara galloped down the stairs. "One of my old sweaters. I'll bet Joy took it. You don't think it's too tight in the chest, do you?"

"Yes," said her mother.

"No. Looks great," Will replied, dangling the bakery box by its strings. "Sticky buns and bear claws. I'll bet you can't get these in California."

"If we could, my personal trainer would have forbidden them. For heaven's sake, Mother, let him in. The house is cold enough already. The heater seems to be on the fritz. I'll need to get the kids some footie pajamas. But, coffee is made. I thought we were meeting at the farm."

"I didn't feel like eating at home and decided we could get an early start if I came here. My assistant is out today, and I thought you could hold my stick—I mean, the stick for me. The surveying equipment is computerized now, but someone still has to stand on the other end of the line for me to get a sight."

He'd argued with his apprentice, an overzealous young man who believed in giving a day's work for a day's pay, about staying home for a paid holiday. Jesus, at that young age he would have considered a three-day weekend and an extra day's pay a gift from the gods. Jeremy made him feel old and out of it. Will prayed the wind had reddened his cheeks enough to cover the blush caused by his verbal stumble. He handed the goodies to Kara.

"Let's go into the kitchen and enjoy these. The kids are watching cartoons. We can eat in peace." Kara led the way to a large, homey kitchen with a table and four chairs set into a bay window overlooking a lawn and garden full of neglected, frostbitten mums. By the time the adults arrived, the children, as if summoned by the aroma of baked goods, were attempting to climb into a place at the table.

"Cake?" asked Maridel hopefully.

"Cake!" echoed her little brother, who had taken to repeating whatever Mari said.

"You each get half a bear claw and a cup of milk. No more. Understand? Then, you go watch Sesame Street. It will be on in a few minutes. We have big people's business to discuss. Don't touch our coffee. Hot, Alan, hot!"

Kara shifted the cup her mother had just poured

and went to prepare sippy-cups of milk. Alan repeated, "Hot," but still wormed one of his little fingers toward Will's steaming cup.

"No! Hot!" Will boomed in his deep voice, snatching the cup away and following up with what he hoped was a stern look. The little boy began to cry.

"What's wrong!" Kara rushed back to the table.

"Nothing. I just have a way with children. See, I'm smiling. I'm not mad." Will bared his teeth in a wide grin. Smiling wasn't his best talent; he practiced it so rarely.

Maridel, who had managed to push herself onto the same seat as Alan, glared at him. "Big, bad man, Mommy."

"Mr. Collier is big, but not bad, Mari. Say thank you for the treat."

"Thank you."

"T'ank you," Alan echoed, stuffing himself with sweet roll, tears gone. "Want dat."

His mother denied him. "No, sticky buns are too, well, sticky for you. You'll choke on the nuts or spit them out." She helped herself to one. "Just eat your bear claw."

"These come from bears, Mr. Collie?" Maridel asked.

"No, sweetie. They look like bear feet. See, these are the toes."

"I eat the toes." Mari took a bite.

"Toooes," said Alan.

"Mom, you'll take care of the kids for me while I go out to the farm?" Kara licked the sticky off her fingers, one by one, picked up a stray nut, and sucked off the glaze. Will watched.

Della Shafer kept her eyes on Will. "That's what I'm here for. Take your time."

Will, still staring at Kara, said, "The jeans and sweater are good, but I'd change those nice leather boots for shoes you won't mind getting dirty. Bring a jacket. It won't warm up until the afternoon."

"I'll be right back—properly attired for surveying."

That left Will Collier alone with her children and Mrs. Shafer.

"You know, Kara's divorce only went through a month ago. She's very fragile right now, Mr. Collier. You don't look like the kind of man who would take advantage of that, but please, go easy. I don't want my daughter hurt again."

"I'm harmless. Honest." Will held up his big workman's hands as if he were guilty of something and about to be arrested.

Maridel glared at him. She poked his wide chest with her little finger. "Don't hurt Mommy."

"Not me," Will promised. "Not me.

****

"What a glorious day! I missed having autumn in L. A."

The maples in the park across the river blazed with pure yellow or bright red leaves according to their variety, and the oaks added russet and orange to the mix. As the sun rose, the sky became a pure October blue. Tramping through the overgrown fields in the chill air invigorated Kara and put the roses in her cheeks, as the old folks used to say. Those pretty brown eyes of hers shone bright above them. With mud on her sneakers and jeans and burrs caught in her coat, she carried an armload of bittersweet she'd found growing on a fence post. In Will's opinion, she could have modeled for the cover of *Country Roads*, but he didn't dare say so with her being fragile and all.

"Lunch break," he ordered. "You're a good assistant, except for getting a little distracted by the bittersweet."

"The bittersweet will make a nice wreath. I had the electricity and the water turned on in the house. We'll sit in the kitchen. I can make coffee."

"Got some in my thermos and enough lunch for both of us." He did, too. His mother always packed double the amount any man but his father, working in the foundry, could have eaten. Usually, he shared with his assistant, telling the young man a free lunch was one of his perks.

Kara appeared to be more interested in the scenery than the food. "Oh, look! Pumpkins in Aunt Mary's garden. She always planted a few vines of the Halloween variety for the children in the family and some of the other kind to made great fresh pumpkin pies. They aren't as big as usual, but my kids will get a kick out of them. Remind me to take some back with us. "

"Will do."

They stepped inside the kitchen. Will glanced around at all the china roosters staring his way. "Why don't we eat on the porch? This is like a scene from *The Birds*."

"I'm going to box those up shortly. If Alan and Mari aren't terrified of them, they'll break them. Maybe someone on eBay wants a ready-made rooster collection. So, what's for lunch?"

"Ham and cheese on rye rolls, dill pickles, great

local potato chips, apples, and a quarter of a coconut custard pie."

They moved to the back porch steps and took a seat on the worn boards. Will tossed her a sandwich and an apple, poured out the chips on a paper napkin, and offered her a pickle spear. She sucked the pickle thoughtfully and gazed at the garden. Will hardened in his jeans and covered the erection with tail of his flannel shirt.

"I think I'll keep the garden. Mary wanted her ashes scattered there. I'll turn the plants under and have a little ceremony in her memory once I get the place in shape."

"I know all the contractors in the area, and I'm good with tools myself."

"Are you?" Kara finished the damned pickle at last and turned to her sandwich. "I'd love to have your help."

Her eyes sparkled like the October light. She unzipped her jacket in the warming air. "Hot." She fanned her chest in the too-tight sweater with a hand.

"You got it whenever you want it—my help, I mean."

Kara bit around a small apple and pitched the core into the overgrown garden for the raccoons and ants to eat. Will took out his Swiss Army knife and cut the wedge of pie in two. She scooped up her piece with her hands and raised it to her mouth.

"Good," she said. The crust cracked in the middle, sending flaky crumbs down her chest. A glob of custard followed, sticking to the deep, brown wool of her sweater clinging to her slightly sweaty breasts.

"Great," Will agreed. He scooped the dollop of

custard with a long, thick finger and put it in his mouth.

"You want to go upstairs? If we stay out here, we'll get splinters in our butts." Kara looked directly at him with her knowing brown eyes, not a bit of that college girl left in them.

"Huh?"

"I've had enough foreplay. I want to go upstairs with you—to bed—to have sex." Kara spelled out

"Ah, your mom said you're still fragile from the divorce. Are you sure you—"

"I've been horny since the split. Are you coming or not?"

"Condoms. I don't have any condoms."

"I do. With Jeff Ryder for a husband, I always had to be prepared. Sorry, I didn't mean to mention that bastard's name. Let's go." She grasped his big hand and led him away like a bear on a chain.

Upstairs, Kara, like Goldilocks, rejected Aunt Mary's bed and a single cot her aunt kept for the vagrants she tried to rehabilitate. They settled on the third bedroom with its double white iron bedstead all made up with clean, if dusty, sheets, and a worn crazy quilt warmed by the sunshine flooding through a small window.

Kara toed off her sneakers, peeled off her jeans, and flung the sweater over her head while Will still worked on unlacing his boots. She knelt on the floor and did it for him. He reached around her back and unhooked her bra letting her breasts spill into his hands.

"They're as spectacular as I always thought they'd be."

Kara looked up, surprised by the compliment. "Really?"

"Your breasts were a big topic of conversation at Heck House. Real, fake, or padded. None of us ever found out." He squeezed them gently. "Real. Get up here." Will kicked off his boots and flung them against the wall leaving marks on the faded paper. He treated her panties the same way, tossing them across the room. Then, he sat Kara on his lap and let her lower his zipper as he settled back onto the quilt and pillows.

****

"Just so you know, I'm not disappointed either." Bigger and thicker than Jeff, his penis lay stiff in her hand. She applied the condom grabbed from her purse in passing and set herself on top for a good, hard ride. With her eyes closed and her head flung back, Kara startled when Will took control and flipped her on to her back, his thrusts coming harder now and much more urgently.

She clawed under his shirt and down his buttocks, spurred him on, until he came with one hard push. He continued surging until certain she had her pleasure, too. His weight, his size, all so different from Jeff Ryder as was the crisp, curly hair on his chest and the top of his head, now resting on her breasts. Kara did something she'd always wanted to do with Will Collier. She took one finger and drew it down his long sideburn to his chin, then across his beautiful lips. He sucked in a breath and her finger with it.

"Sorry if I rushed you. It's been a year for me." She reclaimed her finger and ran it down his chest as he rolled over on his back.

"Longer for me. Not since Corky. Didn't mean to bring that up either," he said, eyes closed. "I meant to ask you out to dinner tonight, but this is good."

"Hey, I still want dinner. I'm not easy."

"I thought Goodies for crab cakes, but if you'd rather have lobster some place fancier, you got it."

"Crab cakes would be great. Are we done surveying for the day?"

"We can leave the rest for tomorrow."

"Good. That gives us all afternoon."

"Kara?"

"What?"

"I think we really missed out on something in college."

"Me, too."

****

Kara and Will bathed in the big, claw-footed tub, teasing each other with their toes under the water, but she dressed before calling her mother and asking Della to babysit. Will got a duffle from his truck and changed into clean khakis, a blue chambray shirt, and athletic shoes. Kara insisted she couldn't go out in a stained sweater and jeans, so they swung by her mother's house.

Her hands hovered over the killer red dress. After all her hard training, she'd regained some of the weight during the divorce proceedings, but she thought the garment from her past might still fit. Heck, the time and the season weren't right. She settled on the classic little black dress with the lettuce-edged sleeves and hem and wore the web of glass beads purchased so long ago in Seattle rather than any of the trove of jewels she'd charged to Jeff. She could wear her highest heels and not worry about being taller than Will or bruising his ego. What an unexpected small pleasure even if they did pinch.

Her mother had the children fed and ready for bed. By the time Kara came down, Will perched on the sofa, his lap covered with stuffed toys. He rolled a red Nerf ball to Alan, who captured it with both small hands and brought it back, laughing all the way. Maridel elected not to play. She sat with a picture book on her lap, telling herself a story she'd heard dozens of times, and keeping a sharp eye on Will.

When Kara entered the room, Will gave a low whistle, and Maridel ran over to hug her mother's legs. "Pretty Mommy."

"Ditto," Will added.

"Don't be late. I worry," Della Shafer said as they went out the door.

Kara shook her head. "I guess you are always sixteen to your parents."

"I know the feeling. You do look great, Kara, but you do know Goodies isn't a fancy place?"

"I know. I haven't dressed up for a while and just felt like it. Let's go. I'm ready for the best crab cakes in town."

****

Will parked his truck on the gravel lot behind the old brick building. They entered a dimly lit foyer. He pressed a button and waited.

"Yeah," said a voice over the intercom.

"Will Collier and a friend."

The diamond-paned door in front of them buzzed open. They descended a dark staircase, Will keeping one hand on Kara's elbow in case she missed a step.

"My dad brought us here sometimes. I always thought this place used to be a speakeasy disguised as a social club back in the Twenties."

"You bet it was. When my father died, my mother insisted I join the club to replace him. The members all chip in a dollar when someone dies and send it to the widow. She was very touched. She used to like to come here with my dad and have a beer and the full turkey dinner with the dried sweet corn, potato filling, and giblet gravy. She still does. So, now I'm a member in good standing and belong to the bowling league. I got my dad's spot on his team."

"We always came as guests for the crab cakes," Kara said casually, not letting on that she'd forgotten about the mother problem all day. Now it came back in full force.

Goodies had no hostess. They took a seat at a table for four with bentwood chairs and a red and white-checked plastic tablecloth. A hefty waitress with her gray hair wadded back into a net padded toward them on white nurse's shoes. A long apron covered her ample body, not exactly Hooters. She handed them plastic-covered menus with the special paper-clipped to a corner—pork chops with baked beans, slaw, and applesauce. They ordered the crab cakes.

"Drinks from the bar?" the waitress asked.

"Get me a draft beer. Kara?"

"A-a rum and Coke, please."

She'd almost slipped and asked for chardonnay. This was Goodies for heaven's sake, not Chez Panisse. A curious bartender brought the drinks.

"This is Fritz, the bartender." Will introduced them. "My date, Kara Ryder."

Fritz's bushy eyebrows flew up. "I was hoping you was his cousin, so's I could take you out myself."

Considering Fritz neared sixty and wore a thick

gold wedding band, Kara doubted he told the truth. "That's very flattering."

"God's truth. Right, Will?" Fritz set down the drinks. "Sorry I can't stay and talk. Friday is always busy. Nice meeting you, Kara."

The crab cakes came accompanied by slaw, fries, and homemade applesauce in little side dishes. She and Will reminisced about college days, sometimes shouting over the noise from league bowling going on in the four lane alley in the other half of the room, balls clicking on the pool table, and bets being placed on an air-hockey game. They finished up the meal with apple pie for Will and chocolate layer cake for Kara, lingered over coffee and another round of drinks, and finally rose, heading for the stairs.

"Where to next," he asked Kara.

"Back to the farmhouse?"

"Sounds good to me if you have any condoms left."

"I restocked at my mom's house. Why do you think my little black bag is bulging?"

He smiled so broadly she could see his teeth in the dimness of the stairwell.

Chapter Twenty-Five
Unwilling

Will left Kara at her door around 2:00 a.m. Creeping into the house like a high school kid breaking curfew, Kara paused in the foyer to make sure all her clothes were on straight. She peeked into the living room where her mother dozed in her father's old leather lounger, a cup of cold herbal tea by her side. The TV, playing an old movie, lit the room.

Guilty as heck, Kara quietly made her way up the stairs, checked on her children asleep in the same room in borrowed cribs, and went into her room to change into her nightshirt. She sniffed herself for any lingering scent of sex, even though she'd washed the important parts over at the farmhouse. Having passed her own inspection, Kara went down and gently woke her mother.

"Mom, bedtime. Thanks for watching Mari and Alan."

"Huh? It's two a.m. How long have you been home?"

"A little while. I didn't want to wake you. The kids probably wore you out."

"Kara Shafer, don't you lie to me. You, a mother of two, were out scratching an itch tonight with a man you hardly know. You should be ashamed, asking me to babysit while you—"

"You should talk! Dad hasn't been dead two years yet, and there you were out in California trading dirty pictures and who knows what else with Mr. Matsumoto."

"*Shunga* is erotic art. That just shows what you know, Miss College Girl. I told him I was curious about pillow books, and he went to all that trouble to find me one, that dear, sweet man."

"He's nothing like Dad."

"No, he's not. You think I don't remember your father? At first, I had your sister's wedding to keep my mind off losing him. But as I walked her down the aisle, all I could think was that Mike should have been doing this. After Joy moved out, I could barely make myself go to the Altar Guild meetings or any of my other activities. Then, you came back and needed me so badly. Going to California away from Mike's grave and Mike's house and Mike's chair—caring for the children, that helped me with my grief, Kara. As for Yukio, he helped, too. We are two lonely people grieving for our spouses, don't you see. I…" A tear rolled down Della's cheek.

"I'm sorry." Kara hugged her mother. "I behaved like a rotten teenager. I won't do it again."

"You're over twenty-one, Kara, and can do as you please, but I worry you are jumping into b—, a relationship too soon after your divorce. You need to remember your children and put them first."

"I know. I will."

"Let's get some sleep. Those kids of yours will be up in four hours."

****

Will let himself into the old row home stuck into

the side of Mount Penn at 2:35 a.m. Despite a couple of empty beer bottles sitting on the coffee table, his mother waited wide awake and was on him like mud at a construction site.

"I worry. Ya know I worry!" Greta Collier's thin robe fell open over the flannel granny gown she always wore as soon as frost set in. Her big, sloping breasts quivered with her anger.

"Ma, you know I go out with the guys on Fridays, have a few beers, relax."

"Ya weren't with no guys, Will Collier. I called the Goodies. Fritz said you left with a woman. Where'd ya pick her up? On Cherry Street—like your pop did when he wanted a woman?"

"No one picks up girls on Cherry Street any more, Ma. You live in the past."

"Where'd ya find her? You tell me that!" Greta pounded a clenched fist on a pile of tabloids littering the table. The empty bottles clanked together.

"Kara and I went to college together. You met her once coming out of church—a nice girl, Ma."

"Those college girls aren't so nice. All they want is to catch a man with a good future, and they do anything to get him."

"Kara has more money than I'll ever make. She used to be married to Jeff Ryder, the pop star."

"Kara Ryder—Secret, Secluded Wife? No shit? Then what does she want with my son? Y'er nothing to a person like her. Wait and see. The tabloids'll read, 'Kara Dumps Toy Boy'."

"Yeah, Ma. You're probably right. I'm going to bed. You want me to put those in the trash before I go?" He gestured toward the beer bottles.

"I can clean my own house, boy. Get out of my sight."

****

Will didn't call over the weekend. On Monday while Kara wrapped china roosters with newspaper in the kitchen of the old house and packed them in boxes for transfer to the attic, his truck rattled up the farm lane and parked on the barn ramp. Will and an assistant got out and tramped into the fields. Kara ran onto the back porch, but they'd gone beyond shouting distance. She returned to boxing up the beady-eyed cocks and tried to keep her mind off the other kind.

At ten, Kara put on old shoes and trekked into the cow pasture with a thermos of fresh coffee and a sack of blueberry muffins she'd brought along for a break in packing—brought along to share with Will.

"Can I interest two hard-working men in coffee and muffins?"

"Got my own. My mother packed a thermos." Will didn't meet her eyes.

"How about you?" She offered a muffin to the thin and always ravenous Jeremy, who took two from the bag like a bad-mannered little boy. The assistant grinned in the direction of her breasts.

"Thanks," he mumbled, cramming one into his mouth. Kara poured him some coffee from her old plaid thermos while Will drank his from the cap of a sleek, stainless steel container.

Kara held out a muffin on her hand. "Muffin, Will?"

He gave her the wary look of a wild animal uncertain if she would throw a rope over his neck, then grabbed the muffin quickly and backed away. "Thanks.

Your plats will be ready the end of the week. Should I mail them with the bill?"

"No, please bring them over here. I'd like to look at them and see if I want to change any of the configurations we discussed. There might be more work for you."

"Yeah, I can do that, I guess," he said as if he had an idea of exactly the kind of extra work she'd want to pay for.

"I'd appreciate it. Oh, I enjoyed going to Goodies last Friday. Maybe I could treat you to a lobster dinner to celebrate the new development."

"I don't know. I might be busy. Bowling league."

"Oh, here, finish these off. I don't need the calories."

She held out the bag, which Jeremy grabbed. The assistant had enjoyed his break with his back turned, pretending not to listen, but the move betrayed him. Kara gave him a friendly smile and returned across the field to the house.

****

Jeremy watched her go with eager blue eyes. So did Will.

"Man, oh, man! She'd hot for you, Mr. Collier, not bad looking and a really great rack. But you are sooo thick. When a woman says she doesn't need the calories, you say, 'you look pretty good to me.' I wonder if she'd be interested in a younger man about my age? Bet she has money, too, or will have if she sells off this land." Jeremy took of his red ball cap and pushed his shaggy dark hair out of his eyes. He flipped the cap on backwards.

"That's not our business. Get back to work. I need

you down there." Will pointed to a low-lying end of the pasture full of deep puddles where cattle once clustered in the shade of the overhanging trees

"Whatever." Jeremy trudged off, dragging his stick behind him.

Frowning, Will supposed Jeremy would make a willing, eager, and young toy boy if he cleaned up a little. As for himself, he'd never be anyone's toy. Kara Shafer could take her money and pay for sex for all he cared. His mother was right. Kara had money and fame. No way she'd want a blue-collar kind of guy like him for anything but a fling. The sooner he finished this job, the better.

****

Kara stowed the china roosters in the attic and brought Alan and Mari with her the next day. They were no help and got supremely dirty, but she wanted them to become familiar to the farm as their new home. She showed them the huge barn and the stalls for the animals, some with brass plaques saying "Pokey" and "Daisy." Kara vaguely remembered Pokey as a large, swaybacked draft horse of endless patience that the many grandchildren rode around the pasture. All of Aunt Mary's cows had been named Daisy. A little straw and a few dried cowpats were all that remained of a once sizeable dairy herd.

They found wild kittens in the enormous hayloft. The balls of fluff were big enough to scratch and claw when captured, but too small to do much damage. Kara showed Maridel how to cuddle a calico kitty against her chest to preserve both of them from harm. Alan patted a little black captive a bit too hard and got scratched on the chin. Regardless, both children wanted to take their finds back to Granny's house. Kara hoped her mother would forgive her.

In her frenzy with Will she'd forgotten the pumpkins and let the kids pick out one each to carve for Halloween. Taking the children upstairs in the house, she showed them their new bedrooms on either side of the bath and closed the door to the larger room with its still rumpled sheets and quilt. Gradually, she'd make this place a home for them.

Over the next few days, Kara arranged to have the furnace replaced and the chimneys cleaned and repointed before the weather got any colder. She called an electrician to do the rewiring. She discovered old sleds she intended to refurbish in the barn and imagined what fun her California kids would have when the first snow came. Picking a few small sugar pumpkins, she tried her hand at making a fresh pie. See, she had plenty to do, and no time for a social life.

The furnace and chimney men still banged around the house when Will arrived with the plats. All business, he spread the papers on the wide kitchen table, showing Kara her choices for developing the pasture and the hay field, pointing out the low area that required fill, more drainage, or a retention pond if a building went in there.

He ran a strong finger along an access road, and she wondered if she'd ever feel it moving over her body again. "I put a street coming in off the access to the Walmart lot and back to a cul-de-sac with house lots. You don't want traffic too near your house. If you sell for commercial use, it all depends on what goes in there." He finally looked at her to see if she followed the plans.

"I've decided not to sell. I think the money I got for my place in California will cover most of the repairs here, and Jeff finally paid his back child support, so I'm good for a while. Both Mandi McDonald and Kristal Pickens want me to write lyrics for them, and I'm getting some royalties now."

"All this was a ploy, then." Will tightly rolled the wide pages he'd laid out. "You have plenty of money and didn't need my real services, just some amusement, maybe a little revenge for that cold bucket of water Frank Bragg dumped on you in college, Frank, not me. Find yourself another toy!" He shoved the plats into a thick cardboard tube.

"Who put that into your head?" she asked, but thought she knew, a formidable opponent. "I might change my mind in the future and use the plans. I connected with you the way we should have in college. I'd like to go out with you again. The offer of a lobster dinner still stands, my treat. I hear the old Abe Lincoln hotel has been restored. Maybe we could go there for dinner tonight."

"I'm going out with some friends." He kept his eyes on the tube in his hands, kept his lips pressed together.

"Saturday?"

"Promised my mom I'd take her over to Goodies."

"Well, I wouldn't want to spoil that for you." Hard as Kara tried, she couldn't keep the snittiness out of her voice.

Will scrubbed his face with his hands. She heard the rasp of his stubble and recalled the feel of it rubbing against her breasts.

"We go to Goodies every Saturday night. She sits

at the bar and talks to Fritz and some of my dad's old friends, has a couple of beers. I play air hockey and foosball, have three or four beers. She tells me I've had too much to drink and insists on driving me home— every goddamned Saturday since Pop died, and I moved back in."

"I'm sorry." Kara put her hands on his big shoulders. "Look at me, Will. You can change your life if you want to. I've done it twice—with mixed results, granted—but it can be done. Tell her you need a life of your own, a place of your own."

"I'm all she's got, her only child. Pop's gone. My mother isn't the most pleasant person on earth. She's had fights with most of the relatives, the ones she's got left, and no friends that I know of. Cooking and cleaning for me is her life."

"But should it be? Will, she's responsible for her own happiness. Maybe if you weren't around she'd try harder to get along. It's not like she's eighty. She couldn't be much older than my own mother—late fifties, right?"

"Just turned fifty. She had me kind of young. Pop was a few years older."

"Well?"

"I don't think I can. Kara, last Friday was the best night I've had in years. Since you came back to town, I've been thinking I could change things, grab a chance I missed once before, but as soon as my mother found out... It's not fair to drag you into this."

"I'm a fighter, Will. Are you?" She cuffed him gently on the chin.

With his bill secured to the cardboard tube with a rubber band, he gave her the plats with the same big, rough hands that felt so good on her body last week. Sighing, giving up, Kara found her checkbook and paid what she owed.

Chapter Twenty-Six
Unclaimed

On Saturday afternoon after a very long Friday night, Kara stripped another piece of linoleum and handed it to the waiting child. Alan, huge work gloves on his little hands, grabbed the discarded flooring, ran to the back porch and dropped it on the growing pile. Mari held out her gloved hands for the next piece.

Faith Harvey, dressed to work, gave the child a square she'd pried up. "I swear there must be three layers of this stuff, plain green, roses, and checks. It's like an archaeological dig in here."

"I think hardwood flooring is about to emerge. Thanks for giving up your Saturday for an old friend, Faith."

"I have no Saturday to give up. At five, I'll go over to the church and see that the altar flowers are in place and everything is set for worship tomorrow. Then, I'll go home, make dinner, grade papers, and work on next week's lesson plans." She dumped another piece of flooring into Alan's waiting hands. He toddled off to the pile, proud to be helping.

"So, the celibacy thing didn't work out for you?"

"Oh, I'm still celibate, but you know that old saying about meeting nice men in church, not in bars—untrue. The ones you meet in church can be just as slimy, and the rest are married and dragged in by their wives. But you, girl—I can't believe you slept with Will Collier after all these years."

"Quiet!"

Alan was back already. "Nighty-night," he said to participate in the conversation.

"He doesn't understand. Here you go, Allie Oop. Take it to the pile." Faith offered him a checkered square.

"Alan got more pieces," Mari pouted.

"I think we need a break. Juice boxes all around. You and Alan sit on the porch for a while. Here, wash your hands first." Kara stripped their gloves and held the children up to the spigot, supplied them with juice and boxes of animal crackers and a push toward the door.

"Coffee, diet drink, or wine for the adults?"

"Wine."

"Faith Harvey, I'm so shocked. Of course, you're as thin as ever and probably don't need diet drinks or caffeine to live your life, unlike me." Kara worked the cork out of the green bottle and poured the contents into two jelly jars awaiting the next crop of Concord grapes. Both women slumped to the floor resting their aching backs against a wall.

"I drink alone. Sad. And I get horny. Sadder. Just imagining you and Will together ruined a good night's sleep. How was he?"

"Bigger, stronger than Jeff, but not rough, more considerate. He surprised me, being such a mama's boy and all. You know, I don't want to talk about it. It's over. I have no idea what I did wrong, but I have a house to fix and kids to raise. I don't need Will Collier."

Faith gulped the chilled wine. "You know, I envy you your children. Lulu has four now. Hannah stopped with the two girls. I guess all I'll ever have are my students. Dear as they are, it's not the same."

"Hell, no. Yours go home at the end of the day and let you get some rest. Come on now, thanks to the tabloids my life is an open book, but what about you? No one in all these years?"

"An odd date now and then, and I do mean odd, like the ones you went out with on that spree in college after you gave up on Will. Did you know the UCC has an assistant pastor now? You didn't come to church last Sunday."

"And this has to do with what?" Kara topped off both their glasses and settled the bottle on a piece of stripped floor between them.

"He's twenty-six, has this nice, short dark beard, big brown eyes, and a beautiful voice in the pulpit. Pastor Webber is getting ready to retire in a few years. John, I mean Reverend Frick, is being groomed to take his place."

"John is it? I guess I'll have to go to church tomorrow and check him out. I'm presuming he is unmarried, and every mama in the congregation is pushing a daughter his way."

"Right. What would he want with a skinny old maid school teacher like me?"

"Skinny is in, and you are a career woman who selflessly teaches other people's children and serves her church on weekends. It's a match made in heaven. Faith Frick, I like the sound."

"That's bullshit. He's almost five years younger than me, and girls right out of college are suddenly attending church again."

"Oh, my tender ears! Such language! Whatever will the school board say?"

"They aren't here, are they?" Faith took another swig of wine.

"Mommy, Mommy, bad man outside!" Maridel ran in shouting.

"Oh my God, Alan is out there!" Faith stood up, clutching the half-empty wine bottle in a fist like a weapon.

"Chill. It's a phase she's going through. All men are bad. I hope it wasn't something she learned from me. Probably just one of the workmen passing by." Kara removed the bottle before the rest of the vintage spilled.

Will Collier loomed in the doorway. Dressed in jeans, he wore a crisp, ironed shirt that brought out the blue of his eyes. He had his denim jacket slung over one shoulder and held Alan by the hand. "Kara, I got up this morning, and I felt like fighting."

Faith turned from her friend to the guy they drooled over in college, unable to break into their mutual gaze. "Fighting?" she inquired.

"Bad man," Maridel pointed at Will.

"No, no, no!" Alan took a swing at his sister, missing, and hitting the floor on his bottom.

"Alan is a baby! Alan is a baby! He wears a didee. Mari is a big girl. She uses potty," Maridel chanted.

Kara smiled weakly. "She has a gift for lyrics, too. Mari, don't tease your brother."

"Up!" Alan held out his arms to Will.

Will hiked him up on an arm, but Alan demanded "up" again, so he put the boy on his shoulders. Alan threw his hands into the air and looked down on his sister. "Alan big boy!"

"Are not! Mommy!"

"Enough! Sorry. You were saying, Will?"

"I was about to say would you like to go to dinner at the Peanut Bar? No need to dress up. We can finish pulling up this floor, wash, and go. You're invited, too. Faith, right? You and Kara were always together back at State."

"What about your other date, Will?"

Faith's head swiveled back and forth between them trying to decipher the sub-text of their conversation.

"I gave her cab fare. Say, buddy, you want to learn how real men go potty?"

Alan nodded into Will's thick, sandy hair.

"Off we go then. No girls allowed, but we'll remember to put the seat down."

****

Will ripped up old linoleum like a floor-stripping machine until five o'clock, then declared the workday done. The women insisted on going home to change. Not wanting to be the third wheel on a date, Faith said she had stop by the church, but Kara insisted she'd pick her up on her way into the city in half an hour. Going to his truck, Will noticed the two old sleds leaning against the porch. He ran his hand over the rusty runners and the scarred wood.

"These are great. Everything is plastic now. I could sand them down and repaint them in my pop's workshop if you'd let me."

"I think I'd let you do anything you want right about now."

"Oh, Jeez," Faith muttered. "Not the double

281

entendre."

"You're still invited despite that comment. Bring the kids. The Peanut Bar at six. My treat." Will packed a sled under each arm and hauled them to the bed of his truck. "Six sharp."

****

Six came and six went at the Peanut Bar, still located on Penn Avenue and one of her dad's favorite places to dine. At six-thirty, Kara ordered for herself and the children becoming restless, tired of coloring the peanut-shaped menu, and filling up on peanuts cracked open by their mother. Turkey sliders for the kids and coconut shrimp for her since no man would see her scarfing down a generous portion of fried food to console herself.

Faith passed over the fried for grilled fish, and that's how she stayed slim even if she didn't say so. "Now I'm glad I came along to comfort you. Nothing is worse than being stood up. I know. Lots of blind dates."

"It's okay, he ripped out more flooring than all the rest of us combined so I can live with the humiliation. I haven't been left empty-handed."

Faith's eyes roved over the crowd as if trying to make Will materialize for her friend. Instead, they stopped, focused in on a man at the bar where the Rev. John Frick, out of uniform, drank a draft beer. "Kara, over there. The Reverend Frick!"

Kara sneaked a look. The man, getting a little soft in the middle, wore a flannel shirt and resembled Al Borland on the old *Home Improvement* show. He might be more impressive in his vestments.

"Well, the UCC's have been known to have a beer now and then, and this is a decent place, not a dive,

Faith. Who says you can't meet a nice man in a bar? Invite him over."

"Oh, I can't."

"Tell him I'm a new member of the church who wants to meet him."

"You were baptized in that church, Kara. I won't lie to a minister."

"Yes, but I've strayed, and I do want to meet him. Go on."

Faith hesitated, finally got up, and made her way to the bar. Concentrating on her friend's progress, Kara didn't notice Will until he pulled his chair out from the table.

"Sorry, small snag getting here." Between his sandy sideburns, his face appeared flushed.

Kara pretended not to care. "We just ordered. Faith is bringing over the minister from our church to join us."

"Great. I can start feeling guilty early this evening for my dirty thoughts."

"I think he's off duty. Here they come. Scoot over closer to me so he has to sit next to Faith."

"My pleasure."

Kara inhaled the scent of his sharp, clean aftershave, reminding her slightly of the chlorine scent that followed Will in his swimming days. He stood for introductions. The reverend brought his Yuengling lager along to the table. Will felt free to order one, too, along with his burger. He and the minister fell into a friendly conversation about the Eagles' chances of getting into the playoffs this year. Slim as usual. Kara offered the contents of her shrimp basket around in hopes of minimizing the damage to her hips.

The children ate enough of their meals to qualify for dips of vanilla ice cream with chocolate sauce, but by the time the adults finished after dinner coffee, both were asleep in the highchairs, chocolate-smeared faces bobbing against their chests.

"Kara, I don't want to break up the evening, but I never did get to the church to check the arrangements, and you're driving, so…" Faith said.

"I can take you, Miss Harvey. I have to check on a few things myself for the service tomorrow. Will, please feel free to join our worship service if you're interested," John Frick said, but gave his angelic smile to Faith.

He did have good teeth, Kara judged. After years with Jeff, the orthodontist's son, she appreciated fine dental work.

"Faith. My name is Faith."

"Really? Not a name you hear much any more. Shall we go?" John helped her out of her chair. The couple shuffled through the peanut shells to the door, which the minister held for his companion.

When had any man done that for her lately, Kara wondered. Will jumped up and did the same, grasping her hand in a strong grip. "We could stay a while longer and listen to the music, but I think Mari and Alan have called it a night, sorry."

"That's okay." Will wrestled Alan from his highchair after settling the bill and placing a good tip on the table. The little boy snuggled into his shoulder, leaving a chocolate stain on Will's starched dress shirt.

"I'm so sorry. I have some wipes in car. Let me get that out before it sets."

"No need. We'll buckle these two in, and I'll

follow you home and help you get them inside."

"Early evening."

"Yeah." Was that disappointment she detected in his one word answer?

"Want to go to church with me tomorrow? We can watch for signs that the rev and Faith did more than check on the altar flowers."

"I usually go to church in the city with my... There are things I'd rather do than go to church." Will nervously checked his watch.

****

Only eight p.m. By the time he followed Kara home and got back to the city, it would be nine. His mother usually didn't leave Goodies until ten or later, and he'd given her enough cab fare to get to Philly and back again if she wanted. She'd balked and made him late for his date at the Peanut Bar by saying she guessed she'd just have to give up her one evening out because her only child couldn't be bothered to drive her across town. She'd sit at home and watch TV like she did every night. He caved and drove her to Goodies, escorted her safely to a seat at the bar, and tipped Fritz to keep an eye on her and call a cab when she wanted to leave. Not a good fight, not something he wanted Kara to know, but thought she already suspected.

"Lead the way, then," she said to him.

They left the city and followed Penn Avenue all the way to Lost Spring. Will parked his truck behind her Toyota and helped hike the kids up the steps. Felt nice, a small, warm child in his arms. Kara fiddled with the key at her mother's house while balancing Mari on one of her arms. Will held Alan, still fast asleep. Della Shafer came to the door and insisted Will come in and visit for a while after they settled the toddlers in their cribs. Maridel wakened, and Kara soothed her child back to sleep with a quick, warm bath and some rocking upstairs. Downstairs, Della began a gentle grilling of Will Collier.

"Did you have a nice dinner with the children along?"

"It was fine. We ran into one of your ministers, the Reverend Frick. Seems like a good guy. Kara's friend, Faith, sure likes him."

"I like Faith. She'd make a good wife for a minister. The children didn't get on your nerves? They can be a handful." Della waited for his answer, tensely leaning forward from the old recliner as if the fate of the world, or at least her daughter, hung in the balance.

"We did spend a good part of the night picking up dinnerware and crackers off the floor, and there was that little debate over when Alan and Mari had eaten enough to get ice cream. Mari said she had only one tiny space left, just big enough for a scoop of vanilla with chocolate sauce. I admit, I sided with her. I'm still trying to win her over, but Alan and me are buds. I showed him how real men go potty today."

Della seemed a trifle alarmed as if he might have pervert tendencies. "How did you do that?"

"With a demonstration. Let's just say Alan's aim isn't very good, but he's definitely motivated to learn. Thanks to his sister's teasing, he'll be out of diapers in no time. I told him girls can't do it standing up. He liked that. I remember how proud I was to go to the restroom with my dad and not to the ladies' room. Pop would hold me up to use the urinal."

"Well, I only raised daughters. What do I know

about training a little boy? Alan appears to want a man in his life."

"Is he missing his father?"

"No, Jeff barely takes an interest. When he does, there is always a big scene, and he upsets them."

"I'm going to restore some sleds Kara found in the barn. My pop left a great workshop behind when he died." That should score him a few points.

"How nice. I recall Kara saying you lived with your widowed mother." Ouch, this nice, soft-faced woman with the kind eyes had hit the target dead center.

Will felt redness creeping up his neck. He checked his watch. Nine o'clock, early for his mother to come home, but it would be just his luck if she called his cell right now. He took the phone from his pocket, set it to vibrate, and laid it on the coffee table.

"Yes," he answered. "She's been very dependent on me since Pop died four years ago, maybe too dependent. She needs to get out more, make new friends."

Kara's mother smiled brightly. "What a good idea. Why don't the two of you come to Sunday dinner tomorrow at one? I'd love to meet her."

"Ah, we usually do the Sunday brunch at the Reading Inn. She looks forward to that." If Greta didn't have one too many the night before and a morning headache, that's what they did every single Sunday, same as his father had done. She generally complained about the food, too hot, too cold, no good meat selections, or they'd run out of her favorite dessert.

"I've heard the buffet is excellent there. We could all go together. I'd be happy to pay the tab."

"Let me run that by her first. Maybe next Sunday." He could arrange to bump into Kara, Della, and the kids accidently. If his mother got suspicious, she wouldn't budge from the house.

"Here's Kara now, and the night is still young. Why don't you two go have some fun. I'll watch the children."

"Mother, are you sure?" Kara asked.

"Go on, go on. Have a nice time."

Kara was still shrugging into her coat when Della closed the door. "I don't know what to say. I didn't expect that."

"The night is still young, but it's getting older by the minute. Go back to the Peanut Bar for drinks? Late movie? Necking up on Skyline Drive?"

"My first choice would be the farmhouse and a good mattress."

"That's an excellent choice, Madame."

****

"I tell you, Fritzy, that boy of mine dumped me here so he could go off and chase that little piece of tail. Gimme 'nother boilermaker." Will's mother tapped her shot glass on the bar to get attention.

"Greta, I'm cutting you off after this one and putting you in a cab." Fritz set her up again.

"One more little drinky, Fritz. Jus' one more. My kid, he's big and good lookin', like his pop. Smart too, smarter than me and Big Bill put together. Don't know how that happened. Women are always after him. Got to scare 'em away. He's all I got."

"Greta, you used to know how to show a guy a good time. Why don't you cut the apron strings and find yourself a new man? Let Will get a life of his own.

Grandchildren, you know I got six. Now that's something to live for." The bartender wiped up the shot Greta spilled before it got to her mouth and watched her down the beer.

"Yeah, that whore my boy is with tonight got two kids. Jus' wants a man to take care of 'em for her. Thass all it is. I didn't want no kids, then I got knocked up by Bill, and my dumb Pollock of a father made us get married. Bill says he ain't no Catholic, and he ain't raisin' his kid Catholic, so we done the deed with a Justice of the Peace."

"Yeah, I know, Greta. I was there."

"Natural childbirth. Ya know what that's like, Fritzy?"

"No, Greta, can't say I do."

"Like being cut in two with one of them wire cheese cutters, that's what. Didn't want no more kids after that neither. Willie was always a good boy, quiet, athletic, smart. He taught school, higher mathematics, ya know."

"Yeah, I knew that. Bet he makes better money with the survey company."

"Does. I don't like that he's around low-life construction workers all day. No, I don't. 'Course, at the high school, all them young slutty teachers was after him, some of the students, too. Had to show that bitch, Corky, who Willie loved the best. Gimme a phone. Gotta call Willie to come get me."

Fritz put a phone on the counter. He'd tried to get her to take a cab. Will wouldn't blame him. He knew what Greta was like.

On a coffee table in Lost Spring, Will Collier's phone vibrated like a rattler about to strike. Della

Shafer answered.

"Willie, come get yer mama. I need a ride. Ya hear?"

"This isn't Will. This is Kara's mother, Della Shafer. Will left his phone here by accident. They've gone out. I don't know where. Could I take a message?"

"Ya can take a hike, and put Willie on the line. I know he's over there, pro'bly screwing yer daughter right now. Where ya at 'cause I'm comin' to get him, see?"

"We live at 1001 Grandview, Mrs. Collier. I'd be delighted to meet you."

"Yeah? Well get ready 'cause here I come, baby."

Fritz and Gus, the barfly, managed to get Greta up the club's staircase. It took both of them to do it. For a free drink, Gus offered to wait with her until the cab arrived. He paid the cabbie in advance from the roll of bills in Greta's purse, not caring if the tip was enormous. Not his money, and he wanted to get out of the cold and claim his freebie. Frtiz had the drink ready to swallow.

"Say, Gus. Why don't you do something nice for Will, and take Greta for a spin one night? Big Bill would appreciate if you helped out his son."

"That old battle-ax! I had her before she went with Big Bill. I think I got a better deal being married to the bottle."

****

Della Shafer waited an hour for the visitor who announced her arrival with a thud on the front porch and a round of cursing. She opened the door to see a large woman in a loose polka dot dress sprawled across the two carved pumpkins sitting by the sill. Thank heaven, the candles inside the jack-o-lanterns weren't lit, or Greta Collier would have gone up in flames when her breath caught fire. Della reached out a hand to help the woman but was batted away.

"Don't need yer help. Will-yum! Get out here boy, and help your old ma."

"As I told you, your son isn't here. Small children are sleeping upstairs, so I would appreciate if you'd tone down your voice and your language. I've made some coffee, and we can have a nice talk before Kara and Will return."

Greta got to her feet on her own. She drew back a foot to kick the pumpkin she'd tripped over.

"Don't you dare. That's Alan's pumpkin. You'll make him cry if you smash it. Now, come inside."

Although she came up only to the bigger woman's armpit, Della stationed herself under one meaty bicep and steered the drunk into her home and over to a comfortable sofa. Coffee sat ready set to be poured into sturdy mugs. She dumped Greta into the soft cushions.

"There we go. How do you like your coffee? Perhaps, black would be best," Della asked in her perfect hostess voice, as if nothing unusual went on in her living room.

"Ruined my stockings," Greta said mournfully, running her hands over the shredded support hose between her dress hem and some clunky orthopedic shoes.

"Never mind. They were ugly anyhow. I hope you don't mind my saying that you dress like a much older woman. Kara told me you're only fifty, nine years younger than me, and already wearing granny shoes and baggy clothes." Della shook her head in disapproval.

"What does she know? Y'er daughter is a whore who wants my Willie to be a father to her brats. He's a good boy, but five'll get you ten, he's out doing the dirty with y'er girl right now. Men got appetites, and take what's spread out in front of 'em."

"You will not refer to my daughter as a whore or my grandchildren as brats ever again, no matter how drunk you are, or I'll…"

"You'll what?" Greta stood, towering over the smaller woman even though she swayed.

"Let's just say I have a Japanese friend who taught me some moves, so don't you threaten me!" Yukio had taught her some moves, but as a pacifist, none were violent. Della smiled at the pleasant memory.

Her smile only served to infuriate Greta Collier. "I could flatten ya."

"Oh, just sit down, Mrs. Collier." Della cocked her head. "We all have a right to seek our own happiness, but not at a cost to others. Why, with a little fixing up, you could be a very imposing woman."

"Huh?" Greta wobbled, lost her balance, and flopped onto the sofa again.

"Wait here, and let me get a mirror and some makeup, a few pins. I'll be right back." In the sanctuary of her first floor bedroom, Della made a call to her daughter.

****

Propped in bed Will and Kara, shared some post-coital bliss. She toyed with the hair on his chest and gazed out the window at the moonlight shining on the water of the creek.

"I think I'm glad you don't shave your body any

more. Sure, you were sleek, but this is so nice and comfy."

"It itched when the hair grew out, and you really don't want to go to a construction site with shaved legs."

"Good. I like your hairy legs, too, all long and strong, like the rest of you."

A phone rang. Will jumped. "No, no, no, not now," he muttered barely loud enough for Kara to hear over the beating of his heart.

"It's mine," she said. "Maybe one of the children got sick. I have to get it." She crawled out from under the big feather comforter she'd bought recently, the only thing covering their naked bodies, and rummaged in her purse for the clanging phone.

"Hi, Mom. Is there a problem?"

"Oh, yes. Mrs. Collier is here and very drunk. I want you and Will to stay away until tomorrow afternoon. Don't come home."

"We're at the—"

"Details aren't needed. I don't care if you've boarded a luxury barge headed for New Orleans. Stay put until I call again. I can handle this myself."

"Does she want to talk to Will?"

"Doesn't matter what she wants. You just stay put. And Kara, enjoy yourself."

"Okay, Mom." She dived back under the comforter, her skin patterned with goose bumps from the chill in the room. She warmed her body on top of Will's long torso. "My mother. She said we were supposed to stay put and enjoy ourselves."

"Great woman, your mom."

"Oh, she has her faults—like butting in and

accepting erotic art from a Japanese man she hardly knows. Your mother is at her place and in her cups."

"Huh?"

"Drunk."

"Literature majors, can't understand a word they say. Look, my ma can be a mean drunk, and she's not much better hung over. Maybe we'd better—"

"Stay here. You ever read the *Kama Sutra*? I have."

"Wasn't included in the math curriculum at State. You'll just have to show me. I learn better hands on." He placed his hands on her breasts. She went for a handle farther down on his torso under the comforter. Good start.

****

Della's guest stirred. Through a crack in the kitchen door she watched the monster arise from the slab of her sofa. Greta Collier sat up very slowly. The hand-knit afghan fell off her lap and onto the floor. She squinted at the cold mug of coffee on the table in front of her along with another empty cup and a thermal carafe. Pouring a cup of brew, still lukewarm, she tried to steady her hands as she raised it to her mouth. In a nearby by room, the shrill voices of small children sang along with Barney, the big purple dinosaur, on the TV.

"Where the hell am I? Where is Will? We'll be late for church. He needs his toast and coffee." Greta staggered toward the smell of toasting bread, bumped a door open with her broad hip, and ended up in a kitchen. She grabbed a chair and sat.

With plenty of time to resume her place by the toaster, Della held out a plate. "Here we go. Dry toast and two aspirin. Hot coffee coming up. You know, my

Mike wasn't a big drinker, but at a festive occasion, he could get carried away. I recall when he tried to do that Russian dance at Lulu's wedding and ended up on his rear. Anyhow, the few times he overindulged, this did the trick."

"Cripes, who is Mike, and why should I goddamn care!"

"My deceased husband. That's something we have in common. We're both widows, but I can see you haven't adjusted as well to your grief."

"I got no grief. I got a son to take care of me."

"Yes, well. That's not a good idea. We need to take care of ourselves."

Maridel scooted into the room followed closely by Alan. "More Cheerios, Granny." Mari held up a plastic bowl. The rest of the crunchy cereal was probably ground into the rug of the TV room by now, but that's what vacuums were for. Della gave her grandchild a refill of dry cereal. She noticed Greta clamping her hands over her ears.

Mari tugged on her granny's arm. "Is that lady a witch?"

"Of course not. Go back and watch more Barney, dear. Turn down the sound a little. You know which button."

Della took a good look at her guest. Greta Collier's appearance did scream witchy. Her long salt-and-pepper hair had come out of its bun and hung in straggles around her face with its prominent Roman nose. The red lipstick heavily applied the night before smeared the woman's cheeks, giving her a bloody look. Della dreaded thinking about the condition of her chintz sofa cushions. With Mari so caught up in Halloween right now, the child's comment was understandable, if impolite.

"I'm sorry for the rudeness. Mari can't wait for trick-or-treat. Please feel free to wash up in the powder room down the hall. You'll feel much better, I'm sure."

"You tell her I *am* a witch, the meanest witch she ever met. I eat little brats for breakfast." Greta glared at the woman serving her breakfast.

"I said—go—clean up!" An order from a general, not a suggestion.

Greta rose and found the bathroom. When she returned, she'd shoved her hair back in its bun, and wiped her strong-boned face free of makeup. Della refused to think about the condition of her guest towels right now.

"Would you like a boiled egg, Mrs. Collier?"

"Nah. I gotta get home. Where's Will? He can drive me."

"Sit." Della barked the command as if she disciplined a dog. "You might as well accept that your son and my daughter are very attracted to each other. They didn't come home last night at all. Sooo, I believe you need to get a life of your own, or be left behind. Into the bargain, you'd get two really wonderful grandchildren who are very nearly potty-trained. What do you say?"

"I say go to hell. Where's my boy?"

"Mrs. Collier, this might be a case of losing everything or gaining a new family. Think about it. Now, I have to get the children dressed. You eat. Then, I'll drive you home. Tomorrow, you and I are going out. Bring your credit cards. The stores open at ten."

"Won't go nowhere with ya, bitch."

"We'll see about that. Enjoy your breakfast, and do be sober tomorrow because I will be on your doorstep in the morning." Della folded her arms over a chest as ample as her daughter's and stared Greta into submission.

Chapter Twenty-Seven
Winners and Losers

Greta Collier worked on sweeping up the broken glass in her kitchen when someone came knocking at her door with the syncopation of a cheery woodpecker. Still in her robe and slippers, her graying hair in a long ponytail down her back, and very much in the mood to toss any kid selling cookies or a Jehovah's Witness down the long flight of cement steps that led to her home, she needed to scare off the intruder, but didn't have the energy.

Couldn't be Will coming back to beg forgiveness, she figured, not after she'd thrown the coffee carafe at him and told him what an ungrateful, misbegotten son of a bastard he was for coming home so late on Sunday and never calling. He said he'd get breakfast somewhere else and left for work. After that, Greta slumped down at her kitchen table and had a good, long cry. She was losing her son, her only child, her substitute for Big Bill.

The knocking didn't stop, so she tossed the glass shards in the trash can and stomped to the door. Della Shafer, all dressed up nice in tan slacks, an autumn print blouse, and one of them—whatchacallit—microfiber jackets, stood on her sill. Greta wanted to slam the door, but the woman, quick for her age, got inside fast as a sparrow seeking bread crumbs.

"My, it's dark in here. Don't you ever open these blinds?" Della's eyes scanned the living room as if judging her old, scratched, and worn furniture.

"Don't touch my blinds."

"I wouldn't think of it. This is your home, after all. Well, get dressed. We have a big day ahead. It was very difficult to get both a hair appointment and a spa makeover on such short notice. I've been on the phone for an hour. Hurry up. They're working you in."

"Can't afford it."

"When Will came to dinner yesterday, he said to use your credit cards. He'd pay the bills. Anything to make you happy."

"He said that?"

"Yes, he did," Della assured her. "Hurry now. We widows have to stick together."

More likely, her son had said, "Nothing will make her happy", but Greta Collier discovered her feet carrying her toward the bedroom she shared so many years with Big Bill. The large cherry wood four-poster they'd bought early in their marriage still sat in the same place facing a massive dresser of the same veneer. Will didn't know it, but his father's clothing hung in the back of the closet and the top left drawer of the dresser still held Bill's underwear, same as always.

Greta realized she had nothing up to date to wear and threw on the Sunday dress she hadn't worn yesterday. Screwing up her hair to pin using the mirror over the dresser, she took a good look and thought, "Old and ugly." Nothing she could do about it and didn't give a rat's ass.

Mrs. Shafer, like a relentless dynamo, drove toward the outskirts of the city where new hotels sprouted skyward around the huge discount mall that used to be factories where men like Big Bill worked. Now, the blocky brick buildings held racks of dainty underwear and rows and rows of running shoes and electronics. Greta didn't shop there. She rarely shopped for anything but groceries and her son's briefs. The so-called spa was located in one of the hotels next to the beauty parlor, and once Kara's pushy little mother got her ass settled in a comfortable chair, she told the girl Greta wanted the full facial and then makeup for a special occasion, abandoning her to a foreigner named Ludovica.

"I'll be right over there getting my pedicure, Greta. I do love having my feet rubbed. Mike, my husband, gave the best back rubs, but Yukio—did you know that feet have erogenous zones?"

"I usta rub Bill's feet after he worked all day. He liked it, but it didn't get me any. So what's the special occasion?"

"Yukio says every day should be looked upon as a special occasion. I had a hard time feeling that way after Mike died, but he is right. Enjoy being pampered for once. Ta-ta."

****

Will showed up after lunch as Kara put away the jar of peanut butter she'd used for sandwiches for herself and the kids. Alan and Mari had gone for a nap in the upstairs bedroom where she hoped they would stay for a while and give her a break from trying to find a job they could do other than harass their kittens and get dirty. She slouched into a kitchen chair and poured a reviving glass of white wine. "Want some?"

He shook his head and grinned at her. "I like a

butch woman with plaster dust in her hair and dirt under her nails."

"Good, because this is the best I can do. I hope you like peanut butter breath, too."

"My favorite." Will leaned over, kissed her on the mouth, added some tongue. When he finished, he glanced around the place. "You're making good progress."

Kara gave a tired sigh. "The floors are finished in the front rooms, and I'm trying to paint in there with children and kittens in the way. Fortunately, everything that can be ruined is covered with paper and tape. We've already had one spill, and the kids got more paint on their clothes than on the wall. They're down for a nap. I hope they sleep a good two hours. Come and take a look. I'm going for a sort of white-washed farmhouse effect since I have real plaster walls and not wallboard."

Will followed her to the front room where once the china roosters ruled from their perch on the pot-bellied stove. "Looks bigger."

"I had them knock out a wall between the parlor and that old-fashioned bedroom these farm houses used to have to house the grandparents close to the warmth of the kitchen. That's where Pop Shafer spent his last days as I recall. I'm putting in a downstairs bathroom in half the space, and the rest I added to this room. With three windows and the light paint, it really opens up."

Will ran his hands over the mantel, bumpy with old, dark layers of paint. "I could sand this down and stain it to match your furniture. I see the household goods arrived."

"Yes, they did. Right in the middle of the paint

spill. I had them cluster all the living room pieces in here away from the walls. My Pottery Barn craftsman sofa and chairs don't look too bad in here. I would happily pay you to do the mantel."

"Kara, stop offering to pay for everything. Makes me feel like a gigolo. You look like you could use a back rub."

"Could I ever."

"Let me uncover the sofa." He threw a drop cloth aside. "Lie on your stomach. Here we go." His strong fingers dug into her muscles.

"Oh, oh, that's so good. I do love a man with big hands."

"Good, because that's what you got."

That wasn't all she had. She knew this ploy, could feel his arousal prodding between her buttocks as he leaned over her, but she would milk the massage for all it was worth before moving on to other things. Kara had reached the dozing and drooling point of relaxation, when Will turned her over gently and applied his mouth to hers like a coat of luscious wet paint sinking into drywall. She put her arms around his neck and increased the amount of tongue. Will rocked gently against her loins, friction creating pleasure. Kara groaned and looked up drowsily just in time to see the attack.

Maridel flung herself over the arm of the sofa and dug her short sharp nails into Will's neck. "Bad man! Don't hurt Mommy!"

Will jolted upright. Mari slid down his broad back and onto the floor. She got up in a second, made a small, hard fist, and before her mother could stop her, landed a blow right in Will Collier's privates. He doubled over. "Oh, God, that hurts."

"Mari, no! Mr. Collier and Mommy were—ah—play wrestling like we do with Alan. You apologize at once."

"Sorry, Mr. Collie."

Will nodded in acceptance, still rocking back and forth over his bruised balls. He barely noticed Alan, trailed by two kittens, joining the group.

"Hold Blackie." Alan scooped up his cat and tossed it into Will's lap and what remained of his erection. The kitten responded by digging its needle-like claws into Will's crotch, right through the khaki work pants, but the small cat didn't stay there. It climbed up Will's chest until it settled on his shoulder, peering down with green eyes at the children. Blackie curled by Will's ear as if it had found a wide, safe ledge and began to purr.

"Hold Cantaloupe, too." Mari set her kitten into his lap, which Will protected with both hands. The calico kitten made its way to his other shoulder.

Leaning back, but keeping his privates protected, Will gasped, "Funny name for a cat."

"I told her this one was a calico cat, and Mari didn't quite understand that. She loves cantaloupe, so Cantaloupe, it is."

"Cute," he said, his eyes still watering.

"Let me get you some ice in a towel."

"I'm fine. I'm okay. I'm good to go." Will leaned back and closed his eyes.

Go. That's exactly what Kara feared. He'd go permanently, extracting himself from her life before her kids damaged him permanently or his mother, whom Della said during a quick mother-daughter phone call while getting her pedicure, had thrown a coffeepot at her son that morning.

Alan clambered into Will's lap, raised a hand and pried open one of Will's eyes. "Go potty?"

"Sure, buddy, but don't count on me for any contributions." Will stood, still hunched over a little, and removed the kittens to the couch.

"I unpacked their plastic potty. It's in a corner of the kitchen. You won't have to go upstairs. He's in pull-ups now. I couldn't get him back into diapers after your last demonstration."

"Thank God for small favors," Will mumbled as Alan led him from the room.

****

Foundation garments proved to be a big problem. They'd finally found Greta a bra that fit and even had a bit of style to it.

"Your bust is most impressive, Greta." Della doled out another compliment as she'd done all morning.

"Yeah, I got big tits. Y'er not so bad yerself."

"Yes, well, Kara's been blessed in the same way. They're our best assets, physically, that is. Try this black top since you don't like the pearl gray one."

"I like the gray okay, but silk is just another trip to the dry cleaners. I usta iron and starch all Bill's work clothes. Now, it's all permanent press. Sometimes, I starch Will's shirts, anyhow. I like doing for a man, ya know."

"Well, the black looks good with those gray wool slacks. Put on this nice salt-and pepper-tweed jacket, Greta. You look classy in this outfit, and ten years younger with the short red hair. Did you ever consider piercing your ears? You could wear big earrings. My lobes are so small I never bother. Don't forget to shave your legs before you wear that new dress, you hear?"

"Yeah, yeah. Fer who? I ain't shaved since Bill died."

"You want to be prepared. A woman never knows when she'll meet an attractive man." Della must have revealed too much to this crude woman judging by her next comment.

"Like that Jap guy in California? They're all kinda short for me."

Greta checked herself in the mirror, front and behind. "I look damn good for an old broad."

The pile of new clothes on the dressing room chair had grown into a small mountain of debt, but Della figured Will would gratefully pay for his mother's transformation.

"Yes, like Yukio. I don't expect to see him again."

"Would y'er like to?"

"Oh, yes."

"Different strokes fer different folks, I guess. I like a big guy."

"I think we're about done here. Would you like to get some tea or coffee before I take you home?"

"A nice cold beer would go down good. I could eat a burger, too."

"We could stop at the Peanut Bar if it's open, I guess. Won't Will be surprised when he sees you?"

"He'll be surprised dinner ain't on the table when he gets home. Serves him right. Tell the girl I'm wearin' this out soon as she gets the tags and security crap off."

After a light dinner—if beer, fries, and a monster burger could be considered light—Della helped Greta haul her shopping bags up the long flight of concrete steps to her row home. She'd gotten a little winded when they reached the top with all the things they hauled. The sack of expensive cosmetics and creams was especially heavy. Greta must have gotten every item in king-size.

"Ya wanta come in? Will's home. Saw his truck parked down on the street."

"I wouldn't miss this for the world." Della gave Greta a reassuring smile.

"Here goes." They burst through the door like cops about to take down a criminal with heavy shopping bags instead of guns.

Will lay on the sagging brown sofa with an ice pack on his crotch. He sprang up as if the FBI had broken in to take him away for committing a felony. The ice bag disappeared behind a latch-hooked pillow. "Ma?" he said to the stunning woman with short red hair, her harsh features softened by artful makeup.

"Get an eyeful, will ya. Order a pizza for yer dinner 'cause I ain't cooking. This shopping crap wears a woman out." Her words confirmed she was indeed his mother.

****

Clothes might make the man, but they didn't make Greta Collier a more pleasant woman. Still, she took a new kind of interest in Will's life. He didn't know for better or worse. When he said he was going to the farmhouse to do some work for Kara on Saturday, Greta invited herself along.

"I can sling a paintbrush as good as yer pop ever could," she claimed.

She wore distressed jeans and one of his dad's shirts. Had he ever seen his mother in jeans before?

Kara paled when they drove up, but squared her shoulders and marched out to greet them. Her children followed like a litter of tumbling puppies.

Alan reached out a hand and grabbed onto Will. "Go potty."

Mari stared up at the tall woman with the short red hair and squinted her eyes. "You the witch lady?"

"Mari! Alan!" their mortified mother said. Will suppressed a smile.

"Yeah, I'm still a witch, just a better lookin' one. I eat little girls who don't behave," Greta snarled into the child's face. Maridel edged behind her mother.

"Don't believe her, Mari. She's my mother, and she brought cupcakes," Will shouted as Alan dragged him in the back door.

"Hansel and Gretel?" Mari asked her mother.

"No, dear. You may have a cupcake if you eat a good lunch. Thank you for coming, Mrs. Collier. We can use the help. I know you're a great cook, so I'm looking forward to having a cupcake myself."

Greta held up a picnic basket. "Brought enough food for everybody. Wop jobs I made myself. Can't call 'em that no more. Now, it's subs. Same sandwich, though. Won't need to send out for nothing. You can cut the bullshit now. I got your number, honey."

Will and Alan returned in time to hear the comment. He had no urge to smile this time, but Kara handled the situation just fine.

"No cupcakes for me, I guess. My mother is out front trying to think of things for the kids to do, if you want to join her."

"I came to work." Greta literally rolled up her sleeves over brawny arms. "I can work ya into the ground."

"We'll see about that," Kara answered. "Let's get it on, then."

****

Greta could handle her paint. She single-handedly put first coats of pale blue and light pink up on the walls of Alan and Mari's rooms while everyone else worked downstairs. Kara would have preferred green and lavender, but Mari insisted, "Blue is for boys, pink is for girls." Well, she could put up interesting wallpaper borders once the paint dried.

At lunch, Greta handed out huge subs filled with cheese, salami, ham, baloney, thin-sliced onions, lettuce, and tomatoes. Kara cut hers in half, then in half again and gave the children just the bread, ham and cheese, knowing they wouldn't eat anything else. Their eyes seemed glued to a shining gold can full of potato chips and a plate of chocolate cupcakes decorated with candy corn pressed into the icing. Having eaten their little sandwiches, chips, some carrot sticks and milk, they were rewarded with dessert and put down to nap.

Della stretched back in her chair. "My, they wore me out, too. I might take a nap myself up in your room if no one minds."

Kara tried to remember if she'd changed the sex-stained sheets since last weekend. Yes, she had. "Great idea, Mom. Go ahead."

"After the children get up, I thought I'd let them roll down the hill for fun. They'll get grass-stained, of course, but I remember you and your sisters liked to do that, roll in the autumn leaves. I'll make sure they don't go in the road."

"If it keeps them out of the paint cans, I'm all for

it."

"Ready to paint some more, dearie?" Greta asked, making her voice wicked.

"As soon as I get my cupcake." Kara plucked one from the plate and gobbled it down.

****

If the others thought Della had chosen the easier job, they'd never done any babysitting. The children laughed and shouted as they rolled down the small hill in front of the house for the umpteenth time. After several trips up and down, Della, exhausted, settled into the rocker by the grape arbor with the two kittens who enjoyed watching the action from a safe spot amid the leafless vines. Both Alan and Mari promised not to go into the street, and she took their word for it.

Across the road, a gray sedan parked aside of the public recreation area. Possibly, it belonged to some jogger or trout fisherman, Della speculated, closing her eyes for only a moment. When she opened them, a stooped man in a dark overcoat was engaging Mari in conversation. He held a stick of gum toward the little girl, but the trusting Alan reached out and grabbed it. Mari backed away. She tore up the hill as fast as her little legs could carry her, shouting, "Bad man, bad man!"

Mari pelted right into the house screaming, "Bad man, bad man, Mr. Collie!"

Kara sighed and put down her paintbrush. "Protect your privates, Will. Mari, I've told you over and over Mr. Collier is not a bad man."

"Out there!" Mari pointed. All the adults ran for the front of the house. Will's long stride got him to the car across the street before any of the others. He threw open the driver's door and wrenched the man from the front seat. On the other side of the car, Alan stood clutching a second stick of gum in the open doorway. He chewed away on the first.

"Call the police," Will ordered a breathless Kara.

She shot up the hill, passing the older women. Meanwhile, Will flattened the man against the side of the car and patted him down for weapons.

"Ma, get some duct tape from my truck. I'll hold him until you get back."

"You got me wrong. I ain't no child molester. I ran out of gum is all, and the little guy wanted some for his sister and followed me over here." The man didn't struggle.

"Tell it to the cops. Mrs. Shafer, would you get the duct tape? It's in my glove compartment. Ma, if you're just going to stand there, how about getting Mari out of the street."

Greta Collier reached out a long arm and yanked Mari to her side. "You can let him go, Will. He ain't no pervert. That's Phil, the wino."

Will eased up enough to allow the man to speak without having his face smashed against the car window. "You know this guy, Ma?"

"Sure. Phil Deaver. Usta work with yer pop. After the mills closed, he hit the skids bad. Wife and kids left him. I seen him hangin' out near the soft pretzel wagon downtown, holding out a Styrofoam cup begging for quarters for more booze."

Still in Will's grip, Phil told his story. "That's true. I drank more than I should have before I lost my job. After, I had nothing else to do. After Frieda kicked me out, I went to live on the streets. The woman who owns this house, Mary, picked me up one day, sobered me up the hard way, and let me stay here until I got my feet back under me. I got a job now, and a nice little apartment. I'm doing the Twelve Steps. 'Course, my kids still don't speak to me, but I'm hoping they'll come around one day. I came back to thank the old lady. You don't believe me, look in the trunk. I brought a gift for her. Thought these kids might be her grandchildren, but none ever came around while I stayed here. Families, you never know."

Kara returned with the duct tape. Will wrapped Phil's wrists with silver bands of tape, pushed him into the driver's seat, and secured his feet the same way. "We'll see what the cops have to say when they get here."

Phil squinted at Greta. "You know me? How? 'Cause I don't recognize you."

"Greta Collier, Big Bill's wife."

"Yeah, yeah. I heard Bill passed on. Gave a dollar at Goodies toward his funeral expenses back when I still had an address. You're lookin' good, Greta. Red hair becomes you."

"Probably got paint in it, and I'm wearin' Bill's old clothes. Nothing pretty about me. Little brat over there thinks I'm a witch." She nodded toward Maridel who'd claimed her stick of gum from her brother.

"Not pretty, bewitching, I'd say. You always were built, Greta."

"Aw, Phil, don't give me none of that bullshit."

"Bullshit," Alan repeated.

A police cruiser, siren wailing, slid into a spot behind the sedan and the three-ring circus of people crowded around the man bound with duct tape. One officer stayed behind to run the license plate while the other got out to hear their story.

"He claims to have known your aunt, Kara. Said he was here to bring her a present for helping him out," Will told her.

"Well, she did take in strays. That's for sure."

"Please, all of you, stand over there while I speak to the suspect." The officer waved them across the street.

"I ain't no suspect. Look in the trunk. I got a gift in there."

"In a minute. License."

"In my pants pocket." Phil leaned to the side to show the officer where to search.

"Take it out of your wallet."

"For crying out loud, take off the duct tape and I will!"

The officer's partner came from the cruiser. They conferred, unwrapped the duct tape and took a gift-wrapped package from the trunk of the sedan. After a few minutes, the policemen came across the street.

"The man checks out as Philip A. Deaver. No arrests for sexual misconduct, but plenty for drunk and disorderly and vagrancy, all a few years back. Says one of you can vouch for him."

"Yeah, that's Phil Deaver. Knew him years ago," Greta said. "What's in the big box?"

"A gift for a Mary Shafer, he says," the officer answered.

"She died earlier this year, officer," Kara said. "I'm a grand-niece. She left her place to me. We're renovating, as you can see. Perhaps, we jumped to the wrong conclusion when we saw him offer the children some gum."

"We can tell him not to hang around here any more, if you want, but we can't take him in since the child never got into his car, just followed him over there. That's his version, anyhow. Do any of you want to say different?"

All eyes turned to Kara. "No, I believe him. We're sorry we put you to so much trouble. Just let him go."

"No trouble, miss. Better safe than sorry where kids are concerned."

The police went on their way, and Phil Deaver, bearing his gift, cautiously crossed the street.

"I heard Mary is gone. I want to leave this here. A housewarming gift, I guess. Go on and open it." Phil handed Kara the box.

"Heavy." Kara stripped off the bow and paper, which the kittens that had wandered down the hill to participate, got tangled in immediately. "Oh, a cast-iron rooster—a really big cast-iron rooster. Mary would have loved it."

Kara set the brightly painted object in the grass. It stood about a tall as Alan. Maridel gave the rooster a big hug and proclaimed, "My chicky."

"Mine!" shouted Alan.

"Uh, I could try to find another one for you," offered Phil.

"Oh, no, thanks. They have to learn to share. Would you like to come in for a drink, Mr. Deaver— that is a drink of water or a soft drink? I think we have some of Greta's wonderful chocolate cupcakes left."

"Don't mind if I do. Since I gave up the booze, I crave sweets more. Ain't doing my waistline any good." Phil patted his rather scrawny frame, tall when he didn't stoop over and on the gaunt side. Drink and homelessness had taken a toll on his teeth, but he owned a gentle smile and kind brown eyes set in a sagging face that gave him a basset hound sort of appeal. Kara could swear that Greta was checking him out from head to toe.

They made their way up the hill, Phil hauling the iron rooster, children and kittens gamboling along in front the adults: a brawny man, a short young mother, a former wino, and two older women who were certain they weren't past their prime.

Chapter Twenty-Eight
Ding Dong the Witch is Dead

"Halloween! It's Halloween," shouted Maridel, so pumped up she hit her little brother with her plastic pumpkin as she swung it around in circles. "Let's go! Trick or treat."

The excited child, dressed as Dorothy from the Wizard of Oz, clicked her heels together as she'd been shown, but they were all still in the living room of her granny's house in Lost Spring, not out on the street.

"Didn't work," Mari said sorrowfully.

Alan in a lion suit turned to Will and said, "Go potty."

"This should be fun getting him out of that suit, but better now than later," Will said, and took the child to do his duty.

"My boy wouldn't get with the program," Greta Collier said. "He shoulda been the tin man, not a construction worker. Couple of weeks ago, I wouldn't have needed to buy a wig to be the Wicked Witch of the West, right, girlie?" Greta wiggled hairy fake eyebrows at Mari.

"You make an awesome witch, Greta," Kara remarked.

"I sewed this costume myself. I sew good. Got the makeup, wig, and hat at the costume shop. Yer mother had to rent hers. Come on Glinda, let's go."

Kara eyed her plump, little mother, a towering tiara in her silver hair and a glittering wand in her hand. The poufy tulle dress stood out all around her and obscured her feet so she appeared to float along the ground. Maridel called it a "princess dress."

"Don't look at me that way, darling daughter. You're the one who is the party pooper. Even Will dressed up."

"Right. He put on his hard hat and a tool belt over his work clothes. I don't think that counts."

Will came up behind her and spanned her waist with his hands. "I considered coming as an Olympic swimmer in my Speedo and medals, but it's too cold outside to wear the costume, and I would have had to shave my body again."

"Hmmm, maybe some other time you can show me your Speedo," Kara said in a low voice.

"Any time, but right now, the lion has pottied, and we are good to go."

"Off to see the wizard, then."

When Kara opened the door, the wizard in his full shyster regalia waited on the porch. "Phil?"

"Yeah. I hope it's okay with you if I go along. Greta invited me. Been standing here trying to get up the nerve to ring the bell. When my kids were small, I always took 'em out on Halloween. We had a blast."

"Of course, you're welcome to come along, but don't expect much. Six houses and my guess is these two will be done if they don't get scared first."

Greta pushed by Kara. "Phil, ya look great. We're short a tin man and a scarecrow because Will and Kara got pissy about dressing up."

"Hey, I wanted to look studly." Will joined the

group on the porch.

"Nice of you to decide I should be the scarecrow, Greta, but no, thanks," Kara told her. "Being the mommy is enough to handle."

Phil crooked both arms. "Ladies, shall we?"

Greta and Della hooked onto him. Will held Alan's hand while Kara grabbed the exuberant Mari, still swinging the hollow plastic pumpkin that would hold her treats.

"So, you didn't want to be the scarecrow, huh?" Will asked her.

"I was always the scarecrow. Joy would cry until she got to be Dorothy. My dad liked being the tin man, and mom, the lion. Dawn took ballet to help with her weight and had all these tulle costumes. She got to be Glinda every year. That left me as the scarecrow. Mom shoved straw inside my shirt for authenticity. It itched like hell, and then, there was the ugly sack mask. I usually ended the night in tears."

"But not tonight."

"No, tonight shows promise. I like the way your tool belt is dragging your jeans down. Less work for me."

The group worked its way down one side of the block and started up the other. Mari ran boldly up walkways with Alan trailing behind, hanging onto Will who rang the doorbells for them. Collecting compliments on their costumes from other trick-or-treaters, the rest of the group waited on the sidewalk

At the corner house, they stood by a short, stout man whose pudgy daughter preceded Kara's children to the door. Though his child stood as wide as she was tall, Kara made certain to tell him how lovely she looked in her fairy princess costume. The kid hauled a substantial shopping bag weighted down with treats. As she passed Maridel, the little darling thrust a hand into Mari's pumpkin and dumped a cascade of candy into her own bag. Mari howled. Will, who still stood at the door with Alan, turned and asked, "Did someone get hurt?" but Greta handled the situation.

"Someone's gonna to get hurt if she don't return that stolen candy. How'd ya like to be a turned into a flying monkey, kid?" Greta leaned down and got right into the fat child's face. The fairy princess reluctantly scooped out a few miserly sweets. Around eight, she clearly wasn't buying the flying monkey threat.

"I got a broom stick here, and I ain't afraid to use it. Ante up." Greta nodded toward the bulging bag, and the plump princess scooped out a more generous handful, deposited it Mari's pumpkin and waddled down the walkway as fast as her round legs could carry her.

"It's just candy, for heaven's sake. She's only a child," her father justified.

"Old enough to know better. This is our block. Ya should move along now."

The guy took a look at Will and another at his big-boned mother. "Come along, Petula. We've had enough of Halloween tonight." The pair headed toward a parked car with Petula whining all the way about her bag not being completely full yet.

"I know every person on this block. Those were just some greedy outsiders," Della Shafer proclaimed.

Mari tugged on Greta Collier's long, black gown. "Thanks, Witch Granny. Come on, Granny Del. Got one, two, three more houses to go."

"Witch Granny. I kinda like it," Greta said.

"Suits you," mumbled Kara.

They ambled back to the house with Will carrying Alan the last part of the way.

Kara offered everyone cider and cookies and forbid the children to eat anything in their pumpkins until she checked the contents.

"After we have a little rest, I'll like to take the children over to the church. They're having one of those safe Halloween parties, and Faith will be disappointed if we don't come for a while. I think she's in charge of apple dunking. There will be goodie bags for the kids," Della said. "I want to show off my grandchildren."

"They won't be at their best. Alan looks ready for bed," Kara felt compelled to say.

"Wanna go," Alan lifted his head from Will's shoulder.

"Why don't you and Will stay here, start a fire, relax and have some wine? We'll be gone about an hour." Della took Alan and herded all the others before her toward the door.

"I guess I've been overridden. Grandmothers can sure be pushy."

"Yeah. I'm surprised my mother got such a kick out of tonight."

"Oh, I think threatening the fairy princess put trick-or-treat over the top for her. Do you want a beer or some wine now that Phil is on his way to the church?"

"No. Let me get a fire started in the fireplace, then we'll work on the other kind."

"I do love a man in a tool belt." Kara worked on the heavy buckle to remove it. Will stayed snug up against her as she shoved her hands into his jeans.

"Kara, I don't guess you want any more children."

"Not until these are toilet-trained," she answered, saving her firmness for the front of his pants, which she stroked.

"Alan's making really good progress. He's almost got it down."

"That's my boys," she said, referring to more than one thing at hand.

"I really want to know."

Kara stopped toying with his genitals. "Is this some kind of odd proposal?"

"Might be. I know my mother is still a problem, and I'd say we are a few months from being entirely accident free in the potty-training department. There's a ton of work to be done on your house, too." He counted off the reasons they should wait before commitment.

"Making excuses will get you nowhere. To answer your question, sure, give me a couple of years, and I'd consider having more children with a man who really wanted them."

"Would you want to marry this man, or just have one of those Hollywood kind of arrangements where the kids get weird first names and hyphenated last names, but the parents never make it legal?"

"You mean like Taffy and Walnut Shafer-Collier?"

"Yeah. Only it would have to be Collier-Shafer."

"No. I'd want a church wedding this time and only one last name and children called after people I love."

"I could do all that."

"So are we engaged now?"

"Heck, no. I just wondered."

Kara punched him in the stomach, but he saw it

coming and tightened his muscles. It wasn't much of a blow. He took her down on the sofa, checked his watch, and got to work. By the time Della returned with the children and informed them Phil would drive Greta home, a cheerful fire burned in the fireplace. Kara and Will, entirely relaxed, shared that glass of wine, proving a pushy grandmother could be wonderful to have around.

****

The Halloween troupe, plus the Rev. Frick, Faith, and Joy, recently over her morning sickness, gathered in Aunt Mary's garden the following Saturday. The cornstalks, severed and put into shocks, now decorated the front porch along with the bittersweet wreath and the remaining pumpkins. Withered bean and tomato plants had been tilled under to enrich the earth. Kara held the funeral urn while Will carried a heavier box.

With the autumn sun just taking the frost off the ground, the Rev. Frick began. "We are gathered here to commit to the earth the ashes of Mary Jane Shafer and Baxter Legg, also known as Buzz Light. While these persons were unknown to me, God recognizes them and holds them dear."

"I've been told Mary Shafer cared for her father in his old age, sacrificing any chance of having a family of her own, but she gathered others about her, shared what material belongings she possessed, and gave the priceless gift of hope."

"Baxter Legg had a sad youth and an early death. His only family was his band, and his one gift music. Miss Mary would have gladly taken this young man into her home and her heart. If the heavenly choir needed a really great drummer, they've got one now in

321

Buzz Light."

The reverend nodded to Kara who opened the urn and walked up and down the rows of the garden, strewing the ashes to fertilize tender peas in the spring and sweet corn in the summer. Will opened his box and poured the chalky remains of Buzz Light onto the pumpkin patch. They took rakes and worked the ashes into the soil as Rev. Frick intoned, "Ashes to ashes, dust to dust, from dust man came and shall return…in the hopes of everlasting life, our Lord Jesus Christ. Amen."

With some reluctance, Alan and Maridel released two balloons shaped like butterflies and watched them float over the river and the fields until they drifted from sight. Della, Joy, and Kara cried. The children wanted more balloons.

Dry-eyed, Greta announced, "Hot coffee and good food back in the kitchen. Y'er all invited."

They trooped into the farmhouse with Greta in the lead. She put on oven mitts and took an oblong pan out of the oven before the rest shrugged off their coats and found a place to sit.

"Fancy," said Phil as he poked at a square of eggs bursting with bits of onion, peppers, and parsley topping a layer of thin-sliced potatoes. He forked up one of Frey's Best Sausage Patties from a hot platter and held out his cup as Della came around with rich, steaming coffee.

"Frittata. Della's recipe. She made the fruit salad, too. Imagine paying that price for fresh berries when it's nearly winter. I made the shoo-fly pies and a brown sugar AP cake. Goes good with coffee. Kids'll want the powdered sugar donuts, though."

"That's kids for you. I ain't had AP cake since I was a kid." Phil took a wedge of the dry, scone-like cake and dunked it in his coffee. "Good."

"Bill usta do it that way." Greta's eyes got a little teary. She wiped them away with her mitts. "Being out in that cold air, then coming into the warm, is all. Want some more? I remember you was a big man once, Phil."

"Yeah. I ain't been eating so good these last few years."

"We gotta feed you up, then." Greta shoveled more eggs onto his plate.

The children, having refused to eat eggs with red and green pepper flecks, begged for donuts. Kara stirred up scrambled eggs in her new microwave, minced a sausage patty, and divided the breakfast onto two small plates. She added a few bits of fruit and cups of milk to their servings.

"Breakfast first, then donuts." She turned away to fix her own plate. When she turned back to take a place at the long, battered old table, she was struck by the scene playing out in her half-renovated kitchen. Will sat in the chair Great-grandpa Shafer once occupied. On either side of him, her children were tucked into highchairs. They dropped little bits of egg on the floor for the kittens underfoot. Faith and the Rev. Frick sat on one side of the table a few inches closer than normal for pastor and parishioner, though they weren't touching thighs. Greta, loudly voicing her opinions, was seated between Phil and Joy.

"Now, y'er Frey's sausage is real good, but pricey. Let me know when it goes on sale, will ya?" Greta said to Joy, adding an elbow nudge for emphasis. "Eat up since y'er eatin' for two, honey."

Joy blushed. She'd bragged to Kara that in her fourth month she barely showed. Della Shafer moved around the table making sure all wishes were granted like Glinda, the Good Witch.

Kara lifted a small glass of orange juice. "I'd like to thank the Reverend Frick for saying a few words in honor of my aunt and Buzz. I know this wasn't the usual UCC service, but they would have appreciated the blessing. All the rest of you, thanks for coming. I couldn't do it alone. May Mary and Buzz rest in peace."

"Amen," said the gathering, each taking a swallow of whatever beverage they had at hand in sort of a prayer-toast. Even the children raised their sippy cups in imitation and shouted the Amen. Tears flooded Kara's eyes. Her mother came running.

"What's wrong, dear?"

"Nothing. A year ago, I thought I'd never be happy again. I—"

Her cell phone clanged in her purse sitting on one of the new granite counters. Kara groped for it, turning her back on her audience, trying to get a grip. Her "Hello," came out sounding all blubbery.

"Kara, is that you? You been cryin', too?"

"Kristal? No, I'm fine. We just scattered my aunt's ashes along with Buzz Light's remains. Jeff probably told you about him."

"Not that I remember. Sorry to call during such a holy time. But, oh, Kara, Jeff and me, we had the most terrible fight. He's run off somewheres. I can't reach him by phone, and his new agent don't know where he's at either. Did he come back to you?"

"No, Kristal, he did not."

Thank heaven for that. She didn't want or need Jeff

Ryder showing up on a motorcycle and destroying this meaningful day. Kara had a good idea where Jeff went: Thailand to get some comfort from two underage girls who could barely speak English, let alone argue with him or tell him no. The report still rested in its envelope at the bottom of a box of important papers. Her children didn't need to know their father had an obsession with young virgins and paid for their services. Neither did Kristal, barely out of childhood herself.

"So, Jeff dumped Manny?" Kara asked, latching on to a safer topic.

"Oh my, yes. He said Manny took your side in the divorce. Now, I don't think that's true at all, but well, Jeff was pretty darn mad and got himself another agent. He made me switch, too."

"I see. Do you want to tell me what you fought about? I'll help if I can."

"Babies. We fought about havin' babies, sweet little babies. I don't understand how Jeff couldn't want a family. I mean my mama had six, and big families seem sorta natural to me. He said he had two already and didn't want no more. Now he's run off, and I'm all alone in this ole mansion. I can't call my mama or my sisters. Truth is, my family don't like Jeff much."

"Ah, is that so?" Kara recalled the September wedding where Kristal's skinny, celery stick of a daddy, and her three burly brothers stood at the altar looking as if someone had recently snatched shotguns from their hands. Even Kristal's two substantial sisters seemed to be harboring unchristian thoughts about Jeff as they clomped down the aisle in their pumpkin-colored gowns. Kristal, a waif in white following them, appeared to be the only child in the family who didn't take after Big Ma Pickens. Kristal wore a dress speckled with tiny blue flowers and bound at the waist with a wide, blue sash, because, as Ma Pickens said, "She ain't pure and don't deserve to wear white."

"They say he's a heathen. Kara, could I come stay with you a while?"

"Kristal, honey, my house isn't done yet. I have plenty of room, but there's only one bathroom on the second floor, and they haven't quite finished the bath downstairs."

"Plu-eeze, Kara. I don't want to be alone. I won't be no trouble." The girl actually sobbed over Jeff Ryder who didn't deserve a single tear.

"Come, then. Call for a ride when you get in."

"Thank you so much. I'm still so sorry about the divorce and all."

"Forget it. Jeff and I were over long before you came into the picture. I just didn't realize it."

"You're so kind. I'm on my way. Hugs and kisses to the babies."

Kara's tears had dried while everyone at the table listened in, evidently.

"Who and what?" Joy asked, never loathe to inquire about her sister's business.

"We're expecting a guest—Miss Kristal Pickens, rising country-western star, also known as Mrs. Jeff Ryder.

"A celebrity," gasped Greta.

Progress—Greta no longer regarded Kara as the Secret Secluded Wife, splashy tabloid fodder. She hoped to keep her life that way.

Chapter Twenty-Nine
A Match Made in Heaven

Kristal Pickens was, honest to goodness, no trouble as a guest. She dug right in washing walls and painting, ignoring any damage to her fine French manicure. Refusing to put either Kara or her mother out of their beds, she stayed alone at the farmhouse, sleeping in Mary's old room and using the antiquated plumbing without complaint. One day as she raked up a pile of fallen leaves for the children to jump in, she heard the call of nature, ducked into the old outhouse, and nearly had her pants down before she realized the building now served as a tool shed. Kristal told the story on herself at the evening meal.

"Well, I didn't grow up fancy, you know. We had a cabin in the hills with one of them hand pumps at the sink and a wood stove for heating. I shared one room with my two sisters, and we still used our necessary. Mama home-schooled us to keep us away from worldly knowledge. Then, Pa got the call to go out in the world and sing the gospel. If church people didn't put us up, we shared one motel room, Ma and us girls in the beds and the men on the floor. Talk about using one bathroom! Now, I got five baths I don't hardly use in Nashville."

Progress on the farmhouse suddenly accelerated as word got around that a famous and beautiful young woman stayed there. Every workman on Kara's list came to gawk and needed an excuse to remain. They completed the downstairs bath in record time, and tore out the one upstairs, refurbishing it handily. With the new heater working effectively, Kara moved in with her children, more because she worried about Kristal staying alone than because she was in a hurry to have her own place.

Greta, dazzled by fame, got Kristal to sign an entire notepad of autographs addressed to various denizens of Goodies. Right on top of the pad where everyone could see was the inscription, "To my dear friend, Greta, from Kristal Pickens" encircled by a big heart and all the i's dotted with the same. Greta dragged Phil along when she went to hand them out. They bowled a few games, had the crab cakes, and laid off the booze.

Even the Reverend Frick appeared star-struck. Kristal had missed going to church since Jeff would never darken the doors of that institution and offered to sing with the choir. She moved the congregation with her version of *Morning Has Broken* and got them all swaying and clapping along to *This Little Light of Mine*. Afterward, the line to shake her hand was as long as the one forming at the door for the pastors. Kristal did remark at Sunday dinner she wasn't sure she'd done well since no one danced in the aisles or shouted hallelujah even once.

John Frick patted her hand and said the UCC congregation tended to be a bit more formal than the churches she attended, but the congregation applauded its appreciation. Faith's lips went thin as she tried to squeeze out a compliment for Kristal. With the exception of Joy, who felt obligated to eat with her in-laws on Sundays, the group attending the scattering of ashes continued to show up at the farmhouse on weekends. Rev. Frick said he mustn't get in the habit of so much fine food and their good company, as other members of the congregation expected him to dine with them occasionally—at least until he married. Unfortunately, he faced Kristal when the words left his mouth.

Since Greta and Della continued to compete in providing food, Kara and Faith cleaned up the remnants of a glazed ham (Della's), a sweet-potato casserole topped with tiny marshmallows that the kids ate as if it were dessert (Greta's), and buttered green beans found preserved in jars in the basement while the others adjourned to the living room. As the after-dinner coffee perked and Faith cut up two pies, fresh apple and pumpkin with whipped cream provided by the rival grannies, Kara cleared the table and loaded the new, marvelously quiet dishwasher.

"The way you're jabbing those pies, Faith, a person might think *you* were the one replaced by Kristal Pickens."

"I think I have been. Did you see the way John looks at her? She's so young. Everything about her is perfect except her grammar. Up until Kristal arrived, things were going so well between us. John had a free pizza coupon someone gave him, and we went out to dinner together on Monday night, then stopped by the hospital to visit the sick. I don't see that ever happening again."

"Kristal is a married woman, cute, but more naïve than Mari—who knows there are bad men in the world. Not that John is bad. The reverend may be charmed, but

I don't think his feelings go any farther than that."

"Pastors have been known to give into temptation before. We were just getting to know each other. We talked about our childhoods, what we wanted in life, how children should be raised, not the usual date chit-chat people use when they are afraid of scaring the other person off, a conversation with real substance."

"You didn't tell him about your celibacy oath, I hope?"

"No, that didn't come up."

"Thank God," Kara whispered.

Faith loaded a tray with plates of pie, and Kara brought the coffee. The men had dragged the comfortable mission-style chairs in front of the corner hutch holding the television and were engrossed in an Eagles game. Alan, wedged into Will's chair, napped against the big man's chest. The male contingent accepted their choice of pie and coffee hardly glancing away from the screen, but Will did squeeze Kara's hand in passing.

The women gathered on the couch in front of the fire, glowing and crackling beneath the broad oak mantel Will restored and stained to match the hardwood floors. Two chalkware dogs Kara found in the attic when she stored the china roosters she was too sentimental to sell after all guarded each end. Mari slept with her legs resting on the back of the giant iron rooster sitting near the hearth. Accepting that the rooster would be a part of their life, Kara ornamented it with a harvest wreath around its neck. In the future, she intended to give Mari all the china roosters in the attic when she married.

Kristal dithered over which kind of pie to have and

finally took both, shoving the apple onto the same plate as the pumpkin. Della and Greta looked pleased, so Kara took half a piece of both. She'd gained another five pounds because of this rivalry and couldn't afford to let her weight get any more out of hand. Everyone knew that at thirty, pie bypassed the stomach and went directly to the thighs. She sighed, but Kristal giggled.

"I'm just a sucker for pie. Good thing I'm so thin and all. I got this fast metabolism like my daddy."

"Faith is still as thin as she was in college," Kara offered a little too loudly.

"Because I only take one small piece of pie," Faith answered.

None of the men turned their heads, either too wise to comment or too happy that the Eagles had scored the extra point. When the game ended, the group broke up. Della and Greta went to the kitchen to claim their roasting pan and casserole dishes. Will and Kara carried the children upstairs to continue their naps in their cribs. Phil moved outside to warm up his car while he waited for Greta to leave, and Kristal removed to her room trying to call Jeff over and over again.

Faith took it upon herself to gather the dessert dishes in the living room. Rev. Frick rose to help.

"You know, Kristal has the face and voice of an angel," he said, making conversation.

"She's eighteen, John. Of course, she does," Faith answered, without turning to look at him. She clanked two coffee cups together. "She's also married to a rich and handsome man. They sing together."

"Yes, I know."

"I didn't realize you were such a big fan of country music," Faith said, her voice sounding as stiff as her

331

body posture. Any minute now she'd drive him away with her attitude if she couldn't keep the sarcasm out of her voice.

"I'm not. I never heard of Kristal Pickens before I met her. She gave me one of her CDs to listen to after I counseled her about her marriage. Poor child, she's in such despair. This Jeff Ryder sounds entirely too self-centered to be a good husband. He doesn't consider the desire of his wife for children, the natural result of a union of two souls."

"Actually, I think it's another kind of union that results in children, John," Faith said tartly, not showing much sympathy for sad, little Kristal. Very un-Christian of her.

"Of course, but the spiritual union should come first."

"Well, it didn't with Jeff and Kristal."

"We shouldn't judge. We should bend our efforts to support their marriage and make it right between man and wife."

"Oh, I could support helping them to reconcile, and you're right. I shouldn't judge. I'm not a virgin myself. There, I've said it."

Will and Kara had tiptoed down the stairs in order not to wake the children. At the moment Faith spoke those words, Will had Kara pressed against the newly plastered and painted wall of the hallway. He whispered the possibility that Kristal could stay with the children while they took a little stroll out to the barn where he'd recently stored a space heater and a double sleeping bag.

"Dear God, she said it," Kara whispered.

"So? I don't know any thirty-year-old virgins, do

you? What's the big deal?" Will breathed hotly in her ear.

"Listen."

Rev. Frick paused to gather his thoughts. "I shall not judge you, Faith Harvey, by the acts of your past, but rather on the woman who stands before me today."

The reverend continued on after this rather stuffy speech. "Besides, I'm not a virgin either. I did go to college before attending seminary and wasn't the most moral man on earth. I drank, slept with women, smoked a little weed, the usual stuff.

"Then one day, shortly after graduation, I was commuting to a job that paid more money than I'd ever seen in my life. The car in front of me ran a red light and a truck coming in the other direction destroyed it. I parked and phoned for help. The car was smoking, about to burst into flame. The trucker and I dragged two men from the wreck, both badly injured. The driver said they were late for work, and he had been careless. He asked me to pray for them while we waited. I did.

"I got to work late myself, my five-hundred dollar suit ruined with blood. My boss chewed me out, said I shouldn't have gotten involved. That night, I went by the hospital and sat with the conscious driver and prayed for his friend who lay dying. The driver had remorse so great he wanted to die, too. I told him what mattered was how he lived his life from now on, my moment of epiphany. I quit my job and entered the seminary. I haven't been with a woman since."

"There's been no one for me since college, either. Oh, John!" Faith curled into his chest.

"Oh, Faith!" The reverend raised her face toward his for a kiss. A quick peek revealed Faith diving into his beard.

"Oh, Jesus, let's get out to the barn, Will. I can't take any more!" Kara said.

****

Not wanting to face the reverend with a little sin on his soul, Will left for home from the barn. Kara returned to the kitchen where Faith engulfed her in a huge hug. Evidently, they'd missed the most important part of the overheard conversation.

"Kara, can you believe John and I are going to be married! I can't. Everything happened so fast. He said it was just like the day he discovered his calling. He knew me to be the rock he should build his family upon because I was like my name, Faith, steady, strong, and always present."

"I am so happy for you! What can I say, a match made in heaven."

"And he's so nice, tryin' to help me with my marital problems," Kristal added, her face going a little bleak. "We need to have a party for y'all. That'll be fun. When's the weddin'?"

"We haven't set a date yet. Not during the holidays. That's his busy time. But before Lent. Maybe Epiphany—that would be meaningful. Neither of us wants to wait too long."

"No surprise there," Kara slipped up by saying.

"You were listening in!"

"I accidently heard the first part of your conversation. Then, Will and I took ourselves elsewhere."

"Yes, you and Will. How is that relationship coming along? And I don't want to hear about the physical part."

"Good, because that part is doing just fine. I don't know. The children have accepted him. Mari hasn't attacked him lately, and Alan adores him. Phil is keeping Mother Collier busy. My own mother has been pimping for us, if you ask me, always leaving us alone together. I thought on Halloween, he might say something, but the moment passed. I'm guessing he still has some sort of problem going to the next step. Who knows with men? Scared to commit? I just don't know."

"Maybe John could talk to him."

"That's a good idea," Kristal said. "I want him to talk to Jeff—when I see him again."

"Oh, you will. Jeff has been known to pout for great lengths of time, but he'll turn up when he gets horny."

Kristal blushed. "He isn't always that way, just most of the time."

"No need to tell me about it. Everyone's gone but us. Why don't we bundle up the kids and go for a walk in the park. I haven't shown you the covered bridge yet. It's great inside, all these thick, hand-hewn beams and a century's worth of graffiti. The children like to run through because it echoes so. After we have some exercise, we can come home and make ham sandwiches for dinner, finish off those pies, and help Faith plan her wedding."

"Sounds like fun."

****

With the air brisk and the sun sinking they clambered back across the bridge on their way home. As they exited with Auntie Faith in the lead holding the hands of Alan and Mari, Kristal took Kara's hand in hers and swung their arms playfully back and forth. She raised them up as they passed between the stout pilings set to block cars from crossing the landmark.

"Reminds me of being a kid in the hills, crossing the creek with my sisters."

A bush shook by the mouth of the bridge. A man jumped out, a man with a camera. He clicked, flashed, and ran for a parked car.

"Dammit, a paparazzo. I thought I'd left them behind in California. I can't possibly be of any interest to them now," Kara groaned.

"Oh, I think they might be after me. They was always hangin' around our place in Nashville. I guess maybe one of the workmen told them I came here. We had to hire a guard back home. I should just go there and wait. It's almost Thanksgiving, and time to fess up to my folks that things ain't workin' out so well with me and Jeff."

"I can hire a guard, too, if you want to stay."

"No. I'm a married woman, not a little girl anymore. I'll be headin' home tomorrow, but thanks, Kara. You're a good person. I'm so sorry I broke up you and Jeff."

"Please, think nothing of it. I—ah—I've forgiven you. Never mention it again."

"All right. You're such a sweetie." Kristal planted a soft kiss on Kara's cheek.

From the direction of the parked car, a camera flashed again.

Chapter Thirty
For Better or Worse

Despite Kristal's departure, the fiends of the press gathered in the park across the street from the farm, destroying its peace. Their last pieces of garbage absolutely infuriated Kara. *Kristal and Kara a Couple? Jeff left out as Ex seduces Wife.* The best of the lot showed a photo of Kristal laying a kiss on Kara's cheek. In a wider framed shot, her children, standing with Faith, watched the kiss. *Nanny Cares for Kids as Kristal and Kara Coo.* The worst of all, *Kara Rydes Kristal? Jeff Out*, headlined a rather sweet picture of the country-western singer holding her hand.

She decided to take them head-on and marched down her steps. Let them take all the pictures they wanted of her in a carefully chosen, very feminine outfit, and shout themselves hoarse. She held up a hand for silence.

"I have a statement and will not be taking any questions afterwards. Kristal Pickens came to visit Jeff Ryder's children while he went out of town on other business." Yeah, right. She suspected he'd run to Thailand to pout and allow his two teenage mistresses to fawn all over him. "The photographed kiss and handholding were gestures of sisterly affection showing we are not at odds over the divorce. Neither Kristal nor I are lesbians. I have a special man in my life, and I ask you to respect our privacy."

Although Will didn't want her to face the press alone, she insisted he stay inside the house. Now, as the reporters hooted out questions she refused to answer— "What's his name?"—"Is he in show business?"—she heard the clump of Will's work boots on the steps and felt the wall of warmth as his body came behind her. The cameras whirred. Will put his arm around her shoulders.

"My name is Will Collier. I've known Kara since we attended college together. I live here in Reading and own a surveying business. That's all we have to say." He took her arm and escorted her up the hill.

"You shouldn't have faced them. Now, they'll stake out your office and your work sites. They might damage your business. I could have handled them alone." Will opened the door for her and shielded her from more photos with his broad back.

"I doubt if they will want to tangle with construction crews, and they can take all the pictures they like of me hauling the theodolite around. You could have been making me up. Now, they know I'm for real."

"Are you, Will?"

"What's that supposed to mean?"

"Well, you're always over here. The sex is great. But, you've never once said you love me."

"I, uh… You just got back in town three months ago. I'm not rich like Jeff or nearly as good looking. Some of the guys at Goodies think I might be your rebound man after the divorce. They say I should enjoy it while it lasts because you might drop me and go back to Hollywood just like that." He snapped his fingers.

"Remember Frank Bragg and the bucket of cold water?"

"I had nothing to do with that."

"No, but you let the guys tease you out of ever dating me or getting to know me. Grow up, stop listening to your friends, and leave your mama, Will." All her frustrations coming to a head, Kara hauled back and landed a fist in his stomach. The blow had much more force behind it than the one on Halloween, but her hand still bounced off his tightened muscles. She shook the sting from her hand.

"I don't know how you stay so hard the way Greta feeds you. I've gained five pounds on her Sunday meals alone," she complained.

"I work out with weights every night I'm not over here." He gripped her wrists in case she decided to go for his nose or his balls like her daughter. "Before you came back, that was every night. You've given me a life, Kara. I don't want to mess this up by moving too fast."

She struggled to free her hands. Out of the corner of her eye, she saw Maridel and Alan peeking at them from the living room doorway. Behind them on the TV screen, the purple dinosaur sang about happy families loving each other.

"Mari, make Mr. Collier let me go."

Will caged both of her hands with one of his and moved the other to protect his privates, but Mari simply cocked her head. "Do you love my mommy? Are we a happy fam-i-ly?"

"Yes, I love your mommy, and I think we could be a happy family."

Alan raced forward and pushed between Will and

his mother. He gazed up at the big man with adoration and said, "Go potty."

Will set Kara free and took the boy's hand. "Let's see if you can hit the target this time, big boy."

As man and child started down the hall, Kara shouted after them, "You can't take that back, Will, so you'd better mean it!"

"I do mean it. Can I move my weight set to your barn?"

He left Kara to ponder if that meant the same as moving in with her.

****

Despite the battle of the iron chefs—Greta's ham, marshmallow-topped sweet potatoes, and green bean casserole covered with crunchy onions rings versus Della's roasted turkey, Pennsylvania Dutch potato filling, and stewed sweet corn—ambrosia with fresh coconut and more little marshmallows up against cranberry-orange gelatin ring—Thanksgiving proved to be a huge success. Faith brought over a brown sugar pound cake to add to the pumpkin and apple pies congregating on the kitchen counter along with Kara's chocolate cupcakes topped with fat, plastic turkeys for the children. The wise diner took a dab of every offering and went back for seconds. Will, Phil, and John had the good sense to do this.

As the guests left for home, Kara stood by with a roll of foil and a pile of disposable containers trying to get as much of the leftovers out of the house as possible.

"Only one plate, Mom?"

"I'll have it for dinner tomorrow. The corn and potatoes are always better the second day, but there's nobody at home to eat it except me. You have a man to feed now."

"Are you upset about Will moving in?"

"Not really. I suspect he will do right by you in the end." Della gave her daughter a soft smile. "Holidays are the hardest, that's all. I enjoyed being with you and the children, but I'm promised to Joy next year."

"There isn't enough Della Shafer to go around."

"Hmmm, I don't know about that." She looked down at her round little figure. "Enjoy the rest of evening." With a quick hug and kiss to Kara and her grandchildren, Della left for home carrying her single plate.

Greta returned to pick up her second load of dishes. "I left the two of ya some of each, but with Phil moving in, I'll need most of the leftovers."

"Mom should get out more. Do you think she'd like concert tickets to the Sovereign Center for Christmas? She could take a friend along."

"Don't plan on giving me nothing like that. Besides, I know what yer mother wants for Christmas, and it ain't concert tickets. It's that Jap guy out in California. When we go and get our hair done, it's Yukio this and Yukio that. They do that email and Skype stuff."

"I didn't know they were still in touch."

"If ya can call email touching. Bring him here for Christmas, why don't ya?"

"Maybe I will. Of course, he might want to spend the holidays with his son and grandchildren."

"He's a Jap. You think he's Christian?"

"You do know how to make a point, Greta. I'll call him."

Produce.

"Damn right, you should. Phil, we're going!" Greta shrieked. "Kids, come give Witch Granny a kiss." They did.

Faith picked up the remainder of the pound cake, and John piled refrigerator containers under his bearded chin. Faith opened the door for him, but turned back to Kara.

"We checked the church calendar and settled on the week of Valentine's Day before Lent gets under way. We'll have just enough time for a short honeymoon."

"Oh, you're planning to abstain from sex during Lent?"

"I'd rather give up chocolate! I want you and Lulu and Hannah to be in the wedding along with my sister, all wearing red. It's your color, you know. Remember the dress you had in college that was supposed to attract Will's attention and got soaked with water by Frank Bragg instead?"

"How could I forget it? My life changed that day—and I ended up with Jeff."

"Maybe a new red dress will seal the deal the right way this time."

"An interesting thought. You know Will is moving in?"

"That's not the same as having a ring on your finger." Faith tapped her own tiny diamond engagement ring.

"I know John probably doesn't approve, but Will is going from his mother's house to my mine and needs to adjust to two small children. This might take some time on Will's part."

"Remember, he won't buy the cow if he gets all the

milk for free."

"Hey, I'm getting quite a bit of cream myself. And thanks for calling me a cow. My hips are big enough."

"So are your udders. They balance out. I don't hear Will complaining."

"No. He doesn't seem to notice things like stretch marks and extra poundage."

"Because he loves you."

"I think so."

"Don't wait too long." Faith gave her a hug. "Next year, we'll have you over to the parsonage. Pastor Webber says he wants to move to a smaller place and be semi-retired now that it looks like John will stay in Lost Spring. I plan on prying my parents away from my sister's table, too."

"It's a date." Kara waved her friend out the door.

She finished the cleanup while Will kept the children out from under foot. Afterward, she bathed Alan and Mari in the big tub and got them to bed. Will ramped up the fire while she was upstairs and opened a bottle of her favorite California wine. Kara stretched out on the sofa, her head in Will's lap.

"I'm exhausted."

"I was thinking of taking you for a ride on Skyline Drive."

Kara shook her head nestled in his crotch. "No, we'd have to wake the kids and bundle them up."

"I thought about that lobster dinner we never had."

"Too full to talk about food." She shook her head again.

"Then, I thought, here is the place—in front of the mantel I refinished in the home of the woman I love with the greatest kids on earth sleeping upstairs."

"Will, I hate to say this on your first official night here, but I'm too stuffed and too tired to do it on the floor by the fire." Kara closed her eyes and snuggled in more closely.

"If you don't stop moving your head, I may never get this out."

"What?"

"Will you marry me, Kara, and let me be a father to your children?"

Her eyes sprang open. Right in front of them, Will held the traditional velvet box. He flicked it open with his thumb. "It's a one-carat, princess cut stone, the best I could afford. Your mother helped me pick it out."

"No wonder she seemed so weepy-eyed tonight. I should have suspected what was going on. She's a sucker for the sentimental. Does Greta know?"

"Ah—no. I wanted her to have a night alone with Phil before I told her. Tomorrow, I swear. I know Jeff probably gave you a bigger and better ring."

"Jeff never gave me an engagement ring. All the jewelry I have, I bought for myself. I never wear the stuff. It was revenge bling. This is love jewelry."

She held out her ring finger, and he slipped the diamond on, a perfect fit. Kara drew Will's head down to where she still rested in his lap.

"I love you, Will Collier, and yes, I want to marry you."

The ring of the telephone interrupted their tender moment, as it always seemed to do. She should learn to turn the thing off.

"My mom, I'll bet you." Kara answered the phone. "The fiancée of Will Collier speaking."

"Oh, Kara, that's so great. You and Will together

forever. Now I don't feel so very bad a-tall."

"Kristal?"

"Yes, so sorry to bother you. Jeff came home. We had another fight. A great big one. We tried to hide our feelings over at Mama's house today, but it all came out—about him havin' hisself fixed like some ole hound dog so we won't never have children. I cried and cried. I'm still cryin'."

"You mean Jeff had a vasectomy without your consent?"

"That's right. I told Mama. Then, Mama said the purpose of marriage was procreation, and she didn't see how we had much of a marriage if he'd go out and do something like that. My brothers said didn't he know about condoms? And Daddy called him a eunuch like they had back in Bible days. That's man who had his balls cut off, Daddy said. Jeff made me go home right then and said he'd show me what a eunuch could do. I mean, Jeff still has his balls and the rest of his privates, so he ain't really a eunuch, but they're all swolled up and purply brown like those stewed prunes my granny used to eat to stay regular, so I don't see how he can right now." Crystal lowered her voice to impart an intimate secret. "I think maybe he wants me to go down on him. I don't like that much, so I won't. It ain't natural, but really, I just don't feel like sleepin' with him no more 'cause of what he did. He says he made sure the operation can't be reversed."

How had she become Kristal's confidant? Kara ramped up her patience and replied with kindness. "I understand, but there are other ways to have children, Kristal. You could adopt, or have artificial insemination. Jeff's brother seems very fertile. He

345

could be a donor—once you and Jeff have worked this out."

"Oh, I couldn't do that. That would be like cheatin' on Jeff, don't you think?"

"No, honey, I don't. Could you call back in the morning, and we'll talk some more, okay?"

"Sorry. I got off the track and the whole train just follered me. I called because when I wouldn't go to bed with Jeff, he said, okay, if I wanted children, he had children. He's going to go get them and bring them back to Nashville. He said what with your lesbian tendencies according to them ugly tabloids and what with you screwing a construction worker in the same house where his children live, he could get custody. We'd get a nanny, then go on just like before. Oh, I'm so sorry, Kara. Jeff is coming to take Mari and Alan away from you."

Chapter Thirty-One
The Good Fight

"I'm staying home today. There won't be any business right after Thanksgiving." Will sat at the breakfast table like an immovable object. Neither he nor Kara slept much the night before, and not because they were celebrating their engagement. At dawn, they gave up and came downstairs to put on the coffeepot.

"After asking if I knew what the hell time it was in California, Prater Wolfe said to get a restraining order. Jeff is supposed to give me thirty days notice if he wants to take the children for a trip. "

"I don't think a vacation is what he has in mind—and I don't think a restraining order will stop him from showing up here."

"No, but we can call the police if he does. The trouble is, all the city offices are closed for the holidays. The order will have to wait until Monday."

"I'll be here the whole time, most of it, anyhow. I want to make a quick trip to my mother's, tell her our news, and pick up a few things. I won't be gone more than an hour. If Jeff shows up, call me on my cell. And call the police."

With Will absent, the hour passed ever so slowly. The children woke and had their breakfast. Mari, always the sharp one, noticed the engagement ring first thing.

"Pretty," she said.

"More than pretty, Mari. This ring means that Mr. Collier and I are going to be married. He'll live here with us. He'll be a daddy for you and Alan."

Mari considered. "Do I get a ring, too?"

"No, you don't, but you can be in the wedding and wear a fancy princess dress like you did for Auntie Kristal."

Remembering the itchy petticoats, Mari wrinkled her nose. Alan peered all around. "Where Will? Go potty."

"I'll take you potty. It might be too late by the time he gets back."

"Big boy," Alan announced and stomped off alone to the bathroom and his little, yellow plastic commode.

He came back in time to see Will drive up in the truck and dashed out to the back porch calling, "See, see, Alan pee-pee."

Once Will admired his sloppy success, Alan allowed his fluids to be flushed and set off to find where the kitties hid. Mari went with him to look under the sofa. Will motioned to Kara to step outside for a moment. In the bed of his truck lay the two refurbished sleds. The one painted a deep blue bore Alan's name in yellow underscored with lightning bolts. The other was red, labeled "Mari" and had white snowflakes stenciled on it.

"Oh Will, the kids are going to love these. Thank you so much."

"We'll hide them in the barn until Christmas or the first snow. I haven't felt so excited about snow in years."

She drew his head down to plant a kiss. "Did you

tell your mother we're engaged?"

"She wasn't up yet. I left her a note."

"Coward."

"If being afraid to see Ma in bed with Phil is cowardice, I'm guilty. She never sleeps this late. We'll face her together."

"Sooner or later, I guess."

"Sooner."

A car turned into the drive. Greta or Jeff? Greta. She arrived with her red hair rumpled and the makeup that softened the brutal lines of her face smeared on.

"Let's see it," she ordered.

Kara held out her hand.

"Jesus! Did ya hock the business, boy?"

"No, Ma. You have to accept that Kara and I are getting married."

"Accept it?"

"Yes."

"Fine. Where the hell are my grandkids? Witch Granny is here, Mari!" Greta stomped inside.

"That went well."

"It did." Kara and Will looked at each other in wonder. "I don't think things will go that easy with our next guest."

Coming from the direction of the highway, a forest green Escalade SUV, the kind of vehicle Jeff would have made fun of a couple of years ago, muscled its way up the farm lane. Evidently, that sort of transportation indicated success in Nashville. Jeff braked an inch from the bumper of Will's truck and climbed out. He wore his blue-black hair back in a ponytail, and his eyes covered with dark glasses. A poet's shirt open to show his chest hair covered his torso, and designer jeans clung to his thin legs. The tooled cowboy boots made Jeff Ryder almost as tall as Will, but not nearly as brawny.

"Now, isn't this cozy, Kara and her construction worker shacked up with my kids." He glanced into the bed of Will's truck. "Hand-me-down toys? With what I pay in child support you couldn't afford new?"

"I'm Will Collier. I own a surveying business, and unlike you, I finished college—with a degree in mathematics. Kara and I got engaged last night." Will held out a hand big enough to crush Jeff's guitar-picking fingers.

Jeff declined to shake. "You can have the bitch. I came for my kids."

"Jeff, let's take this inside and have a rational discussion, not a pissing contest." Out the corner of her eye, Kara noticed Will's face turning red. Jeff stalked into the farmhouse and headed straight for the sound of children's voices in the living room.

He snapped at his kids, "Put down the damn cats and get your things. You're going to Nashville to live with me and Kristal. She wants you brats."

Alan dropped the black kitten that skittered to a new hiding place. He ran to cling to Will's leg. Mari moved behind her mother. She murmured a frightened little mantra, "Bad man, Mommy, bad man."

"Kristal wants her own, not mine, Jeff. I have full custody. I'll call the police if you don't leave."

"I thought you'd be grateful. With the kids gone you can screw your ditch digger all over the house. I'll be the one who has to lock the bedroom door. Shut up, Mari! You know I'm your father."

"Are you on something? Let me see your eyes,

Jeff." Kara reached out to take his dark glasses. Jeff smacked her hand away, and Will surged forward. Kara put out her arm to stop him.

"I'm fine." Her wrist smarted. "Jeff, I want you out of here. I'm calling the police. If you have drugs in that SUV of yours, you'd better get moving."

Kara rushed to get the phone, exposing Mari to her father. Jeff grabbed the scared child by a hand and tried to pry Alan from Will's leg, but the boy clung to Will like a barnacle to a big, stable piling.

"Mommy, Mr. Collie, bad man got me!" screamed Mari.

Jeff stopped struggling with Alan and slapped his daughter in the face. "Shut up. I said to shut up!"

The phone wobbled in Kara's hand, but she had to continue her report to the 911 operator, the questions coming fast and furious. Her child shrieked louder, hurting her more than the slap on her hand. Help came from an unexpected source. Greta, nearly as tall and broad as her son, rose up from the sofa where she'd been avidly watching the real life soap opera. "Nobody hits my grandkid, ya louse!"

Used to taking care of everything herself, Kara watched amazed as the new family she was forming took over. Greta tore Mari from Jeff's arms and gave him a hard shove in the center of the chest. He came back with a wild swing at Greta's face. Will got between them, blocked the blow, and returned with an uppercut to the jaw. Jeff staggered backwards, tripped on the edge of the hearth, and smashed down on the iron rooster. He rolled over clutching his face and pointing in a fury at Will.

"Oo bwoke ma jaw. Sue 'oo."

"I think the rooster did it, but I'm willing to take the credit. You okay, buddy?" Will looked down at Alan, who had remained attached to his leg during the entire incident. Alan nodded.

"Kitty." Alan pointed. Blackie, who had taken refuge in the cold ashes of the fireplace during the scuffle, pounced out, swiped Jeff's hand with his tiny claws, and retreated under the couch with his sister, Cantaloupe. "Good kitty."

"Good chicky," Maridel said and slid from Greta's grip to grab Will's other leg.

Greta seized the lapels of Jeff's loose white shirt and heaved him to his feet. "Let me help ya out there, ass wipe. For a small cat, that's a nasty scratch. Could get infected. Might lose your hand if you don't watch out. Better get to a hospital."

Jeff pointed at Greta. "I'll get 'oo and yoor widdle cat, 'oo."

Sirens wailed in the distance. Holding his jaw and dripping blood from the scratch, Jeff lurched toward the back door. Tripping down the porch stairs, he made it to the Escalade and tore down the drive.

"Stay with Witch Granny," Kara ordered as she peeled her children off of Will and deposited them in Greta's wide and willing arms. She and Will charged to the front porch to show the way for the cops. Below, Jeff took a hard left on the river road as the flashing lights of patrol cars appeared. Still accelerating, he veered toward the covered bridge coming up fast on the right. Whether his blurry mind convinced him he could hide inside and let the cops pass like some old-time chase movie or he missed the sign saying Closed to Vehicles, Jeff slammed into the heavy posts that kept traffic off the landmark.

"Must have been going ninety," Will murmured as Kara hid her face in his broad, solid chest and took comfort in his warm arms.

Though the air bags deployed, the cops reported they found Jeff Ryder D.O.A. when they caught up with him. He'd crossed one too many bridges in his life.

****

The headlines read, *Live Fast, Die Young. Pop Star Jeff Ryder Dead in Crash. Drugs Suspected.* The following week, the tabloids posted touching photos of Kristal Pickens, pale and trembling and all dressed in black, crying into a hankie as she exited the small white Appalachian church behind the mahogany casket carried by her father, three large brothers, and Jules and Steve Ryder. The rising country/western singer buried Jeff in Gatlinburg where the couple had wed. Jeff's former wife and young children did not attend, but female fans mounded his grave with red roses, the rags reported.

Kristal made a statement to the press that she was going into retreat for a while to deal with her grief. When sifting through Jeff's papers, she found he'd recently purchased a private get-away estate in Thailand. Sure her beloved husband had planned to surprise her with this gift for her birthday in December, Kristal decided to travel to Asia in order to recover from her loss.

"I'm gonna try to regain my serenity by studying Buddhism, but I want y'all to know I'll never give up Christ," they quoted the widow as saying.

The mouth of the covered bridge where Jeff died filled with bouquets, votive candles, pictures of Jeff cut from magazines, and copies of his CDs. The locals were concerned about litter and damage to the structure but figured having a celebrity die on park property could only help the tourism industry.

Kara Ryder gave no statement other than to say she felt her children were too young to attend the funeral. "It's always sad when talent like Jeff Ryder possessed is lost to the world," she offered as her final words on the matter.

Epilogue
This the End, My Friends

The grapes growing on the arbor had been picked and boiled into lush purple jelly. Out back, the cornstalks, grown tall, produced ears as sweet as sugar and now yellowed in the garden. The pumpkins were especially large and mellow this year. Kara didn't know if she'd chosen a different sort of seed or if the spirit of Buzz Light rested in each one.

Faith pointed out the pumpkins she wanted hauled to decorate the church. She crouched to examine one very fine specimen, her belly about the same size as the immense orange globe.

"Don't you dare try to pick that up, Faith Frick!" Kara shouted at her. "Leave it for Will. He'll be back in a minute as soon as he loads the corn shocks into the truck."

"Kara, if I popped right now, I couldn't be happier. This honeymoon baby is two weeks overdue." Faith stood and rubbed the small of her back.

"Well, I got mine the easy way. Y'all should try adoption," Kristal said from her seat on the porch. "They claimed Jeff was her father over there in Thailand, but I just don't care one way or t'other. Look at my little Amy Gail. She couldn't be sweeter, but you know those Orientals, they don't set much store by girls. Why, she makes me feel just like Angelina Jolie."

Kristal raised her adopted three-month-old daughter to her shoulder and patted her back. The infant's large, slanted dark eyes popped open when the screen door slammed, and Yukio Matsumoto came out onto the porch.

"That is untrue, Kristal. I have three grandsons now, but Mari is my precious pearl. Tea is ready. Mari, we have the bear craws today."

"Bear claws! Where is Daddy Will? He loves bear claws." Maridel stopped pursuing Cantaloupe's kittens hiding among the pumpkin vines.

"Remind me to get that cat fixed. She's a great mouser, but I only need so many cats. I didn't realize they could reproduce so fast," Kara said.

"You were quick enough to get Blackie fixed. Cantaloupe had to go on the prowl for her mate," Faith said.

"He sprayed the furniture, you know, the way males do."

"Which reminds me, both Alan and Mari seem to be thoroughly potty-trained. Didn't you and Will have some kind of deal concerning that?"

"We've only been married since June. Give me a break. Okay, maybe I'll go off the pill at Christmas as a little extra gift. Will hated being an only child, but sometimes he worries me. He says he knows we could add bedrooms and an extra bath onto the house without destroying its integrity. I'll admit he did a wonderful job turning the lower half of the barn into his office, exercise room, and workshop. Thank heaven Sadie Fischer didn't want to commute out here. His new secretary is wonderful—and middle-aged instead of ancient."

With Alan trailing, Will rounded a corner of the house. "You ready to help me carry another shock to the truck, son?" Alan nodded.

"No, no! Our tea party is ready," Mari informed the men of the family. "You better wash, Alan."

"Girls!" her brother said, following Will to an outdoor spigot.

The women moved inside and gathered round the table set with brown stoneware handleless cups sturdy enough for children to use. The promised bear claws Phil picked up at the downtown bakery were arranged on a raku plate and cut into easy to manage strips flanked by heaping plates of chocolate chip and oatmeal raisin cookies.

"See, I baked yer favorite, Alley-oop. Shove over and let Witch Granny sit beside ya." Greta took her place between a much heavier Phil than the one who showed up at the farmhouse last year, and her step-grandson.

"Oatmeal cookies are healthier," Della reminded them. "And Granny Del makes the best ones."

She poured milk into her grandchildren's cups. Quick learners, the children accepted one of everything, as did everyone gathered for the get-together.

Della moved around the table serving green tea from the pot Yukio brought her at Christmas when he visited from California after receiving Kara's invitation—and stayed. Kara recalled the little man wading through a foot of snow to her father's grave on the hilltop and placing two bottles of Dad's favorite brew and a pouch of cherry tobacco at the base of the headstone. He'd solemnly asked for Mike Shafer's blessing and promised to cherish his 'Dera'." The offerings vanished by the next day. Kara figured some teenagers cutting across the cemetery made good use of the free beer and tobacco. Regardless, her mother and Yukio, taking this as an auspicious sign, married on New Year's Day in a quiet ceremony at the parsonage, the Reverend John Frick presiding.

"I think we should say a blessing for this wonderful food and good company," Faith prompted.

"Amen to that," Kristal added, cradling her daughter in the crook of her arm as she raised her cup in the manner of a toast. "Thanks be to God for good friends and sweet little babies."

"I'm a big boy," Alan contradicted.

"And for big boys, too." Kara smiled at Will, a big man in so many ways.

"For this fine home that keeps out the cold rains of winter, for warm women in our beds," Mr. Matsumoto added.

Faith seemed a little shocked and Della turned pink, but Greta continued without a pause. "Yer damned right ya should be grateful for that, huh, Phil? And may the bumps in the road straighten out before ya. That's what the Irish say, ain't it? Let's eat."

A word about the author...

Once a librarian, now a writer of romance, Lynn Shurr grew up in Pennsylvania Dutch country. She attended a state college and earned a very impractical B.A. in English Literature. Her first job out of school really was working as a cashier in a burger joint. Moving from one humble job to another, she traveled to North Carolina, then Germany, then California, where she buckled down and studied for an M.A. in Librarianship.

New degree in hand, she found her first reference job in the Heart of Cajun Country, Lafayette, Louisiana. For her, the old saying "Once you've tasted bayou water, you will always stay here" came true. She raised three children not far from the Bayou Teche and lives there still with her astronomer husband.

When not writing, Lynn likes to paint, cheer for the New Orleans Saints and LSU Tigers, and take long road trips nearly anywhere. Her love of the bayou country, its history and customs, often shows in the background for her books.

You may contact Lynn at www.lynnshurr.com, lynn.shurr@yahoo.com, or visit her blog—
lynnshurr.blogspot.com.